ZPL

A DEATH IN EDEN

A
DEATH
IN EDEN

Keith McCafferty

—A SEAN STRANAHAN MYSTERY—

VIKING

VIKING
An imprint of Penguin Random House LLC
375 Hudson Street
New York, New York 10014
penguin.com

ISBN 9780525557531 (hardcover)
ISBN 9780525557548 (ebook)

Printed in the United States of America
1   3   5   7   9   10   8   6   4   2

Set in Warnock Pro

For Karen and Bill Basil

A mine is a hole in the ground with a liar on top.

—Mark Twain

Author's Note

A Death in Eden sends you on a journey upon the sparkling currents that have carved Montana's Smith River Canyon over the millennia. This canyon has been called America's Sistine Chapel by those who attempt to describe a grandeur and beauty that is truly beyond description. I have had the great fortune to float this river many times and invite you to visit my Smith River travelogue at keithmccafferty .com/smith. Here you will find a detailed map of the canyon, as well as many photographs that my brother, Kevin, and I have taken, enabling you to accompany the characters as they make their way down the river, and to see the country as it appears to them. You may spot, among other landmarks, the loo with a view, the silver threads of Indian Creek, the cave pictographs, the abandoned homestead at Tenderfoot Creek, and the strangely ominous limestone formation called Table Rock. Look closely, and you might even see a three-legged dog.

I hope you enjoy taking this journey as much as I have.

PART ONE

HARD ROCK HEAVEN

A Loo with a View

"I have to pee."

Awakened by the child's voice, the woman rolled over in the double-wide sleeping bag she shared with her husband. She spooned back against him.

"I didn't hear that," he murmured.

"I have to pee."

The voice was smothered. It came from the far side of the tent, where a small girl lay curled like a snail, her head buried in her sleeping bag.

"Can't you wait until morning, darling?" the woman said. "It will be light in just a little while."

"I have to pee now." The head was out of the bag, the girl's indignation registering.

The woman let out a sigh and fumbled for the zipper of the bag.

"I'll go," the man said.

"No, I'll do it. She's seven, Larry. She's getting sensitive about that."

"I'm seven and a half on the next full moon."

Now where did she hear that? the woman thought.

"It's all right, darling," she said. "I just have to find the flashlight."

"Take the bear spray," the man said.

"It's packed in the boat bag. We'll be okay."

"Sure," the man said. "I paid the premium on your life insurance. If you get eaten, I'll trade up to a pair of C cups."

The woman swatted him with her pillow.

"What's a C cup, Mommy?

"Nothing, sweetie. Daddy's making a joke."

"I have to pee really bad."

"I know. We're going." The woman had found the flashlight and twisted the barrel to turn it on. She got out of the bag and crawled on her knees to the tent flap and worked the zipper.

"Don't step on snakes," the man said. "We're only a hundred miles from anywhere."

"Fifty-three," the woman said. "We floated six miles after we put the raft in and we take out at Eden Bridge at mile fifty-nine."

"You and your arithmetic."

"Mommy!"

"We're going, Mary Louise. Do you want to hold the flashlight?"

"No. You hold it."

So there was no reason to get lost. There was a path and no excuse for it, except that the woods were a skeleton of branches that stood like bones against the milk spilled by the moon, and the abstract shadows they cast made you step faster than you should, before you were sure of the way.

The woman swore under her breath.

"You said a bad word," the girl said.

"I'm sorry."

"Where are we, Mommy?"

"We're in back of the camp . . . I think." The last two words more to herself than to her daughter.

"Where's the loo?"

That's what her husband had called it. "A loo with a view."

All the designated campsites along the Smith River had pit toilets with hinged seats and BEAR AWARE stenciled on the lid. Some were situated on benches of land above the campsites, so that, sitting, one might contemplate the river that glinted between the walls of the canyon.

"I found it," the woman said.

Her voice was matter-of-fact. Still, she felt relief flood through her body. It was silly to have been afraid, even when the path seemed to be taking them too far from camp. They were on the river, after all. They might make a wrong turn to find a toilet, but they weren't lost. She could even hear the cascade of Indian Springs across the river.

"You go first, Mommy."

"I did earlier, darling."

"I don't want to sit down until you have."

"What do you think's down there, a bogeyman? Okay, I'll go first and warm it up for you. You can hold the flashlight and keep watch."

Keep watch. She recalled the signboards they'd seen along the river yesterday, before they'd entered the roadless area. A yellow circle with a diagonal line slashed through the words SMITH MINE. And underneath, NOT ON MY WATCH.

The Smith River was a crown jewel among Rocky Mountain trout streams. For sixty miles it flowed through a near-wilderness canyon of incomparable grandeur, with towering limestone cliffs that glowed gold and pink in the sunrises, and that were shot through with caves where Indians had painted thousands of ochre-colored pictographs. A proposed copper mine in the headwaters threatened the purity of its water, or so she'd learned from her husband, who had made a charitable donation to a grassroots organization called Save the Smith. He'd done a lot of research before filling out the application for the lottery. Had insisted she kiss it before he put it into the mail. With odds of drawing a permit ten to one against, you needed all the luck a kiss could give you. On the day that the results were posted online, he'd called her into their computer room, and she'd sat on his lap as he tapped the keys.

For a few seconds they just stared at the screen. "I knew you had lucky lips," he'd whispered, and their daughter had appeared at the doorway as he was exploring them.

"You two do too much kissing," she said.

It was true. They did a lot of kissing, and the kissing that night had led to a positive pregnancy test nine days later. One they'd been trying to get for three long years. She thought of that as she sat on the loo with a view. She rubbed the just-noticeable swelling of her abdomen and felt the tenderness in her breasts. Another few weeks, she thought, and he wouldn't have to reach very far to find C cups. She smiled to herself as she watched the moonlight play across the pool below camp. The first weeks of pregnancy had been hard, with almost daily morning sickness. But the nausea wasn't as bad now, and life, well . . . Life, like the river, was wonderful.

"Mommy?"

"What, dear?"

"Why is that man watching us?"

The woman jumped from the seat and yanked her camp pajamas back over her hips.

"Give me the light." Trying to keep her voice calm.

The cone of light flashed through the bushes and trees that surrounded them.

"It's nothing, darling." But then—she swept the light up the hillside—there was something. Just for a second. A silhouette? Like a man on a cross, she thought, his arms outstretched. It looked huge. The light wavered and the silhouette was gone. She saw only trees. Had it been there at all?

She gripped the girl's hand. The girl was crying now. It had taken a few moments for the fear to register.

"Larry!" the woman shouted.

"You're hurting my hand," the girl said. She was crying as she was tugged back down the trail.

The woman again shouted for her husband, waited a beat. No answer.

They fled through the trees, the branches whipping at them.

"Mommy, stop!"

The girl yanked her hand away. Stumbling, the woman turned and put her hands on the girl's shoulders.

"I lost my shoe, Mommy."

"It's okay, we'll get you some more. Come on now." She grabbed the small hand and started off, not running now but walking briskly, the girl hobbling.

It's nothing, she told herself. *Nothing.*

"Larry!"

And to her daughter, "Come on, you can do it. Just a little faster."

In the darkness, the firefly of a headlamp.

His voice. "It's me. Over here."

She ran the last yards and flung her arms around him.

"What's wrong? Did you see a bear?" He had the pepper spray gripped in one fist, a hatchet in the other.

"It was like a ghost."

"What?"

"I don't know. Mary Louise saw it first. What did you see, darling? What did you see?"

"I don't know." She was still crying. "It had b . . . b . . . branches. It was walking."

"Maybe it was a tree blowing," the man said.

"There wasn't any wind," the woman said.

"It had arms. Like a scarecrow."

"You mean like in *The Wizard of Oz*?" the woman said.

"Tigers and lions and bears, oh my," the girl said.

"That's backwards," the man said.

"Larry, your daughter is frightened. Be serious."

"Tigers and lions and bears, oh my," the girl said again.

"That's right, darling. And we're all together now, like Dorothy and her friends. We're all safe if we're together."

"Who am I, Mommy?"

"Who do you want to be?"

It was a game they played when they watched movies. What character do you want to be?

"I want to be Dorothy," the girl said.

"Then you're Dorothy, darling. And nothing can hurt you, not even the Wicked Witch."

"But I lost one of my ruby slippers." And she had. The tennis shoes she'd got on her birthday pulsed red LED lights with every step.

"That's all right. You only need one to protect you."

The girl looked down at her remaining tennis shoe. The battery was starting to draw down, but the lights still flickered when she pumped her foot.

"Tigers and lions and bears, oh my," she sang.

And the words strung out behind them as they walked the path back to camp, the girl hand in hand with her father and the stars losing their sparkle, but the forest holding fast to the terrors of the night, and with every other step a pulsing of the lights.

CHAPTER ONE

Object of Desire

Harold Little Feather lifted his hand from the wheel to scratch at the tattoo of wolverine tracks that circled the lower biceps of his left arm. The tattoo was recent and ran underneath the elk tracks that circled the upper arm, which he'd had inked more than twenty years before. On his right arm, badger tracks circling below wolf tracks. Like the wolverine tracks, the badger tracks were new, but they didn't itch. When his sister had caught him scratching at his arm at the kitchen table that morning, she'd said, "Somebody has too many spirit animals if you ask me. That might have been okay when you worked for the sheriff, but you're a state investigator now. Tattoos are unbecoming for someone of your stature."

"I know," he'd said. "It must be an Indian thing."

She'd smiled, but hadn't laughed. Harold and his sister were Pikuni Blackfeet, though Janice had been called Snowflake by her own people, and could have passed if her orbital bones weren't so pronounced. She hadn't put a foot onto the reservation more than a half a dozen times since marrying a white boy out of high school, the last occasion being her mother's memorial wake the year before.

But Harold straddled the two worlds. In the one, he braided his hair and wore khakis and a badge, newly issued, with MONTANA DIVISION OF CRIMINAL INVESTIGATION lettered inside a blue circle. In the other, he let his hair fall down his back and wore shit-kicker boots, jeans, and one of his three flannel shirts, the long-sleeved one for winter, the two with the arms cut off the rest of the year.

That's the way he dressed whenever he drove up through Browning. Browning was the Blackfeet tribal agency headquarters, at the foot of the peaks that girded Glacier National Park. It was where his ex lived, where a bunch of relatives lived, and where, he'd recently learned, he had a son, born from a liaison with a Chippewa Cree woman. The union had taken place on the Rocky Boy's Reservation eighteen years, four months, and some small change ago, a figure he knew down to the day not because of the woman—he recalled little beyond that her eyes were green—but because it was the last time he'd ever drunk alcohol. That was a long time for a Montanan of any skin color to go without a drink, and except for Harold's grandfather, whom he had worshipped, probably a record for anyone in his family.

He placed his hand back on the wheel and thought about his son, whom he'd made the acquaintance of only because his mother had died in a car accident and his mother's brother, who had taken custody, had decided to divulge to Harold the family secret. Probably, Harold thought, because the man knew Harold had a job in the outside world and figured there could be money coming his way. Not a charitable way to look at it, but it had made Harold bitter, being kept in the dark all those years. Bitter, then mad, finally, only sad. How could you ever make up for the lost time?

He tapped at the Bluetooth in the truck and saw he was out of cell range. It didn't matter. He'd only be leaving the same message that he'd left yesterday and the day before, when he first learned that he'd be heading to the northern part of the state.

"I'll be canoeing the Smith for five days starting the morning of the sixth and could use another hand on a paddle. I've got the food and the gear. Just get yourself to Camp Baker by ten Wednesday and pack your rod and your raincoat."

No "I love you, son." They weren't at that point and might never be, but nonetheless, the words sent through the ether on a bent bow with his heart riding on the string.

Harold geared down to cross a one-lane bridge and found himself in a tent camp populated by the floaters who'd drawn a permit to launch. Camp Baker was run by Fish, Wildlife and Parks, and the ranger, one of those always-smiling men who make you question their sincerity, was busy assigning campsites and getting the floaters on their way. He could use a little help, but the department wouldn't pony up for another position. A shake of his head, a downward pout of his mouth. The sad state of state affairs. Could Harold give him half an hour? The steady stream would dry to a trickle then.

Harold changed his clothes and carried his canoe down to the river's edge. His two dry bags of gear were already packed, his rifle in its case, fly rod, fishing vest, binoculars, ax. He leaned back against a fence post to watch the spectacle. A man with a Jell-O stomach and a face like a beet was loading cases of Pabst Blue Ribbon into an Avon raft, while a woman wearing a camo bikini top raised a skull-and-crossbones flag on the bow. She wore a University of Montana Grizzlies ball cap; he wore a Montana State Bobcats T-shirt. Another couple were helping them load.

"Things might get dicey, huh?"

Harold turned his head. Two young women who looked enough alike to be sisters were carrying a canoe up alongside his. The taller of the two, her hair darker by a shade, slapped at her hip, indicating Harold's gun belt.

Harold patted the grips of his holstered revolver.

He looked back over his shoulder at the two couples pushing off their raft.

"You let a mixed marriage like that onto the river," he said, "the claws have to come out sometime. Never know when you might need some law and order."

"Well, we won't cause any trouble," the woman said. She held two fingers together in a mock salute. "Scout's honor."

"You want a hand with your gear?"

"Sure. A big strong man comes in handy when you're just a bitty little girl." The words sarcastic, her smile anything but. She was openly flirting with him and Harold decided to play along. Why not? He had nothing but time.

The women introduced themselves as Carol Ann McManus and Jeanine Regulio, old college roommates from Duke University, separated now by distance and family commitments. They'd kept in touch, though, and had independently put in for a Smith permit for seven years. Jeanine had finally drawn, and now they found themselves in the doghouse because their husbands, Jeanine's in particular, refused to understand why they hadn't been invited.

"He just doesn't get it," Jeanine said. She was the one who'd done the talking to this point. "He thinks I must be turning lesbo. You understand, don't you?"

"Sure," Harold said. "You just need girl time."

"That's *exactly* what I told him. So why are you here?" she said. "Is it because of the scarecrows?"

A perplexed expression must have shown on Harold's face.

"You don't know?"

"Guess not."

It was Carol Ann's turn to speak. A lanky blonde, she had a sunburn-peeled, not quite straight nose and a space between her front teeth. Her voice had a tinkling quality, like a creek that's polished between ice banks. "Yeah. Floaters are seeing scarecrows up in the cliffs. The ranger gave us a number to call after the float. You know. If we saw one. To report it so they could take it down. Spooky, huh?"

She told Harold that they'd been talking to some of the other floaters the night before around a campfire and had learned that a couple of the parties had got launch dates because of last-minute cancellations.

"Backed out because they were afraid?" Harold said.

"Yeah. Spooked. The ranger told us they might shut the river down. We could be putting in just under the wire. It is sort of weird."

Harold saw the river ranger approaching. "My cue," he told the women.

"Thanks for helping us load," Jeanine said. "Where are you camping tonight?"

"That's up to the man." He gestured toward the ranger.

"We're going to be at Lower Indian Springs. If you want to stop by, we have a beer for you."

"I might take you up on that."

"We don't bite or anything," Carol Ann said.

"Speak for yourself," Jeanine said. "I'm not making any promises."

Harold pushed their canoe off, all of them laughing. He heard Carol Ann say, "I can't believe you said that." And turning her head, her paddle lifted, water beaded on the blade, dripping, said to Harold, "I can't believe she said that."

The canoe grew smaller as it turned downriver. Jeanine, in the stern, waved backward over her shoulder.

"Did you see those arms? I could climb him like a totem pole." The words floated over the water.

"Sssh," Harold heard Carol Ann say. "Sound carries. That's racist."

"I'm just saying . . ."

And they were around the bend out of sight, their laughter still carrying above the bickering of the current.

———

"I think I've been objectified," Harold said. "Must be the gun."

The ranger nodded. "Must be," he said. Then, to himself, under his breath, "Yeah, the gun. I've only been packing open carry for ten years. Nobody ever offered to climb me like a totem pole."

"The braid then," Harold said. "Women, they like a braid."

The ranger, whose shrinking island of forelock hair had separated from the mainland, nodded, sucking in his cheeks and then puffing them out. "I wouldn't know about that. But what the hey? We stole your land. Least we can do is lend you our women."

Harold thought, *Or maybe it's because you got a 295 70R18 around your middle.* Something about the man beyond his offensive remark rubbed Harold the wrong way.

"You want to come on up to my abode, I'll show you our sit-u-a-tion."

"I was told it had something to do with pictographs. Now I'm hearing scarecrows."

The ranger nodded. "May be one. May be the other. May be both. You've been out of the loop, huh?"

"Something like that."

For six weeks that spring Harold had been aiding an investigation into a poaching ring inside Yellowstone Park, working undercover in a sting operation as a tracker and middleman buyer of grizzly bear gall bladders. Bear gall bladders were worth a fortune in Chinese and Korean traditional medicine markets, and out of the loop didn't begin to describe the isolation of living the daily terror of being found out by the two men who were the trigger fingers of the ring, brothers-in-law who called themselves "Rural Free Montanans," which, as far as Harold could discern, meant they didn't hold jobs—not ones that could stand legal scrutiny anyway—they didn't pay taxes, and they didn't believe the laws of the land applied.

As a test, Harold had been forced to shoot at a grizzly bear, a light phase boar with dark lower legs and a cream chest patch, in the Hayden Valley. He had missed, deliberately, blaming his aim on flinching upon being stung by a wasp. In fact he had been stung by a wasp a half hour earlier and could show the men the welt. That had drawn a long, assessing stare from the elder man, who had cold black eyes and a long face under a graying beard, who wore a head scarf like a pirate and had a claw of a right hand dating to the time when he'd set a rifle butt on the ground with his hand resting over the muzzle, accidentally tripping the sear. The hand had healed with a starburst of raised scar tissue across the palm and cockeyed fingers, the little one no more than a flipper.

When the man clenched the hand, a habit he had like a hiccup, the little finger drooped from his fist like a comma. He'd listened as Harold gave his excuse, then finally nodded, and said, "Shit happens."

Then he'd said, "Charlie"—Charlie Two Bears was the name Harold had gone by—"thing is, Char-lie," separating and drawing out the syllables, "if you were to have missed, say, on purpose, I'd have been forced to take the diamond stone to the knife. Wouldn't have no choice." He had drawn a drop-point hunter from his belt scabbard, a whetstone from his pants pocket, and began to run the blade across it. "I take pride in being able to separate out the bladder, Charlie. Why, it's like a' art, and me, a natural righty turned southpaw. Right-handed, left-handed, I never seen no one could work a blade to compare, except maybe Dewey here." He nodded toward his brother-in-law, who looked like a garden gnome, short with a barrel chest and few words. His talents, as Harold had witnessed, lay elsewhere.

"Never done it on a man, though," he continued. "I'd know the general lay of the land—once you get under the skin, a man, he can't be that much different—but I'd have to feel around with the blade, could be some co-lateral damage. Puncture the aorta, something like that. *Oops.* First time for everything though, huh? Next bear, I'm going to count on your aim being better."

The man went by Job, as pronounced in the King James Bible, which he often quoted, having claimed to have once been a preacher. Preacher or not, he was one scary son of a bitch. But there had been no next test because there had been no next bear. The wind had changed and the brothers-in-law had disappeared back into the folds of the Little Belt Mountains—it was at a microbrewery in Belt where Harold first met them—though Job was light on the specifics, mentioning only a compound. Harold envisioned one of the nameless under-the-radar shantytowns, where men who held grudges against the government lived among like-minded individuals who took the rifle off the wall any time they spotted a state vehicle.

The official line, the one Harold had been fed by his supervisor, was that thanks to him they had had plenty to make an arrest, but they were after the men behind the knives rather than the ones drawing them, and they were going to bide their time to find just the right one. That was as much explanation as Harold was given, though it was true that when you busted a ring, you brought everybody in at once or not at all. The brothers-in-law would resurface, they were the kind who always did, and Harold would be called back into the sting. It hadn't been his cover that was blown, and he still had their trust, as far as it went. Not something he was looking forward to, though, not at all.

Harold found his eyes wandering and refocused, his ears picking up the sound of the current.

"Out of the loop's one way to put it," he told the ranger.

"Well, then, what *do* you know?"

CHAPTER TWO

"Not on My Watch"

It was Harold's sister, Janice, who'd taken the call. Harold lived in a renovated barn behind her house outside Pony, and she'd relayed the instructions, which were clear enough, though the mission was vague. Fitz Carpenter, Harold's supervisor, whom he'd met exactly once, had told Janice that Harold was to car-top his canoe to Camp Baker, the launch site for the Smith River float, and to pack provisions for a week. The assignment was in connection with defacement of native pictographs, which Harold knew to be a federal offense. The ranger there would fill in the details. After his previous assignment, it sounded like a vacation to Harold.

He told the ranger as much as he followed him up a set of outside stairs that climbed to the second story of the mortar-and-river-stone structure that served as the Smith River headquarters. He found himself in a large room with small windows, a row of file cabinets along one wall, a big industrial green metal desk in front of another. On the wall behind the desk was the tacked-up skin of a rattlesnake that had to have been five feet long.

"Mr. Friendly there," the ranger said, "was found right here at the launch, path to the outhouse. Woman from La La Land spotted him, started screaming bloody murder. I hitched on the gun belt, shot him betwixt the eyes. He crawled away, rattled some, died some, then rattled some more. I gave him half an hour, and when I went to pick him up, he struck at me and commenced to rattling again. That's what I call a reptile. R-E-P-T-I-L-E." In case Harold didn't know how to spell.

Below the snake's skin was a large-scale map of the Smith River. Harold ran his eyes from bottom to top, south to north, the direction the river flowed.

"What do the colors mean?" he asked. The map was studded with pushpins in green, red, and yellow.

"I'll get to that," the ranger said. They were on his turf; they would address the sit-u-a-tion his way. "But first I want you to understand what we're up against, scale-wise. We're talking about sixty miles of river corridor from here to Eden Bridge, limestone cliffs rising a thousand feet straight up out the water, more caves than you could explore in a lifetime. In *ten* lifetimes."

"Lots of canvas for the artist," Harold agreed.

The ranger nodded. "There are more than seventy pictograph sites documented, maybe that many more that aren't. It's one of the richest sites of cave art in the entire West."

Harold said, "Then that's your red pins." There were more red pins than any other color. "And some of these sites have been vandalized?"

"Well, not exactly. But where you see a green pin right next to a red one, at those pictograph sites floaters have reported finding rocks that are painted with NOT ON MY WATCH."

"Which means what?"

"Are you familiar with the controversy over the Castle Mountain Copper Project?

"What I read in the papers."

The ranger nodded. "Well, every other cabin along the river's got a sign saying NO SMITH RIVER MINE and NOT ON MY WATCH. And every other vehicle at the launch has a bumper sticker saying the same thing. I'm not supposed to express an opinion, never mind that one arm of the mine's going to run directly beneath Farewell Creek, which is the Smith's most important spawning tributary."

"What if you were to express an opinion?"

"Then I'd paint NOT ON MY WATCH on the side of this house in letters ten foot tall. You tell me you're going to mine twelve million tons of copper and there won't be any tailings leak for the next million years, even though the lining you seal the poison with is yea thick?"— He spread his thumb and forefinger a couple inches apart—"then you don't know the history of hard-rock mining in the West."

Harold could hear the passion mounting in the man's voice and tried to steer him back on track.

"So the yellow pins? Those must be the scarecrows?"

The ranger nodded. "Nine to date. You see where they are, the significance of the locations?"

Harold nodded. "They're all by one of the pictograph sites where the rocks are painted with the sign. The same person who painted the signs is putting up scarecrows."

"That's the way I read it. And they aren't just scaring birds. They're scaring the floaters. I had a call this morning from a reporter for the *Bridger Mountain Star*. I had one yesterday from the *Trib*. They're getting calls from the floaters and they're going to run stories that will go out over the wire and I'm not allowed to do anything but state facts as known. I'm going to look like a bureaucratic asshole and fulfill my ex-wife's prophecy. She always said that someday I'd make a first-class asshole and she'd get out when I was still only halfway to my destiny."

Harold could see the ex-wife's point but didn't say anything.

"Still not sure what you expect me to do," he told the ranger. He'd pulled his iPhone from a belt holster to take photos of the map.

"Your job is to catch whoever's putting up the scarecrows and bring him to justice, whatever that is. Personally, I'm rooting for the guy. But we have a film crew on location here starting tomorrow. A couple guides are going to float a honcho for the mining company in one boat and the president of Save the Smith in another. They're going to sit around a fire at night and duke it out, present their cases over the course of their float. They'll be on the river three nights. I already have the campsites for them reserved, but I guess that's not going to matter now."

"What do you mean?"

"Macy, the regional parks director, decided to shut the river down. You're going to be the last one to put in, except for the documentary crew. They launch tomorrow."

Harold nodded. "Who's making this? The state?"

"No, it's an independent television producer. I have her name here." He fumbled in his pocket for his notepad, recited the names he had written. Saw Harold's eyebrows crawl a little. "What?"

"Nothing. I know the guides. Sean Stranahan, I've worked with him. I know the other one, too."

"Six degrees of Harold Little Feather."

"What's that mean?"

"Nothing. It's a small world. Montana, especially."

"Seems drastic to close the river. No one's been hurt or threatened, have they?"

"No, they haven't. But Macy, he's a drama queen. And the department wants to show that they're on the job, protecting and serving the public. I'll be left holding the bag, the one who has to tell floaters who didn't get the word that they have to turn around and go home."

"Guess I'll get to it, then. Might help if I had GPS coordinates downloaded for the sites on the map."

"What do you think I was up all last night doing?" The ranger brought a GPS out of a hip holster on his belt and worked his thumbs to get to the map page.

"You see that all the coordinates for scarecrows are marked with dates. The dates are when we saw them in the course of floating the river, not the time they were first reported by other floaters. So they aren't in exact sequence. But overall the pattern of discovery is downriver. Those the farthest downriver were found last. What's that tell you, Harold?"

He's testing me, Harold thought. Before he could respond, the ranger spoke up. "I don't know what it tells *you,* but what it tells *me* is that our guy is a floater himself, and he put up the scarecrows as he went along. He's not accessing the river by roads through private property. If he was, then you'd expect the scarecrows to be clustered near the access points and they aren't. The scarecrows are in remote parts of the canyon you can't get to without a boat."

"He has to put in somewhere," Harold said. "Would you have seen him if he tried to launch from here?"

"Would I have seen him? Sure, if it was daylight. In the middle of the night, probably not. He could drive in with no headlights, and this house is far enough from the water I wouldn't have heard. Of course he'd have to be dropped off; he couldn't just leave a vehicle here. But if he put in at night, there's a good chance one of the campers waiting to launch in the a.m. would have at least heard him, and no one we've talked to did. So I'm guessing he put in on private property."

"He'd still need a vehicle at the take-out, someone to shuttle or pick him up there."

"He would."

"That would mean there's more than one person involved."

"It would at that. I can see why they made you an investigator."

Harold ignored the remark and returned his attention to the map on the wall. He pointed to the pushpin that marked a point far downstream, only a few miles above the take-out at Eden Bridge. He consulted the GPS. That waypoint was marked with the latest date, a week ago.

"I know what you're thinking," the ranger said. "You're thinking if this is the last scarecrow in the sequence, then he's floated through the canyon stretch, he's put up his artwork, said his blessing or put his curse on it, whatever. He's taken out his boat and he's long gone by now."

"Had crossed my mind," Harold said.

"Thing is, though, this isn't the last scarecrow we found." The ranger shook his head. "No-sir-ee."

Harold waited. He was comfortable in silence. Silence was his friend. Don't say anything and the other person will, that was a working philosophy he brought to any conversation where something remained to be learned.

"The last scarecrow," the ranger said, "was called in this morning just before you drove up. You saw how busy the launch site is; I just haven't had time to put a pin for it yet."

Having said that, he plucked a yellow pin from the margin of the map and placed it on a map location. "Want to guess why this is interesting?"

"Why don't you tell me?"

"It's out of sequence. The floater who spotted it and called it in says it's under some ledge rock where Blacktail Creek comes in. That's only about nine point two miles downriver from this house."

"So you think he floated through once and this is his second time down."

"That's the way I read it. You'll be coming in right on his heels. And something else."

Harold waited.

"A little girl camping with her parents said she saw a scarecrow or a man carrying a cross at the pit toilet at a site a few miles upriver from Blacktail Creek. It was night and she couldn't be sure, but it scared her enough, scared her mom, I should say, 'cause she saw it, too. They got the hell out of Dodge and the mom called it in after they floated back into cell range. This was day before yesterday. I'd be guessing little girl, big imagination, if it wasn't for the scarecrow being reported this morning in the same proximity. That was all Macy needed to close the river, him being the bureaucratic pussy he is."

Harold nodded. He was beginning to reassess his opinion of the ranger. The man worked way down the chain in a "Yes, sir" division of Fish, Wildlife and Parks. It took balls to take any kind of stand.

Harold scratched at the wolverine tracks. "Anything else you want to tell me?"

"There is one thing, though I don't know what it means, maybe nothing."

"What's 'maybe nothing'?"

"One of the scarecrows we were able to hike up to is under a ledge where an old hermit camped back in the day. Ran a trapline up and down the river. Old Scotty MacAllen."

"He still in the canyon, this MacAllen?"

"Hell no. He died, must be forty, fifty years ago. Used to be a copy of an article in the *Helena Standard,* stapled to the wall at the sign-in hut. Something for floaters to read while they waited for campsite reservations. Photo made him look like a coyote with a serious case of mange. The Smith River Watchman, they called him."

"You have a copy?"

"No. You put something where the floaters can get their hands on it, you can pretty much count on it going missing."

Harold nodded. "Do you think it's a coincidence, the scarecrow being by one of his old camps?"

"I don't think any of this is a coincidence." He shook his head. "No, sir, I don't. But they don't pay me to think."

"About the girl. Do you have a number for the parents? Maybe I can call before floating out of range."

"I do, but a belt broke on the shuttle vehicle they booked, so they're hitching back here to pick up their car. You can talk to them in person; they should be here any minute."

"Then I'll wait. Might help if I know exactly what it is I'm looking for. You wouldn't have a picture of the scarecrows, would you?"

"Now *that* I can help you with. There I can do you one better. Last week the crew took one of them down. It was the easiest one to climb up to. The rest are pretty hard to access. Whoever put them up was a mountain goat."

"Then you have it?"

"In the shed around back. Wasn't my idea to put it there. You go in, you'll know why."

"You say a crew took it down. How many people work the river?"

"There are four of us. Three from Fish, Wildlife and Parks and one from Department of Forestry. We rotate duties. One of us mans the launch while the other three float."

"How often do you float?"

"Every week. Make sure campers are obeying regs, hanging their food from bears, clean up the sites if anybody trashed them. Basically, it's outhouse detail and a glorified fishing trip. You think you'd get tired of it. But you don't. It's a different river every time you float it."

Climbing down the steps, Harold looked toward the launch site, hoping to see an old truck or rez-type, kicked-the-shit-out-of vehicle that his son might have driven up in. But there was nothing.

The ranger opened the big sliding door on the barnlike shed. "Ta-da," he said. "You don't mind, I'll wait here. I wouldn't breathe any more than you have to, trust me on it."

CHAPTER THREE

River of Wine

Sean Stranahan was one of those fly fishermen who, like his father before him, had been guilty of comparing a trout stream to a woman. A river could be fickle, his dad told him. There would be evenings when you knew her desires and evenings when she could not be tempted.

This was one of the former evenings that, in the span of a few dozen casts, became the latter. Two species of mayfly and one of caddis sailed the surface of Rock Creek as the sun was near setting, and three species of trout examined the silhouettes that the flies refracted on the surface. Stranahan chose the wrong imitation more often than the right one, caught a couple small cutthroat trout early, then a larger brown with circles like blood drops on its sides. Then, as so often happens as hatches progress, the fish dialed in, setting a higher and higher bar for being fooled until it reached a point that Sean's fly might as well have floated on a river of wine. Intoxicating, but not offering much in the way of solid nourishment. Well, not catching was fishing, too. That was something else his dad liked to say.

He hooked the #16 parachute emerger to the keeper ring on his rod and walked along a fisherman's path, whistling to announce his presence to the cow moose and calf that called the tangled river bottom home. Cow moose weigh about eight hundred pounds and don't react well to surprises, as he'd learned on prior occasions. He heard a crackling in the brush as the moose moved away and picked up his pace, following the path toward a curl of smoke in the distance. His camp came into view, his old canvas tent pitched on the riverbank. He saw Martha Ettinger sitting in a folding chair, reading, setting down her book, drinking from her wine cup, setting it down on a stump, leaning forward to poke at the sticks in the fire. She smiled up at him as he approached.

"Home from the hills," he said. He tilted his bamboo fly rod against a tree.

"How was the river?"

"Finicky as a redhead, as my old man used to say." Martha had auburn hair that shone red in firelight.

"You're saying that just to get me to call you a male chauvinist. It isn't going to happen. Nothing's going to spoil this trip, not even you."

"We're like an old married couple, bickering around a campfire," Sean said. He took the charred stick Martha had set down and rearranged the sticks she had just arranged.

"I wish," she said, just loudly enough that Sean could hear if he chose to.

Almost a year had passed since the walls of Sean's house had gone up, a year of relative domesticity. The tipi he'd borrowed from Harold Little Feather and had been living in—surviving, perhaps more accurately—had come down, and Sean's presence in Martha's bed had changed from once or twice a week to almost every night. It remained to be seen what would happen when the interior of his house was finished, but for the time being he was hers, more than he'd ever been, and a large part of her wanted him to put a ring on it, though a smaller part, the part that remembered two failed marriages, thought to leave well enough alone.

She looked at her left hand, at the fourth finger that ended in a fist of skin between the knuckles. She'd lost it in an accidental shooting and shook her head. You could put a ring on it maybe, but it would slip right off.

Story of my life, she thought.

"It's got to be a record," Sean said.

"What's a record?"

"We've been gone two days and I haven't once seen you packing heat."

"Black Beauty's in the glove compartment. Five chambers loaded."

"I know, but still."

"Well, I got a big strong man to protect me, whenever he's not comparing me to a trout."

"Trout stream," Sean corrected.

"Whatever."

They had chosen Rock Creek because it was outside her jurisdiction in Hyalite County, where Martha was in her third term as sheriff, and where Sean worked as a watercolor artist, a fishing guide, and a now-and-then private investigator. The now-and-then had been few and far apart for months and he'd found himself tapping his foot lately, willing the blood to move more quickly.

"A penny," Martha said.

"I'm thinking of the float coming up with Sam, the Smith River trip." Sam was Sam Meslik, Sean's best friend. It was under Sam's outfitter's license that Sean guided. "Not sure what to make of it."

"All you have to do is row a boat while two middle-aged men argue about copper. I don't have to tell you it's going to help Sam's business, so that means you'll get a boost, too. Really, it's not like you to over-think things. 'Always certain, often right.' The code you live by. Remember?"

"I guess."

"What are you really worried about? That you'll be tempted by Lillian Cartwright and forget all about your girlfriend keeping the home fires? That woman's a snake if I ever saw one. She sticks her forked tongue out, men just roll over and kick their feet." A smile as she said it, at least on the outside.

Lillian Cartwright was the documentary maker who had arranged the trip. It was a coup for her, getting the most prominent mine proponent in the state to float the Smith River with the state's best-known mine opponent, childhood friends at that, who had grown up on ranches on either bank of the river.

"Have you met her?"

"I don't have to. Women know these things. What's your real problem?"

"You'll think it's silly."

"Try me."

"Remember the hillbillies in *Deliverance*?"

Martha shook her head. "I read some James Dickey in college and all I recall is there was a lot of Zen stuff about archery. I never saw the movie."

"Well, one of the hillbillies has this stubble beard and his front teeth are gone. He's the one tells Jon Voight's character he has a pretty mouth. A couple nights ago I had a dream. I saw him opening his mouth and blood was coming out. You were asleep. I forgot about it until now. I don't know why I remembered it."

"You remembered it—you dreamed it in the first place—because you're about to float a river, like they did in the book. It's just you're in Montana and they were in the South somewhere."

"The Chattooga River, in Georgia. They floated it before the dam was built and flooded the valley."

"Then that's your association. If the copper mine gets the nod and tailings leak, it's the same scenario. One last float, then a river lost."

"A river lost, huh? I'll try to remember that."

"What's the worst can happen? The snow melts and the river goes out. What's it running?"

"About six hundred cfs. Clear last time I talked to Sam. Nothing forecast. But you're right, runoff's just around the corner. It could bump up overnight. It could get dangerous."

"You have nothing to worry about." But she rapped her knuckles on the sawed stump she was sitting on. The red wine in her clear plastic cup jiggled, firelight dancing in it. "My grandmother's name was Ruby," she said absently, lifting the cup to look through the wine.

"I know you're right, Martha."

"I am right. Want to cook those deer steaks? I'm hungry."

So they ate and drank wine and stared at the fire. The moon rose. Sean added another split from the pile and the flames shot up.

"The invitation's still open," he said. "Might be good to have another woman on board. I'm told it engenders civility."

"You're already going to have ChapStick Lilly. Word is she pretty much sucks the oxygen out of the room. Or the boat, if you will. Not sure what you'd need me for."

"I haven't met her," Sean said. "But really, think about it. When's the last time you had a chance to float a river as beautiful as the Smith?"

"Never. If what everyone says is true."

"It is," Sean said.

He thought back to his only float down the river. It was during his second autumn in Montana, when he'd been seeing Martinique Carpentras. She had persuaded him to take a trip with her to France. There was a town in Provence that bore her name, where she had relatives and had spent two summers of her childhood. Sean, who had never been overseas, agreed on the condition that they visit Italy as well, so he could see the Uffizi Gallery in Florence and the great architecture of old Rome. He recalled standing in line to see the Sistine Chapel, the two Americans a head and a half taller than the nuns who lined up in front of and behind them, looking, in their white coifs and black veils, like tree swallows perched upon invisible telephone wires, waiting for a mayfly hatch.

Michelangelo's masterpiece was worth the two-hour line, inspiring Sean to pick up a neglected paintbrush upon their return. He had thought, at the time, that the Sistine Chapel was as close as he might ever come to seeing the hand of the God that his mother had so wanted him to believe in. Three weeks later he'd floated the Smith

River in a solo canoe to sketch it for future paintings, and revised his opinion. The hand of God did not reside in Rome, glimpsed through the brushstrokes of a thirty-three-year-old genius. The hand of God was in Montana, in champagne riffles and golden cliffs in a canyon that had been cut and molded over three billion years, and could not be described in words, nor captured by any artistic medium.

And so he was quiet for a while, as was Martha, each with their private thoughts, alone in the night but for the undertone of the river and the bats dipping in and out of the firelight.

"I grew up out of White Sulfur," Martha said. "Used to go into all the bars while my dad shopped for feed and whatnot. Buckskin Martha, I ever told you that's what they called me? 'Cause I wore a buckskin jacket with fringe. That and Annie Oakley."

They were like that now, Sean and Martha, the easy familiarity that didn't require answers to questions, but bred answers to questions unasked.

Martha stood up and took Sean by the hand. "Let's see if we can unworry you," she said.

"You want to get lucky, huh?"

"Honestly? Not really. I haven't had a shower since Sunday. But I don't want to disappoint you."

"You don't disappoint me."

"Then if it's all the same, we'll wait until we get home and I'll see you off for your float in proper fashion."

"You'll wear the blue camisole?"

"I won't wear anything at all."

"You know when we first got together, you wouldn't let a little detail like a shower get in the way. See, we *are* getting to be like an old married couple."

"I wish." This time the words were plenty loud enough to be heard. They hung, ringing, as the night stars shivered in the sky.

CHAPTER FOUR

Stirring the Waters

It took a few moments for Harold's eyes to adjust to the darkness. He hadn't known what to expect, but whatever he could have imagined wouldn't do it justice. For starters the scarecrow was enormous, at least eight feet tall with a corresponding arm span, and it was constructed in the shape of a cross, with a framework of heavy gnarled tree branches that were intricately, even artistically, woven with peeled willow branches. Dried grasses were in turn woven into the secondary framework of the willow branches. No nails to hold it all together, just the binding of the branches, and no clothes except for a scrap of red cloth tied around the neck.

The face was what was arresting. It was a dull purple color, and Harold breathed in a rank odor as he switched on his Maglite for a closer look. He fought back an impulse to gag. The face was a hunk of meat, trapped inside a birdcage of branches that were woven into the shape of a globe. The meat, which had to have been placed inside before the branches were woven around it, swarmed with maggots. White quartz river stones were wedged into holes in the weave to serve as eyes. A dark basalt river stone was the nose. The mouth had been fashioned from a curled section of deer antler. Harold drew his knife and scraped off some of the maggots. A few hairs adhered to the blade, but it was too gloomy in the shed to see them clearly. He set the blade aside.

The scarecrow was leaning upright against a wall. When Harold tried to heft it, to guess its weight, the heaviest branch supporting the torso broke away and the effigy crashed to the floor in two parts. He tried marrying the halves, but without anything to marry them with he left the scarecrow where it lay. He pried out the river stone that made the nose—it was the only smooth surface that might hold fingerprints—and after wrapping it in his handkerchief, he went back outside, where he was grateful to drink in unfetid air. He apologized to the ranger for what had happened.

"Can't leave you alone for five minutes," the ranger said.

"What's the plan for the other scarecrows?" Harold asked.

"I Have No Idea." Saying each word distinctly and as if it began with a capital letter. "Not My Decision. I'm just waiting for Macy to drive up from Great Falls. He wants to see it."

"All right. But don't let him touch it. Nobody handles it until I come off the river. The other scarecrows, leave them right where they are."

The ranger nodded. "Look, don't touch. I gotcha. But I'm a little uneasy about telling the regional director what he can and can't do."

"Then have him call this number." Harold drew out one of his cards that announced his position as a state investigator, and penned a number on the back. "That's the personal cell for the state director." The ranger took the card, then faced his hands in an I-back-off gesture.

"It's just better if we're clear on this," Harold said. "I can't work the scenes if they get trampled on."

He studied the hairs on the knife blade. They were light gray behind tapering blue-gray tips. "You can tell Macy that the face was made from mule deer meat. The liver, if he asks."

Harold turned toward the river as a white van lifted a ribbon of dust from the access road. The van, which was mounded with gear on the roof rack, stopped at the boat launch. Five people got out, two middle-aged men and a younger couple with a little girl.

"That would be Little Bo Peep who saw the Big Bad Wolf," the ranger said. He hitched his pants and Harold followed him down to the river.

The couple were thanking the men for the shuttle. Harold waited for them to say their goodbyes and introduced himself to the family. It took the mother ten minutes of fast talking to tell a story that could have been told in as many words—"I thought I saw a scarecrow but can't be sure." Harold asked the woman if she minded if he spoke to her daughter alone. She glanced at her husband, who said he'd go get the car. She turned back to Harold and said okay.

Harold walked to where the girl was standing by the river a few yards away. She was tossing clods of dirt from the cut bank into the water. The girl had yellow curly hair that reminded Harold of Goldilocks in the Golden Books version his grandmother had read to him.

He squatted to bring himself to her eye level and coached her on her throws, told her to bring her left foot forward, her right arm farther back, let the clod roll off her first two fingers, follow through.

"We haven't been formally introduced," he told her. "My name's Harold." He extended his hand.

"I'm Mary." They shook. "My mother calls me Mary Louise but I don't like it. You're an Indian, aren't you?"

"Card-carrying." Harold found his tribal ID card and showed her. "Says I'm a member in good standing in the Blackfeet Nation."

"Is that like another country?"

"Seems so sometimes. We're a sovereign nation. That means the U.S. government is supposed to stay out of our business."

"What's it like, being Indian?"

"That depends. White people have preconceptions, so they're not surprised if you let them down. If you don't let them down, there are some of your own people saying you have too much ambition. Can be hard to win."

She absorbed the information, then threw another clod.

"There's an Indian boy in my grade. His name's Jimmy. He's nice to me, but when he's with the other boys he's a jerk."

"He's trying to fit in," Harold said. "When he's with you, that's his better nature asserting itself. You'll have to hope he outgrows the other behavior. Some boys do, some don't."

She nodded. "My dad's Irish. My mother says Irish have a problem with alcohol. She says Grandma drinks too much but my dad doesn't because he saw what it did to her. Do you drink alcohol?"

"Not a drop."

"I like apple cider."

"So do I."

The girl brought her hand way back as Harold had taught her and threw a clod that nearly reached the far bank. Harold offered his hand for a high five.

In his peripheral vision, he could see the mother watching him closely.

He motioned for the girl to follow him a few yards farther down-river and lowered his voice. "Why don't you tell me what you saw that night, Mary?"

"I saw God. He had arms."

"God?"

"Like Jesus on the cross. We're Catholic."

The mother had moved up behind them. "First it was a man, then it was a scarecrow," she said. "Now she thinks it was God."

Harold looked at her.

"Pardon me for interrupting," she said. She hesitated, then turned and walked back to the landing.

"Grown-ups," the girl said in a withering voice. "They can be exasperating."

"Your mother says you thought it was moving."

"It did, but nobody believes me. They think it's my imagination."

"I believe you. Was it walking, or sort of like floating?"

"I don't know. It was moving. Then Mommy took the flashlight and I didn't see it anymore. It chased us. It stole my shoe, my ruby slipper."

"It did?"

The girl threw her head up and down in a greatly exaggerated nod. "Both of them?"

"No, just one." She pointed to her left foot.

"Do you still have the other one?"

Another nod.

"You want to show it to me?"

"It's in my backpack."

The backpack was with the pile of the family's gear at the landing. The girl showed him her shoe. She took off her sandal and put it on and stepped on it to show Harold the blinking lights.

"Do you mind if I take it, Mary?"

She said it was okay and Harold looked at the mother, who was shaking her head in small movements.

"It *was* chasing me, it was." The girl stomped her foot down onto the ground.

"No, darling. You have a habit of not tying your shoes. It's easy to step out of them when you don't tie your shoes."

The mother turned to Harold. "She's gifted." As if that explained things. "What are you going to do?"

"Investigate," Harold said. "Going to ask you a couple questions. I apologize in advance for their personal nature."

"That's okay."

"You said you were actually sitting on the toilet when your daughter saw the scarecrow."

"Yes. She wanted me to warm it up."

"So, from where you were sitting, what you thought you saw that might have been a scarecrow, where was it, to the left, right, straight ahead?"

"A little to the right. Up the side of the hill. There's a big rock up there. I'd noticed it before because there's a tree growing out of it."

"How far away, would you say?"

"Maybe fifty feet. I can't be sure. I can't even be sure it was a scarecrow. There was something though. We weren't seeing things."

"Your husband said he wanted to go back there when it got light, but you wouldn't let him."

"We'd have been alone in the camp if he went. I thought we were safer staying together."

"How long between after you saw it and you left?"

"Not long, maybe half an hour. It was still dark enough we had to look around with the flashlights to make sure we didn't leave anything behind."

"You made the right decision. Middle Indian Springs campsite, right?"

She nodded.

Harold turned to the ranger, who confirmed the site. "Think you could reserve that one for me?" Harold asked.

"Already done. As soon as I got the call, I made sure no other parties would be camping there."

"What about before you got the call?"

"I had a party scheduled yesterday, but they canceled and the party that took their place needed a larger site. Nobody's been there for four days."

"Good." That meant the ground wouldn't be overly disturbed. Harold turned to the mother. "Before you leave, I'd like to look at the shoes you and your husband wore at the campsite. I'll take some measurements. That way I can eliminate your tracks and concentrate on any others I might find."

"If you find my shoe, you can bring it back to me," the girl said.

"Of course I will."

"It will keep you safe," she said. "It's magic. And I'm not gifted. I'm precocious."

"We can all use a little bit of magic," Harold said.

The husband had driven up in their rented SUV and Harold and the ranger helped them load the deflated raft and bungee-cord the frame to the roof rack. He took the shoe impressions and had one more question: Had they spotted an unattended boat in the vicinity? No, they hadn't. The husband turned the key, and the girl put her head out of a rear window and waved back at Harold as they drove away.

"You're good with kids," the ranger said.

"I'm trying to learn," Harold said. "That reminds me. My son might show up later today or tomorrow. His name's Marcus. He's seventeen. Do you have a canoe lying around he could use so he could catch up to me?"

"We have an old beater Grumman under a tarp at the house. Canoeing on the upper river can be tricky, though. It's pretty bony before runoff. Does he know his way around a paddle?"

"I don't know. But he's a teenager. He'll say he does." Harold laughed, a one-note laugh. "His mother, she named him Etchemin, means 'canoe man' in the language. Nobody ever called him that, and as far as I know, he's never lifted a paddle. Just tell him to look for my canoe. It will be the only varnished spruce strip on the river."

"I'll keep an eye out for him, and if I see him, I'll tell him what I'm going to tell you. You haven't floated the Smith before. It looks like a puppy dog now, but we get a couple more warm nights, the upper elevation snow's going to go. Once it starts, it goes fast. It cranks up to three thousand cubic feet, four thousand, it's a fucking wolf."

Harold nodded. "Understood. Thanks. My son, he's got a dog, three-legged little mutt. Goes everywhere with him. I read the regulations. Will that be a problem?"

"No dogs on the river. The only exception is for hunting dogs used to find and retrieve game. Is your son's dog a hunting dog?"

"Sure."

"What's he hunt?"

"He hunts his missing leg."

The ranger smiled. "Don't worry about it."

"One last question."

"Shoot."

"You said that some of the scarecrows were difficult to spot. Did anything in particular draw your eye to them?"

"Well, we knew the general areas to look, because the floaters described it for us. But funny you ask, because like three of them, we saw them because crows and buzzards were circling overhead. Strange, huh? Scarecrows are supposed to scare them away. Instead, they seemed to attract them. Makes you wonder if they all have meat in them."

Harold nodded as he pulled on his hip boots. The ranger pushed him off, his smile coming back.

"Indian Springs," he said. "It's like someone had a premonition that an Indian would be coming. In the stars or something."

Harold returned the smile, a thin one. He was beginning to form a theory and stopped himself. Let the river reveal its truth in its own way, its own time. This was ancestral land and he wanted to absorb it, to drink it in with all his senses. The Blackfeet, Shoshone, Crow, Assiniboine, Salish, even the Gros Ventre, had been so moved by the Smith's splendor that they painted images of their passage on the limestone walls. The shadows here were long shadows. The voices carried long-ringing echoes. Harold dug deep with his paddle, stirring up the waters of the past as the notes of a new story, perhaps long covered by the current, perhaps as recent as the last rain, were beginning to surface.

CHAPTER FIVE

Canoes in the Night

Everything Harold Little Feather liked best about camping was sensory. The sound of Indian Springs as it silvered over watercress and moss. The resinous scent of the pine blocks when he split them. The mesmerizing dance of the flames as the angels took the hand of the devil. And the woodsmoke itself, pungent, as salty as a smoked ham.

You could smell the spirits of the grandfathers, Harold thought, if you took the time to and your mind wasn't somewhere else, like it was with most white people and even the younger generation of his own people.

He smelled the sizzling of the trout he'd caught before the sun died, a fine brown whose flesh was as orange as the flames. That was one of the best smells of all.

When she helloed the camp, walked into the firelight dangling four cans of a six-pack from the fingers of her left hand and with a sling-back folding chair slung on her shoulder, he didn't know if he was happy to see her or not. He'd thought about it on the two-and-a-half-hour float from the put-in; even when he told himself to concentrate on the river, he'd thought about the chance that she'd show up, that one of them would, and that it would require a decision on his part, and yes or no, he'd have to extend his neck from his shell.

"How did you know I was camped here?" he said.

"Smoke signals," she said.

"Oh?"

"Our camp's just below the bend, not very far. We didn't know it would be you. Hoping though. You want a Rainier to go with your trout? Mountain fresh, they say."

"I drank a few too many of those once. You go ahead though. I have some cider I made from my sister's trees."

"Can I have that, then? I really don't like beer, just thought you being a guy and all."

She smiled, and Harold noticed the slight gap between her front teeth. She fingered her hair. Her face was guttered by the firelight, but she was attractive in an outdoorsy, straight-haired, flannel-shirt-with-the-tails-untucked way, and standing close to him, Harold realized she was a bit more woman than he'd noticed when she'd stood in the shadow of her more gregarious friend.

"I don't know why," he said, "but I thought it would be Jeanine."

"That's because she couldn't promise that she wouldn't bite you."

"No. She just did most of the talking, as I recall."

"That Jeanine, she's a talker all right. But she's not feeling so well. Anyway, she's more married than I am."

"I'm sorry to hear that. I hope she feels better." He worked a pine chip under the trout and turned it over. "How married are you, Carol Ann?" he said, not looking up.

"Aren't you forward? We haven't even had a drink yet."

Harold lifted his head and held her eyes.

"The truth? More than I want to be."

"Why don't you unfold your chair and tell me about yourself? But first, let's have a little of this brown trout. He's plenty enough for two."

He lifted the flesh from the skeleton of the trout, it pulled away easily, and he pushed it onto two paper plates.

They ate and drank in silence. "I think that's the best camp meal I've ever eaten," she said at length. "You cook good trout, Mister Harold Little Feather."

They tossed their plates into the fire, and Harold refilled their cups.

"Start wherever you want," he said.

It was a small-town-girl story, Missouri on a broad brown river, a tomboy who climbed trees and played second base and rode a head for figures to college, then to grad school, and who for fifteen years had been working beneath her degrees as an accountant for several businesses. A husband from the hometown, two children, one a sophomore in college, one finishing high school, the husband's contracting business being sued for fraud, the fish rotting from the head down, his being the head that would roll. And no, she didn't feel sorry for him because he'd brought it on himself and she and the kids were the collateral damage. In fact, if it wasn't for the kids she'd have left him years ago. When did he change from the young man who quoted Kipling and wanted to sail the globe and share adventures and who adored her, absolutely adored her, and who now looked past her into bankruptcy with his eyes vacant and his sports car repossessed and his catamaran sold for a song?

Sex, she said—on the rare occasions they had sex—was strictly by the numbers.

"Guess how many numbers?" she said.

She held up one finger.

"Richard doesn't think outside the box, so to speak." She drank her cider. "If you know what I mean, Harold."

That hung for a beat or two.

"You look too young to have a child in college."

"I started early. Now you. How does a manly guy like you get called Little Feather?"

"You ever hear the Johnny Cash song 'A Boy Named Sue'?"

She nodded. "I grew up in honky-tonks."

"Well, that was me. My father named me Little Feather knowing I'd have to get tough, and I did. When I was older and could pick my own name, I kept it out of spite for him, and because it had made me who I was."

I'll give you the short version of life on the rez, he told her, and did, greatly to his surprise for it was unlike him, and she said he should be proud, getting out but not deserting his heritage, accomplishing all he had. And she did hope he'd meet up with his son and be patient, the young man would come around and Harold would have his chance of becoming a real father to him.

She hesitated after her last declaration and said, "Look at me, I'm acting like I know you." She said she had a confession. Jeanine felt okay. The real reason she hadn't come was because she knew she wouldn't be able to resist temptation.

"You know. You're tall, you have long hair, and you have a sense of humor. And you have wolf tracks traipsing around your arm."

"And you can resist?" Harold smiled.

"I could if it wasn't for the damned tracks. I mean, deer tracks I can handle. Deer tracks I can stop at a kiss. But wolf tracks? Really? You don't give a girl a choice."

"What are we going to do, Carol Ann? I don't want you to do something you regret."

"Oh, I'm long past that." She rose from the fire, and as Harold stood, she put her arms around the back of his neck and pulled him into a kiss, opening her mouth, pressing the length of her body against him, smelling like woodsmoke and apples. More to her than met the eye, and no doubt about it.

"I have to warn you though," she said. "We've been on the road. I didn't exactly anticipate any extracurriculars. I haven't, ah, exfoliated for a few days. It might be a little scratchy down there."

"I'll risk it," Harold said.

Later, in the dark of the tent, she pressed two fingers to his lips and then back to hers, and they passed an imaginary cigarette back and forth.

"Was that enough thinking outside the box for you?" Harold said.

"I'd say just the right amount. I should say goodbye, get back to Jeanine so she doesn't worry."

"I'll walk you."

"That isn't necessary."

"It isn't, but might be wise." He told her about the scarecrow and the little girl losing her shoe.

"That happened here?"

"Just up the hill."

"Is there a reason to think something might still be around?"

"No. But I'll have a look in the morning. Could be the girl was seeing things. Imagination plays tricks in the dark."

"Will I see you again? We're camping at Sunset Cliff tomorrow, the upper site, I think."

"No, the map that ranger gave me shows three scarecrows between here and there. I have to check them all out. It could take a couple days."

"Then this is goodbye?"

"Probably."

"We were just getting to know each other. I mean, the sex was great, fabulous. But we were really getting to know each other."

"We were."

"You know you ruined me for any man in Missouri. What am I going to do?"

"Follow through with the divorce. You said your youngest will be in college next fall. Get her settled and start over somewhere else."

"Maybe I'll move out here, ring you up."

"Absolutely."

"You'll give me your number?"

"I'll give you my card."

She sighed. "But it's probably not going to happen, is it? People hitch onto each other, they make promises, then they're like this river, they just flow downstream where it takes them. That's where life goes, doesn't it? Downstream through time. We never make the changes we say we're going to make. We never see each other again. In the end all we have is the moment."

She'd been lying on her side, circling a finger around and around the wolf tracks on his arm, and moved her hand down his body.

"You have scars. Don't tell me they're from a wolf."

"No. I got a little too close to a couple grizzly cubs. Mama took exception."

"You're just too good to be true." She kissed a welt of skin on his chest. "I'm going to ask you to make love with me one more time, then you can walk me back. Is that all right?"

"I don't seem to be arguing."

She rolled on top of him and settled herself, rose up and settled herself again, then leaned forward, dragging her breasts across his chest. She whispered into his ear. "I just figured it out. What the two of us are, Harold."

"What are we?"

Rocking with him, smiling down with shining eyes. "Canoes in the night. We're canoes passing in the night."

"Why are you crying, Carol Ann?" He could taste her tears when he kissed her eyes.

"I'm just happy this happened. I've been sort of desperate and I'm just really, really happy."

CHAPTER SIX

Sleeping Like the Dead

Harold was up on five hours' sleep. He was always up before dawn, and while he waited for the gray to come into the sky, he built a small cooking fire and drank a cup of tea. The mother and daughter had visited the toilet just before dawn and he wanted to hike to the "loo with a view" having the same view that they'd had when they'd seen the scarecrow.

He shone his flashlight up the path behind his tent and in a few minutes was sitting on the closed seat of the pit toilet. He'd asked the mother where she'd seen it, whatever it was, and she'd said it was to the right and uphill. But she had grabbed the light from her daughter's hands and Harold had to figure that she'd jumped up from the seat first. That meant where she saw the scarecrow was in relation to where she stood, not where she sat. Still, there weren't that many angles of possibility. Harold broke the forest into sectors and examined them, first with the eyes he'd been blessed with, eyes his grandfather had said were the best he'd ever known, then with the flashlight, but without seeing anything that resembled a scarecrow. His focus settled on three Ponderosa pine trees growing out of the side of the hill. The limbs extending horizontally from the lower trunks could possibly be taken for the outspread arms of a scarecrow, but it was a stretch. And where was the boulder she'd mentioned, the one with the tree growing out of it? Well, he'd come back again when it was lighter, look for tracks.

He was almost within sight of his tent when he saw a flashlight bobbing from downriver, in the direction of the women's camp. He expected to see Carol Ann but it was her friend, Jeanine, and when he got close, she said, "I thought you'd want to see this."

She told Harold to switch off his light, and in the sudden dark she brought something out of her jacket pocket and pressed the heel of her hand against it. Red points of light pulsed weakly. It was the girl's tennis shoe, her missing ruby slipper.

"Where did you find it?"

"At the toilet, just now."

Harold had an "aha" moment. The mother hadn't taken the girl to the toilet above their camp. Instead, she'd got turned around, had followed a different path downriver. The "loo with a view" was the pit toilet up the hill from the lower campsite. He told the woman to show him exactly where she found it and followed her to the toilet, which was situated among several big boulders that walled it from sight, giving privacy. One of the boulders, up on the side of the hill, had a small tree growing out of a crack. Jeanine pointed to a stub of branch on a yellow pine, a spot that was well above her head. That's where the shoe had been hanging from its shoelace. She'd had to use a stick to reach it down.

"Carol Ann told me about the scarecrow," she said. Harold nodded, lost in thought.

"Aren't you going to ask how she is?"

"How is she?"

"She's sleeping like the dead. But she kept me up until four in the morning talking. Talking and crying. She said she'd come to a decision. She was going to leave her husband, there was nothing he could say that would dissuade her now. Just thought you'd like to know the result of your little escapade last night."

Harold started to speak.

"No, you don't have to say anything. She came on this trip to put some distance from her circumstances and make a decision about her

future. It's the right decision, but you helped her make it. I'm not saying you took advantage of a vulnerable woman because you didn't
know she was, but it had consequences. See, it might be over for you,
but when she wakes up it isn't going to have ended for her."

She stood, kicking her toe into the ground. Harold didn't say
anything.

"I don't mean to sound harsh. Meeting you is probably the best
thing that could have happened. You want the truth? I'm jealous. It
hurts my ego. I'm her best friend. I wanted me to be the one who got
her to leave the bastard. Then a guy with wolf tracks on his arm shows
up. Yeah, she told me about the wolf tracks. She went on about them.
I just thought you ought to know."

Harold went back to his camp and crawled inside his tent. He
wasn't a one-night-stand kind of man; it's what he told himself after
every one-night stand. When he'd been with Martha Ettinger, he
hadn't looked at another woman until he did, and that was his
ex-wife, who had a hold on him that he had never been able to
break. He couldn't live with her and he couldn't live without her
and it was a circle and most of the time it was hell and once in a
while it was heaven. He'd been in the part that was hell for months
now. If he needed an excuse, which he didn't. Harold was a man of
very few regrets.

"Well, the turtle came out of his shell all right," he said aloud.

He was exhausted, and sleep came almost immediately.

CHAPTER SEVEN

Born Pissed Off

Sam Meslik scratched his left armpit through a hole in his T-shirt while he watched a curtain of dust lift over the bridge at Camp Baker. The T-shirt's logo read MASTER BAITER—ALWAYS FIDDLING WITH MY WORM. Sam pulled it over his head, trading it for a cleaner one as a champagne-colored SUV turned onto the access road. He tugged on the hem of the shirt—this one read SHOW ME YOUR BOBBERS—straightened to his full six foot three, licked the fingers of his right hand, and ran them through the long ringlets of his graying, copper-colored hair.

"My 'Sunday go-to meeting,'" he said to Sean Stranahan as the RAV4 ground to a stop.

"If I didn't know you better," Sean said, "I'd think you were trying to make an impression."

Sean's eyes scanned the vanity plate that read MYIONU—"My Eye on You." It was the title of a television series that aired on Fox affiliate stations in central and southwestern Montana. Lillian Cartwright, the writer, director, producer, and host, was known for her looks as much as her take-no-prisoners reporting style. Sean had variously heard her called Look-At-Me Lilly, for her vanity; ChapStick Lilly, for her habit of applying ChapStick and drawing attention to her lips; and Lactose Lilly, for cavalierly exposing a nipple for the camera at a Mc-Donald's, sneaking it past the affiliate censors by assuring them it was prosthetic. The segment was on public breast-feeding and her on-air proclamation, "It's a mammary gland. Half the population have them. Get over it," became a slogan when feminist protesters picketed the state capital in response to the introduction of a House bill that would ban breast-feeding in restaurants.

As Sean recalled what he'd heard about her, the woman in question stepped out of the SUV. Older than she looked on camera, a trim-waisted blonde, she wore a tropical-wear shirt the color of a Georgia peach, which Sean had read she'd been once, before dropping the accent, the dear-me manner, and the smothering veil of politeness. She ran her ChapStick routine and approached in a strong athletic walk with her right hand extended. They shook hands and, all business, hands on hips, blowing a wayward strand of hair from her eye, she told Sean and Sam to haul her gear and to be careful, it was expensive.

"We aren't even in the water yet," Sam said out of the corner of his mouth. "Already being treated like help from the neck down. You get what I mean, Kemosabe?"

It took the two men three trips—camp gear, camera cases, reflectors, even a portable generator to run the lighting equipment for sitting-around-the-fire night scenes—and all the while she was drumming her fingers and looking preoccupied, her cornflower eyes focused at some indeterminate distance. Sam looked at Sean and, as he grunted under the weight of a boat bag, said it was good they decided to bring Sean's thirteen-foot Avon raft in addition to a canoe, rather than two canoes as originally planned.

"Shuttles arranged?" she asked.

Sam said they were.

"You reserve the campsites I requested?"

He said he did, adding that it didn't matter now that the river was closed to the public. They could camp wherever they wanted.

"But we're on schedule, right? They're going to be waiting. I don't tolerate tardy and I don't like surprises."

"I'm not their keeper but I suspect they'll be ready. How could they resist the chance of seeing you?"

That brought her head back an inch. "I beg your pardon."

The slabs of muscle on Sam's shoulders lifted and fell. "I'm just saying it could get old, sixty miles of your attitude."

"Are we going to have a problem? This is my show and you've been paid generously. You couldn't buy this kind of exposure for your business."

"No problem."

She looked the big man up and down. "Do you have something else you can wear? You look like a derelict. Do you really want the camera to record what a pig you are?"

"Why thank you."

She cocked her head. She looked from Sam to Sean as the hardness in her face fractionally lost the support of the underlying muscles. A smile came and went, and the voice, when she spoke, held a note of reflection.

"I was born pissed off," she said. "People come around to me or they don't. But you get what you see. I consider that better than what you get from the nodders of the world. In my business it's either take what you want or play the puppet, and some of the guys I've had to work with, grabbing at you, talking like you weren't in the room, saying 'bitch' under their breath, it gets old. Subtract five IQ points and you're dealing with a geranium."

She shrugged. "I don't really care as long as I get the story."

Sam pulled his T-shirt over his head, revealing a pelt of hair that would insulate a black bear in November.

"Hey, man, the dude abides," he said. "This better?" He buttoned up a khaki shirt with his Rainbow Sam insignia stitched above the left breast pocket.

She nodded. "Just try to keep food out of your beard."

"You know, I'm already starting to like you," he said.

Sean felt like a bystander.

"Like I said," Cartwright said, "I don't care."

––––––

That was the note they pushed off on, Sean manning the oars of his raft, Cartwright on the swivel seat in the bow, already with her camera in hand, Sam out ahead by half a bend of river in the canoe and soon gone from sight.

When she turned the camera on him, Sean smiled.

"Don't smile," she said.

He didn't and the river did the work, Sean dipping an oar only for direction. He pointed out a mink, slipping like spilled oil through the bankside grasses. It was being shadowed by a kit from the spring's litter and she swiveled the camera and caught them as they hunted.

"It's helpful to have birds and animals to cut away to," she said. "They give movement to the piece, plus they create empathy for what you're trying to get across. If this mine goes in and the tailings pond ruptures, if trout die as a result, that mink suffers, too. And the little one, for a videographer, that's like striking gold. Or in this case, copper."

Sean nodded.

"You don't have to be afraid to talk to me, you know. I just get wound up tight for a story and I thought your friend might try to highjack my trip, and there's only room for one captain on a shoot. Once I get some good footage, my pulse rate will come down. I can be a good old girl. I work hard. I don't complain. I can sleep on the cold hard ground. I'm not a bitch." Suddenly there was a flash of smile. "She said." And, a beat later: "Said like a bitch."

Then she laughed, a wonderful peal of laughter with the South in it, and Sean saw she was like many interesting people he'd met, a person of layers, one you only got to know over time.

"I'll be honest with you," she was saying. "It makes me nervous not having a dedicated cameraman. I'm good behind the lens, but I'm better in front of it, but there was no room in the boat. *My Eye on You* is a regional show. We're not even in every media market in the state. This is a big opportunity for me. The Smith was just named the fourth most endangered river in the country by American Rivers. People trip over themselves when they talk about it, the grandeur, the splendor."

She waved her fingers like birds in flight. "Personally, I don't see what the deal is. It's a pretty piece of water, but I've seen a lot of pretty water."

"Give it about fifteen miles," Sean said. "That's where you enter the Gates of Eden. The cliff walls climb right out of the river on both banks. Goes on for about a hundred bends of river."

"So you've floated it?"

"Once, a few years ago. To paint it. In fact, I'm hoping to give it another try. Montana Parks is sponsoring an art competition for their new poster."

"That's right. You're a Renaissance man. Painter, fisherman, gum-shoe, spy."

"Not so sure about the spy."

"But you're a private investigator, right?"

"I'm licensed. I haven't worked at it for a while."

"So tell me, Mr. Investigator, what's going on with the scarecrows? There was a story in the *Tribune* last week. Now they've shut the river down. Is there really any danger to the public?"

"I don't know. I do know that one of the scarecrows will be coming up on the west bank below Indian Springs, which is just a couple miles down from where we're picking up our clients. The ranger told us it's about three hundred feet above the water, at the mouth of a cave."

"Then that's going to be the first stop."

"I was told not to get too close. There's a state investigator trying to figure out who's putting them up and he doesn't want anyone mud-dying the tracks. Friend of mine, actually."

"Oh."

"Harold Little Feather. He used to work for the sheriff's department in Hyalite County. I've been contracted by the county a few times to help out in investigations."

"How does that work?"

"It's a manpower issue. Something the sheriff would like to look into, but can't spare the eyes."

"And you're deputized?"

"I have been, but usually it's just a straight contract."

"Interesting. This Little Feather, he's Indian, I take it."

"Blackfeet."

Sean saw a flash in her eyes under arching eyebrows. "And he looks like an Indian?"

"Sure. Hair in a braid and everything. But I haven't seen him since last summer when he came to my place to pick up a tipi he'd loaned me."

"You lived in a tipi?"

"For three winters, that's the way Indians count it. I finally got the walls of my house up last summer."

"This Little Feather. Tell me about him."

"He's not much in the way of small talk, if what you're thinking about is putting him in front of a camera. Tends to say what he means, no elaboration, doesn't suffer fools. Best tracker I've known. Harold even has his mark, three slashes of black on each cheek. Streaks it with a piece of campfire charcoal when he's hunting elk."

"Better and better. Will we see him?"

"He's a day ahead of us, but he's not tied into a schedule. There's a good chance we'll catch up."

She nodded. "Let's see if we can make that happen."

CHAPTER EIGHT

Tracking Tendencies

In his dream, Harold saw fire behind his eyes, saw the black of his soul streaked with flames, the conflagration flaring in a starburst like the world's big bang as he came awake with a start, hearing the crackle of burning branches and smelling the woodsmoke. He felt a cold nose rubbing up and down his cheek. A dog, smelling like two.

He pushed the flap of the tent aside to see his son squatting on his heels, pushing at splinters of wood with a stick. Morning, but the sun well up.

"Hey, Cochise," the boy said.

"Cochise was Apache."

"Not talking to you. Calling the dog."

Harold felt embarrassed. He knew his face was shiny with sweat and lack of sleep. It wasn't the image he wanted to present to a son he'd only met a few weeks before. He unzipped his sleeping bag and coughed as he breathed in the smoke.

"But back home," the boy was saying, "there's some call you that, so he's sort of named after you. I started asking around. Old grandfather named Melvin Campbell said you reminded him of Cochise, you being tall and Cochise being a BFI in his day. Me, I think to be a big fucking Indian you got to be at least six-six. It's like there's something in the water now, BFIs everywhere you look."

"His real name was Cheis," Harold said, trying to make up some ground toward credibility. "It means 'strong.'"

He ignored the eyes that were judging him openly as he climbed from the tent and took a chair by the fire. His right hip throbbed from lying on hard ground, his air mattress having deflated during the night. His head was heavy behind his eyes and his muscles were cramped. He tried not to show any of that.

"Yeah," the boy said. "Strong like an oak. When he died, they painted his face and dropped him into a crevasse in the Dragoon Mountains. Then they killed his horse and his dog and dropped them in. And his firearms, too. He was a fighting man. In the world he was heading for, he would need them. He would fight forever."

"You know more history than I would have thought."

The boy's face made a smirk, even as he avoided Harold's eyes. "I know one thing. I didn't expect to find the great Harold Little Feather sleeping it off like every other deadbeat dad I know. What kind of whiskey you been drinking?"

"Apple cider. I have some more, if you want it. The reason I was sleeping in is I had a friend last night who had some problems, needed a shoulder to lean one. One of the young women camped around the bend."

"You wish. I just figured you for more of a morning person. Up with the robin and all. Guess I was wrong. Should have known."

So this is how it's going to be, Harold thought. In his day, growing up on the rez, no seventeen-year-old would dare speak to an elder as he had been spoken to, not to mention his own father. And then another thought. *I was a boy who spoke out of turn, too.*

"I had to borrow my uncle's car to drive here," the boy said. "He wouldn't give me no money for gas, big surprise, so I had to hose some from a rig at that highway construction site outside Ashland. I coulda got arrested by the pale faces."

"You could have got arrested by me, if I didn't have anything better to do."

"So what's better to do? I got your messages. I only came 'cause I wanted to see the river."

"Solve a crime. Or maybe it's not a crime. That's something we'll have to determine."

"You and me?"

"You and me."

"You going to deputize me, make me your Tonto?"

"Don't have that power. You're going to work off the books, and I'm going to pay you by paying for your education. Already talked it over with your uncle. You finish high school, you can start at MSU next fall."

"What if I don't want that?"

"Then you can stay right where you are. Keep it real, see where that gets you."

Harold saw a veil of uncertainty cross the boy's face, saw his show of confidence was just that. *Why, he's no different than an abandoned bird you lift out of a nest. I will not lose him,* he told himself. *I will not open my hand and let him fall through my fingers.*

"Follow me," he said. "I'll show you the first clue."

They hiked down the trail, Harold filling in the blanks for Marcus, the story as he knew it so far. Arriving at the pit toilet, he pointed out the stub of tree branch where the tennis shoe had been hanging.

"What's that tell you?" he said.

"Is this like a test?"

"No. Like I said, I want your help. Fresh eyes, fresh perspective."

The boy looked at the tree. "Tells me whoever put it there is tall. Looks like it's newly broken. Somebody broke it to hang the shoe on it. On the stub."

"What's the significance of that?"

"I don't know. He wanted her to come back and find it. How long we going to be here? I can't leave Cochise zipped up in the tent too long."

"He'll be fine. And that means?"

"What?"

"The significance of where the shoe was."

"I don't know. He's a teddy bear, got a soft spot for little white girls."

"What's the most important word you've said so far? Think about it."

"You said this isn't a test and here you are making me feel like it's school."

"Take your time."

"I always take my time. I'm an Indian, ain't I?"

He's just like I was at that age, Harold thought. *Has to take everything as a challenge.*

"It's 'whoever,'" Harold said. "'Whoever' put it there. It means the girl wasn't making it up. What she saw was real. It was human, and the evidence says it was tall, so odds-on it's a man."

"She told you he was chasing her."

"That, I think, she *was* making up."

"The scarecrow?"

"Something about it made her think of one." Harold picked up a stick. "My third eye," he said. He told his son to stay behind him, to step where he stepped, and to tell him if he saw anything out of the ordinary. He began to walk in concentric circles, using the tree's trunk as an axis and occasionally tapping the ground or lifting a grass clump with the stick.

They worked in silence for a time. Harold stopped and pointed with the stick.

"What you got?"

"Partial," Harold said.

"Partial track?"

He outlined a half-moon impression with the point of the stick. "That's a heel print. See, here's another one. And over here. He's walking away."

"Man we're looking for?"

"Could be. It's size twelve, maybe thirteen—that usually translates into height."

"Is it old?"

"Three days, four at most. So the same time frame when the girl was here."

"How can you be sure?"

"Because of the nap. I'll show you."

Harold stepped down hard with his right shoe on a patch of bare earth.

"Compare how sharp this is to the partial. That's because dirt is made up of individual grains, and when you step down, the grains at the edge of your boot impression stand up. It's called the nap. As time passes, wind knocks some of the grains down, ants crawl across, a snake wriggles by, but most of the grains that are standing on end just sag or collapse of their own weight. I can tell how old a track is by how sharp-sided the nap is and knowing how long it would take for it to deteriorate to its present condition."

"I heard you give classes on this stuff."

"I teach courses at police academies, teach sportsman groups, wildlife enthusiasts, Sierra Club–type folks, that sort of thing."

"I read an interview with this guy in the Safari Club. He said he took one of your courses and you were almost as good as a Kalahari bushman. I couldn't tell whether he was dissing you or it was a compliment."

"It was a compliment. Those guys, the ones who start out as kids poaching bush meat, they're the best in the world. They can track over stone, shadows in the grass, track by scent. So can I to some extent, but they can track tendencies, too, which takes a lifetime of study. Say you're tracking a lion, it sticks to hard ground, doesn't leave a bent blade of grass for a quarter mile. They'll go to the next spot on the route they think he's taken and pick up the thread, know where he'll stop, where he's heading, what he's up to before he knows it himself. They track the mind, not just the animal. I'm not in their league."

"You're better than any white man."

Harold realized that his son had taken the time to background-check him and tried to keep the pleasure out of his voice. "It isn't something that runs in the blood. Just practice. You go back in time when man lived off the land, you could find trackers of every color. Man I worked with a few times, name Sean, he's good."

"He a blue-eyes?"

"More green. So what do we have here, Marcus? Is it Mark or Marcus? What do you like to be called?" Harold realized that in conversations with the boy's uncle, he had always just been referred to as Emma's boy, Emma having been his mother.

"Marcus, I guess."

"Do you have a Chippewa name?"

"Stands Like a Heron. That's what the family calls me, 'cause I had an infection in one foot and had to stand on the other one a lot. Still do, out of habit I guess."

"Okay, Marcus Stands Like a Heron, the girl says what she saw had its arms outstretched and looked like a scarecrow. What could a man pick up and look like that?"

"I don't know. A branch?"

"Lift your foot."

Marcus had been resting a shoe on a dry branch that had cracked off a Ponderosa pine.

Harold picked up the branch, which was about seven feet long, gnarled and as big around as his upper arm. He hefted it like you would a barbell for a set of squats, resting it on the back of his neck. Holding it balanced, he turned toward his son, the branch swinging around.

"Scarecrow," Marcus said.

"It's the start of one. Look at the break. The color, that green-yellow at the center. This isn't a dead branch that fell. It was taken off with an ax. So now we just have to figure out where he got the branch and where he intended to take it. Then we'll know where to look next."

"Like a bushman," Marcus said. "Track his tendencies."

"Exactly," Harold said.

Working on the assumption that whoever the girl saw had been gathering wood to make a scarecrow, Harold and Marcus separated to canvass the hillside. It was Marcus who found the tree from which the branch had been axed. It was a hundred feet or so away from where they found the limb, which confirmed that it had been carried off, and by a strong man, considering the weight. But they found no cut willow branches or other raw materials needed to complete his scarecrow, which suggested to Harold that the encounter with the girl and her mother had scared him off before he could collect them. This surmise, coupled with the direction of the tracks, painted a picture of someone who was not necessarily aggressive, who would retreat if confronted, at least if given an avenue to retreat.

Harold discussed his hypothesis with his son, man-to-man, trying to keep the teacher-pupil dynamic to a minimum. Marcus seemed to be genuinely interested, and with détente established, if only for the time being, they pushed off in the loaded canoes.

Indian Springs, which poured into the river opposite the camp, consisted of three sparkling fingers that cascaded over a staircase of ledges. They pulled over long enough to fill their water bottles and gather watercress for salad fixings—no charge, Harold said, for invertebrate protein in the form of scuds, snails, and insect larvae that were clinging to the jade green cress.

Marcus made a face, then shrugged. "I'll wait for you to take the first bite," he said. "But just a second, I want to take a picture." He went to the canoe and came back with a battered-looking camera. He fiddled with the zoom and the focus, and it was obvious from the way his fingertips manipulated the settings that he knew his way around the back of it as well as the front. He nodded. Harold held up a string of watercress and dropped it into his mouth, chewing and swallowing. Marcus shook his head, then smiled. It was the first time Harold had seen him smile.

"You any good with that thing?" Harold said. He wanted to ask where he'd got it, but refrained. His second thought was to ask if

Marcus had any images of his mother on the memory card, but he refrained from asking that, too.

"I'm okay, I guess. Better than I am paddling this canoe."

"You'll get the hang of it."

They got back in the water and dug with the paddles. As they rounded a bend downriver, the lower campsite came into view, first a red dome tent pitched on the bank, then the two women standing behind a column of smoke that could only charitably be called a fire.

Carol Ann waved, her long straight hair falling from a watch cap, the same flannel shirt she'd worn the night before, the same torn-at-the-knee jeans. She jumped up and down, waving, a campfire wraith holding a coffee cup, her body obscured by the smoke.

"Hey, Harold!" She kissed two fingers, extended them toward the passing canoes. "I see you found your son. Hey, Harold's son! Hey, Harold's son's dog!" She held her free hand high and waved it back and forth. "Happy hunting, you two. Save us from the bogeymen."

Harold extended his arm toward her, his palm up, felt his son's eyes upon him.

"That snowflake the head on your shoulder you was talking about?"

Harold did not turn toward him, and if he allowed himself a smile, it didn't show on his face.

CHAPTER NINE

Sons of the River

If it hadn't been for the big sign on the front of a shed adjacent to Bart Trueblood's house, a yellow circle with a slash through the words SMITH RIVER MINE and under it, NOT ON MY WATCH, Sean would have assumed that the man standing in hip boots by the bank was the one digging the copper, not the one trying to shut the project down.

Not large but barrel-chested, he was clad in a red-checked stag shirt unbuttoned to show chest hair the same shining black of his goatee. A Marlboro man with a devil's twinkle in his eye, Sean decided, one who'd discarded the cigarette in favor of chewing on a green twig, but who had yet to relinquish his other vices. Or so it appeared from the longneck-at-noon that dangled between his thumb and forefinger.

As Sean's raft neared him, Trueblood repositioned the twig in the corner of his mouth and set his beer down on the grass. He waded out and took the rope that Lillian Cartwright tossed to him. Dragging the bow onto the bank, he steadied it for her to step out—she acted like she didn't see the hand he offered—and she slipped as she hiked her leg over the inflated pontoon and fell unceremoniously, half in and half out of the water, knocking over the beer bottle behind her.

Trueblood kicked at the bottle to right it. "Soldier down," he said. "Soldier down." He laughed, a from-the-bottom-of-the-chest laugh, the same place his voice came from. "Mortal wound. Don't wake the medic." He bent to pick up the empty bottle. "The rest of the platoon is in the cooler on the porch. Let's hope they meet a more dignified fate. Here, take my hand."

Sean watched, amused, as Cartwright grudgingly allowed Trueblood to help her to her feet. Her face was flushed. She rubbed at a grass stain on her khaki pants. "Why isn't Sam Meslik here?" she said. No thanks for the hand. No pleased to meet you. No how are you doing today.

"He was." Trueblood nodded. "But he made better time in the canoe. When you didn't catch up after a few minutes, he paddled on down to Clint's house to make sure he was ready to go. He said you were a woman who didn't like to stand around with her hands in her pockets. Words to that effect."

Sean smiled. He knew that the words to that effect were probably a good deal cruder.

"The McCaine mansion is just around the next bend," Trueblood said. "It's about all that's left of the property. Clint's dad parceled it off over the years, ten acres here, ten acres there, that's how Clint comes by his money. He'll be wearing a cowboy hat when you meet him, snakeskin boots, a belt buckle the size of a painted turtle. But make no mistake, he's a virgin—all hat, no cowboy. Those Tony Lamas never penetrated a stirrup."

"I knew the two of you grew up on opposite sides of the river. I didn't think you were this close, though," Cartwright said. "I mean in proximity."

"Two of the oldest ranching families on the upper river. We were amigos once. Huck and Tom Sawyer, me being Huck, him the guy you'd want to sell snow cones in Siberia. Opposite sides of the river but not opposite politics about its future. More innocent times. Why, we—"

She cut him off.

"This is good stuff, but I think we should save it for the campfire. When I can get both of you into the frame. I want it to be fresh, not a rehash."

"You want mano a mano, that's jake with me," he said. "Come on up to the homestead. Grist for your film."

She put her camera on her shoulder and Sean trailed them to the house, a century-old one-story constructed of blackened logs and yellowing chinking, which was set among scattered tall pines. He couldn't remember the last time he'd ever heard someone use the word "jake."

It was a typical working family's house you'd see in any rural enclave in the state, added onto as the children came, with diminishing regard for aesthetics or continuity. At one end was an addition built of lighter-hued logs, at the other end an L-shaped plywood shed covered with Tyvek sheeting.

"I really should cut some of these trees down," Trueblood was saying. "They're a fire hazard sure as we're standing here in the yard. I even touched up the teeth on the Stihl. But they have sentimental value and I just can't pull the trigger. 'Harsh bark, soft heart,' that's what my mother used to say about me. Don't get me wrong. I'm a hunter and a fisherman, made a living writing about it in the hook-and-bullet rags. You could go into any outhouse in any deer camp in the country and you start leafing through *Field & Stream,* you'll find my byline. I had a column for twenty years. 'Bart's Back Forty.' But then I'm one of those people who rescues spiders and wasps, too, worries about stepping on worms in a rain. We could see some, I've heard. Weather, that is."

"Eighty percent chance of rain by Friday," Sean said. "And it could turn to snow."

"Snow in May. Imagine that? You'd think we were someplace like Montana."

Trueblood looked into the eye of Cartwright's camera and raised a pair of mischievous eyebrows. "By then you ought to have your story, Lillian. Clint and I, one of us, will have shot the other by then. There will be blood in the water."

"Is that a promise?" she said.

He ran his left thumb and forefinger down the opposite sides of his goatee, then nodded. Sean saw that he had a tattoo on that hand, a small snake that wound around the fingers.

Trueblood reached into his mouth and extracted bridgework containing two false teeth, the lower lateral incisor and bicuspid on the right side.

"Left hook," he said. "When you meet him, check out the ring on his little finger. It's got a copper nugget big as a sugar cube. That's what did the damage. But I got in some good licks, too."

He replaced the teeth and crooked a finger to lead them up the steps to his porch, pausing there to collect a beer from a cooler.

"The truth is I don't know how Clint will react to me. We've participated in the same forums, brushed past each other in Holiday Inn parking lots from Great Falls to Livingston, wherever they've held public meetings on the mine, but we haven't spoken in years. And he has everything to lose on this trip. It's me who possesses the rogue charm, and for the life of me I can't figure out why he's given me this forum. The mine's already licensed; they're just waiting for the DEQ's rubber stamp. That's the Department of Environmental Quality. The process will drag on, but the DEQ is basically a lapdog of industry and approval is all but certain. About all I can do is draw attention, put eyes on the project, try to find a chink in the licensing process for a lawyer to find a foothold. Failing that, hope to make a strong enough case that the governor frowns and the politicians think twice or the secretary of the interior steps in. That camera of yours could help me do that. You and the scarecrows."

"Are you the one who put them up?" Lillian Cartwright, coming straight to the point.

"Moi?" He tapped his chest. Bared his teeth, false and otherwise, in a smile.

"It's a 'yes or no' answer."

"I might have if I'd thought of it. I won't be surprised if Clint accuses me of it, or of putting someone up to it."

Trueblood swept a hand at the landscape, changing the subject.

"This was my great-grandfather's homestead, ridgetop to water-line. Came out from Illinois in 1881. His wife, my great-grandmother Charlotte, gave birth to their first son down around Independence Rock. Being imaginative people, they named him Rock. That's on the old Oregon Trail. Dodged arrows and rode out snowstorms and cholera, or so the family legend goes. My ancestor was a cattleman with no money to buy cattle. He moved west to Montana, managed a place out of White Sulphur Springs, saved his nickels, bought sheep because they were cheap, leased these eight hundred acres you're looking at, then bought up three adjoining homesteads one by one. My grandfather, my father, myself, all the Trueblood line was born here. It's the only home I've ever known."

He led them into a low-ceilinged living room and kitchen with a center fireplace built of river stones. Marble eyes watched them from the walls: a whitetail deer mount, a taxidermied brown trout that looked to have been five pounds, the full rug mount of a mountain goat nailed to one of the walls, its snowy hair in stark contrast to the soot-stained logs. And the ubiquitous snakeskin, also tacked on a wall.

"Bill Goat Gruff," Trueblood commented, indicating the goat. "And him"—he pointed to the snakeskin—"I call him Tickler the First."

"Tickler?"

"He tickled my leg with his fangs. By the time I got to Great Falls Deaconess, my calf was as big around as one of those Ponderosa rounds." He pointed to a stack of unsplit log sections by the fireplace. "They performed what was called a fasciotomy, made a zigzag incision down the leg to relieve pressure."

He pulled up his pants cuff to expose the smooth foot-long scar. "Did you know that snakebite victims have a much higher incidence of PTSD than the general population? Almost as high as war vets."

Sean's eye was drawn to a framed portrait of Trueblood above the mantel. It was a charcoal sketch with the face in profile. Sean was always interested by art and idled over for a closer look. The piece was quite good, possessing much the same animal magnetism of its subject.

He read the words scrawled at the bottom.

I drink too much. I smoke too much. I make love too goddamned much.

—Bart Trueblood

In the far lower right-hand corner were the initials BJT. Sean caught Cartwright's eye and she focused her lens.

Trueblood smiled. "Someone I scarcely recognize now. About all I do too much of anymore is talk."

"Is it a self-portrait?" Sean said.

"I'm a dabbler."

"No. It's good."

"Thank you."

"Do you still draw?"

Trueblood nodded. "I have pencil and sketch pad packed for our float. But my current medium is oil. I am presently working on a riverscape for Montana Parks. There's a competition for the new state poster. I see the look in your eye, Sean. Is it skepticism?"

"No." Sean smiled. "It's just that I will be your competition, if I can meet the deadline."

"To adversaries then." Trueblood tapped his beer against Sean's empty fist and tipped it back. They talked painting until Cartwright interrupted.

"I read that you were married, Mr. Trueblood," she said.

"My name's Bart. Bartholomew Joseph Trueblood, that's my given name. But yes, twice. Once by church, once by God. The woman who took my name died of breast cancer two years ago August. I miss her every day."

"You were married by God."

"It was a very long time ago. But that's something I can't talk about. You can lose your soul if you talk about some things." He shook his head. "Enough of that," he said to himself, his voice turning soft.

"Does it ever get lonely, living this far out?"

"Since Dolores died?" Trueblood nodded. "It surely does. But I still have the river, and I can make out what it's saying if I leave the window open. Ours is a conversation that began when I was born and has never stopped. The Smith is my wife, my mistress, my muse, my love. She haunts me. And my mission, to save her, is what keeps my ticker beating. I'm always on the road speaking, trying to raise the funds for legal expenses. It's not easy to go up against the kind of money Clint and his offshore investors bring to the table. Hard Rock Heaven Mining Cooperative is an Australian outfit with money from Canada, Europe, and Australia, everybody, it seems, but our own country. They haven't built the tailings facility or dug tunnel yet, let alone extracted ore, but they have already spent more than fifty million dollars drilling core samples. This is a David and Goliath story with the lifeblood of a river at stake, and all I have is my paintbrush and my charisma."

He showed them his charisma with a wicked grin, a clenching of facial muscles that ran a delta of creases back into his hairline. They were back on the porch, where he shrugged into a fishing vest and picked up a rigged fly rod and a spinning rod leaning against the cabin wall, shook off Sean's offer to tote his hard-sided boat bag, and nodded to him to get the cooler.

"What do you have in here besides beer?" Sean said. It was a heavy cooler.

"Ice breakers," he said.

———

Trueblood was right about Clint McCaine's appearance, as far as it went. He *was* wearing a cowboy hat, a sweat-stained silver-belly Stetson with a rancher crease, but as he also was wearing chest waders, no belt buckle was in evidence, no snakeskin boots. Sean knew he'd been a football player at Montana Tech in Butte, graduated from the School of Mines and Engineering—his bio was on the mine website. Still, he was larger than Sean had thought he'd be, one of those men who go through life looking down on their fellow man from their six-four, two forty. In McCaine's case, looking down with a wink and a disarming smile. He was one of those big men, Sean saw at once, who spread their legs and lean back from the waist to minimize their size and make your acquaintance more comfortable.

Sean had expected an arm's-length personality, a man with a long arm at that. He'd been prepared to dislike him. Instead, he found himself drawn to McCaine, his broad, handsome everyman's face, his crinkled-up eyes, the way he nodded when you spoke, as if what you had to say was of the greatest interest and you, personally, were the best thing to have happened to him that day. His short sandy hair was revealed above a tan line when he removed his hat to greet Lillian Cartwright.

"Lillian, may I call you Lillian, what a pleasure," he said. He bowed slightly, placing his hat over his chest. As he did, Sean noticed a birthmark at his hairline that had been covered by the hat. It was as large as a silver dollar and shaped vaguely like Montana. It lent him the touch of the common man, no doubt an advantage for someone whose job was persuasion.

Cartwright, who was filming, scrolled the fingers of her hand to say keep talking. They were standing on a varnished dock, with a flagstone pathway leading up the hill toward a river-stone-and-timber A-frame house that looked big enough to host a mining convention, which, Sean had read, it had.

"And, Bart"—McCaine shook his head—"whatever happened, it's past." He turned to the rest. "We were like this as kids," he said, pairing two fingers on his left hand. Sean noted the heavy copper nugget in the ring on the little finger.

"I know we have different views on the mine," he was saying, "but can't we please start over or at least turn the page? I'll start by saying I'm sorry. Sorry about letting my temper get the better of me that time. Sorry for all of it. And I'm very sorry about Dolores. She was a fine woman."

He extended his hand. "Bygones," he said.

Trueblood shook his head, then, with visible reluctance, the hand. "Sure, Clint. Whatever you say. But the past isn't dead. It isn't even past."

"What's that mean?"

"If you don't know, you don't know."

McCaine shook his head for the camera. He brought his shoulders up and let them fall. *You see the way it is,* his gesture said.

"Would anyone like to see the house before we push off? Going once?" He flexed his eyebrows. "Twice . . . ?"

Sean said he'd like to, and Cartwright waved the back of her free hand for McCaine to lead the way. They all followed except Trueblood, who said he'd stay at the dock watching over the boats. He flicked the cap off a bottle of beer with the spine of his belt knife and tilted it back. "Can't have the scarecrows stealing our gear," he said.

McCaine stopped. He stood, his back to Trueblood, twenty feet of charged air between them. He turned around.

"You call yourself an honest man, Bart. Answer an honest question. Do you have anything to do with the scarecrows? Any knowledge of them at all?"

"No, Clint, I don't. You're just going to have to accept that someone else objects to what you're planning to do to this river as much as I do."

"I don't plan to *do* anything to the river. The mine is twenty miles from the river. It's not going to affect the water quality whatsoever."

"You're going to tell these good people that you're planning to dig ore under the main spawning tributary of the Smith River, and water quality won't be affected? What planet are you living on?" He shook his head.

"Gentlemen, gentlemen." Lillian Cartwright had taken her camera from her shoulder. "Save your talk of the planet for the fire tonight."

McCaine put his smile back in place and nodded. Determined to get in the last word, he said, "Do any of you really think that I'd mine copper if there was a chance it would poison the river I grew up on?"

"You poisoned this place years ago, Clint," Trueblood said, his voice weary. "For both of us. And that's something I will never forgive you for."

Sean exchanged another glance with Cartwright. Whatever they were talking about, it didn't sound like copper.

"Go on," Trueblood said. "Show them your house. I'm sure they'll be impressed. Don't forget your bedroom."

"I won't dignify that remark with a response." And, wordlessly, McCaine continued up the stone walkway to the house.

Sean looked back at Trueblood, whose Adam's apple bobbed as he swallowed the last of his beer.

"You okay?" Sean said.

Bart Trueblood no longer resembled the man in the self-portrait with the piercing eyes and the devil-may-care countenance. He was smaller than that man now, the stag shirt hung on his frame, the greater part of him was simply not present. What past the two men shared, Sean had no idea, but one seemed to have survived it better than the other. That much was clear.

"I'm fine," he said. "Go see the house. It's a nice house. All the blood was mopped up years ago."

He looked away, and Sean turned to follow the group. It really was a handsome house. McCaine smiled with paternal pride as he showed it to them, the big empty-sky Russell Chatham landscapes, the genuine Navajo rugs, the Western-themed furniture, the bison skull over the fireplace.

He said, "Voilà," and ushered them into what he called his Copper Room, which glittered in the slant of afternoon sunshine pouring in the windows. It was a man's office out of a page of history when men of importance commanded dark offices, heavy mahogany furniture with copper beading, a big dark wood desk with a copper-cornered blotter, twin copper lamps with elk pattern shades, copper picture frames showing photos of copper mining operations, copper knick-knacks under glass, a copper Rolex watch that had to have cost a pretty copper penny, displayed in a shadow box. A cabinet with a hinged glass lid held a core sample taken from the proposed mining site.

McCaine encouraged them to run their fingers over the tube-shaped sample, which was about thirty inches long and as big around as a Louisville Slugger. Sean volunteered, the smooth, flaky-looking surface feeling cool to the touch and slightly slimy, as if it was covered by a film of skin lotion.

"Gentlemen, my lady," McCaine said, "the only other metal with that richness to its texture is gold." His tanned face had a copper tint in the sunlight that angled through the windows.

To Sean, it all seemed like a lot of copper.

But Bart Trueblood had been right. They'd completed the tour of the house, and not a drop of blood in sight.

CHAPTER TEN

The First Scarecrow

It took the better part of an hour for Harold and Marcus to skirt the cliffs and work up through a ravine to the upper plateau. But once on top, finding their way along the rim to a spot directly below the buzzards was simple. They found themselves at the top of a cleft in the cliff face that they'd marked from below as the best route to climb down to the cave.

Harold looked at his son for a sign of nervousness but saw none. "Don't worry," Marcus said as he lashed Cochise to a tree. "My mom's dad had some Mohawk in him. He worked on the Sears Tower, one of those guys you see sitting on a beam and eating lunch a thousand feet above the pavement. Must have rubbed off. I'm not afraid of heights."

Harold wanted to ask Marcus about his mother, what she'd been like, but knew this wasn't the time. He told Marcus to wait until he was in the cave before following, and stepped down into the cleft. The path, if you could call it that, was no wider than Harold's boot, but there were plenty of handholds, including a few stunted trees. Still, it was a sheer drop to the boulders some three hundred feet below, heart in your throat climbing if you stopped to think about it. The trick was not to. The wrinkle in the rock face went down at an angle and Harold had descended perhaps thirty feet when the scarecrow they'd spotted from their canoes came into view. Harold glanced at it but didn't allow it to distract him until he'd safely contoured the cliff face and entered the cave mouth.

From the river the scarecrow had looked as conspicuous as a black widow spider on a scoop of caramel ice cream, and now Harold saw why. It was made of bark-on spruce boughs, dark and twisted, while the color of the limestone cliff rock was ochre with a mottling of yellow. To the right of the cave entrance, on a large boulder blossoming with white lichen, four words were scrolled in black paint: *Not on my watch.*

The scarecrow was not upright but tilting forward, so that it appeared to be leaning out of the cave mouth. Like the one Harold had seen in the shed, the head was woven from red willow branches, with a hunk of rotting meat pierced by the stick that served as its neck. With the warming of the day, hornets that were sticking to the meat were beginning to buzz. As Harold watched, teardrops of blood formed on the meat and dripped with silent regularity into the void. The effigy appeared to be supported by God or sorcery, and it wasn't until Harold walked around the back of it that he saw the cords that extended from the branches to the recesses of the cave, where they were looped around jagged rocks on the cave floor. The engineering of the suspension was almost as impressive as the scarecrow itself.

As his eyes adjusted to the darkness, he began to make out pictographs—swirling red lines that resembled bleeding claw marks, a bearlike figure, two animals that looked vaguely like turtles.

Harold turned around to see his son ducking into the cave, his camera slung over his shoulder.

"Pretty cool," were the first words out of his mouth. "But the scarecrow, man, that head, it's messed up." He wrinkled his nose.

"He's putting venison in the heads to attract birds so that the floaters will spot the scarecrows."

"How do you know it's a he?"

"I don't, but be surprised if it wasn't."

"Yeah, I get you. The Y chromosome. We're the fuckups, no explanation necessary." He was taking photos of the scarecrow, then stepped toward the back of the cave as Harold held up a hand.

"I haven't examined the floor yet. Give me a couple minutes to trace any shoe impressions."

"Yeah. Sure."

Harold switched on his flashlight. The dust on the cave floor had been swept into swirling lines, as if raked with a giant comb.

"Looks like somebody dragged a Christmas tree," Marcus said.

Harold nodded. He looked around for a pine bough that could have left the marks.

"He probably had a branch and threw it out of the cave when he left," Marcus said. "Covering his tracks."

Harold nodded. "Are you filming or just taking pictures?"

"Both. I got extra batteries so I should be good."

"Do you want to look around, see some of your heritage?"

Marcus stepped forward and peered at the pictographs. While he did, Harold scraped up a pepper of granular dust and light gray pea gravel he noticed in a corner of the cave. It was bone residue. He placed it in one of his chest pockets, wondering if it was human and, if so, what it meant. Marcus had been preoccupied with the cave art Harold pocketed the gravel without drawing attention to his discovery.

"I like the abstracts," Marcus said at length. "These finger trailings." He shot with the camera. "And the turtles. A lot of tribes consider them magic. Because they live on land and water, they're travelers between this world and the underworld."

"What tribe do you think made them?"

"A test again, huh?"

"No. You know more history of this canyon than I do."

He said it as a flat statement and saw Marcus looking for the motive behind the words. Finding nothing, he shrugged.

"This was Flathead country in the 1600s and 1700s, far as you could ride in a month. Problem was the Flathead didn't have no horses. So the Shoshone came and drove them out. They had the horses, that gave them the upper hand. Then the Blackfeet, your people. They traded with the Cree and Assiniboine for guns, which they had got from the French. So they had horses *and* guns, that gave *them* the upper hand. Then the white man came with the smallpox. But the kiss of death was killing the buffalo. They say it was the white man's rifles, but our people had guns, too. We shot the hell out of the herds, though nobody wants to rewrite that into the history."

He shrugged. "Bullets don't care who's behind the trigger. You get rid of the buffalo, you get rid of the people. Anyone who stuck it out in this country, the soldiers drove them away. That place we put in, Camp Baker, used to be Fort Logan. Whole reason for its existence was protecting settlers from the likes of our grandfathers."

Harold smiled. He was no longer surprised at the two faces Marcus revealed to him, like opposite sides of the same coin. One was tarnished, the tough rez kid with his sarcastic wit, his seen-too-much-of-the-world eyes, his understandable skepticism and his reluctance to engage this man who was trying to step into his life. And then the flip side, the intelligent, interested young man with a winning smile behind the camera, whom Harold had caught looking at him when he thought he wouldn't notice, perhaps even looking up to him. Marcus had taken advantage of his education, Harold thought, and was not yet hardened to the point where he couldn't find his way back toward hope.

Marcus was speaking again. Harold followed his eyes to the walls.

"I'm guessing it's blood-based. That iron oxide was the key. They'd use animal fat as a binder, make a liquid paint. Pretty durable considering the fragility of the rock, all this limestone like to crumble just if you look at it. Who made it? Who knows? Could be people from a lot of tribes."

"But what does it tell us about the person who put the scarecrow here?"

"The art? Nothing."

"No, the fact that he put one here."

"Another test, huh? But okay, tells me he isn't just getting lucky.

You have to figure for every fifty caves, there's like, what, art in one or two of them? He's not just some floater with a spray can tagging a little graffiti, making a little mischief. He knows the paths of the grandfathers."

"That's my feeling, too. What do you think he's trying to say?"

"Don't fuck with my river."

"As in, please don't fuck with my river?"

"More like, 'Fuck with my river at your peril, dude.'"

Harold nodded, though he didn't agree. He was building a profile of the scarecrow maker that contradicted Marcus's statement.

He walked back to the cave entrance and peered down at the sandbar where they had dragged their canoes. As he watched the light dance on the water, a blue raft nosed around a bend upriver, a man at the oars, one in the stern, and a woman hefting something on her shoulder. Harold lifted a hand and the man at the oars did the same.

"You know that guy?" Marcus had his camera lens directed toward the river.

"The tracker I was telling you about. Sean. The woman, she's the one making the film I told you about."

"I don't want to talk to no white people. They fucked us, man. They gave us the pox."

Harold gave him a look as Marcus shrugged. "I hate them. Just telling the truth. Up on the rez, they're either gassing up at the Town Pump, look at you like a monkey in a zoo when they think you're not watching, or they own some store and look at you like you're a thief."

"I understand why you feel that way. I did, too, for years. But hate is like a cancer. It makes you dead to life."

"You're a psychiatrist now?"

"No. Just someone who's worked with quite a few white people. Something that helped me is remembering their ancestors were tribal, too. You scratch them, they bleed the same color you do. I had a grizzly up in the Madison Range toss me like a toy, lost a lot of blood. When it came to looking for a transfusion, nobody much cared about the color of my skin."

Marcus shook his head. "I still don't trust them. You got scars?"

Harold unbuttoned his khaki shirt and pulled it off, showing the ropelike scar tissue on his upper chest and left arm. He remembered the woman, Carol Ann, tracing the welts with the tips of her fingers.

"Looks like you have snakes breeding under there."

Harold could see that he was impressed.

"My mom never said anything about you fighting a bear."

"She wouldn't have known. This was a long time after." Harold saw the opportunity to ask the question he'd been wanting to ask since the first time he'd met his son. He asked it now, saw the cloud come over Marcus's face in the better light of the cave entrance. Marcus leaned over the void and spat. When he looked at Harold, it was the dark side of the coin that had claimed the expression on his face.

"I asked her about you. She said you were dead, that I was better off never knowing you."

Harold felt his heart sink.

"What, you going to tell me you were a good guy, she's making it all up?"

"No."

"Doesn't matter, anyway, does it? You weren't there. Good guy, bad guy, what's the difference?"

"She didn't even know my name."

"Just some drunk she picked up in Rocky Boy, huh?"

"We picked each other up." Harold knew how lame that must sound.

"If she didn't know your name, how come my uncle knew to call you?"

"I don't know. The rez is a small place. Maybe she recognized me later." *Or maybe she recognized me in you,* he wanted to say.

At Indian Springs, when they were collecting water, Harold had brought his face down to the surface to show Marcus a sculpin, a small, catfishlike creature whose mottled back perfectly matched the colors of the river bottom. For a few heartbeats, their reflections on the surface had been side by side, slightly wavering. Harold had already seen that Marcus walked like him and had other mannerisms that reminded him of himself, and the boy who stared up at him from the surface was his own image, or would be with time.

"But you couldn't remember her face?" Marcus said, not letting go of it. "You did what you did and you never saw her again."

"If I did, I don't remember. That's why I drink cider now, Marcus."

"You don't remember nothing 'bout her?" It was an accusation.

"She had green eyes."

"She was Turtle Clan."

"I figured that," Harold said.

"You know, you ain't stuck with me if you got second thoughts. I just came because I was curious. It's not like I'm looking for a dad."

"No."

Harold felt the silence in the cave. It seemed an odd place to be having the conversation, and he reminded himself that people had been having conversations in caves like this one, overlooking this canyon, for more than sixty thousand years. A long time, but no longer than sons had fought with their fathers.

"When we go down there," he said, "keep your head up. I know lowering your eyes is showing deference to your elders, but to them it's a sign of weakness, that you don't think you're as good as they are."

"This guy, the tracker, will he know who I am?"

"No."

"So are you going to tell him?"

"Yes."

Look where secrets have gotten me, he wanted to say. *They've only stolen seventeen years of my life.*

Instead, he said, "You'll be fine. Just be yourself."

CHAPTER ELEVEN

Writing on the Wall

By the time they climbed down to water level, the canoe with Sam Meslik and Clint McCaine had joined the rafting party and everyone was sitting on logs, eating lunch. There were handshakes all around, Sean commenting on how much Marcus resembled Harold, that add seventeen years and thirty pounds and they could be the same man.

Lillian Cartwright stood to take Harold's hand.

"Heard about you," Harold said.

"Don't believe everything you hear."

"I don't."

Cartwright focused her lens on Harold and asked if he minded.

"The camera stole my soul a long time ago," he told her.

She asked him about the scarecrow. He shrugged, the tracks on his arms rising and falling.

"Just what you see from here," he said. "It's made from spruce wood. Bark-on, that's why it's dark. Red willow to weave the pieces together, venison on a stick for a head. The one back at Camp Baker was driftwood, but the construction followed the same blueprint, right down to the meat."

"I was just asking Sean if we could go up there after lunch. I'd like to film the pictographs."

"Are you afraid of heights?"

"No. Well, maybe a little."

"Then not a good idea. You'll be coming across another scarecrow a few miles down the river. My understanding is you won't have to swallow your heart to climb up to it."

"Any idea who did this?" Cartwright asked.

"He's a tall man with big feet."

"Why do you say that?"

"You heard about the little girl who lost her shoe and thought she saw a scarecrow?" He waited for her to nod, and told her why he'd made the deduction.

"That's why they pay him the big bucks," Sean Stranahan said.

Cartwright didn't smile, just let the camera roll. She made a circular gesture with her left hand. *Go on.*

Harold looked up at the cave. He wasn't a person you could hurry.

"He's athletic. Safe to say he's not afraid of heights. He cut the branches up on top, I'd say an ax, but it was no easy task getting them down to the cave. Like I told Marcus, he's highly motivated, a man on a mission. He's self-reliant, and again, if it's the same guy who was up at the girl's camp, nonconfrontational. May seem contradictory, but he's not trying to draw attention to himself. The mine, yes, but he'd just as soon stay in the shadows. And he's smart. He knows people will be looking for him, and he's doing a decent job of covering his tracks. If he's traveling by boat, I'm guessing he's floating at night and hiding in the daytime."

"Wouldn't that be dangerous?" Cartwright spoke as she panned the camera across the rough surface of the river. "It's hard enough to dodge all the rocks in the daytime."

"It is. But we're two days off the full, plenty of moonlight for the next few nights. I'm guessing that's no accident. I'd bet his first trip through the canyon last month also coincided with a waxing moon. He knows what he's doing."

"And he knows where the caves are with rock art," Marcus said. "It's not common knowledge, so that tells us he knows the canyon. Maybe has a history with it."

Harold looked at Marcus. He was mildly surprised that he'd

offered his opinion. McCaine, who'd been rubbing the head of Marcus's dog, swallowed the last of his sandwich and cleared his throat.

"You're forgetting something," he said. He tapped his chest with his right forefinger. "He's trying to make yours truly look like an asshole."

"Probably no fan," Harold agreed. "Do you have any enemies who would do this sort of thing?"

"Do I have enemies?" His look was bemused. "I'll have to give that one some thought." He cocked his head for theatrical effect. "Maybe that gentleman at the other end of the log. What do you say, Bart? Are you my enemy?"

"Better than half the people in the state of Montana wouldn't shed a tear if you drowned in this river," Trueblood said. "In fact they'd consider it just deserts."

"I don't think you have that figure right, Bart."

"Oh, but I do."

"Then I guess I need to work on my message."

"Why? It's simple enough. You want to make yourself rich, and to do that you're willing to poison the Eden you grew up in."

"I would never do that."

"Then why are you going ahead with the project? You know the legacy of copper mining in this state as well as anyone. It's a ticking bomb."

Cartwright, who'd been filming, switched the camera off and stepped into the fray. "Let's save the pro and con for the fire tonight," she said. "I don't want you to get talked out."

"Oh, I don't think there's much danger of that," Trueblood said. "Is there, Clint?"

"Tonight's fine with me," McCaine said.

"Sure," Trueblood said. "A few hours won't change the facts. You know what Mark Twain said? 'A mine is a hole in the ground with a liar on top.' I hear Clint's honey-tongued spiel, and I need a double bourbon and a beer chaser."

"You have a cooler full of Coors Light. Pop the tab on one of those silver bullets and we can finish this argument here and now."

"A silver bullet, Clint. That's not a bad idea. 'Cept it would be better if it was copper-jacketed. More apropos. Have to have steady aim. Your heart's got to be a pretty small target."

McCaine stood, towering over Trueblood.

Trueblood looked up. "What are you going to do? Hit me?" He fingered out the bridgework on the right side of his mouth. "You already did that, remember?" He waved the bridgework around so the others could see it.

"That's because you said . . ." He paused. "You know I can't say what you said."

"I said her name. 'Rebecca.' There. I'll say it again. 'Rebecca.'"

McCaine's face had gone as red as the willows on the bank. Sean Stranahan stood to move between them. He could see the veins standing out in McCaine's broad forehead. McCaine glowered, then he held his hands up and backed away.

"This was a mistake," he said. "This was all a mistake. Lillian, I'm sorry. But I can't float another mile of river with that man."

"You're stuck, Clint," Trueblood said. "There's nowhere to go."

"I can get a helicopter in on the sat phone."

"You do that. Lillian here can film you tucking your tail between your legs. See how that makes you look to the public."

A measure of silence fell. Then the current lifted its voice, smoothing over the break in the argument. Sam Meslik crumpled up his sandwich wrapper.

"You can shoot each other as far as I care," Sam said. "But do me a favor. Wait until we float a few miles and get the tents up. We get a couple cool nights, we can field-dress you and float you out before you start to stink. Or I got a better idea. Why don't you take the canoe on this leg? The two of you in the same boat. You can kiss and make up, lower everybody's blood pressure a few points. Up to you, really. Sean and I get paid either way."

"You agreed to this trip," Cartwright said. Her eyes flashed from McCaine to Trueblood.

Trueblood replaced his bridgework and smiled out of the right side of his mouth, one that went all the way back past his porcelain canine tooth.

"I'm happy to paddle the canoe with Clint. We should all enjoy this slice of heaven while it lasts."

———

Harold had watched the confrontation with an impassive expression. He folded his arms across his chest and looked across the current to the face of the cliff. The light had changed and the scarecrow had fallen into shadow.

Cartwright focused her camera on him, zoomed in, then slowly twisted the lens ring to its widest angle.

"What do you call that, when you start with a tight focus and go wide?" The question came from Marcus.

"A pullback shot," Lillian said. "Are you interested in filmmaking?"

"Yeah, I guess. They took us to a dino dig where they were shooting a documentary on the *Maiasaura*. I spent some time with the cameraman. We were there a couple days."

"He has a camera," Harold said.

"I have competition, huh? What camera do you have?"

"Canon Rebel XS. Friend of my mom's gave it to me. All I got for a lens is a crappy Sigma, but it takes pretty good video."

"He took some pictures of the scarecrow and the pictographs," Harold said.

Cartwright nodded. "I'd like to see them. What year are you in school, Marcus?"

"I'm thinking of taking some time off."

"He's going to be a senior in the fall. I'm trying to get him to finish up, go to Montana State," Harold said.

Lillian took the camera off her shoulder. "I could put in a word for you at the film school there. It's one of the best in the country. They have a Native American film program called 'Native Voices.'"

"What would they want with an Indian who can't shoot a basketball?" Marcus said.

Cartwright shook her head. "Don't sell yourself short. Being Blackfeet works to your advantage. When I started out, people accused me of using my looks to get ahead. They called me Three Button Lilly. I'd unbutton three buttons of my shirt and show some cleavage when I wanted to get someone to talk to me, then I'd button them back up when I went in front of the camera. I felt like I didn't have a choice if I wanted to get ahead. Television isn't a flat playing field; nothing in life is if you're a woman. You have to use what gets you to the goal line. Up at the university, they need Native American enrollment. An intelligent young man like you, you would have to be a fool not to take advantage of it."

"Okay. Thanks, I guess. I'll think about it."

"You do that."

She turned to Harold. "You haven't taken your eyes off that cliff in twenty minutes. All the time those guys were working up to drawing knives, you're looking at that cave."

"He thinks there's something hinky about the sign," Marcus said.

"Oh? What?"

"Probably nothing," Harold said. "Just strikes me as odd, the way the letters are painted. You would think that somebody who wants you to read the words from down here would paint in block capitals, not write in longhand. But that's what he's done. Only the first letter of the first word is a capital and he's writing cursive, linking the letters together. It's very carefully done, all the loops just so, like in a grade-school primer. What do you make of that, Marcus?"

"This is the kind of shit he pulls," Marcus said for Cartwright's benefit. But there was no malice underlying the words. "Always trying to get me to think, like I know jack shit about it. I haven't written a word in longhand since maybe fourth grade."

"So what's that tell you?" Harold waited.

"Tells me he's old?"

"Old, or old-fashioned?"

"Whatever."

Harold looked into the lens of the camera and gave a slight shrug to go with his smile. *Kids these days.*

Cartwright twirled her finger, urging him to get to the point.

"Printing is a static form of expression," Harold said. "People who choose to print are hiding their identities. Cursive is more revealing of personality and emotion. All these letters have open loops. That's the sign of an open, artistic person. And they're relatively small. From here, when the cliff falls into shadow, you really need binoculars to read them. That tells me he's uncomfortable making a bold statement."

"But the words themselves are threatening, aren't they? And the scarecrow, it's also a threat. That's bold, if you ask me."

"You're right about that. That's what has me wondering. It's like he's driven to create this effigy of a watchman, but he's not so comfortable making his statement with it. His personality conflicts with his mission."

"You're sure you're reading this right?"

"I'm not sure at all. I took a handwriting class, part of my continuing education as an officer of the law. But my initial impression, going right back to the girl's story about her shoe, is that whoever we're dealing with, it's not a caveman with a club."

"Why choose a scarecrow to make his point?"

"Same question I asked myself. I came here yesterday, I was under the assumption the job had something to do with defacing pictographs. But this guy's not defacing pictographs. He's making a connection between the pictographs and the mine. Maybe he's saying this is sacred land that should be protected, but beyond that I'm just thinking out loud."

Cartwright shut her camera off and ran her ChapStick over her lips and capped it, buttoning it in her pocket over the swell of her breast. Harold saw Marcus watching her, Cartwright fiddling with the button longer than she had to.

"I Wikipediaed 'scarecrow' after the story broke in the *Tribune*," she said. "The Vanir were nature and fertility gods in Norse mythology. They were said to keep the settlements safe, and the villagers would build effigies of the Vanir in their fields; hence, the scarecrow. Gods protecting the crops and so on. Sometimes it went as far as offering human sacrifices, one man and one woman."

"God of Scarecrows," Harold said. "The little girl who saw the scarecrow, she said he was God. Like Jesus on the cross."

"The Scarecrow God. I like it," Cartwright said. She nodded. "Native Americans built scarecrows."

"Blackfeet? I never heard any of the elders mention that."

"Zuni. The children had contests to see who could make the scariest."

Harold nodded. "They did more farming, so I'm not surprised."

"Fish could be considered a crop. Maybe these scarecrows are meant to protect the trout."

"Could be. Make for a good story."

Cartwright nodded. "I know this sort of fell into your lap, but your work here *is* part of the story now. Do you think you could camp with us tonight? We're going to be at Canyon Depth. Plenty of room for another tent and I'd like to get your perspective on film. You, too, Marcus. You could help me set up the campfire shoot. And don't take it personally if I snap at you. That's just me. If you can put up with me, I can teach you some tricks with your Rebel. What do you say?"

Harold looked at Marcus, who shrugged. Harold said sure, and she went to get release forms from her camera bag.

"That wasn't so bad, was it?" Harold said.

"Her?" Marcus grinned. "Yeah. She reminds me of my Auntie Gemma. No bullshit. But you better watch out. She's got an eye for you now. You see the way she put that lipstick in her pocket, rolled it around with her fingers? She's giving you the three-button treatment, for sure. And she's got a voice, like to bite your head off, but with you, she's a meadowlark singing. She's out snaggin' for you. She'll be creeping in your tipi you don't zip that flap."

"I'll keep the bear spray handy," Harold said. "But you think about what she said, about the film school."

"I'm thinking about it. White people, man . . ." His voice trailed off as he shook his head, the merriment in his eyes. "Those two guys, I'm not so sure I want to be sitting by no fire with them. They like to kill each other."

"Distinct possibility."

"Like you told me, I guess. Tribal as they come."

CHAPTER TWELVE

War and Peace

If the first scarecrow looked like a black widow spider on a scoop of ice cream, the second was a chameleon, constructed of driftwood in tans and grays that matched the lichen splotches on the rock ledge it was propped against. Harold had the advantage of the coordinates and the ranger's description. Even so it took him a minute to spot it, several hundred feet above the east bank of the river. What finally gave it away was a slash of red that on inspection with binoculars revealed itself as a bandana tied around the scarecrow's neck. The sign—*Not on my watch*—was painted in light-colored letters rather than black this time.

"He's getting cagey," Marcus said. "Making it a challenge."

Harold lowered his binoculars. "Ranger told me that a trapper used to camp under the ledge. An old hermit named MacAllen."

"Do you think Trueblood and McCaine can climb up there? It's steep, but it's not scary steep." Harold and Marcus had been the first down the river; the raft and the other canoe were not yet in sight.

"If they haven't already shot each other," Harold said.

———

No shots had been fired and no one begged off, although the rocks made for iffy footing. As they climbed to the overhang, Bart Trueblood stopped more and more often, leaning forward to put his hands on his knees and breathing heavily.

"Go on." He waved them on and up. "I'm having . . ." His breath wheezed. "Just a mild disagreement with Father Time."

"You sure, Bart?" It was McCaine, with what sounded like genuine concern in his voice.

Harold, who was in the lead, with Sean Stranahan a few steps behind him, caught his eye. Stranahan shrugged. Maybe the two adversaries, in the confines of a single canoe, had taken Sam's suggestion and made up.

Twenty minutes of testing footholds and fighting through thornbushes saw them to the overhang, all but Trueblood, who had dropped farther and farther behind.

The condition of the scarecrow was what drew the eye. In contrast to the one Harold and Marcus had examined upriver, this one was much deteriorated, the branch that made the arms broken off and a large hole in the basket weave of willows forming the head. Something had attacked it, a bird with a strong beak, or an animal with sharp teeth. Perhaps a raccoon, Harold thought. Whatever had done the damage had taken the venison as its reward, and the only trace of the meat that Harold had come to regard as the brains of the effigy were dried brown blood smears and a few deer hairs adhering to the branches. Harold brought one up against the light of the sky. The barred pattern of the hair was different than the hairs he'd examined upriver. It was body hair from a whitetail deer, not a mule deer.

He thought back. According to the ranger, this had been the first scarecrow reported by floaters. The one Harold and Marcus had examined that morning was the last reported. If the ranger's theory was correct, that the maker—Harold still had a hard time thinking of him as a criminal—had completed one long float and started another, then nearly a month had passed between his construction of the two scarecrows. Mule deer and whitetail were both common in the river bottom. Meat from two different animals could be explained by the time difference. A small detail, but it bolstered the theory.

The pictographs under the overhang were ambiguous, mostly

indecipherable swirls and smears, the one identifiable image a sun. As Harold and the climbing party examined the art, Bart Trueblood came wheezing up. He said he'd spoken too soon—the river canyon wasn't a slice of heaven so much as a slice of hell. He took his hat off and wiped at the rivulets of sweat that ran down either side of his widow's peak.

Besides the pictographs, all the evidence of human encampment pointed to the hermit, not to the maker of the scarecrows. A fifty-gallon drum, blistered and rusted out, contained scraps of leather and a number of books, their pages yellowed, the covers gnawed by industrious teeth. Most curious were a pair of ice skates, the blades rusted, all the leather but the hardened soles devoured by rodents.

Harold leafed through the books, mostly novels. The exception was the autobiography of Ulysses S. Grant, in the pages of which was an envelope. The canceled stamp was dated October 6, 1945. Harold slipped out two discolored sheets of paper along with a sprinkling of petrified mouse droppings. The pages were sticking and he drew his sheath knife and used the blade to carefully separate them. They were the military discharge papers of one Scott Henry MacAllen. DOB—April 26, 1900. Place of residence at time of enlistment—Hillardville, Florida. Rank at date of discharge—First Lieutenant. Harold photographed the two sheets and replaced the papers in the envelope.

"I knew him," Trueblood said to the assembled party. "Old Scotty, I saw him skating the river in those. He'd skate the big pools below our property line. Clint, you met him, too, didn't you?"

Though Harold had already seen evidence of a thaw between Trueblood and McCaine, he was still surprised by the tone of voice. It was just a question, nothing in it veiled or argumentative.

McCaine nodded. "He'd stop by, trade my dad a few pelts for groceries."

"Same with my folks," Trueblood said. "The bottom had dropped out of the fur market, all the beaver were gone, muskrats weren't worth a plug nickel, so he was down to trapping coyotes for the bounty. Nobody needed coyote pelts, especially if they weren't prime, but coyote was all he had. My dad treated him with respect and always made it sound like he was getting the better deal. This would be back in the early sixties. He died '71 thereabouts. So I was maybe ten. I can remember he wore this coat made out of elk skin and he smelled pretty ripe. When I made a comment, my dad set me down and told me how he'd got to be the way he was. That he'd fought in the Battle of the Ardennes in the Great War and seen so much blood soak into the ground that he'd said the hell with humanity, came to the mountains, and grew his beard and never left."

"He did though," McCaine said. "He was on Okinawa in '45, before Japan surrendered. Imagine, someone whose only knowledge of the outside world was fighting at the front in two world wars. No wonder he was a little mad."

"He wasn't mad," Trueblood said. "He had a lazy eye that made him look mad, and he had a strange way of not finishing his sentences, but you could understand him fine. One year he showed up with a red-tailed hawk that he'd caught as a fledgling and taught to hunt for him, kill ducks and rabbits. It would be on his arm, but it would fly away when anybody got close. He had it a few years, I recall."

He smiled. "They called him 'Old Red-tail.' Scotty, not the bird. You would think we had good times growing up. I suppose we did at that."

"Sure enough," McCaine said. And then a pause, both men's eyes swimming away to a land and time as faded as the pages of the books. A silence stretched into the corners of the overhang before Marcus's voice broke it.

"War and Peace," he said.

He read the name on the inside cover. "Bartholomew P. Trueblood." He held it out for the lens of Cartwright's camera.

"My old man," Trueblood said. His eyes come back into focus.

He nodded to himself. "Dad would stop in bookstores when we were on the road. Pick up paperbacks in the dime bins. I can remember him saying to me, 'What do you think? Would Scotty like this?' He would have given him the books, but Scotty always insisted on trading. Usually whistles or animal figures. You spend the winter in caves, you have a lot of hours to whittle wood. The last time I climbed up here, years ago now, there were still some of his whittlings lying around. I think old Scotty liked the Russian writers because the books had lots of pages. He wasn't always who people thought he was."

"What do you mean?" Marcus said.

Harold studied his son, once again surprised that he was taking the reins of a conversation until he realized that Marcus was speaking for Lillian Cartwright, prompting the others to develop the story without the need for her to interject questions.

"Well," Trueblood said, "he'd take a bath at the house, shave, put on clean clothes he kept there, and my dad would drop him off in town. Scotty knew people there. He'd stay a week or two, once or twice a year."

"What Bart's trying to say," McCaine said, "is he wasn't a hermit per se. The 'people' Bart is talking about"—McCaine scrolled quote marks with his fingers—"was a schoolteacher in White Sulphur Springs whose husband was killed in the First World War. Scotty was in the same regiment, and after the armistice he would visit her."

"How do you know this?" Marcus asked.

"Because White Sulphur was a town of five hundred souls. Everybody knew everybody's business. The story is that they had a child and the woman, I can't recall her name, she tried to make an honest man of Scotty, but he wouldn't leave the river. You heard about that, right, Bart? About the woman?"

Trueblood nodded. "What I was told is she and her son left the state, went back to where she was from, Florida, I think it was. Same place he was from. Old Scotty wound up ranch-handing for the X-Bar. Room and board if you count sleeping on frozen ground as 'room.' He rode the property boundary with a fence spreader and a few coils of two-strand barbed. Take a week to make the circuit, mend a fence, put up a post, round up a few stray cattle, then do it all again. No more lonely than running a trap line, I suppose. Died when his ATV rolled over on him. One of those three-wheelers. Couldn't get out from underneath and froze to death."

"I'm not sure about that last part, Bart. I heard he rode a horse. Horse came back and he didn't. Had a heart attack and froze to death, that's what my dad told me."

Bart Trueblood nodded. He spoke for the gathered. "That's the way it is out here. You don't get two sides to a story. You get two stories."

"Sure enough," McCaine said. "But old Scotty wouldn't have wanted to go any other way. He'd want his last view to be of the sky. I hope it was a horse. Least then, he'd have had somebody to talk to."

As the men reminisced, Harold had let half his mind and one eye return to the scarecrow. He walked over to unknot the red bandana. *The fewer floaters who were drawn up here the better,* he thought. As the knot ends came free, he noticed a long hair snagged on one of the thin willow branches. Harold buttoned the hair inside the breast pocket of his shirt. He looked down, and there, as he half expected, was another little mound of dust and bone gravel. He pocketed that, too, keeping the gravel from the two locations in separate pockets.

A half hour later they were back at the boats, with another hour and a half seeing them to the mouth of Tenderfoot Creek, and, a few hundred feet below the marriage of the waters, their destination, Canyon Depth. While the tents were going up, Harold found a couple plastic bags and deposited the bone gravel he'd found at both scarecrow sites, zipped them securely, and used a black marker he kept in his fishing vest to mark the two locations, in case analysis revealed they were from different sources.

He trusted his instincts as another man might trust the North Star, and though he didn't understand his reluctance to share this evidence with the party, especially Sean Stranahan, he didn't question his decision.

CHAPTER THIRTEEN

Ghost Town

It was early evening in a month when days died the death of a thousand cuts. Harold didn't need a watch to tell him that sunset was still hours away, and with the question of dinner to resolve, he assembled his six-weight Meiser fly rod, a gift from Martha Ettinger several Christmases ago, and hiked from the campsite to the junction, leaving Marcus behind to put up the tent. Marcus wanted to stay in camp to help Lillian Cartwright set up her reflectors for the filming, and, regardless, the truth was Harold was the kind of fisherman who liked to fish alone.

Through the course of the day the river had swollen with runoff, its opaque current interrupted by a line of silver-black where Tenderfoot Creek added a jolt of clear current.

Harold opened his fly box. In off-color water any color fly will do as long as it's black, and the first cast with a rubber-legged woolly bugger shining with copper and blue Mylar strands—a fly Sean Stranahan had given him—brought a strike. The foot-long rainbow quivered, then went rigid when Harold smacked the back of its head with a stone. He shucked the insides, ran his thumbnail to clean the blood line under the spine, cast again into the seam where the colors kissed, and was rewarded with another strike and a fish the same size. A third trout would fill the pan and it took him a while, but he got it, a brown with mandarin-colored flesh—the meat of the two rainbows was blush pink—and might have caught more if he'd had the inclination.

He didn't. Unlike many fly fishermen, Harold was not a sport angler who practiced catch-and-release. He was a predator, and like other predators, he did not hunt, or in this case fish, after he had satisfied his need. In no hurry to return to camp, he decided to explore a little of the creek bottom. The GPS the ranger had given him had a collection of waypoints that had been added before there was any talk of scarecrows. One marked the junction where he stood, with another nearby but on a higher contour. That one was marked "Ghost Town."

Intrigued, Harold found a path that switchbacked uphill from the creek and arrived on a tongue of flatland bordered on three sides by steep cliffs. Several acres in extent, the plot had Homestead Act written all over it. The main structure—a tongue-and-groove cabin built from cottonwood logs with a river stone chimney—was more or less intact. Four outbuildings whose original purposes had been lost over time hadn't fared well. The roofs were gone. The four-pane windows were broken or boarded up, the chinking between the logs eaten away, so that what Harold was looking at were skeletons of a century past, echoes of a way of life whose participants had never known anything but toil and sweat and tears and poverty, and for whom Harold had no empathy whatever.

True, it was soldiers who had driven his ancestors from the river. But the white locusts, as Harold's grandfather had called the settlers, put down the roots that grew into the trees that multiplied into the forests of humanity that barred any chance of his people's return to their homeland. The bitterness in Harold's heart was well buried, but it was there even as he did the white man's bidding. It was there—it was not lost on him—even as he searched for a person who had the temerity to question those who line their pockets with the profits of the earth, whose assurances reminded Harold of the treaties imposed upon his people, and that were lies before the ink dried on the paper.

The homestead had long since been picked over by human scavengers. What was left, except for the structures, were a few old stove parts, coils of wire and various other metal artifacts, rusting at their leisure into the earth. It was more to satisfy a mild curiosity than with any expectation of finding something of interest that Harold pushed opened the door of the house, which had once been secured by leather hasps but was now held in place by wishful thinking and a few loops of baling wire. He took one step inside.

And stopped. He tapped his right hand to his hip, where his sidearm would be, the belt there holstering only his collapsible wading staff. Good for coaxing snakes out of the path, not a lot else.

Someone had been living here. More accurately, he had been occupying the few square feet of floor space cleared of debris. Harold gave the single room a once-over while his eyes adjusted to the gloom. The plank floor was strewn with the detritus of dreams—a woodstove but no pipe, a stack of white-painted windows, the glass panes cracked, harkening, Harold thought, the early years of occupancy, when there might be hopes of expansion. A bedspring tilted against a wall; a rolled mattress spilled its guts where mice had gnawed the pilled ticking. There were two paint cans, the cemented pigments cracked in whorls. A pine table stood on legs turned by a lathe. One piece of handicraft puzzled Harold until he realized that it was a baby's crib makeshifted from odd pieces of board—the shoddy, haphazard craftsmanship, in contrast to the well-made pine table, made him wonder if the child had come on the heels of the first hard times. Standing against the wall behind the crib was a metal pantry with rounded shoulders, the drawers rusted shut, its facade painted in a motif of red flowers on elegantly curved stems. It was the only woman's touch in the dwelling.

Harold turned his attention to the other side of the cabin, where a military cot stood on steel legs. Beside it, on an overturned wood crate, was a kerosene lantern. Above the cot, empty loops of jute cord dangled from J-hooks screwed into the roof timbers. This was for hanging a mattress or a bedroll, anything you wanted to keep from the industrious teeth of rodents.

He peered down into a wood-slat bucket positioned under a gaping hole in the roof. An inch of evil-looking water floated with dead spiders and earwigs. As a storm had moved through the area a little more than a week ago, Harold would have expected more water. That meant to him that the bucket had been emptied within the past few days, during which the periods of rain had been light and intermittent.

A large wooden picture frame hung not quite evenly on the wall behind the cot. Harold flicked away a few clinging flakes of gold leaf with his thumbnail. He fished his headlamp out of his pocket and switched it on to cut through the gloom. A sepia-toned photograph was trapped under the edge of a partial pane of glass. The photo showed signs of having been folded, the paper worn white in the folds, so that it appeared in quadrants. In two of the quadrants a couple danced, the woman with curly dark hair, her skirt flying, the man wearing a shirt with a small checked design buttoned to the collar. Their faces were blurred, though not so badly that Harold couldn't have picked them out of a room of square dancers. For a square dance it clearly was, the silhouette of the caller, a man wearing a straw cowboy hat and holding a fiddle, elevated on a stage in the background. There was a banner against the wall behind the caller. It was grainy and out of focus, but Harold thought he could make the first letter out as an "I" or maybe an "L," another perhaps a "V." All the other dancers were blurred to anonymity—the camera's focus was on the couple in the foreground, who danced side by side in what Harold recognized as promenade position.

He smiled to himself. Martha Ettinger was a square dancer. She'd dragged him to a dance once that was held in a big barn up out of Wilsall—that's how he knew about promenade position. He thought of her for a second, Martha, then put the thought aside as one might take a shovelful of dirt from one place and set it in another. Not being disrespectful, just being Harold.

He worked the photograph out with his fingertips, taking care not to cut himself, and turned it over. The back was unstained by normal exposure, leading Harold to believe that the photo was a reproduction of a much older photograph. His first thought was that the dancer was the hermit. Not that the old man had actually hung the frame. Far too many larcenous fingers had passed down the river for anything like a photograph to have remained over the decades, but that MacAllen was its subject. And the woman? Perhaps she was the schoolteacher McCaine had mentioned.

He took several photographs of the eight-by-ten, then replaced it under the glass. Harold thought of the mysterious Scarecrow God, as he had come to think of him. *Could he have chosen this place as a base of his operations? And if so, what was his relationship to the couple in the picture?*

He flicked his headlamp from the low to the high setting, engaging all five LEDs. He cast the bright circle along the walls and then the floor. He was looking for something, and it was the breeze sifting through the gaps in the logs, lifting the dust of mouse feces and making him cough, that brought it to light. A hair had been trapped between one of the cracks in the glass and was nearly invisible until stirred by the air. Plucking it, Harold suddenly felt claustrophobic and stepped back out of the cabin into the slant of light.

He was aware that there could be eyes on him, and up until this point he had done nothing that any inquisitive boater who stumbled upon the homestead might not have done also. Like others who move about unarmed in those pockets of the wild still ruled by tooth and claw, Harold had a finely honed sense of danger. But the air did not carry the electrical charge that on other occasions had made him aware of unwanted company. That, coupled with finding no food, water, or sleeping bag at the homestead, made him think that the occupant had left, taking his provisions with him. That was on one hand. On the other, the photograph suggested to Harold that the squatter planned on returning.

Rounding the last bend before camp, he saw a long filament of fly line unfurling over mid-current. The angler was out of sight, but

Harold knew it was Sean Stranahan. Stranahan painted the water with the most elegant line that Harold had ever seen. But dirty water was dirty water, and at Harold's approach Stranahan's shrug told him that all the fish must still be in the river.

Harold explained what he'd found, keeping his voice low, adding that he intended to stake out the homestead on the chance someone might return.

"Let's take a look at the hairs," Stranahan said.

Harold brought them out, setting them side by side on a dark slab of basalt. The one he'd found with the effigy was straight, about a foot long and a dirty yellow color. The other, the one the wind had revealed in the cabin, was perhaps half the length, kinked, and gray.

"Different man? Same man?" Stranahan said.

Harold thought about it. There were the obvious differences, but if the shorter, curly one was beard hair, as he surmised, they still could have come from the same person.

"I think same," he said. "Now look at this." He placed the plastic bags with the bone gravel on the rock.

"Human?" Sean asked.

"No way of telling without analysis. But they were placed in neat little piles, in a dark corner of both caves. Like in a ritual. Someone scattering the ashes of a loved one."

"If that's the case, then they're from the same person."

"That's the way I read it."

Sean again looked at the hairs. "Long hair and a beard in recluse country. Doesn't exactly narrow it down."

"No," Harold said, "but it's got me thinking. If this scarecrow guy is holed up at the homestead, where's he keep his boat? I looked up and down for quite a while, no trace that a boat had been dragged up from the bank."

"Maybe he's floating. On his way to build a scarecrow."

"Then what's he do when he's done? Leave the boat downriver, hike back here to lay his head?"

"You're right, it doesn't make sense."

"What if there isn't a boat? We just assumed he had to be a floater. But you look at the map, this river twists like a snake. You can float for an hour and be lucky to cover a mile as the crow files. But if you climb above the cliffs, it's a plateau. You can walk ten miles on top, cover twenty river miles. And there's hardly anyone lives up there. A lot less chance of being spotted than if he was on the river."

Stranahan nodded. "I'll go with you," he said. "We can split the watch."

"I appreciate the offer, but I think I'll go alone."

He raised his chin toward the tents standing on the bench. "Lillian, if she knew about the homestead, she'd want to set up klieg lights."

"She wants you on camera tonight."

"She'll have her hands plenty full with those two. Tell her that Marcus and I will stay with the party all day tomorrow; that ought to pacify her."

"How will I explain your absence?"

"Maybe I like to sleep apart from everybody, listen to what the river says. You know, me being your mystical stereotype."

"What about the others? The photo you found, if you ran it by McCaine and Trueblood, they might be able to ID him. They knew MacAllen."

"Maybe, but that doesn't change what I need to do. You still have those binoculars, the Zeiss?"

Stranahan nodded.

"I'll borrow them, you don't mind."

"All right, but let me have a look at the picture?"

Harold showed him the photo he'd taken with his phone.

"I thought it best to leave the original in place. I didn't want to arouse any suspicion if he comes back."

Stranahan, enlarging the image, said, "Not to change the subject, but we're friends, right? Martha and I, that doesn't get in the way, does it?"

"Not a problem. Martha makes her own way."

"You never mentioned your son before. I just thought maybe—"

"Nothing to do with it. His mom, she died a couple months ago. I didn't know I had a son. He didn't know he had a father. I introduced him to you this morning, I had to think about it. Do I say, 'This is Marcus, my friend'? Or do I say, 'This is, Marcus, my son'? I do it one way, he thinks I'm ashamed of him or something. I do it the other way, then I'm being presumptuous about the relationship, man who's never been in his life before."

"I see what you mean. He's up there leading the discussion. He's an impressive young man."

"I'm finding that out. He has two or three faces. He's not sure which one to put on about half the time."

Stranahan nodded. He'd had the same experience with Martha's younger son, David. Sometimes they were best buddies; other times David found fault in anything he said and looked at Sean as an intruder.

"Anybody get shoved into the flames yet?"

Stranahan smiled. "Nobody's on fire, but then it's early, the alcohol hasn't kicked in. That bit of bromance you witnessed, it wasn't their better natures coming to the fore. They have a bet. The first to blow his stack owes the other a bottle of Scotch. Label of choice, hundred-dollar limit. Sam doesn't think they'll make it through dinner."

CHAPTER FOURTEEN

Where Love Flows

"It's foolproof," McCaine was saying. He tossed his paper plate into the fire, the greasy residue of Sam's elk steaks flaming up like kerosene. "I know that sounds presumptuous, I could see Bart rolling his eyes if it wasn't dark. But if you really studied mining, you'd know there's nothing to fear. No, I'm not conveniently forgetting that one of our extraction tunnels will reach underneath Farewell Creek, and yes, I'm aware that it is a spawning tributary for trout and that it has an unfortunate name, as our detractors seldom fail to point out. But our mining operation ensures that water cannot run out of the mine and contaminate the creek. All the water used in the extraction process will be treated with reverse osmosis; it will be clean enough to drink. Any contaminants will be sealed in the tailings facility or made into a water-impermeable paste, then backfilled into the chambers that the ore was extracted from. What Bart complained about earlier, what happened at the Gold King Mine in Colorado, that was a result of the entrance tunnels being below the water table. All our tunnels will be above it. That kind of disaster could never happen here, even if there was a breach, if for no other reason than gravity. But, gentlemen, there will be no breach."

He shook his head, a wry smile in the firelight. "Not on my watch."

He moved his chair out of the column of smoke. The smoke followed him.

"Smoke knows hot air when it sees it," Trueblood said. He waved his hand in a dismissive gesture. "Clint talks a good game, but he'd strip-mine Mount Rushmore if he thought there was copper underneath it."

"That isn't fair, and you know it." McCaine shook his head.

"No, it probably isn't. But Clint has the backing of foreign corporations to consider, and all I have are my words. First"—he smiled up into the camera's eye as Lillian Cartwright walked around the fire for a better angle—"there *will* be a breach. It isn't a question of 'if'; the question is 'when.'

"And if it happens after the extraction, say ten years down the pike, or twenty, you can bet that the Hard Rock Heaven Mining Cooperative will have been dissolved. 'Not on my watch'? What Clint means to say is that his watch will be over and no one will be around to hold accountable. Hard-rock mining follows a classic pattern. Ore is extracted, reclamation assurances are indefinitely delayed, and then the shit hits the fan. By the time the company's misdeeds have the inevitable consequence of a tailings breach, poisoning the water, the perpetrators—for that is exactly what they are—are long gone. If and when the original owners are sued, they file for bankruptcy. At that point the EPA steps in, and you replace one crook with another. The EPA delays, politics rears its ugly head, and all the time it takes to work through the courts, the fish are dying from heavy minerals released into the river."

He shook his head.

"And it doesn't have to be a tailings breach. The digging alone exposes sulfide minerals. When the sulfides become exposed to air and water, which is inevitable, they release sulfuric acid. Guess what that does to a trout's gills. Maybe you don't have to drink the poison; they don't get the choice. They go belly-up, just like the geese did when they landed in the Berkeley Pit."

"What the hell does the Berkeley Pit have do with anything?" McCaine said, exasperation in his voice. He shook his head. "Keep your cool, Clint," he said to himself. And to Trueblood and the rest circled at the fire: "That was a completely different kind of mining operation."

Trueblood snorted. "Was it? Anaconda Copper Company dug rock, ran it through the crusher to separate out the copper while the rest leached poisons into the water. Anything that came within spitting distance of the tailings turned belly-up—fins, feathers, or fur. I'm told all those snow geese looked like angels. The winds made two lines of them on the surface of the pit, five hundred dead geese forming the shape of a cross. Maybe that's where the Scarecrow God found his inspiration."

They argued for another hour—permit process, jobs for the community, reclamation timeline, transportation precautions, greater good, the philosophy of multiple use. Spiritual and monetary value of trout. It was an educated give-and-take in a gloom that became a mist, that, with the fall of darkness, became a rain. The rain hissed against the coals. Beads of water dripped from the felt brim of McCaine's Stetson. Bart Trueblood turned the bowl of his pipe down to keep the tobacco dry. Neither wanted to be seen as the first to seek shelter. Lillian Cartwright, who had pulled her camera tripod back up under the edge of the rain fly, kept filming as Marcus held an umbrella over her camera for insurance. One eye to the aperture, she looked at him with the other and winked. Then she caught the attention of Trueblood and McCaine and drew a line across her throat.

"Great job, you two. Come on. Get out of the rain so I can kiss the both of you."

———

Harold raised the heavy binoculars. Relics of the Cold War, they had superb low-light optics designed to help East German border guards spot defectors climbing the Berlin Wall. They could not turn night into day, but now that the rain had let up and the moon had fought free of the clouds, the grounds of the homestead were revealed in a milky glow.

Harold could not only see the cabin forty yards away, but a doe mule deer that was cropping grass within a few steps of the door.

The tree he'd selected was downwind of the cabin, and with branches heaped in front for cover and his back to the trunk, Harold felt sure that no one approaching the grounds would either see or scent him. The deer was a godsend, for she would inform him if anyone came into the vicinity. In the meantime, he could close his eyes and let his mind drift.

Who would tack up a photograph of a man who, if in fact it was Scotty MacAllen, had spent nearly his entire life deliberately avoiding his fellow humans?

This was the question Harold turned his mind to, letting it eddy among possibilities. Though a recluse, MacAllen had on at least one occasion spoken out about threats to the watershed. According to the ranger, the story in the paper called him the Smith River Watchman. Looked at that way, Scott MacAllen himself could be said to be the very first Scarecrow God. Perhaps the current one was paying homage as he drew attention to the dangers the river faced from the mine.

Or perhaps not. Harold was not a man given to speculation, and soon he found himself thinking about Marcus. He had read somewhere that the love of a father for his son is stronger than the love of a son for his father, and that the same could be said of a mother and her daughter. The love that parents shower upon their children even exceeds their love for each other. Love flows downhill, and now that Harold had finally worked past his initial bitterness over being left out of Marcus's life, he had opened his heart and was experiencing that flow of love as a blanket of warmth, and for the first time in his life.

He blinked open his eyes. He was shivering, the warmth he'd felt apparently not having the same affect on his bloodstream as his heart, and after zipping up his fleece jacket, he picked up the binoculars. The doe had grazed out of sight, and with her departure, his all-night vigil began.

CHAPTER FIFTEEN

The Three Amigos

Three empty wine bottles, a fourth with a swallow left, and an empty Jim Beam fifth—the latter one of the so-called "ice breakers" from Bart Trueblood's cooler—stood beside the fire ring. The whiskey bottle glowed like blown glass. Sean found himself staring at it, through it, beyond its warm transparency to where Bart Trueblood sat, a lean and hungry Satan, the black hairs of his goatee glistening.

"Last of the Mohicans," Trueblood said in his gravel voice, and raised his cup of whiskey.

It was true, the rest had retreated to their tents. McCaine, drunk and trying to ingratiate himself, be one of the boys, tipping his hat as he said goodnight; Sam, first to bed and uncharacteristically quiet, but then he was the one who shouldered the responsibility for the trip; Lillian Cartwright, dropping her guard, her Southern drawl returning.

"I thank all y'all for your cooperation and we'll see you in the morning," she'd said. And drawn Marcus to her side and kissed him on the cheek. And then once more, giving him a taste of her lips this time, as she put it, "For good measure."

"If you weren't so damned young I'd eat you like the peach ice cream my Nana made."

Marcus had left the fire when she did, though in the opposite direction, toward his tent, leaving Sean and Trueblood to add the last log.

Trueblood pulled out his pipe. "I noticed the Meerschaum in your pocket," he said. "You treat it with a lover's touch, but you don't light it."

"It was my father's," Sean said. "That and a couple bamboo fly rods he made are all I have left of him. Touching the pipe is a habit, like rubbing a rabbit's foot for luck. Usually I'm not even thinking of him."

"Of course you are. You're thinking of him whether you know it or not. I'm an expert on the subject." Trueblood pointed with his chin. "Down by the river. Let's smoke a bowl."

Sean followed him down to the bank, where the boats eddied on their tethers.

"I'm going to ask you a question," Trueblood said.

"Shoot," Sean said.

"Do you believe in love at first sight?"

"I took you for straight," Sean said.

"Don't joke. It's a serious question."

Sean looked up at the slot of sky between the spires of the pines, the belt of Orion, the Hunter, riding above the southern horizon. "No," he said. "Soon after meeting, but not at first sight."

"It happened to me, though. It happened to me."

Trueblood got his pipe going, then leaned forward to see his reflection in the moonstone current.

"My face is a lot older now," he said. "The river tells me what I already know. But I was young once. Her name was Rebecca."

"She who must not be named," Sean said.

"That was unkind of me, saying it to his face like that. I couldn't say her name either, not to anyone but myself, not for a long time."

"How old were you?"

"I was nine. May thirty-first, 1962. My birthday. My father had driven up that morning with a johnboat in the bed of the pickup. He said he'd got it at a sheriff's auction, that it had been evidence in a murder and had a bullet hole in the bottom. It was old and beat to hell and it did have a hole that I plugged up with a green stick, but I think

Dad was just telling a tall one. My mother had tied a ribbon around one of the cleats. They helped me carry it down to the river. I was standing on the bank, driving in a stake with a sledgehammer to tie the bowline to, when the world changed. That sounds melodramatic, I know. But nothing that's happened before or since in my life has had that effect."

He pulled on the pipe, spoke as he looked out over the current that glittered like mica. He said that about a week before he got the boat, a family had opened up a campground on ten acres they bought from Clint's folks on the west bank, a bend in the river with a stand of cottonwoods. His parents had met the couple who bought the land. They had operated a campground in Maine, on the Bay of Fundy, but they couldn't take the mosquitoes and the no-see-ums anymore. So they'd sold the place, packed up, and just kept driving west until they ran out of bugs. They had put in a couple of picnic tables down by the water, and the day that Bart got his new boat, when he was pounding in the stake, a girl came walking up from the direction of the campground. She took her shoes off and sat down on the bank with her feet dangling in the water. She had yellow hair, but it was difficult to see her face under her hat and she didn't look across the water at him.

So there they were, her on the one bank and him on the other, going whack, whack, whack, beating the hell out of the stake with the flat of an ax head, maybe fifty feet from each other, both acting like there was no one for miles around. Trueblood said it was very strange because he had gone out of his body even before she sat down. He caught himself breathing fast and missing the stake with the sledge. He walked back to his house to see if the light-headed feeling and the tightness in his chest would go away, because he wasn't sure that she had caused it. But it was still there, so he went back out, and this time he pulled the boat into the water and started to row across, his back to her and watching his own house get smaller and smaller. He could see his mother working in her garden and she waved to him, and he waved back, and it felt like he was saying goodbye.

"I was, in a way," he said to Sean. "I was an only child and my mother and father were the most important people in my life, and now there was this girl I had not even spoken to. I was so light-headed that when I got to the shore and stepped out of the boat, I stumbled and fell in the water.

"It made her laugh. The first thing I ever heard from her was laughing. It was an inauspicious start. 'You're going to catch a cold,' she said."

She'd asked him if he could catch a crawfish without getting pinched. He said everybody from Montana could do that, and she said anybody from Maine could, too, and quicker, and it went like that, each of them being patriotic to their state and catching crawfish and watching them shoot away when they let them go. She said she had a younger brother who was always following her around like a dog, getting underfoot, but he couldn't swim and wasn't allowed to go to the river without an adult with him, so that's why she had walked up from the camp. To get away.

He could remember it so clearly, the smell of her skin when their heads were together to look at a little snake he'd picked up, her breath on his forearm, the warmth that radiated from her head, the sound of her breathing. The snake was a rubber boa, not much larger than a big earthworm, and he'd pass it into her hands and she'd pass it back, the snake going from one finger to another and curling around them, so that her fingers were in its coils at the same time his were. It looked like they were wearing identical rings. "Look," she'd said, "we're married." Then her mother rang a triangle and she had to go to dinner.

"So that's where the tattoo of the snake on your hand comes from," Sean said.

Trueblood nodded. "I wear it the way I would wear a wedding ring. It means no less." In the moonlight, Sean saw him bend over his reflection in the water.

After that, Bart said, he and Becky were together every day. Clint wasn't on the scene yet. His parents were summer people, his father was in the state legislature, a bigwig. Every year they'd come for the Fourth of July and stay until school started up in Helena, where they lived the rest of the year. For a month, there were the two of them, Bart and Becky, and when Clint showed up, there were three. The three amigos, Bart's mother called them. Clint was two years older than Bart, three older than Becky, and though he tolerated her, sometimes he treated her like she was a nuisance. That went on for two more summers. Then the third summer came, and as soon as Bart saw her, he knew he would lose her. The ugly duckling had grown into the swan. Clint saw it, too.

He pulled on his pipe.

"I tell myself he never loved her like I did, and I believe that to be true, but no question he was smitten, to use one of my mother's words."

Trueblood shrugged. Clint was older, taller than him by half a foot, went to the big high school, had gone on vacations to California. He'd even seen the Beach Boys, wouldn't let you hear the end of it. He was popular, athletic, and a natural leader. Bart was a river rat who went to a two-room schoolhouse in White Sulphur Springs.

"What chance did I have? I ask you, Sean."

It wasn't a question that required an answer, and presently he went on.

Clint staked his claim and Becky became aloof, finding fault in anything Bart said. He found himself tagging along behind them. "I wish you'd just get lost," Clint told him once, and Becky had, by her silence, echoed the sentiment. He was forced out of their circle, and finally he just stayed on his bank of the river and they stayed on theirs. He was so devastated that he dreamed of killing Clint, even went so far as to take his father's elk rifle and aim it at him from across the river.

"I put the crosshairs of the scope on him, and with a live round in the chamber. For just a second. I didn't push the safety off, but . . . still. That's how mad I was for her."

The next summer the anguish they'd put him through was over. Becky's parents couldn't make a go of the campground. It was too far away from any tourist destination, wasn't on the way to anywhere, and the road in was awful. Becky's family moved back East, where her dad and mom got jobs managing a summer camp at a place called Blue Mountain Lake in the Adirondack Mountains, for rich kids from Boston and New York.

Trueblood knocked the coal from his pipe, shook his head at the memory. "In a way it was like I'd never known her," he said. "I'd walk around where we'd been hand in hand once, but her face began to fade and the country lost its interest for me. I started doing stupid things like climbing cliffs I shouldn't, because I didn't care if I fell. That's how I got bit by Tickler the First, reaching a hand to pull myself up onto a ledge without looking where I was putting it."

He began to load the pipe.

"Aren't you going to smoke?" He held out the bag of rough cut. "Put hair on your pectorals."

Sean said he was fine.

"I'm not boring you, am I? I just thought you ought to know. The real stories are always the stories behind the stories."

"You're not boring me. Did you see her again?" Sean couldn't understand how a childhood crush that was over so long ago could have left such deep scars on two middle-aged men.

Trueblood had the pipe going and drew on it.

"Yes, I saw her."

The cherry coal winked in the darkness.

"There are days I wish I could say I didn't, for everyone's sake."

CHAPTER SIXTEEN

Yellow Ribbons

When he picked up the story again, nine years had passed since the idyll and heartbreak of his childhood. He'd joined the Army right out of high school. Without a college deferment, it was either that or be drafted. Had gone to Vietnam like the unquestioning Montana son that he was, and became one of the lucky, catching two golden BBs six weeks into his tour. He told Sean that his left leg could tell the weather, though climbing remained a bit of a problem. That's why it had taken him so long to get to the cave that afternoon. He said he had a cane but too much vanity to use it. Especially with Clint being such a hail fellow.

As it turned out—he drew on the pipe as he thought back—a couple weeks before his injury a letter came for him in one of the helo drops. It was from his mother, who wrote him nearly every day, and inside the first envelope there was a second one, unopened, that had been sent to his parents' address. A return address, but no name. The canceled stamp read Bangor, Maine. He'd looked at it, his fingers shaking.

"Here I was," he told Sean, "important things to do like staying alive, scared for my fucking life, and I was shaking because of an envelope. It shows how some things never go away, even after you thought that part of your life was dead and over."

Inside the envelope was Becky's senior-class photo, a small one like you'd put in your wallet. There was a note on the back. "I was a fool. It was you all along. Please forgive me." It was signed "Love, Becky."

He'd written back, telling her where he was, and that he feared he might never make it home. He wrote: "I've loved you all my life. Will you marry me? If you will look up at the North Star and say 'I do' before God, then I will do the same."

He wrote that he'd carry the photograph over his heart to keep him safe. And it did, depending on how you looked at it. It was a month later that he took two bullets during a firefight in the Battle of Ap Gu. One chipped his left tibia. The second bullet—Trueblood patted the ribs on his left side—had missed the photo by about two inches on the side to miss it by, if you have to be shot. It sent a fragment into his left lung.

Trueblood tapped the stem of his pipe against his chest. If the bullet had hit the photo, he'd be dead, he said, so maybe her picture did possess a kind of magic. He'd been Hue-ed out and spent a month in recovery at the 6th Convalescent Center in Cam Ranh Bay. That's where he had got the tattoo of the snake on his fingers.

He nodded with the point of his goatee, looking across the water.

"I'll never forget the day I came home. Those trees in the yard I said needed cutting down, one of the reasons I don't is my mom had put yellow ribbons on them, and when I look at them today, I think of that. She told me to take a walk around, that there was a coming-home present behind one of the trees. I didn't let myself think about it, didn't want to get my hopes up, because she'd never written back. I was thinking a horse, maybe a graphite fly rod, I just didn't know."

She was standing behind the last tree in the backyard. She was wearing a blue dress. It turned out her parents had moved back to Maine, and that's where she'd flown in from.

He paused at this point in his narration and looked at Sean. When he spoke again, his voice was scarcely audible over the sound of the river.

"I told you I wouldn't tell you the story of being married by God, and here I have. But what we said to each other that night, that is one thing I think I'll keep private. You understand that?"

Sean said he did.

He'd seen her in May, he said, and they had set a date to be married in the yard on the second week of July. It would have been in Maine, but her mother had died and she was the organizer in the family, so it was better all around if the wedding took place in Montana. The plan was they would build a house on the property, help Bart's father set up a guiding business, and put up a few rental cabins. Becky knew that business and tourism was picking up.

Clint's folks still had their house on the river, but the last time Bart had heard from him, he'd graduated from Montana Tech and was entering law school at the University of Montana. They'd been on good terms by then, and as an old family friend, he was invited to the wedding. That's when Becky had told him that she had a confession. She said that she and Clint had had a relationship, that they'd reconnected after high school and he'd taken a trip to Maine to see her. It hadn't lasted long. Neither was what the other expected they'd be. But there it was. She didn't want their life together to begin with a secret.

Bart assumed by relationship that she meant a sexual one, though she hadn't spelled it out and he hadn't asked. It had bothered him, but then, who was he to hold her to a standard of purity? They had been out of touch for years, and it wasn't like he'd been waiting for her. He wasn't a virgin. In fact he'd been seeing a young woman before he went to war and would end up marrying her ten years later.

The second bowl smoked, he knocked out the coal, murmured something Sean couldn't understand, and said, "I'm drawing this out, aren't I? It's that it's hard to get around to, so you put it off. You speak like you're telling a story, nothing deeper. That's how you keep the soul from leaving your body."

He said that the night before the wedding, his parents had had Clint and his parents over for dinner. Afterward, the three amigos went down to the river. They'd all been drinking and Clint dared them to go skinny-dipping. This being July, the water was warm. Bart wasn't comfortable with it and said so, but Becky had always been . . . unbashful, if you had to put a word to it. When they were kids, they'd go swimming and she would take her shirt off to keep it dry, even after she started to develop just a bit. She wasn't an exhibitionist, but more like an innocent, someone without the usual inhibitions. She started to unbutton her shirt, and Clint had said, "That's what I remember, that's what I'm talking about."

That's what I'm talking about?

Bart told Becky not to do it. She said, "Oh, come on, I'll leave the bits and pieces on, you can too," and Clint was stepping out of his jeans, and said something like, "I'll bet you remember me now," though he later denied it. But Bart heard what he'd heard, and it was a coarse remark, and he had snapped, and the next thing they were fighting on the bank and Becky had jumped between them and was screaming, "Stop it! Stop it! Stop it! If you don't stop, I'll jump into the river and drown!"

But they were rolling around, not listening to her. When they finally broke apart and stood up, squaring off, Clint said, "Where's Becky?"

Becky was gone. The two young men stopped fighting and ran up to the house to see if she was there, not there, and ran back. They got in the johnboat and rowed it out, and shone lights around. But the mist was over the water and it was like looking through smoke. Below, they could hear the river where it started running fast and Bart thought he heard something, maybe Becky calling. So they kept going down and down, but couldn't find her, and hauled the boat back upstream and floated through again, this time with Bart's father in the boat. It was his father who spotted her shirt in the light. She looked like she was moving, but she wouldn't answer and the closer they got—well, they knew. Her body was only moving because it was in an eddy. And her head, it was like she was lying on a pillow of blood. Bart held her while his dad went back to the house to call an ambulance. It had to come all the way from Helena, and Bart was still sitting in the water, holding her to his chest, when help finally arrived. His father had to pry him away from her.

He stopped. His voice had broken, and Sean could see his chest heaving.

"Clint was running up and down the bank like a crazy man, calling for her until he lost his voice. Long after we knew she was dead."

It turned out that she had cracked her skull. That's where the blood in the water had come from, a deep fissure behind her right ear. In the morning, they found an exposed rock in the middle of the river that had dried blood on it. Apparently, Becky had not been swimming, but was wading across the river to get away from the fighting and lost her footing on the slick streambed stones and fallen. The impact with the rock had probably knocked her unconscious, and she'd been swept down the river and drowned. The sheriff questioned them, and Bart admitted hearing Becky say she would jump into the river if they didn't stop fighting. It was just a horrible accident, of course. There were no charges brought. But the two young men had triggered the events that led to her death, and Bart Trueblood and Clint McCaine had been reliving the nightmare ever since.

"So you see," Trueblood said in a quiet voice, "when you heard Clint at lunch, talking about forgiveness and moving on, that I'm somehow not able to do that and he is, don't believe it. He's as haunted as I am. This trip isn't about the mine. If it was, like I said before, Clint wouldn't have agreed to it. The truth is he can't forgive himself and still thinks that the two of us can turn the corner on this thing. That the fondness we had for each other isn't that deeply buried, and if we can revive it, we can share the pain and finally put the past behind us. Well I've got news for him. I've tried getting past it for the last thirty-eight years. I've tried with pills, alcohol, marrying another woman and having two children with her. Rebecca is still as close as you are standing to me."

"Did Clint ever marry?"

"A rodeo queen. Miss Montana once upon a time. Arm candy for the banquet circuit. They divorced. No children. I don't know it for a fact, but I have a feeling she couldn't live with his demons. You get behind that smiling face and he's just a lost soul. Ever since Rebecca, all he's done is wander in the wilderness of his own head. You see what this is? It's Eden, Cain and Abel. Genesis. The whole damn book. Everything but the fucking snake."

"Aren't you being a little dramatic?"

"Of course I am. I drank a quarter fifth of whiskey. But it's true. What was the gift Abel gave God? You remember your Old Testament, don't you?"

Sean tried to recall his Sunday school lessons. "A sheep. Or was it a goat?"

"Fattest of the flock. What did Cain give him?"

"I don't remember."

"Grain. Cain was a farmer. God liked the sheep better. Cain became furious and killed Abel. When God asked Cain where he was, Cain said, 'Who am I? My brother's keeper?' And God marked him, and banished him to the Land of Nod. What did you see on Clint's forehead?"

"A birthmark."

"Is that what it is? Or is it the mark God gave him? That's what I see, and that's what he sees every morning when his face stares back at him in the mirror. You take away a few letters and even his name is Cain."

Sean didn't say anything. They stood, listening to the river rise.

"Aren't you going to ask me who God is in our drama?" Trueblood said in a quiet voice.

Sean didn't answer. He knew that Trueblood would tell him.

"When old Scotty visited us in the winter, I'd give him jerky from the deer I'd shot. Clint, the budding geologist, would give him pretty stones from the river. When they dried, they were just gray. So you see, I was Abel. Clint was Cain, and old Scotty, he was God. Now Clint's only here in the flesh. His spirit is banished, and all that keeps him from eating a bullet is the mine. It gives him a purpose. And if the tailings breach, so be it. The river's been dead to him for years, whereas to me, it's all that keeps me alive. I don't hate Clint. He's my brother. I feel sorry for him."

Trueblood put his pipe in his pocket. "Thanks for listening. Like Clint likes to say"—he spread his hands to encompass the black opal river, the moon-bathed cliffs—"it's a hard rock heaven. But it's a hard rock hell, too."

CHAPTER SEVENTEEN

Blood or Kisses?

"Some watchman you are."

Harold opened his eyes, the light just kissing the horizon to the east. "I heard you coming."

"No, you didn't."

"Smelled you, too."

Sean squatted a few yards away. He rummaged through his backpack for his thermos of tea. "Nothing, huh?"

"A doe kept me company. The river told me its problems. What's going on below?"

"Everyone's asleep."

"Late night, huh?"

"If you call two in the morning late. It went better than I thought. They talked themselves out of politics and remembered they'd been friends once. Lillian was in a good mood, now that she's got her story in the can. Everything from here on down to the take-out is gravy. She has an eye for your son, but I think it's a mentor's eye. He seems to enjoy the attention."

Harold nodded. "He drink anything?"

"Marcus? Just cider."

"Good."

"I did learn something last night. Remember when they were at each other's throats, the forbidden subject?"

"Rebecca." Harold stood up and stretched, getting the kinks out. "Bad blood there."

Sean gave him the short version of the story that Bart Trueblood had told him on the riverbank.

"So they're either going to draw swords or bury the hatchet. Which do you think? Blood or kisses?"

"We'll see what the day brings," Sean said. "Last night was the liquor talking."

———

It was still talking, or so it seemed to their ears, when Sean and Harold walked back into camp. Marcus was fussing with a matchless fire, coaxing new sticks to flame by waving his hat over last night's coals. He looked up, smiled, and rolled his eyes. Swept his right arm to include the scattered campsite, the snoring tents.

McCaine and Sam Meslik were the loudest, sounding like buffalo death rattles. By comparison, Lillian Cartwright exhaled popping noises. Only the tent Bart Trueblood had pitched was silent.

It was still silent an hour later, after everyone else had risen—an optimistic word, staggered to their feet more accurately—and had their coffee and were back among the living.

"Who wants to pull on his toes?" Sam said. "We've got fifteen miles to make today."

Clint volunteered. They heard him say, "Come on, old buddy. It's morning and I need someone to argue with." And then, louder, with urgency. "Bart!" Followed by "Shit. There's something wrong."

Sam was up and three "goddamnits" later was digging into his duffel for his medical kit. "The fucker's got a pulse like a racehorse. But Jesus, he's hardly breathing. Sean, help me get him out of the tent."

Sean did as told and they stood in a circle as Sam, who was a certified wilderness first responder, talked to himself as he began to systematically check the body.

"Drooping eyelids. Skin color is off. Edema in the left hand."

Sam unbuttoned the cuff of Trueblood's shirt and they saw at once the cause of concern—twin puncture wounds an inch apart on the lower forearm, raised like black kidney beans. The skin around them was turning an angry red and looked puffy in early stages of necrosis. Sam licked his fingers and worked the wedding ring off the left third finger. He asked for a knife to cut the leather band of Trueblood's wristwatch, which had bitten deeply into the swollen flesh.

He barked out orders.

"Sean, get the sat phone and find out when we can get a helicopter in here. Air Mercy out of Great Falls is closest. We can float him to Sunset Cliff in an hour and they can land on the bench above the bend. If they can touch down closer, great. Harold, let's sit him up. We need to keep the wound below the level of his heart."

"What can I do?" Marcus said.

"You can see if the goddamned snake is still in the tent. If it is, kill the fucker. Use the ax, whatever. Just don't get bit."

"I'd like to help," McCaine said.

"Then get your shadow out of my goddamn light."

McCaine stepped back.

"Sorry," Sam muttered. "You grew up with him, has he ever been bitten before? Snake? Spider? Does he have any allergies?"

"He was bitten by a rattlesnake on the calf," Clint said. "Back when we were kids. It was my dad who drove him into the hospital."

"Well, fuck," Sam said.

"Is that bad?"

Sam's face was grim. "It means his body has produced antibodies to fight poison once. They've gone dormant, but they're still there, ready to answer a fucking call to arms."

"Isn't that good?"

"No. It means if he's bit a second time with a similar venom, the body can overreact. It might produce antibodies too fast, because they have a head start. He can have an allergic reaction and go into anaphylactic shock, and I don't have a fucking EpiPen."

"I do. I'm allergic to bee stings." It was Lillian, speaking from behind the lens of her camera.

"Then you're finally good for something besides criticizing my shirts. Keep it handy. We won't use it unless he shows symptoms."

Marcus had come back from shaking out Trueblood's tent. He'd found no snake.

"Why didn't it rattle?" Sam said, more to himself than anyone else. "You'd think if a snake crawled into your tent and you moved enough to make it strike, the son of a bitch would rattle."

"Maybe it did and we didn't hear it," McCaine said. "We were all pretty out of it. I know I was."

Sam grunted. "It doesn't matter. The reason you kill the snake is so they can make the positive ID at the hospital. You don't want to give the wrong antivenin. But the prairie rattlesnake is the only game in the state, so it's a fuckin' gimme."

Sean came back from making the call. "They can put down at Cow Camp," he said. "Fifty minutes. They gave me a bunch of instructions for first aid."

"The only first aid that would really come in handy is a fucking forty-horse for the raft," Sam said.

———

Harold and Marcus watched the boats pull away from camp. Sam was at the oars, Lillian Cartwright attending to Bart Trueblood, ready to administer the EpiPen at the first signs of shock. The canoe that Sean Stranahan was paddling with McCaine was already at the bend downstream, out in front to establish the line.

"Do you think he'll make it?" Marcus said.

"Odds are in his favor."

"What about the allergy stuff?"

"I don't know. That was news to me. But with the water rising, they'll make good time. Come on, we got a camp to break."

That was the plan. They'd pack up, put a tarp over the gear, take the valuables in their canoes, and leave the rest to be rafted out later.

"Do you think we'll see them again?"

Marcus had become attached to the party, Lillian Cartwright in particular. That much was clear to Harold, never mind the feigned indifference in his voice.

"No," Harold said. "After they get Trueblood evacuated, they'll haul ass on the oars. Both boats should be through to the take-out in a couple days. But you and me, we still have a job to do."

Packing up Bart Trueblood's tent gave Harold his first clue about what might have occurred. In one corner was a muslin game bag of the sort that hunters carry to put elk quarters in. Harold always packed one himself, for stuffing with clothes to make a camp pillow. This bag looked to be used for the same purpose. It was empty but for a shirt, underwear, some socks, and a mess of greenish-white excrement. Harold dropped his nose to it. The bag reeked of rattlesnake. The door of the tent had been unzipped, and Harold figured that the snake, sensing the warmth from Trueblood's body, had slipped inside and nosed its way into the game bag. At some point, it could have been hours later, the snake had slid out of the bag and struck Trueblood, probably when he rolled onto it in his sleep. Rattlesnakes don't strike without provocation.

Still, it was curious. Like Sam had said, why hadn't it rattled? Why, for that matter, hadn't Trueblood cried out when he was bitten? Rattlesnake bites throbbed like hell. Harold had had a running pal in his childhood days, a boy named Francis whose catchphrase was "Watch this." He'd picked up a baby rattlesnake with the predictable result, a bite that made his hand swell up like a catcher's mitt and turn black with necrosis. He'd screamed bloody murder and three fingers of his left hand had never grown longer. His friends renamed him Baby Fingers.

"What did you say, Marcus?"

"I said, 'What are we going to do?' I mean, after packing camp?"

Harold crawled out of the tent. It was a good question. The Scare-crow God had erected his effigies on cliff faces up and down the Smith River, so far without anyone but a little girl catching so much as a glimpse of him. How could Harold expect to do better, especially if the man was on foot with no boat to give him away?

Something was bothering him, had been for some time now, an apprehension that had built into a foreboding and had started with the loss of a girl's magic shoe. A dread had settled over this canyon. The cliffs reflected on the surface were still beautiful, but there were forces at work that ran deeper, and he regretted not sending Marcus down the river with the rest of the party.

He looked at the boy, who was standing on one foot and scratching at his cheek with his fingernails. *My son*, he thought. And saw himself as a hawk, mantling over Marcus with his cupped wings, protecting him from harm.

"I'm thinking you go on ahead," he said. "You'll catch up to them in twenty minutes. Wherever they camp tonight, stay with them. Take advantage of Lillian's offer to pick her brain."

"What will you do?"

"I'll stake out the cabin in case anyone comes back. You stay with the party until you reach Table Rock. Wait there for me. Don't take any chances with heavy water. If it looks dangerous, line your canoe down through it, or portage. Sean, Sam Meslik, you listen to them. If you reach a stretch they say is too risky to float, don't. Pull over to the bank and wait for me. Worse comes to worse, we'll sit it out until the river begins to drop."

"You're thinking I can't handle myself, I might be a liability I stay with you and somebody shows up."

"Maybe, but I've made up my mind."

"Just like that. I don't have a say?"

"No."

"You treat me like a child."

No, Harold thought. *I treat you like my son.*

CHAPTER EIGHTEEN

The Creature from the Black Lagoon

He came with the first stars, when twilight's curtain was all but drawn and the owl by the river was asking his questions.

Harold was asking them, too. *Who? Who goes there? Who are you? Who?*

The figure was treelike, the trunk stooped forward with the arms swinging loose and long. The head trailed tendrils of hair that reminded Harold of the moss called Old Man's Beard. He focused the binoculars on the figure as it bent from the gloom of the forest into a swath of moonlight. The man—for it was far too large a figure to be female—appeared to be carrying a pack with some-thing thin lashed to the back and sticking up over his shoulder. A rifle barrel? No, it wasn't quite straight, had a curve at the end of it. The figure faltered, then stopped as the man bent to rest his hands on his thighs. Harold could see a knife sheath swinging from a wide belt. When the head dropped forward, tangled hair fell across the man's face.

As soon as Harold was certain that the man had no weapon within easy reach besides the knife, he stood up. He thumbed the hammer of his grandfather's old Model 71 Winchester to half cock, not trying to muffle the distinct click.

The man figure lurched upright at the sound, but the long arms stayed at his sides.

"Who's that? Make yourself known."

"I mean no harm," Harold said. He stepped from the shadow of the tree. "Just want to talk."

The man swung toward him, the mosslike hair shifting in the wind that had been steadily picking up pace through the evening.

"Then why are you holding a piece on me? That's a goddamn act of aggression I ever seen one. Any feller hang a dagum barrel on me, he best be ready to fire it."

"I'll set the rifle down," Harold said. He set it on the ground, raised his hands, turned around. "I'm unarmed."

"You a gol-dang fool, you know it?"

The accent was Deep South, bayou South, kiss-your-cousin South.

"My name's Harold." Harold walked purposely up to the man, holding out his hand. After a hesitation, the man extended his. Fingers long and bone white in the moonlight wrapped around Harold's hand, then quickly released their grip.

"Jewel," the man said. "My old man named me that 'cause I had such big gonads coming out of the womb. Least that's what I was told."

"Where's your accent from?" Harold asked

"You ever hear of *Creature from the Black Lagoon*?"

"No."

"They filmed that movie 'bout five mile up the road from where I growed up, twenty mile out of Tallahassee. People hear you talk this way, they think you must be simple. Call you a cracker, call you a hillbilly. But that's north of wrong by five hundred miles. Where I come from it's flat as a Aunt Jemima pancake." He held out his hand level with his waist.

"I don't think you're simple. I think you're smart. Can we go somewhere out of the wind, sit and talk?"

"What you want to talk about?"

"Just talk."

"You think I'm smart, huh? I coulda been, but I got brain damage. Back when I was in school I could run you your multiplication tables but couldn't hardly sign my name more than print a 'X'; you asked me to draw a horse it wouldn't look like no living animal. Then I got my ass lit up like a Christmas tree when a fuckin' mosquito mine tripped, like to cave half my head in. I never was right after, but I could draw you a horse right down to the breed. You hurt one side the brain, the other takes over, and that's fact. Now I'm artistic but I . . . I . . . it's hard to pick up words. It's like they're on the floor but they got a slime on them or something. So I just sort of stammer around and people think I must be of weak mind. Way I talk, it's like my head's on low speed in a kitchen blender."

The right arm swung toward the homestead cabin. "I got a lantern in the dwelling. There might be a . . . a few drops a kerosene in it. I'm plum outta supplies. This far north it don't matter so much. You can read a book 'til per near twenty-three hundred hours."

"You were in the military."

"They call it that. Bunch of crewcuts and fuckups is what it was. I was a conscientious objector, but they done took me anyway. I was a band-aid 'cause of that. Next to your second lieutenant and field radio operator there ain't no higher rate of fatality than your special forces medic. I liked the country well enough. 'Cept for the kraits, it weren't no different than the swamps I growed up in, just your regular boonies."

"Krait?"

"They call it the cigarette snake 'cause you get bit, you got time for one smoke before you're dead. But really you got time to smoke about half a pack. Then your diaphragm freezes up and it's K-MAG-YO-YO. Kiss my ass, grunts, you're on your own."

He laughed, a slow "hey-hey-hey," then shrugged off his pack and tilted it against the cabin wall. Harold could see that the "stick" that poked from the top of the backpack was actually the neck and fret board of a small guitar, or maybe a ukulele.

"You want to know why that war ended?" the man said. "I give it a real lot of thought."

"Yes," Harold said, to keep him talking.

"It's 'cause of the GI smoking pot. By the end of my second tour, that would be in '69, more than a third of infantrymen were toking, that's a fact. You toke and the war quits making sense, not that it never done in the first place. 'Bout the only thing kept me sane was reefer. I'd offer you, but I'm down to stems and I need it for the medicinal effect. It slows down the swirling. Makes me an intelligent-sounding man, if you can believe it."

Jewel was fooling with the lantern, shaking it, fiddling with the wick, striking a match against his fingernail, and lighting it. The yellow glow revealed the craters on his cheeks and his unkempt hair that was the color of a yellow Lab, though heavily streaked with gray.

Picking up the rain bucket and setting it aside, he sat down cross-legged on the floorboards of the cabin and indicated for Harold to do the same. Above their heads was the hole in the roof showing three dim stars.

"People say I look like Billy Gibbons, but 'cept for the beard I don't see it," Jewel said.

Harold didn't know who Billy Gibbons was.

"I guess you ain't no fan of Southern rock then, one," the man said. "You never heard of ZZ Top? He's the front man, plays a guitar looks like a triangle. People figure 'cause he's a long beard he's got to be a redneck. But he ain't no more redneck than me and I ain't no redneck to speak of. I'd put money down that I'm the only vet in Wakulla County voted for a black man for U.S. president. You know what the significance of 2032 is?"

Harold shook his head.

"That's the year the white man becomes the minority. Can't get here soon enough, you ask me. You ought to know things like that."

"Thanks for informing me."

He shrugged. "I don't have nothing to offer. I had some deer I jerked, but it's all gone. All I got left is a sack of taters growing sprouts. They ain't killed me yet. Course they could and I might not know it. This could be a dream, I s'pose. Sometimes I go a whole day like I'm a bird looking down at the world and I'll touch a tree just to make sure it's there and I got the connection. Like I'm still with the living, you know it?"

He reached out and touched Harold's arm with rough fingertips. "You feel real enough. So what is it brung you up here?"

The man had been leaning back on the heels of his hands and a loose floorboard tilted suddenly with a creak, and Harold was looking down the bore of a revolver. The hole was very large and the blade sight above it wavered over Harold's heart. When he heard the man speak, there was no accent and the words were very clear.

"I'm only going to ask you the once."

Now it was Harold who was looking down from above and for a moment he couldn't summon his voice.

"I'm a state investigator," he heard himself say. "I've been directed to find out who is placing scarecrows in the cliffs. If that person is defacing pictographs, it is a federal offense and I have the authority to make an arrest."

"You got a badge?"

Harold placed a hand over his chest. "Can I reach inside the pocket?"

Jewel nodded and Harold handed him his card. As the man read it, Harold looked at the gun looking at him and guessed it was a .41 or maybe a .45. Double action, so that it wouldn't need to be cocked before firing.

"This ain't nothing more than a business card," Jewel said.

"It's down in my boat," Harold said. "Like I told you, I just wanted to get out of the wind and have a conversation. If you'll set your piece down, we could have one."

"I don't see what there is to talk about. I ain't breaking no laws 'cept thems that make no sense. I don't have a dagum boat so I don't need a dagum permit to float the dagum river. I ain't done nothing illegal to get here but a few steps trespassing in country that rightfully belonged to your people. I don't gather you think that's a crime any more than I do."

"I'm not worried about trespassing," Harold said.

"Then what do you care for? I ain't defacing no native art. Them words on the rocks, they'll wash away you get a strong rain. It's just chalk paint."

"But you are the person who is making the scarecrows," Harold said, stating it as a fact.

"I might be. I might not be."

"It's just between you and me," Harold said. "I really would ask you to put the gun down."

"People, they need to know that someone's watching out for their interest. These mine folks, they want to dig a tunnel under the major spawning tributary. Like that ain't digging a grave by a different name."

"Did you know they call you the Scarecrow God? They've shut the river to all floating."

"The past couple days I didn't see many boats, I wondered why. They figure I'm dangerous, huh? Do you think I'm dangerous?"

"No, but you've created a dangerous situation."

"I don't see how that can be."

"People are going to climb up to look at them. Someone could get hurt."

"They fall, that's on them. Nobody's got a gun to their head making them do a durn thing, not one durned thing."

Harold took a shot in the dark. "Who are you doing this for, Jewel?"

The question caught the man off guard. He started to say something, but the words caught and a look of bewilderment came over his face. His eyes flashed away to the walls of the cabin. A long pause, Harold looking at the sprouting of yeti hair where the top button of his shirt was undone, thinking of making a lunge for the pistol and thinking better of it, remembering how quickly the man had drawn it from under the floorboard.

"Why would I be doing it for anyone but myself?"

"It's just a question," Harold said. "I thought maybe that man in the photograph you stuck behind the glass."

Jewel's eyes went to the photograph, then he looked up at the hole in the roof. There were more stars now, and he appeared lost in them, and there was the owl hooting in the canyon that emphasized the silence. He looked at Harold and slowly then, as if in a trance, he turned the revolver so that he was holding it by the barrel and held out the grips for Harold to take it. Harold took the gun and tilted out the cylinder. All six chambers had been loaded. He set the gun by his side and took a full breath for the first time in ten minutes.

"I ain't but seen him more than six, seven times in my life," Jewel said.

CHAPTER NINETEEN

The Mirror of Water

The first time he'd met his father he was not yet of school age, and what stayed with him was the red wine smell of his body and the odd cadence of speech, in which many sentences were started but very few finished. He had known, of course, that he had a father because all kids did, didn't they? He wasn't sure, sex education being something one experienced rather than learned in the Panhandle swamps of his childhood. He'd even known his father's name without knowing it was his father. His mother, who worked the fourteen acres they lived on, supplemented that little subsistence by raising hothouse orchids and boarding dogs for country club people. She was a woman moved to the verge of tears every day and for as many reasons as there were days. Jewel was used to hearing her say the name "Scott" under her breath, usually while taking the Lord's name in vain—"Damn you, Scott MacAllen" being her most common utterance.

Young Jewel was already nearly as tall as the man who went by Pap during his father's next visit, old enough to understand that his father abandoning them was his choice.

"I ought to have been mad," he told Harold. "But you know a boy, he needs his father. And if he doesn't have him, he needs to justify his absences and make believe he loves you. That there's the one makes it hard to keep up the pretense. You know what I mean?"

The unexpected sentiment hit home with Harold, whose own father had been in and out of his life, mostly out, since as far back as he could remember.

"Is your last name MacAllen, like his?"

Jewel nodded. "He was my old man, all right, and I got the name. They called me Jam 'cause them's the initials, you just swap around the capitals. But Pap, he weren't quite the hermit folks think."

He told Harold that for a stretch of years, three, maybe four, his father visited in March or April, when the Montana snows rusted away and the roads became quagmires of mud and the muskrat and beaver pelts had lost their winter value. He'd come in on the Greyhound and would bunk at the hunting camp Jewel's mother's people had let decay back into the swamp. The only structure remaining was a low, rambling shotgun affair built on stilts out over the water, with the limbs of a cypress tree muscling in through broken windows. Jewel would skip school and sleep on the screened-in porch, and the two generations of MacAllens would pull the crab traps, run trotlines, and net mullets. Jewel had never seen anyone as handy with a cast net as his old man. It was during those times that Scott had passed on his woodcraft.

"It saved my life in 'Nam," Jewel told Harold with matter-of-factness, "knowing what he taught me. He was as much at home in the swamp as these mountains."

Jewel had traveled up to Montana only once, as a teenager, after his dad was decommissioned out of Hitler's war. They had spent the fall and winter running Scotty's trapline and hunting coyotes—you got a dollar bounty for every tail you brought in—staying in caves and makeshift lean-tos except for the coldest weeks, when they sheltered here at the homestead. Already abandoned for a quarter of a century, the cabin had fallen into disrepair, but they had made it livable. It was here, Jewel said, that he had one of only three conversations with his father that strayed beyond the comfortable borders of hunting, trapping, and weather. His father talked about growing up in Shelby, Montana, up on the Hi-Line, a hard life on a hard piece of earth with a hard mother and a weak father who died when he was seven. The words had been coaxed out of him by a bottle of brandy, and the talk ran out when the bottle ran dry.

"Them two wars, they just cut the tongue out of him," Jewel said.

When the spring came, Jewel had hitched into White Sulphur Springs to catch a bus back to Florida. He was sixteen, had all the formal schooling he would ever get, and told Harold that his father had foreseen Johnson getting dragged down into the conflict in Vietnam and told him to keep his head down and he'd come out of it on the other end, and when he did, not to run away from life like he had.

"He said it was too late for him, but it wasn't for me," Jewel said, shaking his head. "Old Pap, he hugged me the only dang time I can remember him doing it. It's been near fifty years and I ain't got the smell out yet." Harold noticed the tear at the corner of Jewel's left eye.

The next time Jewel saw his father, he was ashes in a box that his mother went to Montana to retrieve after receiving a call from the ranch that had employed him. She died two years later. He said he'd brought his father's ashes to spread, the Smith Canyon being the only real home he'd ever had.

Harold remembered the bone chips he'd found at the sites of the scarecrows. One mystery solved.

"How did you get here?" Harold asked.

Jewel seemed to think about it. "I assumed it was the natural way, a man and a woman and a little bit of mischief-making's all it takes. Though some that's seen me may have formed their own opinion, think I'm more like that creature from the lake."

"No, I mean how did you get to Montana? Did someone give you a ride?"

He took offense at the question. "I done got a bank account, got my disability. I got a short-bed Tacoma looks a lot newer than I do."

"Where did you park it?"

"I met a fella said I could leave it at his place. Called it a compound. Weren't like no compound I ever seen, more like shacks is all, couple steps up from this place you want the honest truth. It ain't but a hour hike down to the river from there and wouldn't raise no suspicion."

"You mean hike down to here? The homestead?"

"No, the trail comes down at that Table Rock, on down the river a piece."

Table Rock Campground was where Harold had told Marcus to wait for him.

"Just some folks living off the grid," Jewel was saying. "Call themselves the Rural Free Montanans. They even got a flag. Got no sewer, got no electricity but, like, generators, just living with their middle finger out, saying fuck you to the government. You got your folks like that all over the place nowadays."

Yes, Harold thought. *But how many are this close to the Smith River?*

He was thinking of the man who had called himself Job, whose poaching ring he had infiltrated, who had threatened to separate his gall bladder from the rest of his organs not more than two months ago. He'd called himself a Rural Free Montanan. If it was that man, it was quite a coincidence.

But on second thought, maybe not. Harold knew that Job lived in the Little Belt Mountains, and that he would hang out in bars was more or less a given. In fact, it was at a bar that he'd met him. If you thought of it that way, any two men who lived within forty miles of White Sulphur Springs and had a thirst that only a draft beer could satisfy were destined to meet in one or another of the town's establishments. The odds of Jewel MacAllen striking up a conversation with Job were better than they might appear to an outsider.

"One of these men," Harold said. "He wouldn't have a scarred hand? Big fella tall as you, maybe fifty, hangs around with a short guy looks like a garden gnome?"

"Rayland Jobson." Jewel nodded. "It's his tater patch where I left my truck. Got a right hand with a hump, looks sorta like a blue crab."

Harold felt as if his chest wall was lined with a sheet of ice that cracked halfway into the inhalation. Spears of cold white pain shot through his body.

"And how might you have met this man?" he said, feeling the ice settle in his chest.

"He was in the Mint with his brother-in-law, pretty sure it's that little feller you're talking about. I guess they looked at me and saw a kindred spirit. Wouldn't be the first time people mistook my appearance for my character."

"When was this?"

"'Bout a month ago, I'd say. I hadn't been in town but for a few days. I was stocking up on supplies and wondering how the devil I'd get up and down the river."

"Look at me, Jewel," Harold said. "I want you to tell me the truth. Did you tell these men about the scarecrows?"

Jewel looked down at the floorboards between them.

"I might could have. Yeah, I s'pose I did. I recall telling him I got the idea from the scarecrows I seen in the Mekong in the rice paddies, that I seen one that was a man, like a Jesus on the cross, except he was one from our company and he was dead. That stuck with me. When I heard about the mine they wanted to put on the river and got it into my head to carry on the watch, I thought of that scarecrow."

"They called your father the Smith River Watchman. Did you know that?"

"I heard it from him. He showed me a newspaper with a story somebody wrote about him. Kept it folded in a book."

"Back to this Jobson. What do you know about him?"

"Just what I tole you. He let me park my truck. Why? You got bad blood with him?"

"I don't believe so. Why would you think that?"

"Just that he got himself a hard-on about the Native American. This fellow was out there on the sidewalk, Job, like, made a gun out of his hand and said 'Bang' and blew the smoke out of the barrel. I said, 'What you got against Indians?' He said he'd been betrayed by one, that the next time he saw him he was going to snap a cap on him."

"He said that?"

"Just as sure as you're sitting across from me. Y'all got a beef with this fellow it ain't really none of my concern."

Harold thought of Marcus. He was alone now, his son, in a canoe with cliffs all around shot with caves. What if Harold was the man that Job intended to snap a cap on? What if he was sitting behind the trigger of a rifle in one of those caves, waiting for him to float past?

You're being paranoid, Harold told himself. Job never had an inkling that Harold was undercover. And even if he had, how would Job know he was floating the Smith River? Harold had only known himself two days before he launched.

The logic didn't assure him. Harold remembered the reflections on the surface at Indian Springs, when he and Marcus had knelt side by side to examine the sculpin. He recalled Sean Stranahan's comment that the two looked alike, or would when Marcus grew into his father's frame. It didn't matter if Marcus wasn't Harold. All that mattered was that through the crosshairs of a rifle scope he could appear to be.

"They's something else," Jewel said. "I can take you there, but you ain't going to like it."

Harold breathed deeply. The ice had melted, to be replaced by a feeling of cold water pooling in his gut, shrinking his insides.

He listened to the river below the homestead. Last night, when he'd staked out the cabin, he could barely hear it. But twenty-four hours of snowmelt had changed that. The color of the water had gone from an opaque olive to a sickly tan color. It had doubled in size and would double again and again as the thick mantling of snow shrank from the crags. And somewhere down that river a young man who was the only future Harold could see was caught in the runoff, hurtling toward what, toward whom?

"Not going to like what?" Harold said.

Across from him, Jewel MacAllen turned the key of the lamp, raising the wick to draw the last drops of kerosene. But it was too late. Harold heard him take the Lord's name in vain, and then there was a single flicker before the world went black.

PART TWO

HARD ROCK HELL

CHAPTER TWENTY

A Death in Eden

Sean Stranahan was adding jungle cock nails to the fly clamped in the jaws of his tying vise when he heard a ringing on the travertine floor. The stenciling on the frosted window of the door to his art studio read BLUE RIBBON WATERCOLORS and, underneath, in a discreet script, PRIVATE INVESTIGATIONS. The footsteps stopped at the door, and there was a long moment when he imagined someone reading the words and deciding whether to knock, or would have if he didn't already suspect who it was from the cadence of the steps.

"Come in, Sheriff," he said.

The door opened—Martha Ettinger in her khakis, duty belt riding her iliac crest, cuffs on the back, Taser, .357 Ruger. She drummed her fingers on the grips of the revolver while her eyes roamed the artwork on the walls. Sean saw her looking at a study of a man with a snowy beard who was sitting at an outdoor bar with palm trees. Bony fingers hunted at the keys of a manual typewriter. A small cat perched on the man's shoulder. The man was someone Sean had known, who believed that he could summon the pen, if not the spirit, of Ernest Hemingway. He had devoted the last years of his life to trying to finish a story that he believed the great writer had started, but never completed. Under the table, by the man's bare feet, were three dead mice, courtesy of, presumably, the cat.

"I call it *Three Dead Mice*," Sean said.

"We're painting ghosts now, are we?"

It was a literal assessment. The figure was hinted at rather than boldly stroked, and in poor light might not be there at all, the chair empty, the painting a still life with a wisp of smoke, the typewriter and the three mice.

"You didn't come here to critique my art," he said.

"No. And for the record, I like it." She paused. "I like you, too, but I'm mad at you."

"What did I do this time?"

"It's what you didn't."

"I told you I wouldn't be able to call for a couple days. It's the Bob Marshall Wilderness."

"A couple days was a couple days ago."

"They wanted to stay another night."

Sean had picked up a couple of clients after the party had floated through to Eden Bridge, driven directly to Gibson Reservoir, then backpacked up the North Fork of the Sun River to fish for cutthroat trout. He'd just got back the night before, and, rather than drive out to Martha's place, had slept on the couch in his studio.

"I know," Martha said. "I just wished you'd stuck around."

Sean could sense something was wrong from her posture. She couldn't seem to get comfortable, had been shifting her weight from one foot to the other since she'd opened the door.

"What happened, Martha? Bart Trueblood, he's okay, isn't he?"

"I think so. He had some kind of relapse, something about his platelet count, but he's up and crowing last I heard."

"The snake incident will be good for Lillian's documentary."

"Won't it, though?" She smiled thinly. "But I didn't come here to talk about her, or Trueblood, or the mine. Or even you not calling."

"Then what's up?"

Sean saw the smile die on her lips, and the Martha who took a chair was as sober as he had ever seen her. He sat down opposite her at the fly-tying table, feathers in a half-dozen hues littering the expanse of wood between them.

She looked at the fly in his vise, said "Pretty," then raised her eyes. "What's up," she said, "is a corpse floating in the Smith River."

Stranahan's face must have registered his alarm.

"No, it's not who you're thinking," Martha said. "The floater is Caucasian."

"Harold's okay, though. His son? They came out okay. Right?"

"You're talking like a man trying to convince himself," Martha said. "I did, too, at first. No, I can't swear that he is okay. Or Marcus. Neither of their canoes ever made it to Eden Bridge. Harold's canoe was found about a mile below Table Rock, bent around a rock in the river. Not too far from where the body was discovered. There was a bullet recovered in some of his gear. Point two five six caliber. One of the copper petals that peeled from the core had bits of human tissue lodged in it. Janice Thorp, Harold's sister, has provided her own DNA for comparison. No word yet. Marcus's canoe never did surface, so to speak. I have a bad feeling about this. If you'd bothered to call me, you would have known, you might even have been able to help."

Silence fell across the table. In the breeze flowing in from the open windows, the feathers stirred, looking like colorful birds attempting to take wing.

"No, that's not fair," Martha said. "You probably couldn't have added anything to what Lillian Cartwright and your buddy, Sam, already told us."

"When did this happen?"

"A helicopter pilot on training maneuvers from Malmstrom Air Force Base spotted the canoe Monday. He made another pass lower and that's when he spotted the body. Harold's been missing . . . Well, that's the thing. We're not sure. He wasn't on a timetable, but it's been four days now since he was supposed to meet Marcus and I'm worried."

"Marcus stayed with us one night, said he was going to canoe on down to Table Rock where his dad was supposed to meet him."

"So Sam told us."

"I tried to talk him out of it. We could have made room in the raft and left a note for Harold. But he had his mind made up, and I know he made it safe as far as Table Rock."

"I know that, too."

"What about the body, the floater? Any clues there?" Sean was thinking of the Scarecrow God.

"Well, for starters," Martha said, "he doesn't have a head."

———

He didn't have fingers or toes, either. What he did have was a hole in the left upper quadrant of his chest that was through and through, consistent with a wound caused by a high-powered rifle bullet. That, not drowning, was determined to be the cause of death by the county medical examiner.

Martha stirred her fingers among the feathers on Sean's table as she thought back.

The call from the Cascade County sheriff, Andrew Cashell, had come in the day after the discovery of the body. Martha, who had crossed paths with Cashell before on a dual-jurisdiction case, remembered a chewing gum habit, a moonlike face with walnut cracker cheeks, and cold blue X-ray eyes that betrayed a shrewd mind, one that he invariably kept under the crown of a straw Stetson, winter and summer. She remembered Cashell's habit of arguing with his hands, counting up his points by tapping his fingers.

He told her that the ranger at Camp Baker had informed him about Harold's assignment. He wanted Martha's opinion of Harold, knowing that he'd worked as a deputy sheriff in her department.

Martha had asked how he was sure that Harold wasn't the floater. He'd said two reasons. One, Harold was six feet one, give or take, according to the records forwarded from her own department. The medical examiner's best guesstimate was that the John Doe was at least two inches taller than that, unless he had a squashed head, "like a shriveled pumpkin or something." The other thing, Cashell told Martha, was that the floater's skin didn't contain much pigment.

"He's an albino?" Sean asked.

Martha shook her head. "No, but close. Albinism is a spectrum. Cashell said the dead guy's skin had melanin, just not a lot of it. The clinical term is 'leucistic.' It was a detail they were keeping under their hats to separate out the crazies who would claim responsibility."

"Have you had any? Crazies?"

"What I'm trying to tell you, if you'd quit interrupting, is that Harold has become a person of particular interest in this crime. Right now it's a suspicious death, but it's going to elevate to a murder investigation, pending the autopsy report."

Martha remembered how Cashell, in talking about Harold, had begun his finger countdown. Along with his son, Harold was the last person known to have been on the river after its closure. That was one finger. He was deliberately in pursuit of someone who could be dangerous. That was the second finger. Harold was armed with a rifle, finger number three. The fourth finger pointing to his possible, if not probable, involvement was proximity. His canoe had been found no more than two hundred yards below the John Doe.

Martha stopped stirring feathers and raised her eyes to Sean's, then tapped her fingers the way Cashell had, adding up the circumstantial evidence.

"He doesn't believe in coincidence any more than I do," she said.

Martha had told Cashell that under no circumstances could she imagine Harold killing anyone without provocation. Not to mention cutting a man's head off. A justifiable shooting in self-defense, that was another matter.

"We'll find him," Cashell had replied. "Dead or alive, we'll find him. And if I had to put money on it, I'd say dead."

"What do you mean by that?" Martha had asked. "You don't even know if it was Harold's DNA on the bullet."

"I was there and you weren't. It's hard to believe that a person could make it through the canyon alive under those water conditions. With or without taking a bullet. That's what I mean."

Silence fell across the fly-tying table, stretching into the corners of the room.

"He's right, you know," she said in a voice that was barely audible.

Sean had to agree. The simplest and most likely reason that Harold and Marcus had disappeared was that they had drowned, their bodies wedged between boulders or caught in submerged tree roots. They would surface eventually, just as Harold's canoe had, just as the man with the hole in his chest had. And Marcus's canoe would surface sooner or later, as well.

"You said the floater was six-four?" Sean asked.

"Why is that important?"

"Harold said the scarecrow maker was probably tall."

"You think it's him?"

"I think it's possible, and you're going to get mad again, because I forgot to tell you something." He told her about the photograph Harold had showed him, the one under glass at the homestead, and the evidence suggesting that someone had been living there.

"Harold thought it was the scarecrow guy. It makes sense, Martha. Maybe Harold caught up to him. His plan was to stake it out another night."

"What if he did?"

"Think about it. Both the body and Harold's canoe were found way downriver. At least sixteen, seventeen miles. They could have been traveling together."

Martha worked her chin with her fingers.

"That's a stretch."

"You're right. It is. Was there a search? For Harold, I mean."

"Such as it was. The water was too colored to see anything that was under the surface. They did get a jet sled in there from a private access. They got clothing samples and had a search dog go up and down the banks."

"Who was the handler?"

"Katie Sparrow." They had both worked with her before.

"She find anything?"

"Her dog gave an alert at Canyon Depth Camp. But that's where Trueblood got bit, so it doesn't mean anything. And at Sunset Cliff."

"That doesn't mean anything, either," Sean said. "We all stopped there to eat after getting him into the chopper."

"I think there was another hit downriver. Hawk's Foot? Something Foot. It's up from Table Rock, not too far, I think. And maybe a couple more nearby. But you can ask her yourself if you want to. It's as good a place to start as any."

With that, she placed a manila envelope on Sean's fly-tying table.

CHAPTER TWENTY-ONE

Thunder and Lightning

After Martha's steps faded, Sean turned his attention to the sheet of paper in the envelope. It was identical to others he'd signed that stipulated the terms of his employment for the Hyalite County Sheriff's Department. The inherent contradiction of the phrase "independent, cooperative investigative services" brought a thin line of irony to his lips. Sean had worked for the department on several occasions, and though it paid barely half his day rate, traveling expenses were covered, and to a certain degree it meant the county had his back. The fact was he'd have looked for Harold regardless of financial remuneration. Or, for that matter, any measure of safety or cooperation a piece of paper might grant him.

Sean scanned and printed out two copies of the contract, buttoned one into his pocket, filed one in the lower right-hand drawer of his desk behind a fifth of the Famous Grouse, and locked the original in his safe. He turned his attention to the fly in his tying vise, an Atlantic salmon pattern called the Usual Suspect. He looked critically at it, then dabbed lacquer to freeze the thread on the head and let it air-dry while he packed his Land Cruiser for a trip of indeterminate duration and, as yet, unknown destination. All he knew was his first stop. An hour after tucking the fly into his breast pocket, he idled his Land Cruiser down a steep grade on the right bank of the Madison River, some four miles below its confluence with the West Fork.

The cabin was tucked into an alcove of aspens whose leaves

reminded Sean of money fluttering after a safe was blown, though he'd never seen money fluttering, nor, for that matter, a safe being blown.

Choti bound out the door of the Land Cruiser to greet the dapper-looking man who'd stepped onto the porch. The man was wearing a grass Stetson with a Mississippi gambler's brim and a rattlesnake skin hat band complete with head and rattles. He squatted down to greet the dog, then straightened, shaking his head.

"Every time you darken our door," he said, "I start wondering how to spend the money I'll take from you at the table."

"But we don't play for money, Ken."

It was a fact. The members of the Madison River Liars and Fly Tiers Club, a loose-knit group of anglers that included several of the most heralded fly tiers in the world, played poker for exquisitely tied flies, some worth hundreds of dollars.

"You make my point for me," the man said. "Not only are you an honorary member, which means you drink our whiskey but don't pay dues, the flies you bid aren't worth more than the hooks they're tied on. Yet still we invite you to the table."

"What are friends for?" Sean said. He offered his hand, which Kenneth Winston took in long fingers that were as black as the ebony keys on a piano.

"Watch the hand," he said. "It's insured by Sotheby's." His hands were, in fact, insured, though not by Sotheby's and not because of their dexterity at tying flies. They were insured because Winston had become a sought-after hairdresser who ran several salons in Mississippi, and whose name had been mentioned on the red carpet at entertainment awards shows by grateful actresses. Sean went easy on the grip and ducked inside, where Patrick Willoughby, the club president, was padding about the alcove kitchen barefoot, building a bacon, lettuce, and tomato sandwich.

He turned his owl eyes on Sean. "Strict doctor's orders," he said, "minus the bacon, hold the mayo." He smiled, arching eyebrows that escaped the upper rim of his round-framed glasses. "We haven't seen you since before your float. Sounds like you had an adventure."

"What did you hear?"

"We're rather hermetically sealed here, but the headless body has been the talk of the valley. The scuttlebutt is that it's the man who built the scarecrows."

"That's one possibility. But there's a more urgent matter. Do you think you can spare a few minutes after dinner? I'd like to pick your brain."

"Do I sense that a game is afoot?"

"It's no game, but I might ask you to look after Choti for a week or so."

"My boy, you may pick away. My consultation fee, alas, has risen—bison burgers and Scotch ales at Trout Tails upon your return. We have made the acquaintance of a young woman, one Shirley Metzinger, who makes excellent use of a vulcanized tail."

"I thought Trout Tails was out of business."

"New owners."

Beer and burger establishments came and went in the Madison Valley. Even tiki bars where mermaids wore seashell tops had a hard time staying afloat, or aswim, as Willoughby put it, after Labor Day.

They were three for dinner, four for poker when Max Gallagher drove back from fishing a spring creek up the valley. A crime novelist, he was granted trespass rights because the property owner was a fan of both his books, which featured a "nose" for the perfume industry who moonlighted as a detective, and his dark rapscallion looks. Not to mention his willingness to return her advances on the occasions she found herself in need of reassurance that the opposite sex found her attractive.

As Gallagher put it: "My virtue is a small price to pay for a reliable mayfly hatch."

Gallagher had been at rock bottom the last time Sean saw him, having put his profits up his nose, but was clean now and in good spirits. A production company belonging to a well-known character actor had optioned his series. The actor longed to be a leading man, not to mention he had a serious proboscis that wouldn't need prosthetic enhancement to fit the character.

They toasted Max's success, they toasted a reliable mayfly hatch, they toasted the actor's nose, and the moon was sitting on the shoulder of Specimen Ridge when Sean and Willoughby retired from the card table to chairs on the porch. There they sipped bourbon with a splash of spring water from the creek that crooked to the river. Mayflies swarmed the porch light.

"What do you think?" Sean said. He had told the gist of the story earlier in the evening.

Willoughby laced his fingers across his midsection. When Sean had first met him, the club's president was an enigma. A psychologist by training, he had served as a naval officer during the Vietnam War and had subsequently served four presidential administrations as a terrorist profiler and hostage negotiator. One of the more delicious rumors was that his primary occupation had been that of a Cold War spymaster who dangled his assets on strings, like a deadly spider, working out of dingy hotel rooms in places like Cairo and Istanbul. He still received the occasional call from the Continent and would excuse himself from the table to conduct a long conversation in German or French.

Sean knew Willoughby as the best criminal psychologist he'd ever encountered, and without making a point of it had come to rely on his wisdom, especially on investigations that led him into the complex recesses of the human mind.

He was addressing the subject now in a roundabout manner, which was as much talking to himself as to Sean. Sean caught himself tapping his foot, anxious to be going, but Willoughby would not be hurried. Looking at the sky, where the moon had become obscured by a shoal of indigo cumulonimbus, he slowly nodded the orb of his head.

"I was sitting here last summer, August twenty-first, the solar eclipse. An hour before noon, if memory serves."

"I was beside you," Sean said. "Ken and I were both here."

"Indeed you were. I fear for our country, Sean. That chill and dimming of the light that lasted but several minutes is to me the harbinger of a national eclipse which I fear may be far darker and colder, and much longer in duration."

His eyes, the pupils dilated from contemplating the night sky, narrowed as he observed the flies swarming the light.

He continued. "There exists today a fundamental division between those who seek to preserve the natural world for the enjoyment of their children and the health of the planet, and those who will put it in peril for whatever value they can extract from it, and who would just as soon give their sons and daughters money as wonder. What is happening on the Smith River is a microcosm of the opposing philosophies of the age. Realists versus head-in-the-sands. Haves versus have-nots. The drill bits of industry against those who can only fight back with reason, heart, and scientific consensus. It is trench warfare with no quarter given, no soccer match on the battlefield Christmas Day. I fear the ditches have been dug too deeply now for the combatants to climb out in the hope of finding common ground.

He pulled his glasses down his nose. "Please forgive my ramblings. Despite my former stock and trade, I am not a pessimist. I am instead that most hopeless of intellects, a pragmatist."

They sat in silence. The insects that swarmed the electric light now included miller moths that danced like clumsy ballerinas compared to the stately hovering of the mayflies, and when Willoughby began to speak again, he was looking beyond them, where the swollen cloud tips heralded rain.

"The story you have told me tonight," he said, "is set against the ticking clock of the mine issue. It would be imprudent to dismiss the possibility of a connection to your friend's disappearance."

"Part of me wants to drive up there right now and join in the search."

"I thought it had been suspended."

"It has, but it will be resumed when the water clears. Is it arrogance to believe that I can contribute?"

"Sean, it's always helpful to have someone who knows the missing person and can make an educated guess about what he may or may not do in a given situation."

"Harold calls it tracking tendencies."

"An apt description. Still, I'm not sure that is the wisest use of your time. And time is very much of the essence if he is in fact alive. I suggest that you begin at point last seen and work back upriver, rather than downriver, where the searchers concentrated their efforts."

"To Camp Baker."

"And beyond. Stories have deep roots." He sipped from his cup. "The future can be found in the past; that is the first lesson of history."

Sean had been fingering the fly in his pocket and now held it to the light. He'd meant to bid it in a hand of poker but had thought better than to lose it. He squinted at it, admiring the russet fox fur wing that glowed with translucence.

Willoughby peered through his glasses.

"Ah," he said. "The Usual Suspect. One would assume from the proportions that it is a British tie, but it originated in Swedish Lapland. A very popular pattern there. I didn't know you were planning a trip."

"I'm not. But if I tie the fly, I can fish the river, at least in my imagination. It's a lot cheaper than shelling out five hundred dollars a day for a beat on a salmon river. Have you fished in Sweden, Pat?"

"Indeed."

Sean was not surprised. In Patrick's semiretirement, he only took consulting contracts in places that offered trout or salmon to the fly.

"The largest salmon I ever hooked was in the River Byske, on a size-four Thunder and Lightning. It took me through three sets of rapids. Thirty pounds, and still carrying sea lice. I had to go swimming twice to unwrap the line around rocks." He nodded at the memory.

"By the way, what is Martha's take on this? She and Harold were an item, were they not? Before you were involved, I mean to say."

"She's upset, naturally. If I can get traction, I think she'll take time off and accompany me."

Somewhere in the darkness, a nightjar churred.

"I used to love the songs of birds," Willoughby said. "But for a long time after Marlene passed, their song only reminded me of my grief and isolation. I shut the windows to their music. Now I leave them open again. That is a good sign, I suppose."

There was nothing to say for this and they sat in easy silence, the river below them as black as the basalt stones it had been sanding for eons.

"There's one problem with the strategy you propose," Sean said. "The last place anyone actually saw Harold was fifteen miles below the put-in at Camp Baker. If I start there, how do I get back upstream if something points in that direction?"

A smile played across Willoughby's lips. "You told me something I've not forgotten, that when you take on a case, it's like stepping into a new river to go fishing. You're neither at the beginning nor the end of the river, and because you don't know in which direction the fishing will be better, you go both ways until you figure it out. Also, you keep trading one fly for another until you find the pattern that works. Sean, you are the best trout fisherman I have ever known. I have every faith that you will find your way to the heart of this matter."

Sean tucked the Usual Suspect back into his pocket. "I just hope I won't be too late."

Willoughby stood. "Get some sleep. In the morning I will fortify you with biscuits and gravy like my mother made. Any soldier of mine goes into battle refreshed and well fed. The rest, well, as I said . . . I have every faith."

CHAPTER TWENTY-TWO

Green Gold

Katie Sparrow lived in a one-hundred-year-lease Forest Service cabin some few miles west of West Yellowstone, alone if you narrowed the definition to human company. She'd been engaged once, to a young man who'd died in an avalanche while skiing, and it was watching the dogs search for him that gave her the idea of becoming a handler, to provide a service that might save lives after losing the love of hers. Sean knew her to have little use for the male of the species after Colin's death, beyond their basic utility to scratch a biological itch. He had once provided such a service—he never deluded himself into believing it was much more than physical, though she had flirted openly with him for years. Part of their compatibility was his acceptance by the graying-at-the-muzzle shepherd who greeted him with a wet nose on the porch of the cabin. Lothar, Katie's Type I trailing dog, was her litmus test when it came to men. Nobody got beyond the porch if he raised the hackles on Lothar's neck.

"How's old Ephraim?" Sean asked when she answered his knock. "Seen him around much?"

"That old bear," she said, pronouncing it "bar." Katie had come from eastern Kentucky and lapsed into the idiom with friends, though she could talk in a flat midwestern accent, sounding like a woman with two masters under her belt, which she had, when assuming her duties as a backcountry park ranger.

"I haven't seen the likes of that bar since September last. He got through the hunting season, he'll show up a few weeks from now, when the hyperphagia kicks in. Fatten himself up for winter."

Ephraim was a two-toned boar black bear with coal black body hair and a head the color of rusted needles on a burned lodgepole pine tree. He regularly visited Katie's cabin in the fall, and twice, when she'd heard the squawking of her chickens, she'd shot his backside with rubber bullets. Sean remembered his huge haunches shaking as he lumbered away, as well as the blue streak of profanity from Katie's lips that followed him, for the bear had killed six of her best laying hens.

"I haven't been here for a while," Sean said. "You look good, Katie."

"No, you haven't." A pause. "I do? You said I looked like a wren."

"It's the way you cock your head to the side."

"Like when I'm eyeballing some beetle to peck at?" She cocked her head. "But I suppose a wren's better than a grackle or a magpie. You know what we haven't done in a while? You and me haven't got that wolf pack going for a while."

Sean smiled at the memory, waking Katie in the middle of the night to howl with the Druid Pack on the skirts of Mount Two Top.

"We knew how to get them a-going," she said. "That why you're here asking all innocent about Ephraim, want to sing with the doggies? Not that I'd have qualms. Just I took you for the faithful type. Now that you're shacking with Martha and all."

"I'm here to ask you about the search. Harold and his son are still missing."

She nodded gravely, and when she spoke, the accent had vanished. "I've been afraid to pick up the newspaper. Afraid more bodies might have turned up. But no news is good news, huh? I'm on standby to go back up there when the water drops, unless I get called back into Yellowstone Park for a day or two first. We've had a development in something going on there. You want to come in, have some coffee? All I got's instant."

Instant was fine with Sean. She opened the door for him. Sean shut it behind them and looked around. A lot of dog pictures on the walls, framed certification papers, a cabinet of trophies, dogs up on pedestals, a "Western Women and Their Dogs" calendar, one year out of date. It was the same calendar Sean had seen the last time he was here. Little had changed. Katie was a one-subject woman.

They took the cups to her kitchen table, where Sean filled her in on what he'd learned from Martha. Something lit in her eyes when he talked about the bullet found in Harold's canoe, but she didn't interrupt.

"I came to ask about the search," he said. "Martha wasn't too clear on what Lothar did or didn't find."

She sipped her coffee, her head cocked thoughtfully. She said that Lothar had picked up Harold's scent in three locations, starting up-river at Canyon Depth Boat Camp, which was to be expected, because Harold had spent two nights there. The dog also found scent at Sunset Cliff Camp, seven miles downriver, and there was a third hit at mile 32 at a camp called Crow's Foot. Sean was looking at the map he'd unfolded from his pocket. He noted that Crow's Foot was only a mile and a half upriver from Table Rock, where Harold was supposed to hook up with his son.

The river search, Katie said, had started the day after the body had been found, four since Harold and Marcus had last been seen. That was the outside edge of the window for Lothar to be able to pick up a scent. And because the water was rising, the only hits were well back from the banks. There could be many places where Harold or Marcus stepped out of their canoes, separately or together, but any scent they left would have fallen under rising water and been swept away.

Sean smiled.

"What?" Katie said.

"You know how most guys will walk a few feet from the bank to pee? Harold, he'd just step out onto the bank and unzip, pee right into the river. He did that one time Martha was with us, and she just gave him a withering look. He shrugged. 'It's traditional,' he said. Traditional covers a lot of transgressions with Harold."

"Yeah, that sounds like him. Sounds like Martha, too. Does she know you're here?"

"No."

"You going to tell her?"

"Probably, if you tell me something worth telling her."

"Probably?"

"I'm working for her, well, the county."

"How's she swing that? That body was found like a hundred and fifty miles north of the county line."

"Yes, but most of the people involved are in Hyalite—me, Sam, Lillian Cartwright, Harold. It's a joint investigation."

"Just checking, see if you're legit. In case I want to tell you some government secrets or something."

"You have government secrets?"

"I might."

"Let me ask you another question. Since Harold and Marcus were both on the river, could Lothar mistake one's scent for the other?"

"You mean them being father and son, or them being Native American?"

"Either."

"I see what you're getting at. Same ethnicity, same smell. It's sort of a taboo subject 'cause it can be interpreted as racist, but there's definitely an ethnic component. That doesn't mean that Lothar would mistake Harold's and his son's scents, but they would be more similar than, say, Harold's scent and your scent. You want to know about smell?"

Sean sat back in his chair. He was prepared to listen to anyone who thoroughly knew their subject, whatever the subject.

"A person's individual odor has four components," she said. "No, that's not accurate. Better to say that odor is influenced by four factors. Foremost is genetics. Genetics determine the kinds of oils our skin produces. Everybody has a unique chemistry, but Harold's and Marcus's DNA will be more similar to their family's than to yours or mine. And in turn their family's chemistry will be similar to other related families, so that there is your tribal component. Blackfeet will smell different than Northern Cheyenne and both will smell different than whites.

"Then you factor in diet. You go to parts of India where people eat spicy foods, like where I was in Uttar Pradesh for a couple years, their skin is going to smell different than, say, an Eskimo's who eats a lot of fish. That's a cultural difference more than an ethnic one."

"You smell like what you eat," Sean said.

"Yes, but it only goes so far. When I was working on the fish farm, one of the guys I worked with called me Milkshake, because he said I smelled like milk. That's because even though I ate Indian food, my bacterial makeup was still different than theirs. You inherit a lot of your bacteria from your mother. So you will smell more like her than, say, your father. You still with me?"

"I think so. There seems a lot to it."

"There is. And then some races just smell more than others. Odor is produced when your bacteria breaks down your sweat. If you're of European or African descent, the result is BO. But many Asian people, especially Koreans, possess a genetic mutation that alters the composition of their sweat. It still gets broken down by bacteria, but it doesn't hardly smell at all. But your question was could Harold's odor be mistaken for his son's. The answer is no. The only thing that could stump Lothar would be if Harold had a twin. The scent of twins is almost identical, even if they live in different parts of the world and eat the local cuisine. Interesting, huh?"

It was, and Sean said so.

"When did you work in India, Katie?"

"After Colin died. I just needed to get away, so I signed up for the Peace Corps. I got to see a tiger once. It was chasing a sambar deer and when it got away, the tiger roared. This was like fifty feet away, by the fishponds. People think tigers can't catch fish, but they can. We had one of those game trap cameras and the tiger, he'd come in at night and scoop mahseer fish out of the ponds."

She smiled up at him. "You want to know what you smell like? Curry leaves. Sort of a soft spice smell. A bit of swamp mixed in, decaying leaves and roots. A little fecund."

"Sounds like a bad wine."

"No, it's a good vintage. It smells good to me. That's why we hit it off. We smell good to each other. That's how mates find one another, or should. Today people cover up their scents. Then their attraction becomes based only on the visual, which doesn't cut it when it comes to biological compatibility. It's part of the reason for a high divorce rate, let alone fertility issues. Anyway, you have any other questions? I know you want to get going on this."

"How about Marcus? Any alerts?"

She nodded. "One at Canyon Depth, again, no surprise. And one near Table Rock camp."

"That's where he was last seen. Martha said he alerted a couple other times. Or at least he picked something up that interested him?"

"That Lothar, he's interested in a thing or two."

"Martha said maybe another dog."

"It's happened."

"There was a dog on the float. It was Marcus's."

"I wasn't told that. Was it a dog? Lothar wouldn't pay attention if it was a bitch."

"It was male."

"Then that could explain it."

"Just to satisfy my curiosity, where did he get interested in the scent?'

"Let me get my GPS." She did and showed him two waypoints. The uppermost was at Cow Coulee Camp. Marcus had caught up to the group there, so that explained fresh dog scent in the vicinity. The second, again, was at Table Rock.

"Not far from where Harold's scent was found at Crow's Foot," Sean said.

"Not too far," Katie agreed. "Crow's Foot, there's a trail there you take up to some pictographs. They're under some ledges. A lot of floaters stop along the way."

"Is that where you picked up Harold's scent?"

"No, more down by the river."

"Did you climb up to the pictographs?"

"Yes. I thought, it's a natural place for either of them to have gone. And it's protected there, so a better chance of the scent lingering. No luck, though. Doesn't mean they weren't there. Just too much time had passed for Lothar to alert."

Sean took a shot in the dark. "You didn't see a scarecrow at Crow's Foot, did you?" The map that the ranger had given Harold had not shown a scarecrow at that location, but Harold had been there. He had stopped for some reason.

No, she hadn't, but it was rugged country. She wasn't looking for a scarecrow.

"What does he actually do there?" she said.

The question caught Sean off guard. "Harold?"

"Yeah. Division of Criminal Investigation. What's that all about?"

"I'm not sure," Sean said. "Criminal investigation, I guess."

"I heard there was undercover work. Hush-hush stuff."

She cocked her head. "I was telling you we have something going on in the Park? It's a long shot, but it might connect. It's got to do with a poaching problem."

"Isn't there always a poaching problem in the Park?"

"Oh, sure. Trophy hunters wanting to get into the Boone and Crockett Club with a big six-point elk and not too picky about where it stands. Wolf haters, they'll shoot at anything gray. But this spring we've found six G-bear carcasses since May first, mostly in Hayden Valley or south of the Lamar River, places like Specimen Ridge, back of beyond country. That's after the low-elevation ground snow melted but before there would be many tourists to report the sound of a shot. Or tracks to follow once the scent's blown. Deliberate planning if you ask me."

"What were they taking?"

"Only taking gall bladders. They didn't even cut off the paws for the claws. Whoever did it was a surgeon. Didn't make any more cuts than necessary. Imagine killing such a magnificent animal for a few ounces of bile."

"I've heard about the gall bladders. Can they really be worth that much?"

"To some old Chinese dude who thinks it's going to cure his hemorrhoids and erase his hangover? Sure. We're talking tens of thousands of dollars for just one bladder. In Tokyo, powdered bile brings a couple hundred dollars a gram; that's four times its value for the same weight in gold. That's even what they call it—the 'green gold.' Here, I want to show you something."

When she came back, she set a sealed plastic bag on the table between them.

"I found it yesterday with another ranger. We were visiting the last bear carcass. The bear was actually discovered last month, but the team that investigated didn't have a metal detector, and you know me, I like to sweep, you never know what you're going to turn up. This was headwaters of Nez Perce Creek, all that open rolling country. There was a clump of pines about fifty yards away, perfect place for an ambush. I tuned the detector to brass and got a hit right away. It was just under some grass."

"Can I open it?" Sean could see through the plastic that it was a cartridge case.

"Better not. I'm supposed to return it to headquarters in Mammoth, but by the time I called it in last night, they were closed. I'll send it by courier, then they'll log it and forward it on to the crime lab in Hyalite. The Park uses the state lab because the federal facility is Quantico, and they got bigger fish to fry. They'd drag their heels 'til Christmas."

Sean turned the bag until he could read the caliber designation on the case head.

PPU
6.5×54 MS

"Are you familiar with the cartridge?" he said. "It's a new one for me." Something was ticking at the back of his brain.

"New for me, too. But don't you see, you said the bullet in Harold's canoe was two five six caliber."

"That's what Martha told me."

"It's the same thing. Six point five, two five six, no difference. One's in millimeters, one's in inches."

"Did you just do the math?"

"I did it in my head as soon as you told me about the bullet in the boat."

Sean was impressed.

"Careless for someone to have dropped it," Katie said. "Most poachers, they're pretty careful to pick up spent brass."

"Do you think I could bring it up to the crime lab?"

"No way. It's got to maintain chain of evidence. But I can call Mammoth, tell them we have a lead and to get it to the lab ASAP."

"Okay. That'll do."

Katie held his eyes. "I was going to say, you know, you could have just called me. You would have got the same information. But I guess that's not true. We might not have got around to the bullet."

"No. And I wouldn't have had this cup of coffee with you."

They were out on the porch.

An awkward pause. How to say goodbye.

"Eskimo kiss," Katie said, and rubbed noses with him. She hugged him. "You'll tell me if anything comes up, I mean about Harold."

"I'll tell you."

Her eyes were shiny. She looked away and then squatted and rubbed noses with Lothar. "Be gone with you now," she said, her back to him. "You stay any longer and we'll be making the wolf pack howl."

She stood up as he drove away. Cocked her head, all set to peck a spider.

———

Sean was six miles down the road when his phone vibrated in his pants pocket. He pulled to the side, knowing he'd lose the connection once he'd summited Targhee Pass.

It was Katie, telling him that after he'd left she'd remembered something else. Like the cartridge, it was maybe nothing, but then again, you never know.

CHAPTER TWENTY-THREE

Price of Admission

Sam Meslik, his T-shirt reading THE TROUT ALSO RISES, bounced his two-year-old daughter on the great shelf of his shoulder muscles.

"Six point five by fifty-four MS, what's that have to do with the cost of corn?"

"Not sure," Sean said. "But Katie Sparrow found a six point five case where a grizzly bear was killed inside the Park. It had MS on the case head. Just thought you might know more than she did."

"I thought you were looking for Harold. I don't see the connection."

"There probably isn't one."

"If you're looking for a reason to knock on her door again, Uncle Sam says no. You go once, you come away with a peck on the cheek, no harm, no foul. You go back, she's exploring your gold molar with her tongue. Next thing you know, your Tony Lamas are at the foot of the bed. Just marry Martha and get bored like all the rest of us."

"Are you bored?"

"A little. I mean, I love Molly, I'd be a derelict without her. You know that better than anyone. Hell, if she hadn't made me go to the dentist, I'd still be scaring children. And then this little girl here"—he swung around to show Sean the child's face, shrouded in copper-colored curls—"she's all the reason I need for living. But I miss getting into a little trouble as I go downstream. You know what I mean, Ke-mosabe? You settle down, all of a sudden you start living your life at one remove. You retreat into your own little world. Like wearing reading glasses. Everything more than an arm's length away is out of focus. Safe, but not exactly exciting."

He went into his mudroom to fish a couple cold ones from a defunct top-loading washing machine that was filled with ice.

"Better than a fucking igloo," he said.

They took the beers to the porch, where Sam waved a hand at the swallows that were dive-bombing for chukar breast feathers wafting across his fly-tying table.

"Get lost, little darlings, line your nests with somebody else's feathers."

He drained the can in one swallow, said "Ah," said "Six point five by fifty-four, interesting cartridge, hmm," and looked away for a moment.

"Austrian design," he said. "First unveiled in 1900 at the Paris World's Fair. Rifles made by Mannlicher-Schönauer, there's where the MS comes in. Distinctive rifles. Forward bolt, full-length stock, rotary magazine, short barrel.

"Six point five seems small for grizzly bear."

"You'd think so, but it shot a long hundred-seventy-grain bullet with great sectional density, a real penetrator. Karamojo Bell, the old ivory hunter, shot about five hundred elephants with it. But it's a fairly small caliber and with a muzzle velocity of twenty-three hundred feet per second, there's not a lot of muzzle blast. You aren't saying 'Here I am, come and get me' each time you pull the trigger, the way you would with a .300 Weatherby. No, you think about it, it's a good poacher's choice. Compact. Lightweight. Quiet, accurate, effective."

"But six point five is uncommon?"

"Depends on what you're asking. If you're asking if the bore diameter is uncommon, then no. You've got your 6.5 Creedmoor, your .260 Remington, .264 Winchester Mag. There's a lot of cartridges that shoot the same bullet. But if you're asking about the Mannlicher round specifically, then I'd have to say yes. The rifles turn up at gun shows now and then, always a couple on the website listings. Bring a couple grand depending upon condition. But there aren't too many floating around on this side of the pond."

"How do you know all this?"

"I owned one. Oak leaf engraving on the bolt, nice rifle. I used to do a lot of horse trading. It went off on somebody else's horse. Ten, maybe fifteen years ago."

"Whose horse?"

He shrugged. His daughter bounced. "A woman. She wanted a deer rifle that wouldn't kick her fillings loose. A looker, maybe early sixties. Real style about her. Her husband was on the way to the promised land. Cancer, I think. She'd be on the downslope herself now. Marnie Post. Yeah, that's the name."

"Is it possible that it could have been the rifle that fired the case Katie found?"

"Well, one thing, a rifle doesn't fire a case, it fires a bullet, but I know what you're saying and there's an easy way to find out. But you're probably pissing in the wind."

A moss green Subaru Forester scattered gravel as it came up the drive. Molly stepped out, two bags of groceries in her hands. She gave Sean a peck on the cheek, Sam one, took her daughter, and went into the house, followed by Sean with one of the bags.

"When are you going to make Martha an honest woman?" Molly, straight to the point, setting the milk on the top shelf.

"Always the same question," Sean said.

"That new deputy lives up by Three Forks, he looks at her the way men looked at me in my mermaid days. You think she'll wait forever, she won't."

"Thanks for the advice, Molly."

She shrugged. "That's right. Keep it lighthearted. Just don't come moping around here when she moves on."

"Maybe it's her who's not sure."

"If you believe that, then you're as hopeless as the rest of your gender."

Sean found Sam in a nook off the fly shop that he had turned into a reloading room, with a heavy pine bench dominated by a squat, insect green RCBS reloading press. The surface was scattered with tools and measures, bullet boxes, powder cans, with reloading dies stacked like books on a wall shelf. The wood surface of the bench glinted with brass shavings from case trimmings. Sam reached down a plastic box marked 6.5×54 mm and opened the lid to a mix of reloaded cartridges and fired brass that had yet to be resized and primed for the next loading. He extracted one of the fired brass cartridges and bent a gooseneck lamp over it, showing Sean the rim and the dented primer.

"Anybody watches TV knows that you can identify a gun by a fired bullet, because it retains rifling marks and no two groove patterns are alike. But you can make the ID from a fired case as well. The dent the firing pin makes in the primer is peculiar to the rifle and there are other marks. Your girl Friday, Wilkerson, she wouldn't even have to strain those Olive Oyl eyes of hers."

"And these were loads for your old rifle?"

"Yeah."

"Why didn't you give them to the new owner?"

"Same reason I never shoot bullets reloaded by someone else. If the gun blows up, you don't want to be the one who provided the ammo."

"Do you mind if I send one of the fired cases to Katie?"

"Not at all. I haven't been out killing grizzly bears. The only thing I've been shooting lately is blanks."

Sean's look was quizzical.

Sam lowered his voice. "Molly wants another kid, doesn't want them to be more than a couple years apart. I do, too. What the hell? As soon as you have the one, your freedom's fucked anyway, so why not make her happy? But my salmon aren't swimming upstream as fast as they're supposed to."

"I'm sorry, Sam." *What else is there to say?*

Sean thought about Molly's comments. There was a part of him that wanted to settle down, to have the kids, coach Little League, be a man of the hearth, as the French put it. It was a part of him that had been growing. But Martha already had two sons. Maybe she wouldn't want more children. They had never discussed it, had never got any further than Martha's mention of a ring when they'd gone camping.

"Why the fuck did you come here, anyway?"

Sean put the lid back on his thoughts. "I wanted to borrow a couple of kayaks. The two sit-on-tops with the luggage straps."

"So you're going back up to the Smith, look for Harold?"

"If he doesn't show up before I get there."

"See, this is what I mean by losing your freedom. I like Harold, except when he pulls his 'I'm-an-Indian' face, that stoic shit. It's just an excuse for not being engaged. I've called him on it, too. But sure, I'd like to go back up there and help you find him. But I can't do that and stay married to Molly, and I don't want to be one of those divorced dads whose kids only think of him as a gift fairy."

"Rock and a hard place," Sean said.

"Well, it's something to think about if you're considering tying the knot. Who's the other kayak for? No, don't tell me. It's her, isn't it? She and Harold were sharing the sheets back when, she's going to want to get in on it."

Sean sought to veer away from any more discussion of Martha or marriage or, for that matter, sharing sheets with Harold. He asked Sam what he'd got in return for trading the Mannlicher rifle. The big man picked up a cartridge case from the reloading bench and rolled it in his fingers as he groped through the cobwebs.

"It'll come to me," he said.

Sean followed him outside to the big barn where he stored his boats.

"You want to hitch up the trailer?" Sam said.

"I'm going to car-top them. I'm not sure where this thing's going to take me and might get off on some twisty roads. I don't want to be worrying about a caboose."

They cargo-strapped the kayaks to the roof rack of the Land Cruiser and stored paddles and life jackets. Sean was ready to go.

"Hey, I got it," Sam said. "What she traded for the Mannlicher. It was a Brittany. Starter dog. I called her Samantha. Hunted her first time for sharp-tails and, dumb fuck that I am, I neglected to buckle on a skid plate. She got all torn up by some barbed wire and it got infected and I had to put her down before a single feather fell out of the sky. No wonder I couldn't remember the trade. I might as well have given that rifle away."

"Do you think she'd still have it?"

"How the hell would I know? But something to keep in mind. You find a spent cartridge under a tree, you think it was ejected when the shooter worked the bolt to chamber another round. But a Mannlicher has a rotary magazine. The empty case just revolves to another position in the magazine. So if it was found on the ground, it was dropped there on purpose, or else it fell out of someone's fingers when he was loading or reloading. Understand?"

Sean understood.

"You'll be looking for the old Lazy L place up Bear Creek. You know, the 'L' laying down short side up, like it's asleep? Cute. I don't think Marnie's sold out to the Californians yet."

———

She hadn't sold out, but she had got rid of the rifle after her husband passed. The outfitter who leased the hunting rights had taken it off her hands for a song. This was before a banker from Pittsburgh had put a bullet through a hindquarter of one of her horses, mistaking bare aspen branches for antlers and thinking he'd shot at a bull elk. Luckily, the bullet had missed an artery. The damage bond the outfitter put up for the lease paid the vet bill, and the mare came out of the ordeal with a scar and a jumpy disposition. But it had left a bad taste and she had shut down the operation. Now she only let a few friends and family on during the elk season.

As she talked, Marnie Post drew lines in the pollen covering her porch with the toe of her boot. She was a tall, hips forward, still-elegant woman wearing jeans, an untucked pink shirt decorated with white horses, too-bright dentures that matched the color of the horses, and she answered the first of Sean's questions working her toe against the porch floorboards and the next on the linoleum floor of her kitchen, where she set a cup of ranch coffee before him that had no more kick to it than stained water. Sean blew the steam off. As a veteran of knocking on doors in rural Montana to ask if he could fish, he understood that the price of admission was, as often as not, coffee so hot it could scald your lips, and simple conversation over a cup of it. Or two. Or three. Depending on how many children's lives you were going to hear about.

A half an hour later she was showing him "all the horseflesh I have left," her two remaining horses that were grazing in a pasture behind the house. Marnie tuck-tucked with her tongue and both of the horses ambled over to visit, the half-thoroughbred mare that had taken the bullet and a mountain horse with white stocking that Marnie said she rode up on the trails. Flies buzzed at their nostrils.

"You ride alone?" Sean asked her. He fed the apples Marnie Post had given him to the horses. He rubbed his fist against the mare's bulging jaw muscles.

Marnie Post shrugged. "I don't have anybody to ride with me, now that Martin's gone."

Sean was past being astonished by the number of people he met, many of them octogenarians, who lived in drafty old farmhouses with no neighbors for miles, and who, like Katie Sparrow, had nothing but the dog and the barn cats for company. Or the occasional bear, come autumn. Or horses. Or children who visited twice a year wanting the best for old mom, not to mention all the money they'd pocket by selling the place once they gained power of attorney.

"Maybe you could find me a fella," Marnie Post said, taking Sean's arm for support as they crossed an irrigation ditch bridged by an old barn door. "That's what I really miss, just Martin walking by my side like you are, somebody to look at the birds with and talk to. But most of the men my age are looking for someone to take care of them, and I've been nurse enough for any woman's lifetime."

She squeezed his arm and crinkled up her eyes, the skin of her cheeks thin and finely wrinkled, as if it was waxed paper that had been balled up in a fist and then spread back out. "You want to hear what my three requirements are?"

They were confidants now, walking a fence line to nowhere in particular. Sean looked east to the great limestone reef of Sphinx Mountain, where he'd almost died once. It seemed like twenty years ago, but couldn't have been more than five. One thing about etching PRIVATE INVESTIGATIONS into the frosted glass of his studio door, it had put him on the road to an eventful life. He was on a road now. True, it was a detour from the one he'd taken only a few hours before, when he'd agreed to search for Harold. But the question was, were the two roads diverging? Or were they parallel tracks? His instinct told him the roads had the possibility of bleeding into each other at the horizon. The cartridge case that he had in his pocket shot the same caliber bullet as the one found in Harold's capsized canoe in the Smith River. It was an uncommon round, too uncommon to ignore the possibility, and Sean, who was always certain and often right, didn't believe in coincidences any more than Martha Ettinger did.

He lowered his gaze from the peak.

"No walker, that's my number one," Marnie Post was saying. "Any man of mine's got to be able to get around. No oxygen tank, can't be trailing that through the grass. And no catheter. His plumbing's got to be in working order. You get a thirty-below night, you want to get as close together as God made a man and woman to be. Yes, even at my age." She laughed and squeezed his arm. "You're going to leave here thinking, 'What will this old bird say next?'"

Sean didn't leave her thinking about what she might say next. He left her while pondering the name of the outfitter who had bought her rifle, which he had inked onto the back of his hand. He rolled the cartridge Sam had given him in thoughtful fingers.

CHAPTER TWENTY-FOUR

Harold's Mark

The steel Quonset hut outside Bridger that served as one of Montana's two forensic crime labs looked more like a place to judge cattle at a 4-H event than run a fingerprint analysis. In fact, the first time Sean had visited it, the hut was an uninsulated storage facility for Montana Fish, Wildlife and Parks, and confiscated game animals were gutted and hanging from rafters, ready for public auction. That day he had found the Region 3 elk biologist, Julie McGregor, helping Georgeanne Wilkerson, the county's top crime scene investigator, drop a skinned deer carcass onto the antlers of a six-point bull elk, to measure how far the tines penetrated. They'd haul the deer up a ladder, poise the carcass over the elk's head, and when Julie said "One, two, three," they'd let it drop, then howl like schoolgirls when the carcasses smacked wetly together.

As McGregor was part of the FWP team that investigated game poaching, Sean had called her on his way down the valley. She met him in the parking lot behind the building.

"Aren't you going to ask me what's new?" she said.

"What's new?"

"I got knocked up. Yep, bun in the oven, preheated and timer set. Seven months and counting."

"Good for you, Julie."

"I know. I feel like a princess. And a biologist. I'm not sure you can be both at once."

"You're living proof," Sean said, and she smiled like Christmas morning. They went into the lab, where they found Wilkerson at her desk, wearing latex gloves and looking red-eyed behind her gogglelike round glasses. The two women air-hugged, Wilkerson careful not to touch anything with her blue-sheathed fingers.

"Dropped any deer lately?" Julie asked.

"Those were the days," Wilkerson said. She placed a clean Mason jar upside down over the object she'd been examining, a tooth chip, she told them, and smiled the tired smile of the regional laboratory chief she'd recently become. It was a mantle of authority she wore heavily. Though both were average-sized women with short-cropped hair, there the outward similarity ended. Julie was tomboy head to toe, with freckles and a sun-peeled nose, smooth hard muscles, and leather hands, where Georgeanne, whom everyone called Ouija Board Gigi, had an indoor pallor, a slight build, and didn't look as if she'd possess the hand-eye coordination to swat a fly. One thing they did have in common, Sean suspected, was that neither had worn makeup in her adult life, if you discounted the camo face paint that Julie used when she hunted whitetail from her tree stand.

"Did you get the package the Park sent?" Sean asked Wilkerson. He'd called Katie Sparrow from the road, who'd assured him that the cartridge had been overnighted from Park headquarters to the regional crime lab.

"Not in the a.m. drop, but we'll see if it's here now," Wilkerson said. She tapped an extension on the desk phone. Yes, it had arrived.

"While we wait, show me what you got from Sam Meslik."

Sean handed the cartridge case over. Wilkerson frowned at it.

"I'm not familiar with the caliber, but that's neither here nor there." She bent a magnifying lens over the rim.

"Distinctive primer indentation with a shallow sickle mark. Six parallel striations made by lateral movement when the bolt closed over the case head. Mark closest to the primer indentation is boldest, third mark shortest. Concentric breech marks. Pronounced. Don't you just love old firearms, they're so"—she searched for the word—"idiosyncratic."

She put the glass down. "This one's going to be a lead pipe cinch, one way or the other." The smile, not so tired now. "What have you been up to, Julie?"

"Besides getting pregnant and throwing up? We've been capturing bighorn from the Beaver Creek herd and airlifting them up to Bear Creek. Talk about a rodeo."

They talked about the rodeo of sheep catching as they waited for the cartridge case. When it came, there was no knock at the door, there being no door. A young man in scrubs handed over a sealed envelope with a diagonal strip of evidence tape across it. Wilkerson opened it and shook out the cartridge case onto a sheet of lab paper cornered into her blotter. She placed Sam's case beside it. They were identically proportioned, though Sam's was age-darkened and the one found in the Park had blotchy discoloration from exposure.

"The cases are of different manufacture. One is Norma, one PPU," she said. "Both show evidence of being resized. Note the dimpling in the shoulder area on the one from the Park. That's caused by using too much lube during resizing. Usually those marks disappear with the pressure of firing, but not always. And on this one"—she tapped with a steel tool that looked like a dentist's probe—"that hairline crack in the neck indicates metal fatigue. It's been resized once too often and is ready for the trash bin."

"Does it make a difference that they're from different brass manufacturers?" Sean asked.

"It shouldn't. The marks caused by firing or chambering will be the same." She examined them again with the heavy lens and then, expressionless, passed the lens to Sean.

He saw the striation marks she'd mentioned and compared them to the marks on the case Sam had given him. They were similar. So were the breech marks that resembled the concentric rings left on the surface of a pool when a trout rises.

"Gimme," Julie McGregor said.

She looked for a minute, set the lens down, and beamed her smile. "I think you got yourself a bingo."

"No question then, right?" Sean asked.

Wilkerson nodded. "I've sat as a firearms expert in the witness box with a lot less. Do you have an ID for the person Sam sold the rifle to?"

"It was a ranch owner in the valley. But it's the guy she sold it to who's of interest. He was the outfitter on her place. A Rayland Jobson. Have you heard of him?"

Neither Wilkerson nor McGregor had, though the elk biologist was nodding to herself.

"A lot of poachers are outfitters. That's the way some of them get their start. They know all the access points and where to find the trophies."

Wilkerson's eyes behind the thick glasses settled on Sean. "You inquired about the possibility of tying this case to a bullet found in the canoe that Harold Little Feather was paddling up on the Smith River. I can't do that. Number one, it's in evidence at the Cascade County Sheriff's Office. Number two, it wouldn't tell me the story you want to hear. I can match the slug to the rifle, and I can match the case to the rifle, but I can't match the slug to the case. The bullet doesn't transfer distinctive marks to the case when it's fired, and vice versa. But"—her eyes went away as she thought—"say this Jobson got rid of the rifle. You could still link him to it through Sam and the ranch owner; you could prove he had possession of the weapon in such and such year. It's circumstantial, but it's a brick in the case for the prosecution if you had other compelling evidence. It would help string him up by his turkey neck. Sorry, but I'm always thinking like a D.A. Occupational hazard."

"How do you know he has a turkey neck?" Julie McGregor fingered her own neck.

"Everybody has a turkey neck after a six-foot drop," Wilkerson said.

———

"She forgets we're not a hanging state anymore," Martha Ettinger said. "The last one dropped in 1943. Phillip Coleman, aka Slim Coleman. Murdered a couple at their home, spared the child who found the bodies. Converted to Catholicism after the arrest, then he fessed up to another robbery-murder for which he got twelve whole cents. Makes you long for pioneer justice.

"So what were you doing talking to Wilkerson? Why are you here, for that matter? I didn't expect to see you until there were developments. Were there?"

She pushed her wineglass away with her first two fingers. Sean took the empty glass and set it with his own on the counter. He'd driven straight over from the crime lab, just in time for a glass of red and Martha's spaghetti with venison meatballs.

His back to her, he put the question that had brought him to her door.

"You'll want the evidence summary," she said.

She brewed two cups of tea and they retired to her home office, a desk computer on a five-hundred-year-old sawn Ponderosa stump illuminated by track lighting. She tapped her way to the report that had been forwarded to her from the Cascade County Sheriff's Office and ran her eyes down it.

"Two fifty-six caliber," she said. "Minimal fragmenting. One hundred thirty grains retained weight. Passed through the bow decking, penetrated the waterproof boat bag with Harold's gear, put a hole in the stock of his rifle, which was in a scabbard lashed to the middle thwart, and came to rest in a stack of firewood on the boat bottom. Penetrated four three-inch-thick pine splits before running out of steam. As I told you before, somewhere along the way it struck human flesh. Trajectory angle estimated at thirty-seven degrees indicates a shot from above and downstream of the canoe, assuming the canoe was going downriver at the time of the shot. The good news, if it can be called that, is the trajectory suggests that the person the bullet struck was in the bow seat. That tells me two things. One, that Harold had a passenger. Two, it suggests the passenger was the one who was hit."

"Harold could have been in the bow."

"Possible. But it was his canoe. I can't see him letting anyone else sit in the stern. Can you?"

Sean closed his eyes. He could picture it, the shooter lying on a ledge, in the shadow of the cave mouth perhaps, the scope of the Mannlicher to his eye, waiting for Harold's canoe to round the bend upriver, waiting until it came so close he couldn't miss.

"It could have been Marcus in the bow," he said. "He could have wrecked his own canoe so they were traveling together."

"You're right, it could have been. But if it was, it still doesn't explain why his canoe disappeared. There's a photo of the bullet." She clicked an attachment.

The bullet resembled a much-scaled-down mushroom cloud from the explosion of an atomic bomb.

"Is two fifty-six caliber the same as six point five millimeter?" Sean asked. He already knew it was, just wondered if she did.

"Yes," Martha said.

"Can you do the conversion that fast, or is it in the report?"

"I'm good with numbers."

"I didn't know that about you."

"There's a lot you don't know. It's sort of your choice," she said, the last part under her breath.

There was a moment of silence, not altogether comfortable.

"Sorry," she said. "Why are you interested?"

"You're going to say I'm stretching, but I think the rifle that shot that bullet is the same rifle that shot a grizzly bear in Yellowstone Park this spring. Katie Sparrow found a cartridge case near the carcass that was six point five millimeter. I took it to Wilkerson and she matched it to an old handload Sam Meslik had. It used to be his rifle, a 6.5×54 Mannlicher-Schönauer. He traded it to Marnie Post for a bird dog, and she sold it to the outfitter who guided hunters on her ranch up Bear Creek. Guy named Rayland Jobson. I was hoping you had some background on him."

"Sure." She wrote the name down. Now there was a different kind of silence, and a bemused look on Martha's face when she lifted it.

"Katie, Sam, the widow Post, Wilkerson. You've had a busy day. You're going to have to explain this very slowly."

He did, as Martha listened with her hands laced behind her head. When he finished, she frowned at him but said nothing. She looked at the clock on the wall. A long minute passed. Then, the three-note hoot of a gray owl in the canyon.

"He's late this evening," she said. "Used to be you could set your watch by him. Okay," she said, turning to face him. "I give up. What's the connection to the bullet in Harold's canoe with the cartridge case Katie found? I mean besides the caliber. There are a lot of calibers that shoot a six point five bullet. Heck, my son David has a .260 Remington I got him for his eighteenth birthday. Are you accusing him of shooting at Harold's canoe?"

"No. But I told you I went to Katie's house. After I left, she called and said she'd thought of something else, something about the place where she'd found the case."

He fingered his phone from his pocket and clicked on the email attachment he'd had Katie send to him. It was a photograph showing three parallel lines.

"What am I looking at?" Martha said.

"Those are cuts made in the trunk of a limber pine tree a few feet away from where she found the case. Katie said they were about a half a foot long and a couple inches apart. She guessed they were carved by a knife blade. They're hard to see now because they're shallow, but you can see where the bubbles of sap formed in the deeper parts of the wounds."

"I see that. If there was one more slash I'd say it was a bear made it. Or a lion."

"Three slashes on the diagonal. Have you seen that before?"

Sean saw the dawn of understanding. Then her eyes swam away.

"Harold," she said softly.

And for several moments she was somewhere else, far to the north, up in the Two Medicine country. It was a November day, snow falling straight down, and she was riding Petal, her gloved hands blocks of ice on the reins. Harold had invited her to join his hunting party, which included his brother, Howard, and Howard's wife, Bobbie. Harold said he'd leave his blaze on a tree where she should take a spur trail to the left, that the tipi was pitched on a bank over Badger Creek. But she'd seen his horse before she saw the blaze, the big paint ghosting through stunted aspens, the rider obscured until the horse stepped into an opening, steam columning up from its nostrils. Harold sat on the horse with his hair falling over his shoulders. Martha had never seen him without a braid and he looked wild to her, his hair blowing, three char-coaled black lines striping his cheeks. Later, in the tipi—the second tipi, the one he hadn't told her they'd be sharing—she'd stood awkwardly, shifting her weight from one foot to the other, and gone rigid when he'd kissed her. She'd turned her head away. Then something had broken inside her and she'd turn and pressed herself against him and opened her mouth with a hunger that had been building for weeks. For months.

"We'll have to be quiet," she said. Ever Martha. And had been. Ever Martha.

Afterward, she'd lain naked beside him under an elk robe and traced the lines on his cheeks with her fingertips, there being just enough moonlight bathing the walls of the tipi to see the marks.

And she'd thought, *What the hell are you getting yourself into, Martha May?*

CHAPTER TWENTY-FIVE

The Masterpiece

During the hours he thought he might be dead, he remembered Jewel MacAllen saying that he'd felt the same way at times, like he was a bird looking down at the earth, and that he'd touch a tree to reassure himself that he was still grounded and alive. But in the cave there were no birds, nor trees to touch, nor sky to look down from. There were only the rock walls blackened with the smoke of long-dead fires, and stalactites formed drip by drip over the course of millenniums, bats hanging from them like fig clusters.

The tether was a chain of metal links about the size of the rusty chains that suspended the swings he remembered as a child, the broken set in his auntie's yard. One end of the chain had been passed through a two-inch-wide slit cut through the skin on the thin part of the ankle in front of the Achilles tendon. It was the same cut Harold had made dozens of times in order to pass a rope through the hocks of a buck deer to hang it by its hindquarters for skinning. When the clawlike right hand had jerked the first link through the slit, in one side of his ankle and then out the other, the pain had seared so sharply that he gasped, and for long moments couldn't breathe back in. Then more of the chain had been pulled through, link by agonizing link, the man who pulled it keeping up a running commentary.

"What do you think, Charlie, do you want one more? No, I keep forgetting, your name isn't Charlie is it . . . Harold?"

Or, sometime later, "How about you, Dewey?" speaking to the

gnomelike man who sat cross-legged at the far end of the cave. "What's the verdict? One more link, or two?" And the small man replying, "How many more you got?" And then laughing, a slow, tenor laugh, "Ha, ha, ha?" ending on a quizzical note, as if he'd forgotten what was amusing. And all the while pressing the muzzle of a revolver to Marcus's ear, the boy sitting on the hard rock with his head hanging down, his hair covering his face.

And so the links were jerked through the slit, Harold's nerves screaming, until by the time that the chain had been pulled through to half its ten-foot length and both ends padlocked to an iron ring, he was mercifully only semiconscious, though that had as much to do with being smacked into submission by a stone earlier as the pain from the chain. He did not hear the blows of the flat of an ax that drove a railroad spike through a circular opening in the iron ring and into a crack in the rock wall. Nor did he see the men leaving, the tall man he'd known as Job, followed by Marcus, shuffling, stumbling, finally the gnomelike man trailing a wake of body odor, who spit on Harold as he passed by.

An hour later, the daylight that seeped into the cave from some unseen recess had been replaced by a darkness so absolute that Harold could have been soaring through a black hole in space, and sometimes felt he was. Then, swimming back from that fathomless ether, he had envisioned his son's face, the finely sculpted cheek that was his own blood, and then, without his bidding, the vision changed, the head turning to reveal the grotesque swelling where Marcus had been struck unconscious with a river stone, perhaps the same one that had been used on him, though the details of his capture were written in a disappearing ink that he had yet to find the catalyst for. The hand that held that stone was the one that had pulled the links of the chain, and Harold remembered it well, had come to despise it apart from the man to whose arm it was attached. The starburst of scar tissue, the flipper of a little finger, the claw of hand clenching and releasing, clenching and releasing, as if it was in spasm, a body dead, but the hand yet to receive the message.

Is he alive? Is Marcus still alive?

It was all Harold thought about, for after Marcus had been led from the cave, Harold had not seen him again. When the vision of his son began to reel away from behind Harold's eyes, he pulled it back with an effort, and then it paid out again like rope, Marcus's face turning over and over until it was as small in the distance as a locket photograph, where it held for a few beats of Harold's heart, and then was gone.

———

Harold, lucid now, his pain a dull throb, looked around the walls of his confinement. He judged by the relative light that it was middle of the day, and glanced down at the lines he'd scratched onto the rock floor with a piece of charred wood. The lines told him that he was in the sixth period of a paler gloom. His stomach could have told him as much. Except for a few pieces of venison jerky and an apple that he'd shared with Jewel MacAllen, Harold hadn't eaten anything of substance since launching his canoe at the camp below the homestead at Tenderfoot Creek.

He had relived the day many times, but now did so again, beginning with finding MacAllen at the homestead. Taking him down the river with him had been a gamble. He could have left him with MacAllen's promise that he would do no more mischief among the cliffs, for the man's eyes had admitted to being the Scarecrow God, taken pleasure in it, even if his words hadn't. But Harold hadn't trusted him to leave of his own accord, and felt that Jewel's volatile nature could escalate a confrontation should someone else cross paths with him. In that case Harold would be morally responsible for the consequences. Then, too, Jewel's words before the lantern had flickered out had haunted him.

"They's something else. I can take you there, but you ain't going to like it."

Take me where? Not like what? Jewel would not elaborate.

"What-chew think I got around in, in them swamps?" he had said, when Harold had gone over with him the rudiments of handling a canoe paddle the next morning. "You best worry about your own paddle. I'll take care of mine."

And he had been true to his promise, his facility with the ash blade better than adequate in a river that didn't suffer fools under the best of conditions, and conditions were far from good and deteriorating hourly as upper-elevation snow melted from the south slopes of the Big Belt and Little Belt mountain ranges.

Two Creek, Sheep Wagon, Sheep Creek, Cow Coulee where the helicopter had picked up Bart Trueblood, all the boat camps in the next sixteen miles, even Sunset Cliff, the most majestic of all with its rose-colored rock buttresses and resident pair of golden eagles riding the thermals—it all swept by in the periphery of Harold's vision. All his concentration was needed to navigate the current, Harold saying "hup" when he wanted MacAllen to dig his paddle in on the other side, Jewel pointing out barely exposed boulders that Harold would not have been able to spot from the stern in time to avoid collision.

And all the while Harold was thinking of Marcus; Marcus, whom he had sent down ahead of him, thinking at the time that it was the safe thing to do; Marcus, whom he'd told to wait for him at Table Rock, which they ought to make by late afternoon at the current rate of flow. They were still a mile or more from the destination when Jewel had said "Pull over here," indicating the west bank of the river. Harold J-stroked to spin the canoe and nosed it upcurrent into a cove in a willow-choked bottom.

"You see that overhang yonder, wraps under the cliffs?" MacAllen had pointed with his paddle. "Bunch of swallow nests plastered against the walls? You get back up under there, it's all pictographs, must be three, four dozen. I came by here about the last day you could wade across. It seemed like a good place to build 'cause a lot of floaters would notice, and then when I saw what I saw, I backed away like a yeller dog."

"Show me," Harold barked, betraying his impatience to get on down the river and find Marcus.

"You're antsy as a worm in hot ashes. Won't take but a few minutes," Jewel had said.

From the bank, a well-trod trail led uphill from the willows, passing a discreet sign requesting floaters not to touch the native art.

"You made a scarecrow here?" Harold had not seen a scarecrow marked at this place on the map the ranger had given him.

"Done about half of one," Jewel said. "Like I tole you, what I seen squelched the appetite."

The overhang was tall enough for Harold to stand, the ochre-colored pictographs appearing to be as sharp as when they'd been made. A handprint was most prominent, and Harold had to stretch to his full height to raise his own hand to cover it.

"Tall sum bitch," Jewel said.

"For his time." Harold nodded.

"It's around to the right. Just got to foller up around this ledge a piece."

He had told the truth. The top half of a scarecrow was propped against a rock, its head woven from green willow shoots.

"He'd have been my masterpiece, I ever got around to finishing him. I had plenty material and this overhang's 'bout as good a location as any. It's protected, but not too dark under the ledge a body can't see it from the river."

He led Harold across a scree slope scattered with slabs of limestone that had cracked off the overhang. His bony index finger pointed to the right, where two gray jays were industriously digging their bills underneath the edge of a flat rock.

"They had to be a dozen last time I was here. I got to work and paid no never mind, but you know how it is, you got a curious nature to you. I never did lift a rock I didn't know better, and me from Florida, where you as likely to find a moccasin underneath as a nightcrawler. I seen stuff worse, that's for sure, but all the same I'd as soon not repeat the experience. I'll stay right here, guard all these pictographs from miscreants the like of me while you have your look."

Harold remembered the river ranger pointing him to the scarecrow in the barn and saying be my guest. His gut told him that whatever these birds were working at would be worse. With the day warming, the breeze had shifted and Harold skirted the rock to get upwind before scattering the jays. The rock was heavy enough he had to use both hands to turn it over.

Harold swallowed. What he was looking at was a human head. It was facedown, and Harold was looking at two whorls of stiff blonde hair encompassing bald spots, one above the left ear, the size of a nickel, the other on the crown, as big as a fifty-cent piece. There was no apparent injury if you didn't count the fact that the head was unattached to a body. Harold took photos with his phone, then glanced around for a stick, finding a suitable one a short distance down the slope. Careful not to touch the head with his hand, he worked the stick under it and turned it faceup. No sign of injury on that side, either. The decapitation appeared surgical, a clean, nearly bloodless cut with a pepper of bone chips where, Harold guessed, a saw with close-set teeth had sawn through the joint of the second and third cervical vertebrae.

He heard a rock tilt, then Jewel's voice. "He was clean-shaved I found him. Folks say hair and fingernails grow after a body's dead, but I seen corpses two and three days in the heat and what it is, it's the skin dehydrates and shrinks and it exposes the hair under it."

"Where did you find it?" Harold said.

"Right where you're standing."

"Was the rock covering it up?"

"Yeah. You could see a little hair you bent down. You'd think the sum bitch that done it would have buried it a little deeper."

"You'd think," Harold said. "The head, was it faceup, or facedown?"

"Down. I didn't turn it over."

"Were there this many maggots?" The severed head seethed with the writhing of tiny white worms.

"Not that I recollect."

"You sure?"

"I woulda recalled."

Harold knew that maggots appeared within twenty-four hours of tissue becoming flyblown. The man had been dead only a short time before MacAllen had discovered the head, or else he would have seen maggots.

"What day did you say you found it?"

"I didn't. But it was day before yesterday."

Harold photographed the face, the everyman's countenance of regular features, bloated now, the pale skin, the ghostly blonde hair, the strange red tint of the sunken eyes.

"I ain't knowed but one albino in my life," he heard Jewel say. "Black kid I growed up with, got out of the draft 'cause his eyes was so bad. What about you? You know this feller?"

Harold, tight-lipped, shook his head.

CHAPTER TWENTY-SIX

The Wisdom of Beavers

It was, now that he looked back upon it from the perspective of a man chained in a cave, not technically a lie.

Fitz Carpenter had not been part of the interview process when Harold was hired, and their conversations, the few they'd had, were conducted by phone. He had met his supervisor at Division of Criminal Investigation face-to-face on only one occasion. That had been back in early March, at the Willow Creek Cafe and Saloon on the Jefferson River. Carpenter had picked the meeting place, he told Harold, because it was partway between Helena, where the state office was located, and Pony, where Harold lived at his sister's place. They had taken a seat under an eagle sculpture at a back table, and it was when Carpenter turned his head to the waitress taking their order that Harold noticed the unusual whorls of hair. It had reminded him of photographs of hurricanes approaching a mainland that were taken from space, the counterclockwise cowlick of the whirling white clouds.

Carpenter told him that the department had decided to take advantage of Harold's anonymity—he had yet to wear the uniform and was relatively unknown outside of Hyalite County—and insert him into a sting operation involving the poaching of grizzly bears for the Asian traditional medicines trade.

The man who had acted as a go-between bridging seller to buyer had been discovered and turned, the charges against him dropped in return for photographs, incriminating documents, and a sworn statement. But he had failed to meet an appointment with Carpenter and had never given his statement; in fact had never been heard from again. Carpenter suspected he had been blown and then eliminated. He gave Harold the name of a bar in Belt, the Harvest Moon Saloon, where the leader of the poaching ring was known to favor the Arndt Burger, a hefty patty of prime Angus slathered in sauerkraut and topped with Swiss cheese.

Carpenter had paid the bill for the lunch and they had gone outside, where he handed Harold the details he'd need in a sealed envelope that, besides containing background on the poaching ring and possible avenues of introduction, included topographic maps showing the locations of several bear carcasses, two inside Yellowstone National Park, three others in the greater Yellowstone region to the north.

"Welcome to the big leagues," Carpenter had said, and told Harold to burn the contents after memorizing them.

At the time it had seemed like a bit much, and Harold had smiled at the subterfuge. That was until he insinuated himself into the ring and met the man who threatened to cut out his gall bladder with his knife.

"I done know what it looks like," Jewel said.

Harold, returning from his thoughts, said, "What's it look like?"

"Like I done it. You still going to let me free, we reach Parker Flat?" Parker Flat was a boat camp four miles downstream from Table Rock. "That compound I was telling you 'bout, where I left my truck, it ain't but far from there on a two-track, you get on up above the cliffs."

Harold had fully intended to let him go, having no reason to suspect that MacAllen had committed a serious crime. But now there was a dismembered body to consider, and the circumstantial evidence linking Jewel to what looked certainly to be a murder was impossible to ignore. Yet he was puzzled. If Jewel had killed the man, why did he lead Harold to the crime scene? The half-built scarecrow wasn't visible from the river. They could have just floated by, Harold none the wiser. And there were larger questions, starting with what the hell was Fitz Carpenter doing on the Smith River only three days after he'd ordered Harold up here to investigate the scarecrows?

Words echoed from a not-so-distant past as he stared at the maggots swarming the severed head.

Why, handling a knife is an art. All my life, I never seen no one could work a blade to compare.

"This man you met at the bar in White Sulphur," Harold said. "I believe you called him Jobson. You think he could have something to do with this?"

"Hell, man, that's why I done showed you. He's trying to put it on me, the dagum sum bitch. Somebody finds this head, he sees the scarecrow, they gonna think I had a hand in it."

"But how would he know you would build a scarecrow here?"

"It was him suggested it. When I told him what I was planning on doing, for my Pap and the river and all, he said he sympathized and knew this place that would be perfect, that it weren't but a few miles from the compound. I was saving it for last because it was going to be my masterpiece. Anyway, you best hope it was him that done it."

"Why do you say that?"

"'Cause if I didn't do it, and he didn't, then there ain't nobody left but you."

With that thought to chew on, Harold had scribbled a note, folded it several times, and sealed it in an empty sandwich bag. He used his handkerchief to tie it to the half scarecrow. Then he went back down the scree and wrapped a lock of hair around his right forefinger to lift the head, which was as heavy as the bowling balls in Mark Lanes, the six-lane alley in Browning where Harold had whiled away hours as a child. Hiking with MacAllen back to the river, Harold had to stop to rearrange his grip twice when his fingers became white and numb.

At the bank, he washed as many maggots off the head as he could and then placed it on the canoe bottom under the rear thwart. From his seat in the stern, Harold could see it roll back and forth as waves rocked the canoe, the eyes staring up at him like coins turning over.

He stepped out of the canoe, and after some rearranging put the head in the smaller of his boat bags. They pushed off and had paddled perhaps a mile when Jewel said, "You best have sealed that bag. We make the turn and get a headwind, you going to be sorry you didn't zip it 'cause it's you going to be the one smelling it. You ask me . . ."

But he never finished the question. As they rounded the bend in sight of the uppermost campsite at Table Rock, Harold looking past the bow to try to spot Marcus's canoe, he saw Jewel MacAllen pitch forward, then jerk back sideways, his body twisted and his mouth coming open in the instant that the crack of a rifle carried the distance. Later, Harold would think that he had seen a puff of smoke from Table Rock itself, though, as modern cartridges use smokeless powders, that seemed very unlikely.

Everything in the next few moments seemed to occur in slow motion. MacAllen spilled over the gunwale, his mouth working like a fish's, and Harold, going over too as the canoe capsized, heard the dull thud of a second shot from underwater. Panicking, he fought to free his legs from Jewel MacAllen, the two of them having become tangled. He kicked free and thrashed to the surface, grabbed a lungful of air and ducked back under, but found that he was buoyed by his life preserver. He unbuckled the preserver and let it float away, hoping the next shot would find it with no one home.

The canoe had capsized in a boulder field and Harold was being pinballed from one rock to another, even as he tried to stay under the surface. Below him the current slackened, and he realized he would become exposed, dead in the water for all practical purposes, if he continued on course. He surfaced for a breath and craned his neck, looking for any option that didn't draw him closer into the crosshairs of the shooter.

Where the river bent to the right, the current had undercut the cliffs rising from the west bank, making a deep cavity where water swirled with foam. Harold kicked for it, making for the darkness. He was going to be too late, was going to sweep by just short, when he saw a tree limb protruding from the recess. Grabbing it, he pulled himself against the current back up the limb, dragging his waterlogged hip boots until he was under the bank and, he hoped, out of sight.

Exhausted, he collapsed onto the damp rock floor of what appeared to be a small cavern just above the water level. For a time, ten minutes, fifteen, he listened to the lapping of the water and concentrated on little more than breathing. Harold saw that the limb he'd used to haul himself up was anchored in a mound of sticks that he at first mistook for piled-up driftwood. As his eyes adjusted to the darkness, he recognized it was a beaver's house. He saw movement back in the gloom, heard a shuffling, then saw the animal itself as it climbed on top of the mound.

"Ksisk-staki," he said, using the Blackfeet name for beaver. "Nitsiniiyi'taki"—I thank you.

The shiny black eyes turned away as the beaver retreated out of sight.

When Harold's adrenaline subsided, he began to shiver. With trembling hands he pulled off his boots, dumped the water out, and then stripped off his soaking clothes and wrung everything out, including his wools socks, the only item of clothing besides underwear he put back on. The plan that he had half formed, to wait until darkness before slipping back into the river and floating until he was past the danger zone, simply wasn't going to be an option. His body was shuddering with cold, and he knew that if he was to make a move it had to be soon, before the blood in his extremities rushed to protect his core, rendering his arms and legs useless.

Like most who have lived a life of exposure, and who have witnessed the impersonal malevolence of which nature is capable, Harold was a fatalist. *If I die, I die,* he told himself, and not for the first time in his life. But still, he looked around for the beaver for guidance, for among the people the beaver was a symbol of wisdom. Not seeing it, Harold smiled to himself, shook his head with the slightest of gestures at the lip service he'd paid this ancient bit of folklore, and slipped back into the river.

To his surprise the water felt warm, at least it was warmer than the air, and he floated on his back with his legs downstream to kick off the boulders as he came up against him. How long had he been in the beaver's den—an hour? Probably only half that time. It was still far from full darkness, but the sun was riding the shoulders of the cliffs, the river running from glitter to shadow, and from shadow to glitter, as it wound a serpentine course between the canyon walls. He'd be harder to spot now, and if he was lucky, the man behind the trigger would have given up, figuring that Harold had been killed by the shots or drowned.

He estimated he had covered about a mile and the squeezed-chest feeling had abated when he spotted the fire on the east bank, the welcoming lick of orange flames, and then, a voice that couldn't be, yet was.

"Da . . . !" The shout echoing across the river, the last consonant lost in the echo. And again, "Da . . . !"

Dad?

Holding the bundle of his clothes in one hand, he stroked with the other, making for the column of light. He could see a canoe now, pulled up on the bank, its red sides catching the glow of the firelight. It was the canoe that the ranger had lent Marcus. Harold knew it could be a trap, but he also knew that he had to take the chance. Marcus could need him. But even if he didn't, Harold needed the flames, for his survival kit had gone down with his canoe, taking with it any chance of starting a fire. He touched the bottom and crawled onto the shore, where he collapsed. When he caught his breath, he rose to his knees. He could see a silhouette, dancing at the edge of the light.

"Marcus?"

No answer, the figure dancing, though Harold knew that to be an illusion. It was the fire dancing, the figure warping at the edge of the updraft could be standing still, and Harold rose unsteadily and began to stagger toward the flames. A small shape was darting into and out of the light. Cochise? Harold felt his chest expand as he drew in breath.

"Marcus!"

Then a sudden beam of white light blinded him, and a figure separated from the flames and came toward him. A voice said "tut-tut-tut," the tone feigning exaggerated disappointment.

"Isn't like me to miss like that. Not like me at'll. But then, I recall a time you missed a bear as big as a house, and with this very rifle. I hain't had occasion to fire it since. Must be a screw loose on the scope mount. Either that or you jinxed it. What do you think? You wouldn't have a 3/32nd Allen wrench handy? No? Well then, I guess if it comes to shooting you, I'll just touch the barrel up under your chin. Won't matter where the sights point then."

"Marcus," Harold said, his voice quaking.

"I'd be worrying more about yourself right now." Harold could see the rifle as the figure drew near, the black river stone in the other hand. He felt the cold steel of the barrel against the soft skin under his chin, the sharp bite of the blade front sight. The pressure lifted his head up and the man he knew as Job was smiling down at him, his beard glowing as if it had caught a shower of sparks from the fire.

"Marcus decided to take a little nap," he said. "Just a wee one. I had to hit him a little harder than I meant to."

"Marcus!" Harold called out, swallowing against the steel muzzle. And once more, "Marcus!" the name echoing across the river.

And then the stone in the man's hand swung in an arc to send a shock through his head. Harold fell, one eye catching the reeling of the stars, the other a red starburst that pulsed and drew down to a point, then pulsed again, opening like a flower before everything went to black.

————

And now the merciful nothingness of the rest of that night was six periods of indigo darkness behind him, long hours without stars and even the bats gone hunting, and after saying his son's name one last time, he took the burnt stick and drew another line onto the floor of the cave.

CHAPTER TWENTY-SEVEN

Close to the Chest

Even as Sean stepped out of the Land Cruiser, she was walking toward him, her arms folded across her chest, her body pulled to one side, looking small and vulnerable in too-big Carhartts, as if she'd been hit and was preparing herself for another blow.

She came right up to him, high cheeks under black eyes, and not really a small woman at all. "Whatever you didn't tell me on the phone," she said, "tell me now. Is he dead? Is my brother dead?"

"I don't know, Janice. I'm trying to find him."

She shook her head. "You're the first person who's come here since that woman who wanted me to spit into a cup. He must not count for so much."

"That isn't true. We didn't know when he planned to come out so we didn't know he was missing. And someone drove his truck away from the take-out. Harold had the key. It was logical to think he'd done it. You know how he is. He's not the kind of guy who calls in from the road unless he has something to say."

"So was it him who was hit? The bullet? Did they do the match?"

"Those things take time."

"I guess they do for some people. So why are you here then? Because now they think he's a murderer, that's why. I guess that goes without saying. You think he popped the guy in the river. But he's no killer. If he killed anybody, it was self-defense."

"I know that, Janice."

They'd been standing a few feet away from the Land Cruiser, close enough they could hear the metal expanding and contracting as the exhaust cooled and ticked down. Sean saw her eyes dart past him, then the small shake of her head. She looked levelly at him. The first words had come in a rush, but she appeared calm now, now that there remained the chance that Harold was still alive.

"Is there a call out on the truck?"

"I'm sure there is," Sean said.

She shook her head. "You're just like he is. Driving a piece of shit when you don't have to, like it's a badge of honor. I'd tell him his old Jimmy has rez written all over it. He should take my truck when he was paying a call on white folks 'cause they notice things like that, but he'd just laugh."

"Can you help me find him, Janice?"

"I don't know how. It's not like I'm in the loop. Harold's his own loop. He doesn't need another soul on earth." She looked down and again shook her head. "Except for that witch," she said under her breath.

Sean didn't need to be told that she was speaking about Harold's ex, Connie.

"What I'm trying to find out is what he was doing before he was sent to the Smith River."

"You'll have to ask his super at DCI."

"Martha Ettinger's working that end."

At the mention of the name, she stiffened. Then shrugged.

"None of my business," she said. "Yours maybe." A pointed look.

"I know about Harold and Martha," Sean said. "We're all grown-ups."

"Sure you do. The three of you are so evolved. But you don't know Connie. That woman, she never took the claws out. You can't talk to him about it. All you can do is hope she takes too much of that poison and dies."

"Is she a meth addict?"

"No, she's riding the horse. Harold pulled some strings to send her to rehab. That's that place down in Phoenix—Native American Connections, they call it. All she got out of it was more sources. I could have told him that before she ever went in."

"Would Harold have told her what he was doing?"

"I don't know. He didn't tell me. All I know is he was associating with bad people. He got those new tattoos, you saw them?"

"Yes, the tracks."

"I told him it was unbefitting to flash ink around like that. He'd cross his arms so his muscles popped out, and you wouldn't be looking at his face, you'd be looking at the tracks, think he was a savage or something. He's such a gentle man, what did he want to do that for? He said he had to look tough. But that was just an excuse for it. Harold, when we walked to school, he'd pick up nightcrawlers in the street after a rain and toss them into the grass so they wouldn't get stepped on. But he said the people he was associating with, they would sense any weakness in him."

"These people. Who were they?"

"I don't know. I think he was undercover, but when I came out and flat asked, he wouldn't say. Said he'd signed a confidentiality clause. But I heard him speak into a cell phone, one of those burners, and he was using a different name. He said, 'Charlie here.' When I asked him, he told me I heard wrong. Bullshit. I heard what I heard."

"Did he mention anything about Yellowstone Park or drop any names? Job? Jobson?"

She shook her head again. "All I know is he was nervous, and you know Harold, he's never nervous. That impassive face he puts on, the one you can't think what he's thinking, it's like his calling card."

"Can I have a look where he stays?"

"Okay. There's not a lot to see. He never needed possessions. I'm the one has to make sure he has clothes. He'd wear those flannels 'til they were nothing but threads."

As Sean followed her to the barn, he realized that he had never actually seen where Harold lived before. He'd been to the house several times to pick him up, but Harold had always been standing in the drive, ready to go. He'd never been inside the farmhouse, let alone the barn where Harold had insulated and furnished a room.

The barn door was open and they passed four horse stalls, all empty, the horses out to pasture. Nothing but a bobtailed orange tabby perched on a divider rail that arched its head to get its whiskers scratched as Janice walked past.

"That's Pumpkin," she said, "world's worst mouser."

She led him up rough pine stairs and into Harold's room. To call it furnished would be a stretch. The dry walls were up, but had yet to be spackled and taped. An insulated Carhartt jacket hung from one six-penny nail; a cracked felt cowboy hat hung from another. Otherwise, just bare walls. There was a floor mattress by a window that faced east, a wood chair and a simple table with a Mason jar and a gallon of water on it by a window that looked north, up the spine of the Tobacco Roots Range. A lamp with a cracked calfskin shade perched on an overturned crate, serving as an end table. An old issue of *Smithsonian* was beside a pair of dollar-store reading glasses. Two pairs of cracked cowboy boots stood by the door, and that was all, three hundred or so square feet of nothing much, where someone might sleep, but not really live.

Janice encompassed the room with a wave of her hand. "You see how neat he is in a place nobody sees. His truck, anything visible to the outside world, he's conscious of where he came from. Can't bang out a dent, 'cause that's saying my truck's better than yours."

"Does he have a closet?"

"His closet is the rear bench of the truck. He has two pairs of jeans, and three shirts minus one that I gave to that dog handler who needed his scent, and some Muck boots. I know, I bought all of it at Murdoch's. Harold travels light."

She shook her head. "He could dress presentable if he wanted to. I know how much money he makes. He supports this place now that Don can't drive the truck."

Sean knew that her husband was a truck driver who hauled horses

ranch to ranch throughout eastern and central Montana, and who'd
recently had to take a desk job in Bridger at half the pay because a
sciatic nerve made sitting behind the wheel impossible without pain
killers, to which he'd become addicted before Janice drew a line in the
snow and he'd kicked the habit.

"Money doesn't mean anything to Harold," she went on. "If he
didn't sink it into the horses or the property, he'd just give it away to
some do-gooder organization for kids."

"I don't see a bathroom," Sean said.

"You're facing the wrong window," she said. "Yeah, I caught him
peeing out of it one night. He just hauled up the window and let fly on
my tomato plants. Do you know what he said?"

"It's traditional," Sean said.

And both had started to laugh—Janice, who never laughed, wiping
at her tears. Then, abruptly, the tears were the more familiar tears, the
ones she'd been crying every night for the week now that Harold had
been missing.

Sean reached out for her and she pressed her head against him, so
that her voice was smothered by his chest.

"You'll find him for me. Tell me you'll find him for me."

"I'll find him," Sean said.

When she had gained back her control, wiped at her shiny cheeks
with an angry hand, she asked Sean if he wanted to come into the
house. She and Harold shared a desk computer. He followed her up
porch steps and shut the screen door behind him. It was a single-story
rancher not too different from others he'd spent time in, all the rooms
built for small people, a living area comfortable if dark, dusty, mis-
matched everything, an old yellow Lab thumping its tail as it lay before an unlit fire in a stone fireplace. It was the echo of a life that hung
on behind hundred-year-old doors while the world outside changed,
one subdivided property at a time, the vista compromised as the
houses went up, the trout in the overfished rivers becoming as sophis-
ticated as the chardonnay sipped on wraparound decks at six.

Janice booted up the computer. On the evening before Harold had left to float the Smith River, he'd tapped his way to a floater's map of the canyon with mile markers and all the camps labeled, had Google Earthed the river corridor and clicked on two websites focusing on the rock art in the caves. *Nothing unexpected there,* Sean thought.

"Harold tell you about his reason for going there?"

"No, he wouldn't even have told me he was going to float the Smith River. The only reason I know is I'm the one picked up the phone when his supervisor called and took the information."

Sean nodded. He gave Janice one of his cards, promised to call if there was news, and said goodbye to her at the door, though they lingered.

"What do you know about Marcus?" he asked her.

"I never met him. I heard the mother was Northern Cheyenne."

"Chippewa Cree," Sean said.

"You see how much I know. Does he look like Harold? My first thought is that it was a scam, somebody trying to line their pockets. Harold being the soft touch that he is."

"It's Harold's son all right. He never mentioned he might join him on the river?"

"He never even told me he existed. I had to read that in the paper." She made a dismissive gesture with her hand. "But that's Harold, right? He plays it close to the chest. Sometimes I don't think I know him at all."

Sean got to the end of the drive as he had so often in his life, water all around, surfaces hiding secrets, and a bamboo fly rod for a compass. But this time he had no interest in fishing, and after a minute of indecision, he turned north, and then the phone rang in his pocket and he adjusted his course, still heading north but, as he listened, east now, too, on his way to the end of the world.

CHAPTER TWENTY-EIGHT

The End of the World

It had taken Martha the better part of the hour to run down the name on the various search indexes, and then to put the name with an address. That was because Rayland Jobson had legally changed his name after his last brouhaha with the law, as convicts and bankrupts often do, to throw creditors, potential employers, and doubters off the trail. As of the past October, he was Job, no other name, and after finding the residence, Martha had drawn a red circle on a Montana map over a blank spot some thirty miles northeast of Winnett.

Martha knew the area slightly. Her uncle Ike had raised sugar beets some fifty miles to the south, out of Roundup, and he and her father hunted turkeys there up in the Breaks, where the Musselshell River flowed north toward the Fort Peck Reservoir. She remembered Winnett as a nothing town with a sense of humor, its slogan written in block letters over the grocery store:

**WINNETT, MT: IT'S NOT THE END OF THE WORLD,
BUT YOU CAN SEE IT FROM HERE**

Martha selected a blue pen from a jar on her stump desk and drew a squiggly line to represent the Musselshell River, which the mapmakers had deemed too insignificant to award notice.

They wouldn't overlook the river if they'd been stuck in gumbo up there, she thought. She was recalling the one time she'd joined her father and uncle on their annual hunting trip. On the second day in, the Cat Creek Road had turned to snot in the rain and she had missed her senior prom as a result. And so instead of petting on the front bench of Jimmy Ferguson's dad's pickup and enduring the boy's fumbling fingers trying to unsnap her bra, she had huddled under a rain fly before a smoky fire, feeding sage and cow chips to what passed for flames. It was tick season, and she had picked the ticks off her uncle's and her father's backs by the light of a Coleman lantern. Then had had the favor returned.

Later, they'd taken turns dancing her around the fire, her father playing the harmonica, the three of them talking and laughing until the whiskey ran dry. Her dad had kept apologizing for her missing the prom, but she hadn't cared. She liked being one of the boys, far more than being one of the girls. People got her wrong; they had all her life. They thought she hated men. Some even thought she must be lesbian. The truth was Martha loved men. She was practically one herself. She just hated the assholes.

None of this she told Sean as he drove up the 287 past Harrison, to Willow Creek, to the junction with I-90, where he pulled into the Pilot station and put her on speaker as he gassed the Land Cruiser.

"So he's done this kind of thing before?" he said. Martha had told him that Jobson had a record of game violations.

"The gamut. Outfitting without a license, outfitting with a suspended license, failure to obtain landowner permission to hunt, unlawful possession of trophy game animals, guiding unlicensed hunters, illegally obtaining licenses for out-of-state clients, facilitating transfer of game animals and parts across state lines. So on."

"Any consequences? Most game violations don't bring more than a slap on the wrist." Sean replaced the pump and waited for the receipt.

"Actually, yes. The last conviction for outfitting without a license and possession of an illegally killed elk landed him five years in the Sweet Grass County jail. Plus twenty grand and change in fines and restitution, and loss of all hunting, fishing, and trapping privileges for ten years. That's been, uh, three years ago. But I think he only served one year in the khakis."

"Any violations in the Smith River vicinity?"

"Maybe."

Sean could hear Martha click keys.

"Crazies, west side," she said. "Bear Paws, UL Wildlife Refuge, that's up in the Breaks, but not far from the current residence. Here's one, though. Carroll Ranch in Meagher County. I know that place. It's up off the Millegan Road. That's the road up above the Smith, the route you take to shuttle cars to Eden Bridge. Crossing private land without written permission to retrieve a whitetail deer shot in the national forest. I remember because I know Joanne Carroll. Jobson got into it with a ranch hand who told Joanne, who turned him in. As a result, she pulled the ranch out of block management and closed twenty-two hundred acres to public hunting."

"What's the address?"

"The ranch or the residence?"

"Where he lives."

"Tell me when you're ready." He was ready, jotted down the location on the gas receipt, and was set to go.

"It's not that simple," she said. "You need more than GPS to find places up there. I can get you to the ballpark if you'll just listen." She gave him country directions, working from memory, left after the second cattle guard, left again at the Y, and so on, with the caveat that the roads could have changed.

"The Musselshell," she said. "Nobody who builds there drives into Lewistown to buy a welcome mat. There's a lot of people this side of loony or that side, take your pick. This Job is a career criminal. He could be cooking meth or building bombs. Either way, you can bet he's armed."

"You're being dramatic, Martha. He has a record of sneaking around behind people's backs. I didn't hear one conviction for assault or anything violent in his record."

"Still, I don't like you going there."

"You know me. I'll be careful."

"I do know you, and that's not the word I'd choose."

"I'll check in and let you know I'm okay."

"From where?"

"From wherever I get back into cell range."

Changing the subject, he asked if she'd got anywhere with Division of Criminal Investigation. She had and hadn't. Martha's contact in the department, Kevin Whatney, whom she'd worked with before when a case overlapped, and whom she'd thought well of because he hadn't tried to bigfoot her, could or would only say that yes, Harold had been working an investigation, but that the state wasn't at liberty to divulge the details. Certainly she of all people should understand. And by the way, how's Jack? She wouldn't know, she'd told him, they'd been divorced seven years. Oh, I'm sorry to hear that. I'm a little busy now, as if Martha wasn't. Did she hear a condescending note in his voice? Or was he just a man who had the phone halfway to the cradle?

"Is it anything to do with poaching in Yellowstone Park?" she'd asked him.

A pause. "What makes you say that?"

At least she'd got his attention.

She'd told Whatney she'd like to speak to Harold's supervisor. Whatney said the man wasn't in, that he'd flown to Tampa Bay, Florida, where his elderly mother was in hospice care, and nobody in the office knew when he'd return.

"Who?" Martha asked. "I need the name."

Another pause.

"Fitz Carpenter, but he's not authorized to tell you what Harold was involved in."

Martha told him there was no law against talking to him, and Whatney grudgingly gave her a number. Martha called it on her cell phone, keeping Whatney connected on the landline. Straight to voice mail, mailbox full.

"So, nothing?" Sean said. He had already turned onto I-90 East.

"I didn't say that. Whatney's agreed to meet with me tomorrow morning, at the DCI offices in Helena. I'm sure he sees it as a one-way street—me talking, him listening. But I think I can persuade him that it's in our mutual interest to give and take. I'll just have to drip a little blood into a coffee cup and drink it or something, swear an oath. Harold could be trying to catch a grasshopper poacher with a BB gun and they'd claim it was secret state business."

Sean thought, *Helena will put her that much closer to the Smith River.* Sean told her to throw a dry bag with her sleeping bag and gear into her vehicle, just in case the events of the day ended up taking them to the river's edge, that he already had two kayaks on the roof rack.

"I still don't like you going up to the Musselshell," she said.

CHAPTER TWENTY-NINE

House of Quilts

It was Breaks country, a harsh, arid sagebrush and tumbleweed landscape with cracked earth and buttresses of sandstone rock showing the layers of the ages. For many people, it was the kind of place where you put pedal to the metal, making fast for anywhere else. For Sean, who examined all country with an artist's eye for geography and geometry, it was beautiful.

As he drove east on Route 200, putting Grass Range and then Winnett in the rearview mirror, he began to register the touches of menace—the NO METH, NOT EVEN ONCE signs, with their skulls and crossbones, the gophers eating their roadkill sisters, the tire-squashed rattlesnakes strung up on barbed wire, placed like mile markers on this road heading for hell, even while meadowlarks trilled from fence posts and bluebirds flitted gorgeously over the grasses, turquoise angels in a land that had been bled by the sun until it was almost without color. It struck Sean as biblical, though he had never been to the Middle East, and had no point of reference.

He glanced at the map he'd drawn from Martha's directions, found the road she'd said was unmarked, took the scribbled Y and found himself stopped before a locked gate. That wasn't on his map. He dug out his GPS and extrapolated the route he'd need to take to the coordinates of the last known residence for one Rayland Jon Jobson, aka Jon Jobson, aka Job. It was five miles to approach the location from the other side by what would probably be a sketchy road, only about a mile as the buzzard flies from the locked gate where he stood. He pulled on his boots and ate a sandwich and stalled. What gave him pause wasn't the hike in so much as the story he'd tell when he got there. Discounting the three hours he'd spent taking a stab at sleep in the back of the Land Cruiser at the truck stop in Edie's Corner, he'd been more than seven hours on the road, plenty of time to concoct a plausible reason for his visit.

He had thought to come right out with a part truth, say he was a gun collector who'd heard from a friend that Marnie Post had sold a Mannlicher-Schönauer in excellent original condition, he would pay top dollar for it, and she had pointed him in this direction.

But what if Jobson saw through the cover and felt he was under suspicion? He'd bury the rifle before a court order reached the door. No, that strategy wouldn't fly.

A traveling salesman? Actually there still were a few in remote parts of the state, smiling hucksters who traded their company to the isolated who desperately needed it, and who were willing to part with a little cash for something they didn't need to get it. Garden gnomes and rooster weather vanes, antler section dog chews, ranch implements you couldn't find in the local Murdoch's or North 40—they sold all this and more. Sean had been visiting a house once when a white shaman with the outline of a Skoal chewing tobacco tin on his back pocket had tried to sell the owner a divining rod. Even litters of puppies were shopped door to distant door.

But Sean didn't have any weather vanes, or gnomes, or puppies. His fallback, to pass himself off as a hunter asking for permission, he had abandoned because turkey season had closed and archery deer was still three months down the road. Now he considered it again. He could say he was scouting, trying to line up properties to hunt before landowners were swamped with requests. Hunters' knuckles had undoubtedly rapped on every door in the county; the addition of Sean's would raise no suspicion. It could easily get a door shut in his face, though. Well, it would be his job to make sure it didn't. He climbed up and over the fence, swinging his leg high so as not to rip his pants on the rusted barbs.

The road skirted the upper edges of jump-across coulees that crooked like broken fingers, deepening and widening as they fell to the riparian corridor of the Musselshell River. Sean could see the river as an intermittent milky slash a mile or more below, and for a while he thought that the house would be tucked in a lee down there. But then rounding a bend, he saw it in front of him, less a house than a two-story industrial middle finger, a "Fuck you, I'll do what I want with my land" structure with metal siding and a metal roof, an eyesore in a countryside full of them, though possibly no others for several miles. There was a jacked-up silver-and-black Silverado in the drive, caked with dried gumbo except for the two window crescents cleared by the wipers, the sleepy half eyes through which Montanans in mud country see the world. Sean found that he was whistling, trying to keep his mind nimble if he was to get beyond the door. Provided anyone was home. The fact that there was no ranch dog tugging at his pants cuffs wasn't encouraging.

But at his knock he heard footsteps start and stop, and the woman who opened the door was preceded by a shotgun barrel, which she tapped in front of her as one might tap a walking stick, with nothing in its sights but her own purple-painted toenails peeking out from pink flip-flops. She was blonde, or chose to be, for her eyebrows and lashes were as black as crow wings, and sturdily built, with fingernails painted the same color as her toes, and jangles of charm bracelets on both wrists. She looked like someone who would wear silk scarves and give you back ten for a twenty before reading your fortune, assuring you of a long life and the woman of your dreams. Sean told her why he was there while watching her face go through changes—a nodding, I'll-hear-you-out look, pleasant enough, then a rolled eyes you-must-be-kidding look, a level stare, finally an assessing look at an angle, the hooded eyes conveying that she wasn't buying it.

"I saw a couple bachelor bucks about a half mile west. I think the one would go one eighty, once he gets rid of his velvet," Sean finished up. The book was the Boone & Crockett record book, the points awarded to a trophy deer a sum of the length of its tines and beam circumferences, minus points for asymmetry.

The woman's laugh was musical, and not as hard as her eyes.

"They's all bachelors this time of year. No nookie 'til November. But I know what you're here for," she said, "and it isn't permission to hunt deer."

Sean waited, trying to keep a neutral expression and hoping she'd clarify.

"I'll tell you what I told that other fellow," she said. "It's my house free and clear, it's my name on the deed. I'm not indebted to the man in any way, we're not cohabiting on a regular basis, and I've not entered into a common-law arrangement by mutual consent or agreement. So if you want to talk restitution, you'll have to dig him out of the compound and you can leave my property out of the equation. For that matter, you can leave my property."

Sean, winging it, said, "If you cooperate, you will be left out of it. It's Job who owes the government back taxes and penalties, not you."

"Good to hear. At least you got the name right."

A yard of silence separated them, and Sean could feel it growing longer. *Where was Choti when you needed her?* In rural Montana, a dog was an ice breaker; it gave you something to do with your hands, a reason to turn your head away, and a little more time to think about what to say next. But he'd left her at the clubhouse on the Madison with Willoughby and company, and now he was seconds from being kicked down the road.

She was speaking again. "The last fellow didn't even know he'd changed it. He's still Rayland as far as I'm concerned, which isn't very. But you haven't shown me any paper says you're who you say you are, and if that's all the business you got, you can back up a step so I can close the door without being rude about it. I have a show coming up this weekend and I need to be working."

"What is your work?" he heard himself saying. The piercing eyes that were like java chips narrowed as she smiled, and Sean saw where a tooth was missing on the upper right side.

"It's the quilting show in Hardin. We got two more until the big one in Lewistown, the Harvest Moon Celebration. Next to the state fair, that's the biggest around."

"My sister quilts," Sean said. Well, he thought, she appreciates them, anyway. He'd never seen her sew so much as a button onto a shirt.

"Where's your sister?"

"Adams, Massachusetts. It's about six miles from the Vermont line."

"That's quilting country, it sure is. I used to live upstate Connecticut and I'd give anything to be there in the fall again. All those colors, just rolling hillsides of them, and pumpkins and that crisp feel to the day. If you're a landscape quilter, it doesn't get any better for material. Not like this country at all. Here you just go from fires and haze one day to rain and mud the next. I might as well be living on the moon. Who wants a quilt looks like that? We got weeks on end here you can't get out to the road. You don't have pickle jars and a pig hanging, you'll be counting your ribs by Christmas."

"Would you show me one of your quilts? My name's Sean, by the way."

"I'm Darlene Cook. My husband was one of the Hardin Cooks. He's gone now, ten years, three months, and six days, and God rest his soul. He was a good-hearted man, that man. If I hadn't gone on the pill, I might of had somebody to stick up for me by now, but you know how it is when you're young, the time is never right and you think you have forever."

She looked past him over his shoulder. "I suppose you might come on in. It's my house, isn't it?"

"It says so on the deed," Sean said. And risked a smile.

"Okay then, but just for a minute. I never know when he might be coming back. He finds you here it wouldn't be good. He can get wicked mad. It's when he's shifting his weight, like a mountain cat switching its tail. That's when you keep your head down. If you can't look at him right, then don't look at him at all. Somebody sang that, I can't recall who."

And Sean was in the door.

The house was airy and, despite its stark exterior, inviting. It had an old-fashioned shabby-chic feel, with comfortable furniture, calico throw pillows, everything round-edged except for the Mesa-design, faux Navajo rug that commanded the living room. It was a place you could sit back and put your feet up without taking off your shoes, while you admired the ribbons that hung above the fireplace mantel and the quilts that won them.

The quilts were everywhere—folded on the backs of chairs and sofas, hanging from all the walls, draped on racks like ironed newspapers in a London gentleman's club. Some were no larger than place mats. One looked big enough to warm a moose on a Berkshire winter night. The quilt that drew Sean's attention had photographs imbedded or rather fabric patches with some kind of photo transfer that had been stitched into the quilt. The photos looked to be of a family—father, mother, two daughters, a son, dogs—taken at various ages. One photo showed a young woman sitting on a horse with some kind of banner diagonally across the front of her Western shirt. A Stetson tipped up to reveal a face that could sell soap.

"You were beautiful," Sean said. When in doubt, he thought, flatter.

"I was Miss Nebraska 1984," she said, coming up beside him. "They took that photo for posters to promote my appearance at the state fair. I went to a lot of ribbon cuttings and all the fairs, but that Nebraska State Fair, that's where I saw my first quilt show. They just took my breath away, the colors, the intricacies, all so beautiful. I thought, 'I want to do that.'"

"How did a professional beauty get from Omaha to Connecticut to nowhere Montana?" Sean wanted to ask. But she was opening up and he didn't want to interrupt the stream. She began to talk quilting then—mixed media, glue sticks, machined versus hand-pierced—it was a foreign tongue to Sean. As he half listened, his eyes walked the furniture and climbed the walls. She'd said she was a landscape quilter, that was where her heart was, and Sean took in and went by a mountainscape that looked like Glacier National Park and another that had to be the White Cliffs of the Missouri River, and yet a third quilt that showed a peculiar rock formation up in cliffs above a bend of a river, and then his eyes came back to that one and he tapped his lip with a forefinger, thinking, as a slight crawling sensation worked up the back of his neck. He knew the place, had seen it from below rather than from above, or would have recognized it immediately. They had floated past the formation the day after Bart Trueblood had been flown out by the helicopter.

She said the name that had already come to him—"Table Rock."

"It's on the Smith River," she said. "The one you have to draw a permit to float it?"

Sean nodded. "I've heard of it."

"We drew last year. Judy did, that's my sister-in-law. I went with her and her folks. You couldn't get Job to go with that much company. You put three people in a room and he takes his plug tobacco and heads for the hills. It was really a little too low to float, we had to drag the raft a lot, but it was beautiful. Breathtaking. The Portals of Eden is what they call it. We climbed up to the rock and I took a lot of pictures. Such a strange formation. Like a mushroom. That top of the table, it must be big as a queen-sized bed. I told Job it sounded like the title of an old Western—*Showdown at Table Rock*.

"I wouldn't have picked it for a quilt, but Job, he saw the pictures I took and told me to put it in a landscape. See, that compound he's always driving off to is near the river there. So he knew the place. I didn't think it was material for a quilt, but it turned out better than I thought. It was People's Choice at the Quilt-O-Rama in Bismarck last February. Shows to go you, you never know."

She led him up the stairs to the second floor, where she had her quilting room looking out over the landscape. Halfway up the stairs, Sean stopped at a framed photograph on the wall. It was a campy, staged photo of the pitchfork couple in *American Gothic,* the painting by Grant Wood. The man was tall, narrow-faced, and serious, the woman in her colonial print apron, a younger Darlene Cook, trying for stern but playing with a smile.

"That's Rayland and me. Back before he blew his hand up. Better days, those. When he lost his son, it changed him. Lost his faith after that. Started saying he was like Job in the Bible. Always did the right thing, and still God made him suffer and wouldn't say why. He became bitter. One of those world-on-his-shoulders people, much as one can be who can't hold down a job. That's how come he changed his name."

"What happened to his son?"

"He was taking his wife to the hospital after her water broke and tried to beat a train to a crossing. It stalled out on him. Him, his wife, the unborn son, all gone in less time than it takes a train to whistle. Job says that railroad track is the river that divides his life. He used to be a preacher, you know. Lutheran. He could talk real eloquent."

"Darlene, I really would like to talk to him. I won't say I was here."

They'd reached the landing and she studied her toes.

"He'll know. I just can't." Her eyes were pleading when they finally looked up at him. "I already told you more than I should."

"Why don't you leave him?"

"You say it like it's simple. And go where? I sank every dime I had to build this house. His specs, but it's my house, my land. Why this place, that's what I asked him. He says it's beautiful, the Badlands of Montana. I said I don't want to move to no bad lands. I want to move to good lands. I didn't really want to move at all. I liked where I was.

"He says, 'You'll love it,' so I looked it up. I'd never been to Montana and he's wanting me to buy land sight unseen. So I looked up Montana Badlands and it really was beautiful, all these cliffs, like drenched in molten gold. I thought, I can work with that. The quilter in me can work with that. It might be nowhere, but it was somewhere, too, if you had the eyes for it. Then I make the down payment and wind up here in the Missouri Breaks. Rayland, he thought Breaks, Badlands, it's all the same. But it isn't the same at all.

"You know what I call it, this place—Folsom, Montana. Like the song. It's a prison and he's the warden, and guess who's in lockup? But you never heard that from me. And him gone half the time anyway. He comes back from the compound, it's as romantic as an oil change. I'm just something to grease the gears and get him back down the road. It isn't rape 'cause I let him, knowing what he'd do if I didn't."

Her eyes implored Sean. This is my lot in life, they were saying, and abruptly her shoulders sank. "He wasn't always a bad man. I found the heart in him once, it's who I hitched onto. But it's like a slipping down, isn't it? You take one step in the wrong direction, and you get something good out of it and nothing bad happens to you after, so you take another step."

Was she talking about Job, or about herself?

Sean knew there were women in her predicament all over the world, who made the excuses and wouldn't help themselves if they could. Who had such low esteem they believed they deserved what they got. He had never understood it, but then, he wasn't a woman.

"What's he do at the compound, Darlene?"

"You mean beside plotting to overthrow the U.S. government? That's a joke. They just like to feel like they're important, that they're making a statement by not paying taxes and squatting on federal land like it was their own. They call themselves the Rural Free Montanans, though there aren't more than about five of them. Job had me stitch up a flag, a copper rattlesnake winding through the initials—RFM. Rayland said it was copper country, that you dig under their feet and there was a fortune there. Not that they could do anything about it because it isn't their land, it's BLM and Forest Service checkerboard. I still don't understand why they don't kick them out."

"This is the place up near the Smith River?"

She hung her head.

"Could you direct me how to get there?"

"I don't know how to get there. It was dark. If you think this is nowhere, it's that place that's nowhere."

"How many times have you been there?"

"Only once, for the flag raising. There's like three houses, glorified shacks if you ask me, the one that's the biggest, it's called the Appalachian Hilton. That's what this guy and his woman call it. Job introduces me to them, and the guy says when he first built the house the outhouse was off by itself. But then as he added on, the outhouse became the in-house. You had to go, you didn't even have to walk outside anymore, just open a door off the living room. He showed it to me, proud as a peacock. Can you believe that? How would you even empty the vault?"

She shook her head. "Even Rayland can't take it for more than a few weeks at a time. For him, it's mostly just a place to conduct his business out of."

"You mean the big-game poaching?"

She looked at him. "I didn't say that."

"You aren't not saying it."

"I don't know. I just know that Rayland says that the long arm of the law can't reach him there. I don't ask what he's up to. I saw a dead wolf in his truck once, I told him to get it off my property."

Sean heard a thump on the porch. Darlene Cook startled, jerking upright.

"It's just the dog," she said. "Like to scare me half to death."

"Are you going to let it in?" Sean asked. And wondered, why hadn't it barked or greeted him when he walked up the drive?

"For pity's sakes no," she said. "No telling where that critter's been. It stinks to high heaven." She paused. "His brother-in-law dropped it off a few days ago. I said I didn't want another dog. But he said Job said to drop it off, and he does whatever he tells him. Rayland, he's the kind of man likes to kick a dog. This one, he must figure he can put the boot to it. Most are too quick for him. He misses and then he gets all sullen like it was my fault. You better go now. You look like you could take care of yourself, but you don't know him. It would be like fighting an animal."

He gave her his card, not the one with the eye on it, one that advertised Blue Ribbon Watercolors.

She frowned. "You're an artist, too? What's that have to do with the federal government?"

"Nothing at all. But you call that number if you want to get out. I have friends who won't be afraid of him."

"That would be their mistake."

When Sean pushed open the front door, a dog of dubious heritage came up to nuzzle his thigh, his tail thumping on the porch floorboards. Sean knelt and worked his hand into the thick fur at the nape of the dog's neck. When he stood, he had a moment of vertigo. The woman was talking but the dog had taken him to a different place at a different point in time, and to regain his bearings he again knelt and let the dog bury its wet nuzzle into his palm.

"He don't have a voice, the poor thing," she was saying. "Just thumps his tail and shambles like. Wonder what happened to his leg. Probably hit by a car, that's usually what it is." Her voice softened. "Why, he acts like he knows you. He's a mite skittish around me."

"Oh," Sean said, keeping his voice level an effort, working a smile, "dogs and me, we get along."

"You want him, you take him."

"When did you say Job's brother-in-law brought him here?"

"Day before yesterday, no, it was the day before that. How time flies amid all this splendor," she said, waving at the monochrome landscape, glancing up at the darkly pregnant sky. It was the first attempt at humor she'd managed.

"What's his name, the brother-in-law?"

"Dewey Davis. Rayland calls him Blackie sometimes, 'cause he's got a real heavy beard. It's like his cheeks are purple. Imagine being kissed by a man like that. Make a woman shudder. But you take that dog if you want. It's sure enough going to rain. It don't take much to get you stuck."

"What about Job?"

"I'll tell him it run away. Dog with three legs, he wouldn't last long hereabouts. Coyotes get him if Rayland doesn't kick him to death first. You'd be doing him and me both a favor."

Sean told her to throw in a bar of soap and they'd have a deal, and a few minutes later took his leave, the dog hobbling in his shadow and the woman shutting the door on the light that had come into her day, and all the rest of her life to count the years and hours since she'd lost a good-hearted man.

CHAPTER THIRTY

A Hope, a Prayer, and
a Three-legged Dog

Sean worked his fingertips on the drive from Winnett to Camp Baker, filling in Martha when he finally came within range of a cell tower. She agreed to meet him at Bart Trueblood's house a few miles below the put-in. Trueblood knew the river as well as anyone and might be able to offer some insight into what Harold would be facing, river-wise, provided that he was alive. That was the plan, as far as they'd got, and Sean stepped on the gas and was washing Cochise at the put-in when the ranger ambled down from the stone house. He had his hands on his hips and smiled crookedly.

"Whatever you do, don't tell me he's hunting for his other leg. Where did he turn up?"

"Up on the Millegan Road," Sean said, the lie coming easily to him, having rehearsed it on the drive. "A FedEx driver saw him, heard on the radio about a dog with three legs being with the film crew, and figured we'd want to know."

The ranger worked his mouth around, giving some thought to the statement or acting like it—with him it was hard to tell posturing from reaction.

"Betty Griggs drives that route," he said. "She delivered here just yesterday, five boxes of T-shirts with 'Save Our Rivers' on it. Parks Department idea. Make some money, everyone being aware of the mine issue. But nothing like being nonspecific, huh? Why not 'Save the Smith'? It sure as hell needs it. I went to the hearing in Lewistown last week. Gave my statement to the Department of Environmental Quality. As a private citizen, you know. Twenty-six speakers, three minutes each. All but one against the damned thing, but what does it matter? By fall they'll have dotted the T's and crossed the I's, DEQ will wash its hands of the matter, and after that it's going to take legislative action. The political climate being what it is . . ." He shrugged. "I wake up every morning hopeful. I turn out the light every night fearing the worst."

"Did you get in trouble?"

"For speaking up? Oh, I'm sure of it. Macy's coming down next Tuesday to decide whether to reopen the river to floating. We'll see if I still have a job when he leaves."

He shrugged. "You want a shirt? They run big so I'm thinking extra-large. Funny, Betty Griggs, she didn't mention the dog."

"Maybe it was USPS. All I heard was a delivery truck." Sean was backpedaling—so much for his rehearsal.

"Maybe, but I haven't seen but a couple dozen postal trucks up on Millegan since I started here. They don't deliver over fifty pounds. But what the hell? I don't see everything. Where was the dog? Upriver? Down at the take-out? It's sixty miles of gravel."

"I don't know. I'm picking up someone who knows more. You wouldn't know if there was a compound up above the cliffs somewhere? Maybe near Table Rock or Fraunhofer. Maybe Parker Flat. All that middle section. It wouldn't be visible from the river."

"What exactly do you mean by 'compound'?"

"One of those places where off-the-grid types squat on public lands. People who have a bone to pick with the government."

"Lot of people with hard-ons about rules and regulations around here, that's for sure. Why do you ask?"

"Just something I heard."

"You think the dog's going to be able to find the Indian?"

Sean didn't know.

"You're about as noncommittal as those T-shirts," the ranger said.

———

Bart Trueblood was thinner than Sean remembered, a gauntness in his face and an unhealthy pallor to his skin. His goatee drew up, his lips revealing his canine teeth as he greeted the dog before sitting back in one of the two Adirondack chairs on his porch. Martha had arrived earlier and occupied the other. Trueblood picked up the beer bottle that had made a wet ring on the arm of the chair.

"I know, I know," he said. "I look like Satan on his deathbed." He took a pull at the bottle.

"I was thinking drained by Dracula," Martha said.

"Well, I did get snake bit." He tapped the dressing on his left forearm. "Damn near met my maker. I think I deserve a little sympathy." He made a gun of his hand and cocked it at a cooler. "Have at it."

Sean found a bottled water bobbing among the bottles of beer.

"You're as much fun as a blood transfusion," Trueblood said.

"He means that literally," Martha said. "Guess who provided the blood?"

"I give up."

"Clint McCaine," Martha said.

Trueblood nodded. "They said I was out of the woods, and then the bottom fell out of my platelet count and the coagulatory properties of my blood were so fucked that they were looking for a supply of AB negative pronto." He nodded and took another swallow. "I knew his blood type was mine, because when we were in the canoe together he said he was going to the Seychelles islands to fish this fall and had to get his blood mapped and a bunch of vaccines and other shit. Being the asshole I am, I said you mean you're going all the way to Africa to fish for bonefish when there's blue ribbon trout fishing in your own backyard. But oh, yeah, I forget. You're poisoning the well, so I guess it makes sense. Anyway, his blood was my blood, and they did the transfusion in Great Falls and it's been, what, four days ago Friday? And here I am sitting on my porch and enjoying a beer and your company, thanks to my archenemy on the environmental battlefield."

"So you've buried the hatchet?"

"One of them, the one we each wanted to bury in the other's heart. Clint was right. We blamed each other for Rebecca's death, because it was easier than blaming ourselves. It was past time to move on, try to find a little peace before we leave this world for the next. I think that works for me better than him, though."

"He told me just the opposite," Sean said.

"Well, he would. But he's just trying to convince himself. He lives in that big castle alone, with all its echoes. He doesn't even have a dog to warm his bed. What do you think he's thinking about when he turns out the light? I don't think it's copper."

"Where do things stand with the mine?"

Trueblood looked at Sean and shook his head. "That's the other hatchet. There's no common ground there. Clint's still drinking the Kool-Aid, believing his own bullshit about the mine being benign, forgive the rhyme. Part of me thinks the thaw in our relationship is due to his largesse because, truth be told, they have the momentum now. There's only a couple more meetings left where concerned citizens can speak up, and that's where our strength lies, with public opinion. It's easy to be the nice guy when your team's two touchdowns up."

"I thought they still had to conduct an environmental impact study."

"They do. The deal is the developer foots the bill for it, and just last week the mining cooperative shelled out a half a million bucks to hire a consulting firm that I believe, from its track record, is prejudiced to support its new employer. By law they will have one year to complete the study, then, if the verdict is favorable, and barring government or divine intervention, it will be time to sharpen up the bits."

He drained the bottle, said "Fetch," and threw it into his yard. Cochise wagged his tail, but stayed where he was at Sean's boots.

"I can't even get the dog vote," Trueblood said. Then he shrugged. "Fuck it. At least Clint and I have got to the point where we have more than one subject to talk about."

"We were hoping you might have some insight into where to find Harold," Martha said.

Trueblood shook his head. "And here I just thought you wanted to admire my profile and have me shuttle your rig down to Eden Bridge." He struck the "I drink too much, smoke too much, make love too goddamned much" pose of his self-portrait.

"I only know what I've read and what you've told me," he said. "My first thought was everyone's else's. He drowned. His son, too. They'll find the missing canoe and the bodies when the water clears. But now the river's dropped far enough to think that something would have surfaced."

He looked at Sean. "And this morning you find the dog way to hell and gone up the Musselshell, and now you think that Harold might have run afoul of this Jobson character who's living in some kind of freeman compound. So sue me for being a pessimist, but if there's any truth to that, then you've just traded one worst-case scenario for another. Would you fish me out another one of those Horsetail Thief IPAs? Drink 'em when you got 'em, that's my new philosophy." He nodded to himself. "It was my old philosophy, too."

Sean got the beer for him, and they said their goodbyes when the bottle was still half full, for the day was already in decline and there were more than twelve miles of river to cover if they were to make Canyon Depth, which had been the plan.

"Are you going to stop at the scene of the crime?"

"You mean where the little girl saw the scarecrow? Probably," Martha said.

"No." Trueblood tapped his forearm. "Where Tickler gave me a kiss."

"That's where we're camping tonight," Martha said.

"Well, if you see him, you give him a stern talking to. But don't kill the poor darling. He was just doing what he was supposed to under the circumstances. Not his fault if he didn't have a rattle."

They left him exercising his new philosophy and schlepped Martha's gear down to the river, where Sean had tethered the kayaks.

"What did you do, tow one of them?"

"Yes. I thought it would be easy; it wasn't."

"Which is mine?"

Sean indicated the smaller of the two. "You sure you can paddle it?" he said, expecting a rebuke and getting one.

"I learned on the Colorado River. My oldest, Christopher, spent two summers as an apprentice guide. Is that good enough for you?"

Sean smiled. "Water's still murky," he said.

"The water or the situation?"

"The canyon, the scarecrows, the body, Harold, Marcus, everything."

"On the contrary," Martha said.

"Do you know something I don't?" Sean crisscrossed bungee cords over the loads, testing them for balance.

"I'm not sure yet." She hadn't told him about her meeting at Division of Criminal Investigation in Helena earlier in the morning. "Maybe. I need to process it."

Sean's look said "Be that way," and he extended her the paddle. When she reached for it, he drew it sharply back, then inched it forward again.

Martha rolled her eyes. "Really. You're a ten-year-old now?"

He extended the paddle.

"Hunh-uh. Nope." She started to cross her arms over her chest, then lunged and grabbed for the paddle blade. After a brief struggle, Sean surrendered it.

She glowered at him, breathing heavily. Then she closed her eyes and shook her head. "Men," she said, blowing out a deep breath.

"Okay, I forgive you. Can we go now? Where's the damned dog fit in this corps of discovery? Your dugout or mine?"

———

Cochise ended up in the copilot seat, just ahead of Sean in the two-seater kayak. An awkward arrangement, for the upper river was a rock garden that demanded vigilance and the ability to spin the kayak on a dime with a nickel left over, and the overloaded craft was bulkier to maneuver than ideal. But with the water cooking along, the five miles to Indian Springs passed quickly, and they found themselves standing before the "loo with a view" with the afternoon sun glancing off the surface of the river.

Martha sat down on the toilet seat. "So the scarecrow would have been about there?" she said, pointing ahead and up the hill.

"By the big rock, that's what Harold told me. He found the shoe hanging on a stub of branch. Maybe that yellow pine."

"A scarecrow with a heart, humpff," she said.

"Humpff, what?"

"Nothing. Let's look around. If this was a movie, we'd find some crucial piece of evidence about now."

But it wasn't and they didn't, and they covered the remaining miles to Canyon Depth and had the tent up and a fire burning down to cooking coals before speaking of anything beyond deciding the line or other technicalities they'd faced while negotiating the river.

"What's on the spit?" Martha said.

"Speedy goat," Sean said. "Antelope, onion, mushroom, pineapple, tomatoes. I speared them up before leaving Bridger and they've been marinating in a homemade teriyaki. Do you want to eat now, or hike up to the homestead first, while we've still got the light?"

"Let's save it for the morning. We've had a long day and I'd like to bring fresh eyes to it. Besides, there's something else to put our minds to this evening. Is that my marinade?"

"Your recipe, yes. But I'm afraid tomorrow we'll be eating out of cans unless I can catch a trout. In this dirty water . . ."

"Oh ye of little faith," she said. She flicked a mosquito that had settled on the back of her hand. Then, in a voice with a sober note: "I might have a lead on the body."

Sean placed the shishkebabs on his fold-up grill. He raised his eyes.

"I saw my guy Whatney at DCI this morning," Martha said. "He hemmed and hawed, brought in a department lawyer who said a confidentiality contract was involved. They weren't at liberty to say what Harold was doing, and that there were layers of insulation for undercover projects and they didn't exactly know themselves what he'd been up to. The thing was, my involvement could throw a wrench into a larger operation and raise an alarm with the people they were building cases on, and all their work over the past couple years could be for nothing. Yada, yada. Pretty much just what I expected to hear."

She flicked away another mosquito.

"This lawyer, she looked like she'd stepped out of an office in a New York firm, that or a coffin, all buttoned up in black with a red scarf and lips, hair like cigarette ash. She introduced herself as Miz So and So Utgoff, looked at me like I was something she'd found underneath her heel. I said who am I talking to. Am I talking to you, or to Whatney here, who was giving me his 'This is out of my hands' shrug. She said I was talking to her. Martina, that was her name. Martina Utgoff. I said, Miz Utgoff, here's the deal. I don't give a shit if my concern for Harold Little Feather throws a wrench into your operation. I know he was undercover with a poaching ring, I know what gun was used to shoot the grizzly bears, I know who it belongs to, and I know where he lives. If you don't want me knocking on his door with a warrant, then tell me something that helps me find Harold Little Feather.

"She said I couldn't get a warrant. I said I wouldn't need one if all I wanted to do was ask questions. Either way, it would blow her case out of the water."

"Good for you, Martha," Sean said.

"Yeah, I was proud of myself. You know how it usually goes, you don't remember what to say until you're out the door. Well, Miz Utgoff, she retreats under the 'I don't know myself' mask, so that puts us back to square one. I say, then put me in touch with his supervisor. Whatney speaks up and tells me what he did over the phone, that the guy who pulls Harold's strings, Fitz Carpenter, had gone to visit his sick mother and can't be reached. Maybe I could call back, say, end of next week.

"I got out of my chair and said thank you very much, I got a long drive ahead of me. I start walking to the door, it's like I can feel a camera on my back, and I'm reaching for the knob when the lawyer clears her throat.

"'He's missing,'" she says.

"What do you mean, he's missing?"

"She says sit back down. I sit back down. She says that Carpenter left word that he was visiting his mother in Tampa Bay, who had the Big C, and would keep them updated. But it had been seven days and he hadn't checked in and his mailbox was full, so finally someone had got worried and pawed back through the mail in his office. The mom had sent him a birthday card. She was contacted through the return address. She did live in Tampa, but she hadn't seen her son since Christmas. And she did have cancer, but it was in remission and she felt fit as a fiddle. In fact she cocaptained the champion shuffleboard team in the retirement home. Had a trophy to prove it."

"The lawyer told you this?"

"No, Whatney. He's the one who called the mother. The point is, if I was being told the truth, then this guy was lying to them about where he'd gone. Jump forward a few days and we find a body in the Smith River. We assume the dead guy must be the Scarecrow God, because who else was on the river, right?"

"Plus, Harold was looking for him," Sean said. "That puts them on a collision course."

"And that. But sitting in that chair, I'm thinking no, this guy, Carpenter, he could be our John Doe. The more I think about it, the more likely that seems. Carpenter sends Harold undercover to infiltrate a poaching ring honchoed by this Jobson character. Then, after he pulls the plug on the sting, for whatever the reason, he sends Harold to investigate the scarecrows on the Smith River. At roughly the same time, Carpenter goes AWOL. A few days pass and somebody winds up in the drink without a head, no more than a hundred yards or so from where Harold's canoe is found. You factor in that this Jobson might be living in the same neck of nowhere, and that's too much coincidence by two. But here's the ace. I asked to see a photo of Carpenter and they took me into his office. And here he is, all smiles for the camera, holding a walleye he caught in Canyon Ferry Reservoir. Guess what?"

"What?"

"What did I tell you about him?"

"You said he was tall."

"And . . . ?"

"And dead."

"Come on, think back."

Sean smiled. "He was an albino."

"Yeah. They call it leucistic."

"So it's him?"

"What are the odds of another albino dead in the water?"

"Did you tell Whatney and the lawyer?"

"No. And remember I told you that Cashell was holding that detail back from the press, so they could weed out any crazies who wanted to confess? That means no one at DCI knows, because they weren't one of the agencies contacted by the sheriff's department. No reason they would be."

"So who else does know?"

"That the dead guy is Carpenter? No one, just you and me. But Whatney and company aren't stupid. Now that Carpenter is officially missing, it's connect the dots. They'll find a blood relative of

Carpenter, the mother, a sister, whoever, and they'll request a DNA comparison to the headless horseman. If it comes back positive, you can bet that the lawyer will step all over us with her pointy heels and we'll be out of the picture."

"So why are we sitting around this fire instead of finding the road into the compound? I think if we don't find anything tomorrow or the next day, we take out at Eden Bridge and drive up the Musselshell and lean on the quilter. She wanted to tell me this morning. She was just too scared to."

"If we brace her, what's to stop her from telling him? For all we know, there's cell reception where he is. No, that's not the route. Sean, I've had some experience with types. You send child services in to take custody of the kids because they're being neglected or used as labor, or someone with a federal warrant shows up to investigate tax evasion or squatting on land they have no paper to, and word gets out. By the time you get around to knocking on doors, the so-called compound is deserted, or the few who are present are actually minding their business. We find that road, go through the gate, if someone's got a hammer cocked at Harold's head, they'll drop it. No, our best bet is to go through the back door. This is the back door." She waved a hand to indicate the river, which was fading into its bass notes as the shadows climbed the canyon walls.

"Are those shishkebabs done, or not? I'm hungry."

They ate in silence, Martha occasionally stirring the coals with a stick, Sean feeding tidbits to the dog. Both were absorbed in their thoughts.

"Cochise, huh?" Martha said, sipping at her wine. "Seems like wishful thinking. But that's what we've brought to the river, a hope and a prayer and a three-legged dog."

CHAPTER THIRTY-ONE

Telling Secrets

In the gray of dawn the homestead cabin and its outbuildings looked skeletal, the eroded bones of a bygone era, people with hard hands and broken dreams lost to the pages of a history that nobody read, there being no poetry in the words, no reward in the labor, and no better life than the one that had been left behind.

Harold had told Sean that the photo was on the wall above the cot, and that he had tucked it back under the broken pane of glass after photographing it. He found the frame hanging a little crookedly, but no photograph. A kerosene lantern with a cracked globe sat on an overturned wood crate. When Sean shook it to see if there was kerosene in it, a triangular piece of glass broke off the globe.

He and Martha exchanged glances. Martha shrugged.

"It's called police work," she said. "You walk in one direction, turn over a stone, and nothing's there. You walk in another direction, you turn over a stone, and nothing's there, either. You keep walking, you keep turning over stones. As opposed to what you do, play hunches and step into shit."

Sean had noticed that the end of a short length of floorboard near the cot was raised above the ones to either side. He tugged at it. It didn't move. He pushed down. The other end levered up just enough for him to insert a couple fingers. He raised his eyes to Martha, who met his expression and reached for her Maglite.

"Here's to stepping in shit," Sean said. He lifted the board up and set it aside.

The beam of Martha's light made a bright circle in the cavity under the board. Sean saw a rag cut from burgundy cloth, similar to those found in gas stations. He pinched the edge between his thumb and forefinger and brought it to his nose, then Martha's.

"Gun oil," she said. "Smells like the mutton lining of my shotgun case. Harold mention anything about a firearm?"

"No. But he was planning to come back here after we left the campground. Stake it out another night. At least that's what he told Marcus."

Sean set the rag aside and scraped at the layer of fine sawdust that had accumulated under the floorboard. Droppings of deer mice were scattered like wedding rice on a church step.

"Regular hantavirus hotel," Martha said in a dry voice.

Sean's fingernails scraped against metal. He answered Martha's flexed eyebrow with one of his own as he extracted a tin box with a fitted lid and blew the dust off. It was a two-deck playing card case, the cover embossed with live oaks dripping moss in a swamp. The raised lettering read: WAKULLA SPRINGS STATE PARK, HOME TO THE CREATURE FROM THE BLACK LAGOON. The rubber band holding the case together was so dried out that it snapped when Sean tried to take it off, spilling the contents of the case onto the floor. A quick inventory revealed a stack of photographs—Kodachrome snapshots gone to sepia, sepia photos faded to black and white, black-and-white photos bleeding into unrecognizable patterns of light and shadow. Six pencils had been cut to fit the case, the ends showing the distinctive scallops of being sharpened with a knife blade.

"Two H, two B, four B," Sean said.

"What's that mean?"

"They're sketch pencils. Different hardnesses."

The apparent target for the lead was a soft-sided notebook with an elastic band, black and unlined, similar to the Moleskine sketch pad that almost always rode in one of Sean's shirt pockets.

He tapped one of the photos, a four-by-six folded once to fit the compartment. "An enlargement of this one, that's what was in the picture frame."

Martha nodded. "Let's take this stuff outside. I don't want to breathe in any more mouse poop than I have to."

Among the scattered farming implements were rusty spools from a disk harrow that had once been used to plow furrows behind draft horses. Sean tipped one upright to make a flat surface, spread his handkerchief over it, and fanned out the photographs. Most were of the same person, a thin, wiry-looking man with black hair and hollow cheeks. In one photo, the man was bare-chested and holding a dead snapping turtle by the tail, the shell so large that it covered his entire torso. In another, he was bearded, wearing a herringbone Jack-Shirt with the tails hanging long, displaying a beaver skin on a round stretching board. Behind him was a forest of pine, the boughs laden with snow.

Two photos, one black and white, one color, depicted a woman sitting on a rocking chair on a porch with a trellis growing around the columns supporting the awning. She was holding a baby in the black-and-white. In the color photo—same pose, same half smile, only the angle of sun different—the baby had grown into a toddler and balanced on her knee. There was only one photograph that showed the three subjects together, but it was arresting because only the woman and the boy were actually in the frame. The boy, a stripling of nine or ten, was wearing a straw hat, his short-sleeved shirt buttoned to the collar. The woman wore a summer dress, her face plain, her countenance stern. The man who'd been absent most of the boy's life, if what Sean and Martha were looking at was the family they thought they were looking at, was behind the lens. He was the ghost in the photo, visible as a cast shadow, perfectly positioned between the woman and the boy.

"The lost father," Martha said.

Sean nodded. "She must be the schoolmarm Trueblood was talking about. And the boy, he's the son. Are we looking at the future Scarecrow God?"

"Fifty years down the road." Martha nodded. "I think so, anyway. But I'm not sure how Harold fits into the equation."

"It was his job to find him. I think he found him. Let's have a look at the notebook."

A cursory thumb-through was enough to show that if information was to be gleaned from the pages, it would not take the form of the English language. The writer—artist, to be more accurate—was a man of few words, though he spoke eloquently with his pencil. It was, Sean decided, a form of wordless diary, each page including a date in the upper right-hand corner, a short notation, usually nothing more revealing than the weather or water clarity, and a sketch or two. Animal sketches were most numerous, not just the big animals but the minor denizens—mink, muskrat, red squirrel, pine marten. Trout. A kingfisher swooping low. Cliffs. Pictographs. Whatever, Sean guessed, had struck the artist's fancy that particular day.

The most detailed sketches were the scarecrows. Sean counted eleven, most large enough to merit two facing pages, with one or two preceding pages of cursory sketches showing the scarecrow as it was in progress, and revealing that each one entailed two or three days of labor.

Sean unfolded the river map that the ranger had provided him. It was a photocopy of the map the ranger had given Harold and was marked with the locations of all the scarecrows seen by floaters, including GPS coordinates. The scarecrows in the illustrations had been penciled in sequence, the first, Sean surmising, representing the farthest upstream scarecrow and the last, the farthest downstream. This was confirmed by the descriptions. The first scarecrow, for example, was marked:

¼ mile downstream Rock Creek, 300 ft. above left bank,
cave mouth.

That was the scarecrow Harold and his son had climbed to before the documentary party met them on the sandbar below the junction. The pencil sketch was an accurate rendition of the scarecrow in the photos Harold had shown the floating party.

"There's one missing," Martha said. "It's in the book but not on the map."

She tapped the last page of the notebook. The sketch was a partial scarecrow, no head or legs, only skeletal branches supporting the torso, with the head suggested with a few willow shoots. It was dated May 15.

"That's two days before we floated through," Sean said. He read the description.

Pictograph site above Crow's Foot, left bank, ledge rock
overhang.

"Why are you nodding? Do you know the place?"

"McCaine pointed it out. Crow's Foot is a boat camp; it's a long mile upstream from Table Rock, where Marcus said he was going to wait for Harold. Lillian Cartwright wanted to stop and climb up there because there were pictographs, but we vetoed her. I did. The river was coming up fast and I didn't want to lose any time."

"If we find the guy behind the pencil," Martha said, "I think we find Harold, too."

Sean took out his own sketchbook, picked up a pencil from the card tin, and with a few deft strokes sketched Harold in profile. He tore it out and did another one, also a profile, but of the other side. He handed the first to Martha, tucked the other into his shirt pocket, and answered the question she hadn't asked.

"For luck," he said. "When I was a boy, my grandfather told me I would have better luck fishing if I first envisioned the fish I wanted to catch. I was always drawing, so the night he told me that, I went home and sketched a bass. I put it in my pocket, and the next time we went fishing, I caught a bass. When I moved to Montana, I envisioned catching a ten-pound trout so I sketched one, a big brown with a kype jaw."

"Did you catch it?"

"I had the sketch in my pocket for six years, but I finally did, fishing the Madison last summer. Swimming a deer-hair mouse at night."

"You never told me that."

"I never told anyone. The river told me a secret that night, and I decided to keep it. Besides, I didn't think anyone would believe me."

"I believe you."

"That's why I told you."

"No, I think it's because you want me to know your secret. That's a good omen for us, I think. I don't know about Harold."

She crossed her arms over her chest.

"How long did it take to catch that fish? Six years, did you say? Let's hope it doesn't take that long to find Harold."

CHAPTER THIRTY-TWO

The Gift Fox

On the day when Harold added the sixth line to the cave floor—after he had roused from a state of delirium that had lasted half the night, a terror of tremors and visions brought on by hunger and cold as much as by pain—he heard a scuffing on the rock. The bats made scratching noises when they climbed the stalactites with the claws at the tips of their wings, but this wasn't that sound.

Harold turned his head to see an animal that at first he took for a dog. He immediately thought of Cochise, Marcus's dog that he'd last seen on the night he'd been struck unconscious. Harold remembered seeing Marcus curled before the fire, the dog hopping on its good legs around the silent, unmoving form, nosing him. Then Job had swung the rock that sent the stars of Harold's universe reeling.

But this animal was slimmer, and it had something that drooped from its jaws. When Harold saw the big bush of a tail he knew it was a fox, its silhouette standing out against the light that was slowly infusing the cave. The fox whirled as Harold caught its eyes and was gone in a single fluid motion, but in its panic it dropped what was clamped in its teeth. All Harold could make out was an indistinguishable lump on the cave floor. He kneed to the extent of the chain and found that by lying down, he could touch what he now realized was a rabbit. He scissored a leg of the rabbit between his first and second fingers and inched it toward him until he could pick it up.

Ever since his capture, Harold's diet had consisted of a single slice of bread, tossed to him in the morning when either Job or Dewey Davis checked in, and, in the evening, another slice along with a packet of ramen noodles. The noodles he softened by holding the opened packet so it collected water that seeped through the rock ceiling and dripped, Harold had calculated, at a rate of about a quarter cup of water every hour. Before he had the packets to collect water in, he'd had to lie down on his back and catch water drops with his open mouth. He had spent many hours each day in this manner, doing little else but trying to stay hydrated.

The fox's teeth had ripped the rabbit's hide and by inserting both forefingers through the slit and pulling in opposite directions, Harold peeled the skin from the rabbit like it was a sock, the way his grandfather had taught him. He tore at the flesh with his teeth and gulped it, and almost immediately felt like throwing it up. He told himself to slow down, that the morning visit from his captors was still a couple hours away and he had plenty of time to eat the rabbit. He forced himself to chew before swallowing, first the flesh, then the guts, even the dead marble eyes, saving one hind leg for later, figuring it would keep in the cool of the cave and wouldn't bulge out his pants pocket enough to draw attention.

When he was done eating, all that remained was a scatter of the bones he'd sucked clean, the head, the clawed feet, and the two pieces of skin. He put a piece of skin in each of his socks to help warm his feet, and setting aside the larger bones, threw the remaining evidence of his meal as far as he could into the dark recess of the cave behind him.

Though his captors had meticulously swept rock chips and other debris from the part of the cave within Harold's reach, removing anything that could be used as a weapon or with which he might free himself of the chain, the limestone floor remained an abrasive surface. He now began to rub the edge of one of the thin scapulas against it, sharpening the flat shoulder blade as his ancestors had sharpened similar bones with sandstones. They had used razor-honed scapulas for hide scrapers, to prepare skins for tanning, but Harold envisioned another use for it, one that brought back the pulse of hatred that had been building in him for a long time, going back to the day when Job had talked about removing his gall bladder.

Harold recalled that day as he worked on the bone, how he had deliberately shot over the bear's back and then had extracted the empty cartridge case from the rotary magazine and dropped it onto the grass, and hastily cut the diagonal lines into the nearest tree trunk. He had done the same thing two days earlier, a different bear, that one not so lucky, and with a different man behind the trigger. Not Job, but Dewey, who, Harold came to see, was the better shot. In fact Harold had been witness to three of Dewey's kills, and in each location he'd been able to drop a fired cartridge case and replace it in the magazine with another empty, because he acted as the gun bearer, and the gnomelike man took the rifle from him only when its use was imminent.

Harold's purpose in leaving the cases was to provide evidence that the men were in proximity to poached bear carcasses, should legal proceedings be brought. At the same time, he knew that if he was caught doing it, his fate would be that of the bears.

The entire operation had left a bad taste, and so when the young grizzly offered a target, Harold, who already had blood on his hands from his participation in earlier hunts, had almost shot it. Only at the last second had he pulled the crosshairs high, and as the bear ran into the forest, Harold had hurriedly unscrewed the cap on the horizontal adjustment turret of the rifle scope, then used his thumbnail to turn the knob several dozen clicks to the left. He had meant to do the same to the vertical adjustment, which would certainly throw off the next shot from the rifle, perhaps by as much as several feet at a hundred yards. Then he could use the scope misalignment to explain away his miss and, in the process, perhaps save the life of another bear. But the two men, who'd remained behind when Harold made his final stalk, were approaching and Harold barely had time to screw the cap back on before they came into sight, Job making the tsking sound with his tongue that Harold would grow to hate.

With time to think it over, Harold had arrived at the conclusion that the only reason he'd survived the shots on the river was because he'd tampered with the scope. But if that was true, it was probably also true that moving the adjustment ring had caused the bullet to strike Jewell MacAllen in the bow. Harold was not a man of regrets, and better the Scarecrow God than himself. Still, the unfamiliar feeling of remorse had haunted him during the long nights, when his spirits were lowest and he had no one to talk to but the few bats that weren't out hunting.

One question had plagued him at all hours. He might be alive due to fast thinking in the field, but why was he *still* alive? And as he *was* alive, did that mean Marcus was, too?

He had finished sharpening the first scapula and was beginning to shape the femur into a point, sanding to the metronome of Marcus's name, repeating it over and over, when he heard the footsteps. From the cadence he knew it was Job, and he quieted his voice and quickly pocketed the bone.

"What are you up to, Harold? Singing for your son?"

The tall man towered over him, trapping Harold in the aura of his scent and vitality, then strode by to sit down opposite him, only inches out of Harold's reach. As the days had passed, Job had begun to crowd him more, four long steps becoming two, now one, as if he were daring him to react. Dewey, by comparison, kept his distance. Harold believed that the little man's bravado was an act, that underneath was naked fear. Dewey would be the easier to kill, but the more difficult to lure within striking range.

"I asked what you are up to? Sounded like you were saying something."

"No. I was just scraping my heels on the rock."

Harold demonstrated, the grit caught in the soles making a rhythmic scraping sound, and as he did so, he backed away, to try to get Job to come closer. There, at the far end of his tether, he coiled, ready to strike.

"I suppose this place gets lonely," Job said. "The bats can't be much company."

"Where's my bread?"

"Almost forgot," Job said. He tossed the single slice of bread.

Harold wolfed it down. "How about my soup?"

"No soup for you. My woman, she likes to watch the TV, says there's a cook in New York they call the Soup Nazi. You look at him wrong—'No soup for you!'"

"Why don't you just kill me, get it over with? Be one more piece of bread for you at the end of the day."

Job made the tsking sound. "But then you'd never see your son again. You want to see him, don't you?"

Harold tried not to give him the satisfaction of a reaction. His face was stone.

"You see," Job said, "I know what you told me is a lie. That he is nothing to you, a distant relation, that you are doing his mother a favor by taking him off her hands. You sit there, you give me your stoicism, your Indian eyes. But he is your weakness. Six days ago, if I told you your cooperation would ensure his safety, you would not have believed me. No, you would have schemed against me, and I would not be able to trust anything you said. But you are no longer that man. You are broken, and despite your eyes, you will do anything I ask without question. Am I correctly assessing the situation?"

"Just tell me what it is you want."

"I will. Very soon."

"Tell me now. And bring the boy to me. You want to loosen my tongue, show me he is well." Harold coughed. He rubbed his stomach. His hand dipped into his pants pocket.

"Still hungry, huh? Or are you just happy to see me?"

Harold's fingers fanned along the edge of the shoulder blade.

"Tsk. Tsk. Shush now. Sing to your bats." The tall man stretched to his height,

Harold's thumb and forefinger clamped on the bone. *Just take one step forward, just one.*

But Job skirted him, well out of reach, and ducked out of the cave. When the sound of his footsteps faded, Harold found that the muscles of his hand had cramped around the bone. He flexed his fingers, and slowly his grip relaxed. He looked down at the lines on the cave floor. Instinct told him there would be no more, that either he would be gone or that he would be dead by the next morning. He drew out the scapula. It could be made sharper, and he picked up his mantra—"Mar-cus, Mar-cus"—as he honed the edge against the cave floor.

CHAPTER THIRTY-THREE

Sinner or Saint

Martha stood under the overhanging ledge and took in the pictographs—the recognizable turtle, the coyote or maybe wolf, the might-be bear, the rattler with its forked tongue.

She set her hands on her hips. "Where's the scarecrow?" she said.

"Half scarecrow," Sean said. "That's what it said in the sketchbook."

Martha grunted. She lifted her hand toward the red ochre palm print.

"Tall," she muttered. "If I recall right, Katie Sparrow's dog alerted at this place when the search team was looking for Harold. You think if there was a scarecrow, they would have found it."

"Half alerted," Sean said. "She said they had another thirty miles of river to check. Unless Lothar got really excited, they didn't look in any place for long."

While they talked, the three-legged dog had wandered out of sight. Sean called his name, and a few minutes later, when Cochise hadn't materialized, he and Martha split up and began to look farther afield. A minute later Sean heard a short whistle and found Martha standing before the half-formed skeleton of the scarecrow. A red handkerchief tied to one of the willow shoots stirred in the breeze. Martha saw a piece of paper peeking out of it and untied the handkerchief.

This is a crime scene. Do not touch anything. Immediately report anything that might be construed as evidence

of a crime to the Hyalite Sheriff's Department, Bridger,
Montana, attention Sheriff Martha Ettinger.

The note was dated six days previously and signed *H.L.F.*, followed by two telephone numbers. One was the department dispatch, the other Martha's direct line.

"I wonder why he used us," Martha said. "Why not say 'Report to Division of Criminal Investigation'? That's who he works for. Do you think he knew something was off with Fitz Carpenter?"

"Maybe he just knew he could trust you."

"Maybe." She seemed distant. "We're, what, a mile and half upriver from Table Rock?"

"About."

"And his canoe was found a mile below Table Rock."

"About."

"So whatever happened to him, it happened somewhere between here and there." She nodded to herself. "Let's keep our eyes peeled. The river's dropped quite a bit since the searchers were here. They could have missed something."

They had.

———

For the six years he'd known him, Sean had heard Harold Little Feather complain about his brown waterproof boat bag, saying that you should never buy a dark-colored bag, because you'll never be able to see what's inside it without a flashlight. But he was Harold, and too stubborn to trade up.

So what might have been overlooked by another set of eyes, or dismissed as a piece of weathered driftwood, was immediately apparent to Sean for what it was. He slid his kayak paddle through the bag's shoulder strap as he swept by the driftwood collected on an exposed boulder, where the bag had fetched up, and a few minutes later pulled to the shore at the uppermost Table Rock campsite. He waited for Martha to rope her kayak to a post before unsnapping the straps of the duffel.

"What did you find?"

"It's Harold's boat bag. Must have fallen out when his canoe capsized. Feels like there's a bowling ball inside."

He pinched the top to break the watertight seal. The eyes were staring at him, and he gagged reflexively. Overcome by nausea, he made it as far as the riverbank before retching. He took in his wavery reflection on the surface and just breathed for a minute, then washed his mouth out.

Martha was regarding the head with her hands on her hips.

"I've seen worse," she said as Sean walked up.

"How much worse?"

"Considerable." She nodded. "He won't win Miss Montana anytime soon."

"Is it Carpenter?"

"Oh, yeah."

"What the hell was Harold doing with his head in his boat bag?"

Martha hitched up her duty belt. "That's not a question I thought we'd be asking this morning. It's a game changer, all right. Come on, let's get the tent up while it's still light. We can figure out the next step after we have a fire going."

———

There was a scraping sound, and a small flame danced in the darkness. The man lit the crooked cigarette as if it was the fuse of a firecracker, holding it in front of him, then put it in his mouth and drew a long breath. Slowly, he let the smoke out.

"Harold, Harold, Harold," he said.

He patted his pockets and drew out a stub of a candle and went about lighting the wick, dripping wax from the molten cup and twisting the candle into the puddle so it stood upright on the cave floor.

"There, that's better. We can see each other now."

He had come when nearly all the light had drained from the cave, and at first the sound was so faint Harold thought it could be the returning of the fox. Then he heard the familiar footfalls on the cave floor. *Maybe he's brought Marcus*, Harold thought. But the tall man was alone.

"I want you to understand that I did not choose this course, Harold," he said. The man, Job, drew on the cigarette and expelled another lungful of smoke. "You betrayed my trust. By doing so, you have forced my hand. Surely you understand the position you put me in. But what you don't know is how I discovered your treachery, how I came to lie in wait for you on the river. Did I make a mistake? That is the question you ask yourself. What misstep put me in these chains?"

Feed his need, Harold thought. *Give him license to ramble and maybe he will be the one who makes a mistake.*

"I'm asking you," Harold said. "How did you know?"

Job drew on the cigarette. "How does the saying go? A little bird told me."

"What bird?"

"Fitz Carpenter," Job said.

Harold had no reaction. But he said the name as a question in his mind. *Fitz Carpenter? The man who sent me to Job in the first place?*

"So as you betrayed me, he betrayed you," Job said, nodding. "I will preempt your next question." He smiled across at Harold, a concerned, paternal look. "You want to know why a man in his position turns from the light to the darkness? It is the same reason some would risk poisoning this river—not for the resource it provides their fellow men, though that is their mantra, but for the money it puts in their pockets."

"'All that is bitter will be sweet,'" Harold said under his breath. "'All that is copper will be gold.'"

"What is that, a proverb?"

"Spanish. The man who built the scarecrows told me. Jewel Mac-Allen."

"That crazy cracker. But funny you should mention the name. You see, MacAllen provided me the solution to the problem you pose. When we came back from our foray into the Park, Fitz approached me, never mind how he discovered where I lived. Understand, I had never heard of the man."

"What's this have to do with Jewel MacAllen?"

Job cocked his head. "I am trying to explain to you how you ended up talking to bats and shitting in a corner, yet you interrupt. Is your intention to aggravate me into doing something I shouldn't? In that case you will have a long wait, and only part of it while among the living."

"I'm sorry," Harold said. "Go on."

Job stubbed out the cigarette against his belt buckle. "Fitz told me that he wouldn't turn over the evidence you had gathered against my operation if I cut him into the profits. He insisted it wasn't blackmail because he didn't demand money up front, that what he was proposing was a business arrangement. He knew the ropes of the smuggling trade, had even met a couple of the Korean brokers who trafficked in animal parts. His contacts would prove an invaluable resource. With my knowledge of the country, your tracking skills, and his connections, we could grow rich together. Greed, you see. That is the true religion of our country."

"How are you any different?"

"Who said I was? But you are right, Harold. I am different. What Fitz Carpenter aspired to was an office with a view, not the windowless cubicle that defines his position on the ladder. I do not aspire to an office with a view. I aspire to the view as my office. At the present time, our government has taken that view from me against constitutional authority and has restricted my access to it and my activities upon it. People look at my beard, see my middle finger raised against the tyranny, and they say militiaman, they say conspiracy theorist, they say Christian patriot, they say white supremacist. But I have no ax to grind when it comes to the color of a man's skin, nor Bible to thump with my knuckles. All I am is a rural free American man who wants the right to walk into the Montana horizons and hunt, fish, and camp on lands that rightfully belong to me. To have the freedom of the view."

"And kill bears for their gall bladders and leave the carcasses to rot on the forest floor."

Job again smiled. "Did God not give us dominion over the animals, Harold?" He shook his head. "All my adult life I have hunted under onerous restrictions and been persecuted for the slightest, ah, misinterpretation of such restriction."

"One year, seven months, and five days," Harold said. And thought, *Provoke him. If you make him mad, you make him careless.*

Once again, Job looked at him askance. "Are you mocking me?"

"I know how long you spent in Deer Lodge prison," Harold said. "You've told me the story more than a dozen times."

Job lit another cigarette. "I am a man of resolve, but how one quits this pernicious habit is beyond me." He exhaled, the smoke columning up to hang in a haze under the rock ceiling.

"Prison is something that sticks in the craw," he said. "And then, less than a year after my release, I pick up a rifle that has spiderwebs in its bore from disuse, yet before I can fire those eight-legged darlings out the spout, along you come, flexing your tattoos, playing hard to get, then coming around to me as if you'd just found a blood cousin. I welcome you, treat you with respect, and what is my reward? That you scheme against me. You, a man whose blood should boil at the oppression of a government that gave your people disease, that killed your buffalo and raped your women and stole your land, that hasn't uttered a word of truth to you in more than two hundred years?"

He smoked. "I misjudged your character, Harold, but at the time I thought, 'Here is someone who can follow a track, but more important, a man whose heritage puts us on common ground. I can trust this man.' And I did, right up until the crack of the rifle. You placed a stone of doubt in my heart when you missed that bear. Still, I was willing to give you the benefit. And then one morning I wake up under the flag that flies over my compound, and who do I find in my drive but Fitz Carpenter with his promises of our future. What arrogance! To come to *my* compound, *my* sanctuary. All we have to do, he says, is convince you to get on board. If you resist, we can make you disappear and find someone else for our project. The truth is I think he wanted to get rid of you. It would make us brothers bound by blood. By your blood. Sharing that guilt, we would be less likely to betray one another."

Job flicked the ash from the cigarette. "I never smoked before I went away," he said. "It was another way of doing the time. You can get high if you try hard enough, let your mind soar. But you aren't interested, are you, Harold? You have no vices. Yet here you are."

Silence settled in the cave. Then the faint sound of the bats, their claws scraping against the upside-down candles of the stalactites.

"You interrupted my train of thought," Job said. "Where was I? Oh yes, Fitz. I told him to give me a couple nights to mull over his offer, and all this time he sat across from me I was looking past him and seeing you. What was this evidence you had collected against me? Where was it? Would it surface if Fitz was to die? Would it surface if you were to die? Or would it go to the grave with your body? These things I needed to know. Truthfully, I was at an impasse. I did not see how I could eliminate either of you without a shadow cast in my direction. I even entertained the notion of tucking my tail and fleeing the state. And now we come to your friend, the Scarecrow God."

"He's no friend."

"Then my mistake. It is of no consequence. What is important is that he crossed my path, call it providence, destiny, what you will."

He looked at the cigarette between his fingers and stubbed it out against his belt buckle.

He nodded to himself as he began to tell the story.

He said he'd been in the Mint Bar in White Sulphur Springs when he overheard a man, with long hair and eyes that moved without settling, saying that he was looking for a place to park his truck near the river. The man introduced himself as Jewel MacAllen. Job had stood him a beer. "Can you keep a secret?" the man asked him. Job said he could.

Had he heard about the dagum mine? That was the word Jewel had used, one that peppered his speech. Job had heard, and yes, he agreed that the copper mine was a travesty. Jewel said he had a plan, had driven all the way from Florida to execute it. The plan came out with the alcohol, a little incoherently, but Job got the drift. He prodded the man to keep talking, but to keep his voice down. They were in the lion's den, after all; nearly everybody in White Sulphur Springs supported the project. It was the only town in the state that stood to profit.

Job told the man to follow him to the compound, where he was welcome to leave his truck. He gave him directions from there to the homestead, told him he'd be able to keep a roof over his head there and be undisturbed as he went about his work. Jewel had asked what he could do to repay Job for his generosity. Job had replied that Jewel could honor him by constructing the largest of his scarecrows in a place of his selection. Job provided a hand-drawn map. The site where he wanted the scarecrow was the pictograph ledges above Crow's Foot boat camp.

At this point in his narration, Job focused his eyes on Harold.

"Now the stage was set," he said. "Now I had to be patient."

News came to him first by word of mouth. Someone was building scarecrows along the river, putting up signs that read *Not on my watch*. A name for this mischief-maker was coined—the Scarecrow God. Who was he? Devil or watchman? Sinner or saint? Could he be dangerous? The state thought so. They responded by closing the river.

Job bided his time. He had to wait until Jewel built the scarecrow at the ledges. The location was chosen with care. Far enough away that it wouldn't draw attention to the compound. Close enough to check on Jewel's progress at regular intervals. From the compound, an old Jeep road climbed to an overlook. Every day, Job would take a four-wheeler and set up a spotting scope. Day after day, nothing. Finally, when Job figured that Jewel had forgotten his promise or lost the map, he saw something in the scope. He cranked up the power of magnification to fifty. And there it was. Not a complete scarecrow, just the beginning of one, but that is all he needed to move forward.

He paused, and smiled at Harold.

"Let me ask you a hypothetical question. Imagine that you found yourself in a predicament that could only be resolved by killing a person. Possibly two people. The killing would be easy. Keeping the finger of the law from pointing in your direction would be the catch. What would you do?"

Go along with him, Harold told himself. *Keep him talking until he forgets I'm here, until he makes just one mistake.*

He said, "I'd stage the deaths in a way that placed blame for them on someone else. Ideally, someone who had a motive, but didn't have an alibi."

"Very good," Job said. "So who did you think that was, who could be blamed for the deaths?"

"Jewel MacAllen," Harold said.

Job smiled. "I see that little unpleasantness at the river, when I had to quiet you with a rock, did not impair the function of your brain. You are, of course, correct."

He said that his next step was to contact Fitz Carpenter. He was, after all, the man who had put Job in the bind he found himself in, and one of the people who had to be eliminated. He called him. Said he'd been thinking over his offer, that he was amenable, and would Fitz drive to the compound, where they could discuss their joint venture in person? But first, he wanted Fitz to do him a favor.

Again, Job smiled.

"What favor do you think that was, Harold?"

"I don't know."

"It was to call you. To send you on a fool's errand to find the Scarecrow God. Because you were . . . Finish the thought for me, Harold. Who were you?"

"The second person you had to kill. Get rid of Fitz, get rid of me, and there's nobody to tie you to your crimes."

"My, you're smart. I really do wish we'd met under other circumstances. Where was I? Oh, yes, Fitz. I told him that I would post a sentry on the river, either Dewey or myself, and we, whoever, would wave you over as you floated by. That way, we could present you with the details of our venture on my terms and on my grounds. If the discussion headed in a direction that was not to our liking, then you would not live to see another bend of the river. Your death would be a drowning, natural enough given the height of the water. But if you offered resistance, a bullet would do in a pinch. In that case, the suspicion would fall upon the Scarecrow God. Obviously you had caught him in the act. You died in the line of duty, your body found not far from the scarecrow."

Job relit the crooked cigarette he had stubbed out on his belt buckle. Took a lungful, blew it out, and continued.

"If Fitz had thought it through, he would have realized that I asked him to come to the compound for the same reason that I asked him to send you down the river, to draw him into the sights of my rifle. When he saw that instead of partnering with him I was eliminating him as a witness, he pleaded with me. I told him that his only hope was to tell me what evidence you had gathered. He said that your report hadn't been filed, that you were dragging your feet, but that he knew where it was. If I released him, he would bring it to me. Where? I asked. He said your sister's house. Where in the house? He hesitated. In a trunk, he said. In the basement. I lied and told him I had been to the house and that it didn't have a basement. The crawl space, then, he said. I watched him try to squirm out of the trap, heard him begin to embellish, watched his eyes go anywhere but to mine. Don't lose your dignity, I told him. Just tell the truth. It will set you free. He began to cry and admitted then that he had no idea where your report was, or even if there was one. At that moment I had no more use for him, and I do not think he heard the shot that killed him."

"You cut off his head."

"I wanted to—" He stopped, and frowned down at Harold.

"My, you've been busy," he said. "What happened, did a bear dig it up?"

"Birds found it. Jewel MacAllen followed them."

"Curiosity killed the cat."

"No, it didn't. He was alive after you shot him, and he knows it was you who killed Fitz Carpenter."

"He never surfaced. He's dead." But his voice did not sound as certain as his words.

"So you tell yourself."

"No," shaking his head as he said the word. "I don't think so." He seemed to be somewhere else and when he came back, his voice had reclaimed its authority. "No. You, Harold, are my sole remaining problem. You wonder why I have kept you alive. I have—"

"Why cut his head off?"

Job hesitated. "Again, you try to provoke me. It won't work."

"I asked a question."

"Fair enough. Dewey and I wedged his corpse under a logjam where the river banked. It would be found when the water dropped, but without a head the assumption would be it was the body of the scarecrow maker. A man who possessed no name and no identify. A figure in the night that caused a little girl to lose her shoe. A ghost, when all is said and done. And even if the body was identified, where would the blame fall? It would fall on you, Harold. You worked for the victim. Perhaps you felt betrayed by him. As I was about to say before you interrupted me, it always comes back to you. I do not expect you to beg for your life, like Fitz, but I do expect you to plead for the life of your son. He is the innocent in this matter."

"What do you want?"

"I want the report you were writing for Fitz Carpenter, of course, and any video or photographs that could incriminate me. You see my situation. You could offer me the top of a carrot, and I would have no way of knowing how much more remained buried in the ground, or when it might be dug up. The leverage I hold is Marcus. Who, by the way, I admire. He is an intelligent young man of singular spirit, and he has been treated well while you have been given the time to ponder your choices. Here is my promise. If you tell me where to recover this evidence, and it is as promised, then I will set the young man free. I could say I would set you free as well, but you and I, we are men of strong character. False promises do not become us."

"If you know Marcus as you say, you know he would never go along. He would come after you."

"Not if I held the life of his sister in my hands. You see, just as I have come to know him, he has come to know me, that I do as I say I will. You look surprised. Did you not know he had a sister? Half sister, to be precise. Irene. She raised him, understand. She was older and their mother had her demons. A familiar story—the absentee father, the mother whose mothering leaves something to be desired. It is a story familiar to all families, regardless of their heritage. It is my story, too. That, in part, is why I give you my word."

Harold closed his eyes and listened to his breathing.

"I will give you tonight to think it over," Job said.

"I can give my answer now. I will turn over all that I have to you tomorrow morning. You should be able to retrieve it without any problem. I have one request."

"You are in no position to ask favors."

"I know that. But I'm asking anyway. Look into your heart and allow me to see my son. I have only just met him. You have spent more time in his company than I have. If you will allow me to be with him tonight, to have a few hours so I might know his heart and keep it with me on my journey to the next world, then tomorrow I will keep my end of the promise."

"You play on my emotions, knowing my past."

"I'm asking you as one father to another. Let me see my son to say goodbye."

"I will think about it."

CHAPTER THIRTY-FOUR

Bone Magic

At first he thought the voices were his imagination, for the small hours belonged to the bats, and with nightfall Harold had all but given up thinking that he would stay alive long enough to see his son. But then the chamber thudded hollowly and Job entered, carrying the ax in one hand and a lantern by its wire handle in the other. Marcus shuffled behind him, prodded by Dewey with the Mannlicher rifle. Harold heard the slight clanking of a dragging chain. He rose to his knees to reach toward Marcus, who seemed not to acknowledge his presence; then the hands that held the rifle jabbed, and Marcus stumbled forward and fell to the rock floor, where he curled on his side.

It took no more than ten minutes for Job to drive the spike into the cave wall, and the ends of the chain that passed through the small of Marcus's ankle to be padlocked to the iron ring. Marcus flinched but made no sound during the pounding, and neither Job nor Dewey spoke. It was as if they were mute laborers who had shown up for a shift, a double-checking of the length of the chain, a few grunts as the ax head fell, a simple going about of a half hour's work.

"There," Job said when the ax had rung for the last time. He came to stand over Harold. "Wait for me outside," he said, not turning to face Dewey.

When the shuffling had faded, he nodded toward the form of Marcus.

"Don't be alarmed. He is unhurt in any substantial way and he

understands why he has been brought here. He thinks that by remaining mute that he punishes me, denying me the satisfaction of a
response. He doesn't know my history as you do, nor that I require no
other ears but my own as an audience for my voice. I will leave you
alone with him now. I have made the chain just long enough that you
may touch his hand. When it becomes light, you and I will get to the
business of unearthing the carrot."

———

He was gone then, and the lantern light that had made the bats flutter
died with his leaving. Momentarily night-blind, Harold saw his son as
an outline that changed as he came to a sitting position. After fearing
that he'd never see Marcus again, Harold could find no words to express what he felt. But it was no time for sentiment.

"How long have you been chained?"

"They brought me to a cabin," Marcus said. His voice was a rasp.
"Someplace that's nowhere. That's what he called it, the 'Nowhere
Suite.'"

"Where in relation to here?"

"I don't know. Above. It seemed like we climbed all night, but all I
know is that it was morning when we got there. The last couple miles
were on a four-wheeler. Every time it hit a bump, it was like spears of
pain going through my brain."

"But you're all right now?"

"My head is. I lost my voice screaming, but I might as well have
been on the moon in that place."

"How about the chain?"

"It just makes my leg throb. But I don't think it's infected."

"Did they give you food?"

"Yeah, Job came by every evening, cooked for me like I was his
guest. He likes to hold forth. Finally I just said fuck him and wouldn't
talk back, 'cause what he wants is the attention. He said you and him
have an agreement? He said ask you about it."

As Harold told him, he saw the shadow of Marcus's face waver. "That's fucking bullshit, isn't it? He'd never let me go."

"I think *he* thinks he might. He can justify killing me because I betrayed him. But you didn't do anything but be in the wrong place. He hasn't said so, but I think you remind of him of the son he lost. He was about your age when he died. In the end, though, I don't see how he can let you go. You know who he is. He'd be looking over his shoulder the rest of his life. Marcus, I . . ."

Harold's voice broke. "I should have never."

"It's okay."

"I was a fool to ask you to come on the trip. If I'd had any idea." His voice faltered. "I'd give up my life if I thought—"

"It's okay. We're here now. We just have to figure out what to do."

Harold heard the words, the calmness in the tone, and it came to him that their roles had switched. Harold, always looking forward, one plan fails try another, never giving in to doubt—now that was Marcus's role. Part of it was Harold's infirmity. Besides his ankle, he was weak from malnutrition. And the periods of delirium had become debilitating, robbing him of his spirit and resilience. It was hard to be Harold when you couldn't keep thoughts together or bridge gaps in your memory.

"I don't remember anything between here and the river," he told Marcus. "I remember hearing your voice and Cochise dancing around the fire and you were there, and then the next thing I was here in the cave with a weight in my head. When I opened my eyes I was seeing two of everything."

"You had a concussion, Dad."

Dad? It was the first time Harold had ever heard Marcus call him that. No, that's what he'd called out when Harold saw the fire. "Da . . . ," the final consonant drowned out by the echo.

"Where's Cochise?"

"Job said he ran away, but I don't know. He was hanging around the cabin for a couple days. I could hear him shuffling and pawing at the door, and then nothing. Maybe he did run away. I hope so."

"Did they chain you up with a combination lock?"

"Yeah." A short laugh. "A bicycle lock. Four numbers. It took me like a couple minutes to roll it. He must have figured I was such a good kid, I never stole a bike before. I would have got away, too, but when he left me that time he forgot something, and when I opened the door, he was standing there. Man, when I pulled that chain out, I almost passed out. After that he put on a key lock I couldn't pick."

"What was the combination on the lock you picked?"

"Six five five four."

"Six point five by fifty-four. That's the caliber of his rifle."

"So is that what you have, a combo lock?"

"Yes."

"You try the caliber numbers?"

"No." Harold began to shake his head and caught himself as the pain sharpened. "I haven't been thinking too straight." He shuffled over to the cave wall where the chain was locked to the iron ring.

"Can you see the numbers?" Marcus asked.

"No. It's too dark. Could you teach me how to pick it?"

"Be pretty hard unless you read Braille," Marcus said. "But once it gets light, we could try it. Maybe he bought a two-pack and programmed in the same combo."

Once it gets light they're going to take you away from me, Harold thought.

He said, "Sometimes I think I can hear the river running. Can you?"

Marcus shook his head. "But I don't think we're too far from the water. After we were walking, I started counting steps and got up to about eight hundred before we climbed to this cave. I used to run the eight hundred in track. That's about the same in yards, so you figure a yard a stride, that's a half a mile, give or take. And then maybe three hundred more feet up to get here."

"What's this look like on the outside?"

"The cave? It's sort of a comma shape. You have to duck in and then there's a passage that angles back and gets wider. Job cut some little trees to hide the mouth. It's not easy to see until you're standing in front of it."

"Doesn't surprise me. I'd hear planes going overhead and once I thought I heard a jet boat. But nothing for days now."

They fell silent. Harold breathed slowly, the weight of hopelessness hanging on his shoulders. When he tried to speak, no words came out.

"We'll get out of here, Dad."

Again, that word.

"You're my son," Harold said simply. He stretched to the length of the chain and held his hand out. When Marcus did the same, he grabbed the boy's hand and squeezed it.

"I didn't mean it," Marcus said. "When I told you the only reason I came was to see the canyon. I just wanted to see you. I'd heard so much, you're the big success and people admire you. I thought when my uncle told you about my mom that you'd deny it. Say you never met her. But you owned up right away. It's just hard putting myself out there, so I act like a hard-ass."

Silence. A slight ticking of the bats.

"Most of them are still out hunting," Harold said. "But the little ones are practically hairless and they can't fly yet. I thought about catching one to eat."

"I guess maybe you have enough hot sauce to choke it down."

They listened to the bats making their small clicking sounds.

"That's called echolocation," Marcus said. "I read that most of the sounds they make are like two or three times higher pitched than humans can hear."

Harold thought, *In a little while it will be dawn, they'll start flying back to the cave.* Three hours, four at most, and he would never see his son again.

"If I had a knife," Marcus said, "I could cut my way out like that guy did in Utah. The one who got trapped by a rock and cut off his hand with a multi-tool."

"What are you talking about?"

"That guy. You don't know?"

"I remember something about it."

"If I had a knife or a sharp rock, I could cut through the Achilles tendon and get the chain off. But it looks like they swept this place pretty good. You can't even find a pebble."

Harold felt the scratching against his thigh, where the pieces of sharpened bone dug through the fabric. He drew them out, the two scapulas not much bigger than soup spoons, the femur ground to a point.

"What do you have there?"

Harold told him.

"A fox, huh?"

"I think he probably brought food here before and just panicked when he saw me."

"No, he gave that rabbit to you. He knew you'd see me again and I could cut myself free. He knew the bones were magic. Give them to me. I can do this."

"No. Best if I do it. I don't know why I didn't think of it right away. I wasn't thinking beyond weapons."

"Can you even reach your ankle?"

"Maybe." Harold sat and drew his left leg as close to him as he could. "Barely." He spoke through gritted teeth.

"It has to be me," Marcus said. "And you're too weak. You couldn't go for help. I can."

"I don't know how much pressure you can put on a leg with a ruptured Achilles."

"Better than us sitting here waiting to die. Let me try. If I get free, I can get a jump on them. I can push one off the ledge and kill the other. I can go for the rifle."

"Don't even think about it. You'll die for nothing. No, if I give you the bone, you have to promise me you'll get as far from here as you can."

"I can't leave you here."

"You can. You have to. I would only drag you down. What did they do with your canoe?"

"They stashed it in the bushes. They were planning to go back for it, but I don't think they did. If I can get across the river and find it, I can float down to the bridge in one day."

"No, that won't work," Harold said. "Once they know you've escaped, they'll find another access farther downstream. They'll pick you off from the cliffs. They can cover country faster in a truck than you can in a canoe."

"Then I'll only float far enough to find the first road or house. Or maybe somebody will be on the river."

"The river's shut down. Or was."

"I'll find something. I'll get help for you."

It would come too late, Harold knew. But at least Marcus would have a chance. He lay down on the cave floor and stretched his arm out, his fingers clamped on the bone.

"Promise you'll go," he said.

"I promise."

He felt Marcus's hand clasp one of the scapulas.

Marcus took off his shoes and sat cross-legged. He placed his left ankle on top of his right thigh and poised the scapula over the raised ridge of the tendon. Harold saw him bite with his upper teeth at his lower lip.

"You'll bite right through your lip. Just clamp your teeth together," he said. "And don't shut your eyes. It focuses the pain and makes it worse."

"You got any other advice?"

"Find a way to get away from yourself. Get your mind out of this cave."

"Maybe I should wait until a spirit animal comes to me, like your fox. Or maybe dream of a woman like that one at Indian Springs. The one who needed a shoulder to lean on." His voice was jittery. He was just talking, stalling.

"Whatever works," Harold said.

"I'll try thinking about Cochise, see where that takes me."

———

The first cut was shallow, a black smile forming as the scapula sliced across the back of Marcus's ankle. Harold watched as the smile grew pregnant, then the quarter moon was obliterated as Marcus cut down harder and the blood flowed freely.

"Come on, Marcus," Harold heard his son mutter. "You can do this." His face contorted with the effort as he bore down on the scapula.

He sat back, panting.

"Just do it," Harold heard him say. Again he pressed with the blade, sawing now, his face a mask of pain and his jeans black with blood.

"The fox isn't working." His sharp laugh rang off the cave walls. A small cloud of bats lifted from the stalactites and ticked in the darkness.

"Aaaugghh!" And again. "Aaaugghh!" The air was suddenly filled with bats.

"Are you through?"

"Not yet."

"I thought I heard a pop. Are you sure?"

"No, goddamnit. I'm not through. Give me the other blade. Maybe it's sharper."

Harold stretched out his hand with the second shoulder blade.

Marcus's entire body began to shake. "I don't know if I can do this." But then his outline stilled, and Harold heard Marcus breathe in once, then once more. He pressed down with a grunting effort, and when the tendon ruptured, his leg sprang from his thigh and jumped around as if in the throes of a seizure.

Marcus grabbed his knee and squeezed it to his chest. Gradually, his body stilled.

"I've still got to pull the chain out through the cut. God, it's going to hurt."

"You can do it," Harold said.

"Let me breathe a minute."

"Yank it through. The longer you wait—"

"I know. I have to turn the chain so the link is flat. It has to come out sideways. Okay, okay, I'm ready."

When he yanked on the chain, his prolonged scream echoed on the cave walls.

"Are you okay?" No answer. "Are you okay, Marcus?"

"No."

After a while: "That's one way to get rid of a bunch of bats. Huh, Dad?"

CHAPTER THIRTY-FIVE

The Stardust of Heaven

"Your dog wants out." Inside the tent, silence. "He wants out. Should I let him out?"

"So he's my dog now?"

"Make a decision."

"Sure then." Sean's voice was muffled by his sleeping bag. "How much trouble can a three-legged mutt get into?"

Kneeling, he unzipped the tent flap. The dog bolted past him into the black. Sean could make out the bed of the night's campfire coals, a soft cherry glow. Usually, he was meticulous about putting a fire out, but in this season of rain and drizzle there was no need, and the coals would make starting the breakfast fire easier.

Martha had climbed out of her bag and was pulling on her shoes. "Where are you going?"

"To the loo," she said. "Where else would I be going?"

"Don't get lost."

Sean pulled on his shoes and walked down to the riverbank. He lifted his eyes from the stars reflected on the pool. To his east, a thin band of teal over coral. Dawn's lie. He recalled that it was during this hour of false promise that the girl had seen the scarecrow. It was coming full circle, he thought. He could feel a charge in the air. He smiled to himself and peed into the water, the stream of urine raising a steam.

"That one's for you, Harold," he muttered.

Back in camp, he fed sticks to the coals and fanned them to flame. He set his pot on the collapsible grill over the fire.

Martha's flashlight bobbed as she came back up the path.

"What's for breakfast?"

"Cereal and powdered milk."

"How exciting. I've been thinking and thinking, and I'm still not sure what the best plan is."

"Follow Cochise," Sean said.

"I knew that's what you were going to say, but he isn't a search dog and too much time has passed. Even Lothar can't follow a scent after five days. Isn't that what Katie told you?"

"Maybe he won't need his nose. Maybe he'll see something familiar, find a trail we can follow."

"Speaking of, where did that damned critter go?"

———

To his relief, the pain was manageable, if constant. Marcus could put more weight on his foot than he'd thought. He couldn't go uphill, or come to tiptoes, but he didn't need to do any climbing. The long swale he'd been marched up nearly a week ago, a lifetime ago, with a gun barrel in his back, offered a gentle descent to the river. There, the pearl ellipse of water seemed not to move. It was moving, though, and even if Marcus could hobble to the bank, a part of him still doubted that he'd be able to summon the strength to wade or swim to the far side.

And it was to the far side that he'd have to go to find the canoe, and, in it, taped under the stern deck with duct tape, the cheap revolver he had traded a dirt bike for when he was sixteen, and which he had not told Harold about initially, knowing he would disapprove, or a half hour ago, because he knew Harold would make him promise not to try to rescue him. When Job had taken him captive on the riverbank, neither he nor his companion, Dewey, had bothered looking under the deck before carrying the canoe well back from the bank to stash in the bushes. How Marcus would climb back up to the cave to rescue Harold, if in fact he could find the canoe and the gun was still in it, Marcus didn't know. But get there he would, even if he had to crawl.

To his right, silhouetted against the sky, was the long ridge terminating at Table Rock. Job, during one of his soliloquies, told Marcus that he'd lain down on its rough surface, four hundred feet above the river, for two days and two nights, trading shifts with Dewey, before Harold had come by in his canoe. And then he had shot the other man by mistake. Later, he'd found that Harold had screwed with the sighting turrets on the scope. He hadn't said this in a spiteful way, in fact the opposite.

"Your father," he'd said, "I admire him. He's like a cat, but he's down to his last life now. He's become mortal. It will pain me to take the ninth life from him."

"He'll kill you," Marcus had replied. "The last thing you'll see is my dad in your dying eyes."

"You're quite bold for a young man in chains."

"I'm telling the truth," Marcus had said. "You'll die with him in your eyes."

Job had laughed. His laughter had filled the tiny cabin. But he had not mentioned Harold's lives to Marcus again.

Now the long grasses were paling, and Marcus hurried on. He tried not to think about Harold, who had brought him to his chest and hugged him with surprising strength before they'd parted. They had debated, briefly and coldly, whether Marcus should free Harold in the same way that he'd freed himself. Harold had argued for it, saying it would give him the element of surprise when the men returned. He could lie in wait, unhampered by the chain. He might die bloody, but he had the sharpened femur of the rabbit, and it wouldn't be all his blood.

Marcus had feared that Harold was in such a weakened state that cutting the Achilles might send him into shock, in which case he could offer no resistance at all.

In the end, and despite misgivings, Marcus had brought the bone to bear on Harold's ankle. The tendon was much thicker and stronger than his own, and for minutes he sawed at it, while Harold made not one sound. It was the set of his face that Marcus remembered, the look far away, as he had wondered if Harold was thinking of the woman or was running with the fox.

———

Thirty yards down the bank, the river reached its widest point before funneling into a riffle. Marcus knew that the wide tailout would offer the shallowest ford, and as he made his way down the bank, more and more of the bend upstream came into view. Glancing back over his shoulder, he saw a glimmer of light. The light was coming from the east bank—perhaps, he thought, the uppermost of the two Table Rock campsites. It was a few hundred yards away, and for it to be visible at this distance, with dawn approaching, it had to be more powerful than the beam of a simple flashlight. *A fire?* If so, whose? It would not be Job or Dewey. The compound where they slept was on the same side of the river as the cave, and at least several miles away.

Whatever it was, the light gave him heart, for here was an unexpected chance of help at hand, and heart took him into the river, where he managed to stay upright for only a few steps before slipping on the boulders. The cold water was like a slap. He struggled up, fell again, and was swept downriver into the riffle. Backstroking with both arms and kicking with his good leg, he angled toward the far bank, trying to keep his face above water. The first time his head went under, he saw the dancing of the dawn stars from beneath the river's surface, each star refracted so that he was was seeing two, and fought back up to see two stars become one all across the sky. The second time he went under, he found this heaven on water so fascinating that his chest hurt before he fought back to the surface. A lungful of air and he went under again, at peace with the world now, and as his mind reeled away, the stars blacked out abruptly as something slammed into his chest. A moment later, he felt pressure on his pants leg, and kicked to free himself of it. He surfaced, still kicking at his tether and wondering if he'd become snarled in a piece of old barbed wire.

Marcus struggled to his hands and knees, finding that he was in shallow water and had nearly reached the far bank. He dragged his bad leg up onto the mud, where the dog that never barked shook itself, jumped over him, jumped back, tugged again at his pants leg, and then dug its muzzle under his chin.

For a moment, able to comprehend but not to believe, Marcus thought he must be under the water again, traveling across the universe patterned on the river's surface, and that, having crossed to the far side, he had crossed into the stardust of heaven, where all men are reunited with their dogs.

"Cochise," he said.

———

Harold felt his heart beat against the rock floor of the cave. How long had he been unconscious? An hour? Two? Enough light suffused the cave that he thought the latter. He'd been lucid when Marcus had left, had, for a time anyway, managed to distance himself from his body, discarding the pain as if it was a suit of clothes that one had only to unbutton. He'd told himself it was too early for Job to be returning with his morning slice of bread, and thought, *I'll lie down for just a few minutes, summon my strength. And then I'll get out of this cave and . . .* and do what? Anything, he'd thought, even die, just as long as his final ceiling was sky. But rest first.

He rolled over and looked at the stalactites. Where there had only been a few bats in the night, there were dozens now, further proof of the dawning hour. Harold glanced around the cave, the tangle of the discarded chains, the dark stains of Marcus's blood where it had dripped onto the rock, his own blood. He'd had a plan before passing out. What was it? Something about the blood. Yes. He'd told Marcus to remove his shirt, and then had bound it tightly over his son's ankle. There were no major blood vessels ruptured, and what little blood Marcus dripped would be hard to see if he kept to the grasses on his way down to the river.

Harold found that he was thinking more clearly than he had in days, and that for the first time since his capture, moving his head abruptly did not bring a wave of pain. The rabbit he had eaten had not sated his hunger, but it had given him unexpected strength. He'd lost a few hours, true enough, but what he had gained more than offset it.

The problem of what to do, however, remained. Without any definite plan, he started to limp toward the light that betrayed the cave entrance, and then he stopped himself. Something that Marcus had told him nagged at his brain—what was it? Yes, the combination lock. It might be light enough now to read the numbers. He went to where it attached the chain to the iron ring. By canting the face of the lock to catch the directional light, he could in fact read the face. He tried 6-5-5-4, as Marcus had suggested. No luck. He thought back to his time in the Park. Job had a second rifle, also in a metric caliber. It was a heavier rifle than the Mannlicher, his "stopping rifle," as Job put it. He carried it when he had to follow a blood trail and might provoke the charge of a wounded grizzly bear.

Nine point three by sixty something. *By sixty-four?* Harold aligned the numbers. No dice. *Sixty-two, maybe?* He used his thumbnail to turn the tumbler two clicks. And was not as surprised as he might have been when the lock came open.

Harold wrapped the freed chain around his waist four times and knotted the ends. Maybe he could use it as a weapon.

He limped back to the cave mouth and ducked outside. He came to his height for the first time in a week, and stood, fighting vertigo.

Though morning was dragging its feet, it was to Harold almost blinding in its intensity, and he found himself blinking as his eyes adjusted. Below him was a thin belt of aspen saplings and thornbushes, and below that a grassy swale, and below that was the river, flowing like gunmetal in the hour's deep shadow.

He knew now what to do. He would lay down a trail, a blood trail, one that led away from the river and Marcus. With luck, Job would be alone or, if not, both men would follow his trail, giving Marcus that much more time to escape. At the very least, it would split the men apart.

A game trail worked to Harold's left, contouring the rocky hillside. He gingerly put weight on his left leg, then stepped ahead with his right foot, brought the left up parallel, shifted what weight he could onto it and again reached ahead with the right. In this halting manner he worked along the trail, stopping once to pick up a broken limb to employ as a walking stick. Every few feet he deliberately dragged his left pants cuff against the rocks. He was leaving a blood trail a blind man could follow and told himself to keep moving while he still had the strength.

A quarter mile after taking up the trail, he came to a rockslide. The trail continued across the slide, but the footing was iffy and twice he almost fell. Where the slide ended, the trail skirted the bole of a big pine tree, then angled along the top edge of a cliff before reentering forest. Harold got down on his hands and knees for this part, for if he fell here, he fell off the cliff. He peered over the edge. The cliff was only about a ten-foot drop from top to bottom, but the rocks at the base were jagged. Anyone who pitched over could easily break a leg, or much worse.

He retreated to the tree, whose lower limbs shaded the only bit of flatland for some distance in either direction. An elk had chosen this as a bedding site, leaving as its calling card two piles of pellets. Harold squeezed a few between his thumb and fingers. The pellets, shaped like small acorns, were soft with an insect green slime, and smelled sweetly of wild cattle. Harold guessed that the elk couldn't have been gone for more than an hour.

Ever since peering over the cliff, a plan had been taking shape in his mind. He unwound the chain, which was about twelve feet long, and tied one end to the base of a pine sapling five or six feet on the far side of the footpath, then crouched behind the big pine. He stretched the chain tight. That it would trip anyone who followed his blood trail, Harold had little doubt—provided, that was, that the person didn't spot the chain. Harold scooped up a handful of dirt where the elk's hooves had bitten deep and scattered it over the chain. He continued to do this until he could no longer see the steel links. Then he placed small bits of stick, pinecones, and dead leaves on top of the duff. Again he got behind the bole of the tree, first having draped the end of the chain over a low branch. The chain was invisible now, and if he yanked on the end of it, it would spring up taut about a foot off the ground. With a bit of luck, anyone who tripped on it would fall over the cliff.

Harold had one remaining chore, and carefully picked his way along the rim of the cliff until the trail reentered forest, and then came back on his tracks to the tree, dragging his cuffs. Anyone following him would think that Harold had continued on. Their eyes would be on the smears of blood, not on the tree Harold was hiding behind. He thought about his grandfather, who had taught him to trap animals and birds in all the old ways. He remembered snaring gophers and being shown a very simple trick to catch hopping birds by tying a string to a forked stick that propped a cardboard box up. When the bird hopped under the box, you yanked the string and the box fell, trapping the bird inside. The first time Harold tried it, he'd baited his trap with a nightcrawler pinned to a chip of wood with a fishhook, and caught a robin. He'd been hiding behind a tree and remembered racing to the box, hearing the flutter against the cardboard, and lifting it, the robin flying up, so close that the tips of its wings brushed his face. The moment had been magic, but he had felt bad about the robin's panic and had never trapped another bird in this manner.

And now this, a different tree, a different trap, with a different quarry, and the bait his own blood. This time, Harold thought, there would be no release, no wings beating to freedom. He reached into his pocket to worry the femur bone of the rabbit. He felt the sharp point dig into the pad of his forefinger.

Come on, you bastard. Come to Harold.

CHAPTER THIRTY-SIX

Showdown at Table Rock

Through the scope of the Winchester rifle, Martha Ettinger watched Sean's slow progress as he backtracked Marcus's trail.

"What's taking you so long?" she muttered under her breath.

She swung the crosshairs away from Stranahan's back and painted the circle of magnification across the landscape—the staircasing cliffs, V-shaped patches of pine forest, the bony ridge opposite the camp, knobby as a crocodile's back, that terminated in the mushroom-shaped architecture of Table Rock. Below the rock, the cliff fell away steeply to the river.

Once and once more, she cursed herself for having dropped her binoculars onto rocks earlier in the float, which had thrown the ocular alignment out of whack. And for what? A closer look at a pair of Canada geese and their puffball offspring, trailing them like corks. How many geese had she seen in the last three days—five hundred, a thousand? You've seen one gosling and you've seen them all. But she had dropped the binoculars, and so was reduced to looking through the scope, which was half the power of the 8×42 glasses and a more limited field of view at that.

Behind her, some twenty yards away, in a runoff channel that was running bank-full with snowmelt and couldn't be seen until you were standing directly over it, Marcus sat on a patch of sand with his hands around his knees. Already thawed once by the fire, he was now twice warmed by Cochise, who lay with his head in his lap.

When Sean and Martha had found him on the riverbank, Marcus's body was shivering so violently that the dog on his chest appeared to tremble. His teeth were chattering so hard that he was impossible to understand.

"We've got to find my dad," was the first definite sentence they could decipher. He'd insisted that he'd take them there, that there was no time to waste. But as he'd been unable to walk the hundred yards to the fire without assistance, *on level ground*, guiding them to the cave was out of the question. This presented a dilemma, because it meant someone had to stay behind with him, with every likelihood that either Job or his henchman would come looking. Stranahan was the tracker, so that left Martha to hold down the fort, the "fort" being a cottonwood tree felled by beavers. The tree and its stump were still attached by splinters of green wood, and the natural V between the trunk and the stump, cushioned by Martha's hat, made a solid rest for her rifle.

Thirty yards downriver stood their blue dome tent, and just beyond it, the fire ring. Before taking cover, Martha had built up the fire; then, flashing to the image of the half scarecrow at the pictograph ledges, she'd laced together a few sticks and limbs and hurriedly draped them with the wet clothing they had peeled off Marcus. On top of this effigy, she placed his hat. It would never be confused with the artistic creations of the Scarecrow God, but from a couple hundred yards away, and partially obscured by wood smoke, it might pass muster. The last touch, the hat, had been Marcus's suggestion, which in turn gave her another idea. Assembling her fly rod, she tied a big fly called a Sofa Pillow to the leader and hooked it into the hat. Then she paid out line as she walked from the fire to the downed cottonwood. One jerk of the line and the hat would come off, and the decoy would look alive.

Maybe.

Repositioning herself behind the log, she swiveled the rifle so that the scope once again drew crosshairs on Stranahan's back. He was still working out the trail on the apron of grass, but was nearing a line of trees. Ever since he'd taken his kayak across the river and started backtracking, Martha had half expected the serenity of the morning to be split with the thunder of a shot.

"Where is he?" It was Marcus's voice from the depression.

"He's at the top of the opening, working to his right. Okay, he's in the trees." Now that he'd made cover, she found that she was breathing deeply for the first time in minutes.

"Look up from there. Can you see something blue? I tore off a strip of my shirt and tied it to a tree. It's just below the cave."

"I see it. I wish I'd known so I could have told Sean. He could have stayed in cover."

"I'm sorry. I forgot, I guess. I wasn't thinking real clear."

"It's okay. He's there now. So far so good."

"He's a good man, right? I mean with a gun and all."

"He couldn't hit sand if he fell off a camel."

But her eye was back in the scope and she didn't hear herself speaking. She'd seen something flash. It was to the south of where she'd last seen Stranahan, quite some distance away, where a scree slope made a break in the forest. There it was again, a quick glint like the turning of a trout in clear water. And . . . ?

And nothing. It was gone. She placed two fingers against the artery in her neck. *Calm and steady, Martha,* she told herself. And to the two men who meant more to her than all the rest in the world put together. *Don't you dare die on me. Not on this river. Not here, not now.*

———

When Harold heard the rock tilt, and then settle back, he put the sharpened femur between his teeth and took up the slack in the chain that was wrapped twice around his right hand. He gripped the chain with his left hand a foot farther up and waited. Earlier, he had stripped off his flannel shirt, thinking that his skin tone offered the better camouflage, being similar in hue to the patches of lichen that splotched the limestone rocks. Once more, the scuffing sound, drawing closer now. Harold squeezed his eyes to slits. He could feel his bare chest thudding against the forest floor.

Just don't look down, he thought, trying to will this message to the man he could hear now, but not yet see.

But when you are following a trail of blood, and you have a rifle in your hands and a finger on the trigger, your eyes are the eyes of a predator. You are looking forward to the last splash of crimson, not at your feet. Harold could hear breathing and knew it to be Job, the slight wheeze of his inhalations as distinctive as a fingerprint. He had reached the elk's bed, was probably giving it a cursory glance, the hunter in him assessing the size of the animal that made it. Almost as soon as the thought came to his mind, Harold heard the mutter of Job's voice.

"Good bull."

Another footfall. Harold could see the right shoe advance and tap for foothold. Now the left came up to join it. He'd be looking at the precipice now. His next step would be shorter, more carefully placed. The boot inched forward, the sole coming down squarely on the camouflaged chain. Would he look down? No, he'd just think he'd stepped on a stone. Harold saw the foot kick at the obstruction and cringed, knowing it would expose the chain.

Just one more step.

And even as he willed it, the right foot lifted and inched forward. *Now!*

Harold jerked the chain, felt the vibration as it came taut between Job's boots. A sudden hard tug as Job's left shin caught the chain, and he was stumbling, reaching out to break his fall with his right hand. Harold heard the clatter of the rifle as Job dropped it and then the sharp smack as it hit the rocks below the cliff. Now Job was scrabbling at the loose rocks on the edge of the precipice, and Harold, looking full into his face, saw his wild-eyed grimace changing to a look of inquiry. And that's the way he went over, a question on his lips. A moment later, Harold heard a cracking sound as the body struck the rocks.

He edged to the lip of the cliff. The rifle came into view first. It had ricocheted off the rocks and slid down the slope in an avalanche of small gravel. Job was lying on his right side, both hands clutching at his left leg, which bulged grotesquely. He emitted a thin scream. He screamed again; then, stretching out his neck in a fishlike way, he twisted until he was staring up at Harold. He looked from Harold to the rifle, which was thirty feet down the slope. Wrenching himself onto his stomach, he began to roll down the hill toward the rifle, grunting with pain each time his left leg went under the weight of his body.

With no time to find an easy way down, Harold let himself over the cliff face, still holding on to the chain. He had descended no more than a couple feet before the knot holding the end of the chain to the tree slipped, then broke. He hit the rocks feetfirst, the chain cascading on top of him. He struggled to his knees, looking around for the bone that he'd instinctively spit out when he was falling. Not finding it, he began to half crawl, half stumble in a race with Job to get to the rifle.

Harold could move faster and was closing the gap, but Job had a head start. Realizing that he was going to lose, Harold lunged, grabbing at the leg Job had been favoring and yanked on it. Job screamed, but the rifle was in his grip now, and as he swiveled with it, Harold felt the world slow, saw the bore of the rifle peer his way like a lazy, unfocused eye, and as he pulled with all he had on Job's injured leg, the crack of the rifle and the man's scream were simultaneous.

Harold grasped at the barrel as the rifle jerked in recoil. He saw Job working the bolt to chamber another round, and again the bore crossed his body, its black eye no longer lazy but swimming in tight ovals, and then he both heard and felt the concussive blast of a second shot. The big body tensed under Harold's hands, then abruptly released.

Has he shot himself? No, that wasn't possible. Harold tore his attention away to look for the rifle, which had fallen from Job's grip, even as the muscles of the big man's arms surged back to life, the claw of his hand seeking Harold's throat. Harold brought up his hands to fight the death grip on his neck. His right hand was still on the chain, and seeing an opening, he wrapped a loop around Job's head and pulled, released to make enough slack to get a second wrap, and pulled.

As Job twisted onto his back, Harold placed his right foot against his shoulder for leverage and leaned back, the constricting steel coils biting into Job's throat. The fingers of his scarred, crablike hand flew around his face like the bats in the cave.

Time bled away and Harold found that he was staring at his reflection in the man's bulging eyes. The tongue came out between purple lips and the face pearled a sickly gray color, then darkened into a mask, and the eyes slid away to look into space, then came back, found Harold's eyes, focused briefly, then again slid away. Harold closed his eyes with the effort and was still pulling when the red behind his eyelids began to spot with color, green at first, then black. He felt something release from his body, and then he was no longer in the canyon of the Smith River fighting for his life, but was a small boy running toward his grandfather's outstretched arms, and running, he leapt into the air and was a bird, soaring, and then as he settled back to the ground, the bird was gone.

————

When Martha heard the first shot, she shouted "Stay low" to Marcus. The sound had reverberated from the area where she'd seen the glinting from the rockslide. It had been a rifle barrel, she knew that now, even as she tried to empty herself of thought, although a part of her couldn't help but wonder if Sean or Harold had been hit. Then the second shot sounded. It also was from the vicinity of the slide but different, not a split of thunder that echoed off the cliffs like the first shot, but muffled, lower in decibel. Lower in decibel generally meant lower in velocity. A handgun? *Her* handgun? She remembered pressing her service revolver into Sean's hands before he crossed the river.

No more shots followed, and in the silence the minutes ticked. She wanted to be doing something, anything, to crack the tension.

"What's going on?" she heard Marcus say.

She spat back at him to stay quiet. Then said "Sorry" under her breath.

"You said there could be two of them, right?"

"Yeah."

"You ever see either of them with a handgun?"

"Yeah."

"They both have rifles?"

"Yeah."

"Well, shit."

She put her right eye to the scope. The rockslide was too far away, at least a half a mile, and the detail too small, to see anything unless someone was standing right in the middle of it. She was too busy looking to notice Marcus scrambling up beside her.

"I told you to stay back."

"Can't you see him?"

"Who?"

"Can't you see him? It's Dewey, Job's brother-in-law. He's got a rifle."

"How do you know?"

"I know his hat."

"Where?"

"He's behind Table Rock. Maybe twenty yards back of it. He must have been following my track."

"But you didn't go there."

"He's skirting to get a vantage. There he is. He's coming closer."

Still, she couldn't see him.

"Are you sure?"

"Pretty sure. He went out of sight."

"Why wouldn't he be heading toward the shots?"

"He does what Job tells him to do. If Job said, 'Follow that trail,' he's going to do it, no matter what he hears."

"You think he spotted our fire?"

"How could he miss it?"

"Wouldn't he think there was something didn't add up, you right out in the open like that?"

"He doesn't use the same numbers they teach you in school." His voice rose in excitement. "There he is. See him? He's got a green hat."

Now Martha saw. There was a patch of color, like the quilted patterns of moss on the rocks. The color shifted.

"Are you going to shoot him?"

Martha didn't respond. It wasn't a justified-use situation. She couldn't see a weapon, and as yet there was no proof of imminent threat. And it was too far for her to shout and announce her presence.

"You see the fly rod?" Martha said, without taking her eyes from the scope.

"Yeah. You want me to give it a pull?"

"I want you to crawl away from me farther up the log, so if he shoots at me, he won't hit you. Take cover there. Then when I give you the word, pull the line."

She heard the reel spool click as Marcus paid out line.

Something in the circle of her scope shifted, suddenly resolving into the shape of a man. He was lying prone on the ground, just behind the limestone pedestal of Table Rock. The old K-4 Weaver on Martha's rifle had been sharp and bright for its day, but its day was forty years ago, and the figure in the crosshairs was fuzzy.

"Shit," Martha uttered under her breath. And to herself, *If you get out of this, you're going to buy a new Leupold scope, one you can crank to a higher power than four.*

The gunshot startled her. Or rather the sharp smack of the bullet that beat it by a split second. She hadn't signaled to Marcus to pull on the line, hadn't seen the hat come off the effigy. She craned her head to see beyond the fire. The effigy swayed back and forth. There was a second smacking sound. As the air rent with the thunder of the shot, the flimsy effigy broke and pitched forward, falling into the flames.

Martha's right eye centered the figure in the scope. Targets across an expanse of water always looked closer than they really were. She calculated the range at three hundred yards, a distance where the 180-grain boat-tail bullet from her .30/06 would drop sixteen inches.

She raised the crosshairs to what she judged to be the right height, yet still she hesitated. If the shooter thought he'd killed Marcus, wouldn't his natural course be to walk closer to make sure? The shooter would present a bigger target if she waited. She might even be able to take him alive.

The explosion of bark came an instant before the cracking echo. Martha ducked. She felt a burning sensation in her right eye and frantically rubbed at her face, feeling the stubble of splinters digging into her cheeks. She looked at the blood on the backs of her knuckles and blinked, wincing at the pain as her eyelids caught on the bits of bark showered by the impact. She brought her head to the scope. More sensing then seeing the blob, she fired.

A third shot from Table Rock came in the echo, the bullet thudding into the bole of the cottonwood.

Martha could feel the heat of Marcus's body next to her. *How did he get here?*

"Keep your head down!" she said.

She crawled to her right a foot, then shifted the rifle from her right shoulder to her left, so she could take aim with her left eye, which she could still see through a little. Keeping her right eye shut, she looked through the scope and saw the patch of green. Indistinct, but not as blurry as before.

A fourth shot from the rocks, the bullet whining away over the log.

Martha ducked. Slowly she brought her head up, centered the green hat in the crosshairs, and raised the rifle to allow for the bullet drop. Breathing in, then letting out half the breath, she pressed the trigger with her left index finger.

The butt of the rifle slammed against her shoulder with the shot. The barrel lifted in recoil, obscuring her sight of the target.

"Did I hit him?"

"No." She could hear the breath coming rapidly as Marcus spoke. "You're too high. I can see the dust where it hit the rock."

Martha deliberately slowed her breathing. For a second she flashed to a vision of the whitetail buck she'd hung in her barn last fall during hunting season, the red wine color of its hollowed-out body cavity that turned in the wind when she slid open the double door. She'd shot it as it ran past her at forty yards, leading it like a duck in flight.

You can do this, Martha.

She jacked in another cartridge. Again she brought the crosshairs to bear on the green shape and raised them, but only by a few inches this time.

The rifle thundered, then rang away in echoes.

"He's hit." Marcus's voice seemed to come from under water after the concussion of the shot. "You got him!"

Martha looked toward Table Rock through the scope. She saw movement there, then a shower of small rocks falling off the cliff, and then, suddenly, the figure of a person was going over and she saw a glinting of metal, heard a cracking sound, then another, and a moment later a heavy thud. Then, silence.

Martha found that she'd bitten her lip and spat out blood.

She could hear Marcus say, "He's still rolling. Okay, he's stopped. He's dead."

Setting down the rifle, she got to her feet. Marcus was beside her and she leaned against him. "Help me down to the river."

"Don't you think we should stay here? The other guy might still be alive. We don't know where he is."

Of course he was right.

"The channel then. It's protected."

Reaching the bank of the runoff channel, which was a few yards wide and flowing with off-colored water, she knelt down and cupped water with her hands to try to wash the debris out of her eyes.

"Can you see?"

"A little with my left eye. There's still some grit." She waded into the shallows, braced her hands on the cobblestone bottom, and dipped her face under the water. Using her thumb and forefinger to open each eye as wide as she could, she blinked, feeling the cold against her eyeballs. In her blurred vision, she saw a stonefly nymph, magnified by the water, crawl up on the top of a submerged stone, the gills on its middle body segment feathering. It seemed to be looking at her, and she remembered the card case at the homestead, the Creature from the Black Lagoon. She brought her face up, took a breath, and dipped under again. The little monster was gone.

"Better," she said when she'd stood up. She saw Marcus standing on one leg ten feet away, leaning on the butt of the Winchester for support. She had completely forgotten that his Achilles tendon was ruptured.

"If you were Harold, you'd probably pee in the water. Act like nothing of significance had happened."

And then she thought, *Harold.*

CHAPTER THIRTY-SEVEN

Last Leg to Eden

Even from three feet away, Harold looked dead. But under Sean's hands was a string of pulse, the heart song quiet but the notes clear and distinct. Sean pried his fingers from his grip on the chain, releasing them one by one.

He'd already checked the ABCs—airway, breathing, circulation. No apparent injuries, though his right calf was distorted compared to the left, swollen tight against his pants cuff. The left side of his face showed an old bruise, yellowed with brown patches, an ellipse of green under the eye.

Sean felt around Harold's body for blood, careful not to push against his back in case he'd incurred a spinal injury when he fell off the cliff.

Shooting with Martha's revolver from the top of the cliff, Sean had aimed for the lower part of Job's body, so that even if he was off by several feet the bullet wouldn't strike Harold. He turned his attention to that man now, whose back was on top of Harold's chest. Sean did not recognize the man, but knew it had to be Rayland Jobson. There was a stain of blood on the shirt. He ripped at the buttons and saw the dark worm of the entrance wound. As he watched, a bubble formed at the hole and broke. Then another as the gases escaped, the air turning fetid with the odor of bowel.

Sean remembered that the man had jerked and stiffened when he shot him, but then seemed to recover. Perhaps the slug had creased the spinal column, the shock rendering him momentarily unconscious. No matter. He was dead enough now, his eyes staring at something, or maybe that's what eyes that stared at nothing looked like.

"Is he dead?"

Sean turned his head. Harold coughed. Sean saw his chest heave.

"He's dead," Sean said.

"You kill him?"

"I gut-shot him. I would have shot him again, but he was on you and I couldn't take a chance. No, you killed him."

"Good," Harold said. "Drag the son of a bitch off me."

A look crossed Harold's face, as if he'd forgotten something of importance and just remembered.

"Did I hear shots, or was that just in my head?" Words formed at his lips, were said silently, then aloud.

"My son."

———

It was a battlefield reunion—Martha, her face full of splinters, eyes red under sandpaper lids, each blink feeling like claws raking; Marcus, propped on one good leg, a stick for a crutch, Cochise crow-hopping beside him; Harold, his right knee sprained in the fall, limping on a severed tendon, his mind clear but his tongue having a hard time making words.

As the only one who hadn't left a trail of blood during the course of the day, Sean took charge. His first priority was to use the satellite phone and call in the Air Mercy flight out of Great Falls. Harold's infection, when they had managed to get the swollen leg out of his pants, didn't look good at all, with angry red lines running up his calf. Sean was put on hold, then told the helicopter was engaged. By the time it completed its current mission and returned to the hospital, it would be too dark to attempt a landing on the Smith, even with night-vision goggles, unless the situation was life or death. Neither Harold's infection nor ruptured tendon reached the bar.

That left the dead to deal with, and Sean eventually thought it best to leave them where they had fallen. He called in the GPS waypoints to the Cascade County Sheriff's Office. The coroner and a forensics team would be dispatched. Birds would lead them to the bodies if the coordinates didn't. In fact, a pair of gray jays had already found Dewey Davis, and Sean's inclination was to let them have at it. He walked over to see the rifle that Davis had dropped over the cliff as he began to fall. Like the Mannlicher-Schönauer that Job had carried, and which Harold had fought him for, the rifle was a European-made bolt-action, but with a caliber of 9.3×62. It had a peep sight. Not a long-range weapon at all.

Martha walked up behind him as he covered the rifle with rocks, so it would remain undisturbed until the forensic team appeared on the scene.

"You got lucky," he told her. "If that rifle had a scope, you'd be dead. You were sitting ducks behind that log."

"Don't I know," she said.

Davis's body lay a few yards away—crumpled, lifeless, small. An insignificant man in death, as in life. He had survived the fall after Martha shot him. At least he had survived long enough to blow a bubble of blood, which burst and spread obscenely over his face when Martha touched it with a twig.

"Here's your hillbilly," she said. "Your nightmare from *Deliverance*. Everything but the missing teeth."

"What do you think it means?"

"It was your dream. You tell me. On second thought, don't. I don't want to know."

Twenty-six miles of river remained between Table Rock and the take-out. That was too many by half to cover before dark, and the river was in gloom when they reached Ridgetop Camp, where they decided to stop for the night. While the others stumbled about, pitching the tents and gathering wood for a cooking fire, Sean flashed a small streamer called a Black Ghost and caught three trout in a run opposite camp. Enough to fill the pan.

"So who's got the head tonight?" Martha said. "What, no takers?"

When no one volunteered to bring Harold's boat bag inside their tent, Sean treated it the same way he would hang food from bears. He tied a rock to the end of some paracord, tossed the rock over the stout branch of a pine, and tied one end of the cord to the heavy bag. Then he pulled the bag up under the pine canopy to a height of ten or twelve feet.

"You've been complaining about that bag for years," Sean said to Harold, as everyone looked up, the bag swinging over their heads like a metronome, gradually slowing. "Now you have an excuse to throw it away and get a new one."

"Nothing a little soap and water won't fix," Harold said.

Of the Scarecrow God, they had found not a trace. Nor would they find one in the fifteen miles they covered the next morning before reaching the take-out at Eden Bridge, where an ambulance met them to take Harold and Marcus to the hospital in Great Falls.

"We'll do this again someday," Harold said.

And Martha just shook her head. *Men.*

CHAPTER THIRTY-EIGHT

The Silent Tickler

On October 1, four months after the head of Fitz Carpenter was re-united with his body in the cold storage facility at the Cascade County morgue and the story of their separation became public, a late-season floater intent on a bit of Montana cast-and-blast—fly rod in one hand, shotgun in the other—found a prairie rattlesnake at the Canyon Depth Boat Camp. He had nearly stepped on it, and the snake gave no warning before it struck. Fortunately for the floater, he was in his camo waders and the heavy boots deterred the fangs. The man promptly decapitated the snake with a charge of #4 tungsten shot from his Ithaca Model 37 shotgun. It was only then that he discovered the reason that the snake hadn't shaken its rattle. It had no rattle to shake, only a single segment formed at its last skin shedding. Bad luck, as he'd had plans of making it into a hatband.

After finishing his float, the man called the *Bridger Mountain Star* and asked to speak to Gail Stocker, the reporter who had written a feature story about the making of the documentary, which had aired in September. In the documentary, Bart Trueblood had christened the snake that bit him "the Silent Tickler." The story she wrote after interviewing the floater ran under the headline "Silent Tickler Strikes Again." Along with a summary of the documentary, which had reached 1.4 million viewers in its first airing, it included a photo of the cast-and-blaster, holding the Ithaca in one hand and the terminated serpent in the other.

When Sean Stranahan read the story, he smiled, then peered critically at the sketch on the drawing table in his art studio. One of dozens of pencil studies of the Smith River he'd made before putting paint to canvas, this one included a few strokes of graphite to give heartbeat to the landscape, a pair of sandhill cranes flying low over an inside bend where Indian Springs hooked and crooked its silver threads to the river.

Sean again looked at the newspaper, and then, for a long minute, his eyes were somewhere else. Then the smile came back, and he picked up a gum eraser and the cranes flew no more. Selecting a pencil in 2B grade, he sketched in a small rattlesnake, coiled discreetly among rocks, in the lower right-hand corner of the study. This one had rattles.

"You son of a gun," he said aloud. "You scheming son of a gun."

———

At the Camp Baker boat launch, the ranger stood with his hands on his hips, watching Sean and Martha pack gear into Martha's Mad River canoe.

"I suppose you're going to tell me those are hunting dogs," he said, taking in the playful leapfrogging of Choti, Sean's little sheltie, and Goldie, Martha's bright but aging Aussie shepherd. "But I can't imagine what they're hunting," he said, "seeing's how you have no rifle and no shotgun."

"The truth," Sean said, and the ranger shook his head and said, "Go on, get out of here. I didn't see anything. Who am I, anyway? Just somebody dropped by to collect money from the box."

He helped push them off.

"You think we'll see anyone on the river?" Sean asked.

The ranger vibrated his lips, making a sound like a dying outboard motor. He shook his head. "Only fools float the Smith this late in the year."

Martha had phoned ahead and Bart Trueblood was waiting for them, exercising his philosophy with beer in hand. He set down his bottle and grabbed the bowline of the canoe that Martha tossed him.

"My favorite season," he said. "Last stroke of the paintbrush before the leaves fall. Call it what you want."

"I call it third week of October," Martha said.

"Did you stop by just to spoil my fun?" Trueblood coughed, the sound deep in his chest. He seemed thinner and even frailer than when they had last seen him.

"You don't sound so good, Bart," Martha said.

"I wish I could say you were mistaken." He looked at Sean, his eyes sharp in a face turned haggard. "Are you still planning to submit a painting to the American Rivers contest?"

"If I can meet the deadline."

"Would you like to see what you're up against?"

"I would," Sean said.

"It's in my studio."

Trueblood's villainous goatee preceded them up to the house, past Billy Goat Gruff and the charcoal self-portrait, then to an east-facing room with tall windows and a flood of natural light that served as his studio.

The painting stood on an easel. It was an eagle's-eye view of a bend of the Smith in the stretch upriver from Sunset Cliff, a full moon over the water in a dawn sky, geese flying in a wedge.

"Acrylic on wood," Trueblood said. "The morning of the super moon, June 16, year before last. The closest the moon's orbit came to the earth in three years, and the last time I would ever be able to climb so high."

"It's beautiful." Sean meant it.

"Thank you. I am at the point when I wait for the painting to tell me if it's finished. Yesterday it said it was. This morning, it's ambivalent. What is your opinion? One artist to another."

"I would sign it, that's all."

Trueblood nodded. "As you are aware, the original of the first-place painting will hang in the Capitol Building. But win or lose, I am commissioning a limited-edition run of one hundred prints, and I would like you to have one. I'm also reserving prints for Harold Little Feather, for his son, and for Lillian Cartwright."

"Not for me?" Martha said. "I'm hurt."

"I should have said one for Sean *and* you. You hang your hats on the same rack, I assume you will be looking at art on the same wall. Or have I misread your relationship?"

Martha felt color come into her cheeks.

"The reason I'm telling you this now," he said, picking up the thread, "is because my body has been at war with a particular malady that I refuse to credit by name. I have been ill for some years, and recently I've been informed that I may not be around for the outcome of the art competition. In that event, you will be contacted by the lawyer handling the distribution of my estate."

He waved a hand as Martha began to speak.

"Your sympathies are noted and appreciated, but they aren't necessary. I've had a full life well lived, if not without heartache. Through the years there has been one constant, this river that flows through my paintings, which I have only to draw the curtains to see. To have awakened nearly every morning of my life to its sight, and fallen asleep every night to its song—I have been enriched beyond measure. That is why I have fought so hard against the mine. When I pass, this place will be sold and the profits will go toward carrying on the battle."

"Has the status changed since we saw you last?" Sean asked.

"No, the ball is still in the DEQ's court, and the environmental impact statement is being prepared as we speak. Our best chance to halt or at least postpone development is by placing a rider in a legislative bill, the way they put a temporary stop to gold exploration on the

Yellowstone Park border last year. We can also request that the DEQ take a hard look at the company owners with respect to bad actor laws. If one of the execs has been neglectful with regard to environmental cleanup in a previous mining venture, then the DEQ has the authority to disbar that person or persons from involvement with the current project. Which could buy us time, if nothing else. I assume you saw the documentary then?"

"Last week," Martha said.

"Then you know it made a powerful case in favor of the river. Not to say Clint came off poorly, and for the most part we were preaching to our choirs. But for anyone on the fence, I predict they'll fall on our side of it. And public opinion always counts where politicians are concerned."

"It made you a celebrity," Martha said.

They had moved back into the living room, where they reluctantly accepted Trueblood's offer of coffee. It was already afternoon, and though it was only a handful of miles to Indian Springs, where they'd make their first camp, daylight hours in late fall were in short supply.

"The snake helped," Sean said, after sipping at his cup.

"Didn't it, though?" Trueblood smiled, exposing his porcelain canine tooth. "Tickler was a windfall. I wish he hadn't come to such an inglorious end, though."

"What I'm wondering is how you did it."

Sean saw Martha glance at him.

"What do you mean?" Trueblood said.

"I think you know, Bart."

Trueblood gave a slight shrug and turned to regard his self-portrait. "I should add one more line to my epitaph," he said. "'I care too goddamned much, too.'" Sean watched his Adam's apple work under his goatee.

"It wasn't premeditated, if you were wondering. I saw the snake in back of the house, where my wife's rock garden used to be. Just weeds and rocks now. He crawled under one of the stones. I didn't think much of it. I share the earth with all God's creatures. But then it came to me that I might better serve the river dead than alive. I didn't really want to die. But either way, being bit during the float would grant me, and the cause, instant sympathy. The disease that can't be named had already eaten away the core of my body, and I'd resigned myself to probably never seeing another summer. What better way to go than making the ultimate sacrifice to save this river?"

The next day he had turned the stone. He didn't really expect the snake to still be there, but there it was. It was like he'd shown himself deliberately and was patiently waiting. Trueblood had taken a broom and coaxed the snake into a pillowcase. His hard-sided gear bag had plenty of room to accommodate the snake for a couple days. There only remained the question of his rattles. Rattles are made of keratin, the same substance that toenails and fingernails consist of. Rattlesnakes grow a new segment each time they shed their skin. That was why, Trueblood explained, that in some cultures they were seen as a symbol of eternity. The shedding of the old skin, the putting on of the new. The continual renewal of life.

Trueblood had pinned the snake's head down, then snipped off the rattle with a pair of pruning shears. It did him no harm. At worst, Trueblood said, old Tickler lost a little dignity. Trueblood told the snake that he'd have his revenge soon enough. And that's exactly what had happened. Trueblood had let him out of the bag once he got inside of his tent. The snake didn't want to strike. It was cold and he was lethargic. Trueblood had to grab him with his hand before the snake completed his end of the bargain.

Trueblood looked at Sean, then Martha, and shrugged.

"All's fair, as they say. But please don't tell Clint. We've arrived at détente and this would open old wounds. I assume you're going to stop by? He's at the house. I saw woodsmoke from his direction this morning."

They were back at the river's edge, where Trueblood wavered a little unsteadily, as if buffeted by an internal breeze.

"I assume you're contemplating this season for your painting," he said, "or you wouldn't be floating so late."

Sean said he was considering it.

"Then I suggest *Indian Summer—Smith River* for a title. Simple, direct. A world at peace before the snow falls." He fingered his goatee, as if the thought had just occurred to him that he might be describing the current status of his own life.

"And you, Martha? Why have you agreed to this misadventure?"

"This one," she said, cocking a finger at Sean. "He insisted."

"Then I'll bid you goodbye and safe passage." He extended his hand, and they took it in turn.

Sean glanced back as they rounded the bend downriver, and Trueblood was just standing there. Sean knew he would never see him again.

"So now I'm 'This one,'" he said to Martha's back.

He watched her dig with the paddle from the bow. "Better than 'That one,'" she said.

———

Clint McCaine tipped his hat back with two fingers as he leaned in the doorframe.

"I know that winter's in the air when my head no longer looks like a two-tone Chevy," he said. "That's something my wife used to say. You wear a cowboy hat in summer, you're white over brown. I told her if she must use an automobile analogy, I would prefer being compared to a Rolls. They were famous for their two-tones. In fact I owned one, a '69 Silver Shadow drophead coupe in tan over black, back during my first midlife crisis. Purred like a kitten. A very large one. Now, like everyone, I drive a truck."

"That new 250 I saw 'round back is copper," Sean said. "Is that an accident, or is it the color you ordered?"

"Technically, it's amber gold metallic. But yes, the possibility exists." He shrugged. "Probably." Held up his hands. "So shoot me."

And ushered them into the house, the big man at his most expansive and hospitable, where they brought each other up to date over mugs of hot chocolate. McCain was interested in what had happened when sheriff's deputies raided the compound of the Rural Free Montanans after Rayland Jobson and Dewey Davis were killed. A photograph of the in-house outhouse had leaked and gone viral over the Internet. Martha told him there wasn't much to report. The several dwellings had been abandoned, the flag with the copper snake entwined around the initials RFM was gone, and there was no evidence suggesting that the grizzly-bear-poaching ring went beyond the brothers-in-law, except for the Korean buyers for the traditional medicines market, who had not been identified or brought to justice.

He also was curious about Jewel MacAllen, whose body had never been found, and who had now become part of the lore and legend of the Smith River. Martha said it was hard to imagine that he'd survived the icy current after Harold's canoe capsized, especially as Harold had seen the man react to the first shot from the Mannlicher rifle, though he couldn't say where he'd been hit.

Sean found himself warming to McCain, even though his Land Cruiser now sported a NO SMITH RIVER MINE bumper sticker.

"Maybe it's appropriate," he said.

McCain said, "What? That he's still missing?"

"All the better to haunt the river."

"This river already has too many ghosts," McCain said. And for a moment, a dark cloud swept over his face. "As well Bart and I know."

"We just left his house," Martha said. "It must be nice that you are friends again."

"Yes. It's good to put the bad blood behind us. To hear him tell it, you would have thought God had banished me to the Land of Nod and given me this mark on my forehead." He touched the birthmark under his hairline. "I have news for him. It is not given me by God. It's just a vascular blemish under the skin." He waved a big hand, the dust motes in the stripes of sunlight coming through the half-shuttered windows stirring to life. "I just wish I'd come off a little better in the documentary. I was promised it would be fair, and then Bart goes and gets bit by a snake. Now how was I supposed to compete with that?"

"You gave him your blood," Sean said.

"It ran across the screen before the credits rolled, but small letters as I recall. More an afterthought than kudos."

"You had the last word."

"I'm not sure about that. But I *will* have the last laugh."

They had entered his copper room, where McCaine showed them the latest core sample in a glass-lidded case.

"That's from the southeast arm of the deposit. A finer core of copper you cannot find in the world. Makes my heart skip a few beats just to see that color. You realize, despite what Bart may have told you about bill riders, public opinion, bad actor laws, political pressure, or anything else he deludes himself is going to stop the mine, he's wrong. A seam of ore this rich creates its own specific gravity. It will come out. There's too much money under the ground for it not to. The question is, do you want it to be dug by someone who's never stepped foot in Montana, or do you want it to be dug by somebody who grew up here and will do the job the right way?"

He shrugged. "The answer seems clear to me."

And with that they went to the door and shook hands, and McCaine went back into the vast house where his heart could skip a few beats over the color of copper.

CHAPTER THIRTY-NINE

The Usual Suspect

At the top of the climb from Tenderfoot Creek, Martha put her hands on her knees to catch her breath. Or, as she put it to Stranahan, to admire the view. "Such as it is," she added, straightening and sweeping a hand to encompass the weathered bones of the homestead.

"Remind me why we're here," she said. "Oh yeah, in case the Scarecrow God survived bullets, drowning, and hypothermia and decided to take up housekeeping."

"It's where he told Harold that he'd spent a winter with his father. It has meaning for him. Unless he's dead or gone back to Florida, this is where he'd come."

"He can go back to being the Creature from the Black Lagoon as far as I care. I forgot to ask you how it went."

"How what went?"

"Talking to the mother."

When Jewel MacAllen's personal effects—the photos and sketches that Martha and Sean had found in the playing card tin—were released from evidence, Martha had had a deputy work the keyboard to find an address. It was a place called Hilliardville, near the Florida Gulf only a few miles from Wakulla Springs, where the horror classic had been filmed. Sean was better at extracting information over the phone than anyone else she knew, so she'd given him the number to call. He had, and got next to nowhere.

Annabelle MacAllen had admitted to having a child with Scott

Henry MacAllen, and a good boy he was, sweet as Tupelo honey. But when he came back from Vietnam he wasn't anyone she recognized, she'd told Sean, and that had been nearly fifty years ago. She'd seen Jewel infrequently since and had last seen him five years ago. No, it wouldn't do any good to send the package of his belongings to her. It would just bring back a bad time in her life, and Sean, hearing the pathos in her voice, had wondered if there had ever been a good time. If that was all he had to say, she'd better get back to her orchids. Sean said if she saw Jewel, to tell him that the tin with its contents had been returned to the place where it had been found. He would know where that was.

"I don't expect you'll be hearing from me," she'd said, and Sean hadn't, and that had been that.

"So that's why we're here?" Martha said. "To turn over a plank of wood?"

"Sam had a guide trip in September. I had him put the tin back. If it's there, then you have nothing to worry about. He's gone. Maybe he never existed at all."

At the cabin, Sean turned the plank. The playing card tin wasn't there. Nothing was there but sawdust and mouse feces.

They looked at each other.

"This place gives me the heebie-jeebies," Martha said.

———

That evening, they fished the riffle below their camp at Sunset Cliff, Sean taking two browns on a cone-headed bugger with blue and copper flash that he called the Smith River Special. Martha passed him on the bank as she hiked back to the tent.

"They're giving me the finger," she said. "I'll get the fire started."

"Here, give one of these a few casts."

He took a pewter fly box from a vest pocket. The lid was labeled USUAL SUSPECTS, #2, #4, #6. Martha's look was dubious.

"I thought this was an Atlantic salmon pattern," she said.

He opened the lid. Held the fly box out toward her like he was offering a tin of mints.

The flies were gorgeous, with rust orange wings, jungle cock eyes, and hackle collars in kingfisher blue. Martha's eyes were drawn to the glinting gold hook that one of the larger flies was tied on. Her brow furrowed. Those glints of gold didn't belong to a hook.

She took the fly box from Sean's hand. She felt her fingers trembling as they stirred the fox fur, guessing what she was going to find before she found it. The gold band was pinned to the sheepskin lining in the box by the hook of one of the flies, the russet wing all but hiding it.

She unhooked the fly and placed the ring in her palm. She looked at Sean, who had knelt in the shallows.

"It was my mother's," he said. "My sister sent it to me after she died."

"Are you asking me to marry you?"

"I'm on my knees in the Smith River in October. The water isn't warm."

The ring was a simple gold band with a Celtic design. She turned her hand so that it glinted.

"Aren't you going to try it on?"

"I don't have a ring finger."

"You have one on your right hand."

"You haven't asked me yet."

"Will you, Martha, do me the honor of being my wife?"

"The possibility exists," she said.

"The possibility exists?"

"Yes," she said. "You've only kept me on the hook for five years."

"On the hook?"

"Quit repeating what I say. Yes, I'll marry you. Of course I'll marry you." She laughed even as she felt herself trembling, and blinked away the tears in the corners of her eyes.

"Can I get up now?"

"I sort of like you where you are. Oh, okay. Only if you'll kiss me, though."

The Wolves of Winter

Harold Little Feather's grandfather liked to say that winter was a wolf. It preyed upon the old who no longer had anything to give back to the herd except the wisdom that they had already imparted. It preyed upon the young who couldn't keep pace and so strengthened the herd by eliminating the weak. And for those who remained living, the wolf was the night song to remind them to be ever vigilant, for danger could lie anywhere.

Harold had first heard this allegory while hunting elk on a frozen breast of snow on the eastern front of the Rocky Mountains. Before him was a small fire, and above, the diamond dust of the stars, and as his grandfather had spoken, Harold heard the voices of a hunting pack floating down from some faraway basin.

"What do you mean, Grandfather?" Harold had said. He tried not to betray his fear. Beyond the old man, the boy could see the firelight glinting off the barrel of the Winchester that leaned against a tree.

"It means that when you hear something approaching in the night, no matter how faint the sound, that you do not respond as one who hears but does not heed, that where another hunter might add a log to the fire and fall back to sleep, you keep your eyes open and your rifle in reach.

"Today," his grandfather said, "I am your ears in the darkness and I am your eyes in the light, as I have been since you were born. So was my promise to your mother, and you will remain in my heart into the next world. But there will come a time when I can no longer be vigilant for you, or be your rifle at hand, and then it will be up to you to avoid the jaws of the wolf."

He had described the animal to Harold, this winter wolf, as being bigger than other wolves, and said that it could change shape and represent any face of danger, whereas ordinary wolves could not.

All through Harold's life, he had heeded his grandfather's warning, although he had never heard another elder speak of winter wolves, either as the spirit of a season or as an animal of flesh and blood, nor had he found mention of them in the histories of the people. Thus it became his story alone, and he never forgot the lesson or the night it was given, even this many winters after his grandfather's passing.

So it was that on this night, when he opened a window to air out the fumes from the lantern he'd been burning, his first reaction to the creaking footfalls in the new snow was to check for the Winchester. Slipping it from its case, which he kept unzipped under his bed, he fingered the hole in the stock, where it had been struck by the bullet meant for him six months before. He walked down the steps to the dirt-and-straw floor of the barn, the beam of his flashlight catching the eyes of the resident barn owl, which remained motionless. His leg was much better now, his limp almost unnoticeable. The stick he used to walk up and down steps was only a precaution. He set it down on a hay bale and scratched at the new tattoo on his left bicep, the fox tracks he'd had inked when the cast on his ankle came off and the doctor said he wasn't going to lose his leg after all.

Assured that there was nothing in the barn but what belonged, he opened the door to the night. He thought for a moment that it might be Marcus, but to Harold's great satisfaction Marcus had gone back to high school for his final semester, and he had talked to him only a few hours earlier, happy, as he always was, to hear his son call him "Dad."

Anyway, if it was Marcus, he'd have driven right up to the barn and there would be Cochise. There was no Cochise, and not seeing anyone, Harold's eyes lit upon his old pickup in the drive. In the moonlight flooding through the windows, he could make out the shoes that hung from the rearview mirror. They were the ruby slippers that the little girl had worn on the night she saw the scarecrow, returned to him, along with his rifle, after his capsized canoe had been recovered. The girl had told Harold that the shoes were magic and would keep him safe. So far they had done so, although they had long since ceased to glow when he pressed on the heels.

The footfalls stopped, and then they started again and Harold saw a figure disengage from the silhouette of the truck, the dark outline bent forward from the waist, the arms hugging the chest.

"Is that you, Harold?"

"It's me."

"What is it, like twenty below? I've never been so cold in my life."

"Something like that."

Now the woman, it was a woman, was illuminated in the light from the naked bulb Harold had switched on. Bringing her fresh cold scent with her, she stepped past him into the barn. He heard the tinkling, icicle quality of her voice that he'd first heard at Camp Baker on the Smith River.

"I parked down at the house. Your sister said where to find you. She didn't tell me how far a walk it was. I got the impression she didn't much approve of me coming."

"When it comes to women, she doesn't much approve of anyone coming," Harold said. "What are you doing here, Carol Ann?"

"You told me if I ever got rid of the bastard and got my daughter off to college, that I could start over and look you up. Well, guess what? I did." Her laugh was music, though her voice sounded a little shaky. "I hope I didn't read that wrong. I know it was just one night. I know it's sort of sudden."

Then she seemed to find her center, and said, laughing, "As I recall, Harold, the first time I saw you, you were packing a gun and here you are with nothing changed. Maybe I better turn around while the get-ting's good."

Harold set the rifle down next to his stick. "How long have you been in Montana?"

"Since about six hours, I guess. I was in Missouri the day before yesterday."

Her breath made clouds.

"Wow," she said. "Wow, that was cold." And she came into his arms and buried her face against his neck, her nose like ice.

"You're so warm. You're just what I need."

She made no attempt to disengage, and Harold, who was ever vig-ilant but too often alone, made no attempt to move away.

He switched off the light and they held each other in the darkness.

"Isn't it beautiful out, though?" she said.

After a while they went up the steps, while below them and above them and all around them winter pulled its satin robe close, and if there really were wolves near enough to hear their songs, whether they were winter wolves or just the ordinary ones, on this night they were silent.

Acknowledgments

A Death in Eden is a work of fiction, and the characters and the organizations in the novel are fictional. However, a very real cloud hangs over the Smith River Canyon. Whether that cloud is dark or light depends on the position you take on a copper mining operation proposed in the Smith's headwaters, which critics fear will poison the river. Tintina Resources, an international mining company with controlling interests in Australia, is the driving force behind the Black Butte Copper Project, which would mine copper ore under Sheep Creek, the Smith's most important spawning tributary. The company promises that its operation will not harm water quality. Environmental groups, including American Rivers, which listed the Smith as our country's fourth most endangered river in 2016, disagree vehemently.

To research this novel, I spoke with many people on both sides of the issue, attended public forums on the mine conducted by the Montana Department of Environmental Quality, which must sign off on the project before an environmental analysis is begun, and joined a tour of the mine site led by Jerry Zieg, the senior vice president of exploration for Tintina. At the time, I thought I might write about this issue for *Field & Stream*, where I am an editor. For their courtesy in answering my questions, and for their thorough and honest presentation of the project from a pro-mining perspective, I thank Mr. Zieg, as well as Bob Jacko and Chance Matthews, who are also associated with the project.

On the other side of the controversy, I thank Scott Bosse, the director of the Northern Rockies region of American Rivers, and Mike Fiebig, the associate director, for answering questions and reviewing parts of the novel for accuracy. I also am indebted to biologist and environmental lawyer Jory Ruggiero, for his help in deciphering legalities involved in licensing and operating hard-rock mines. Any mistakes of fact are my own. And despite the rough treatment I gave them in the novel, I wish to thank the U.S. Forest Service and Montana Fish, Wildlife and Parks' workers who supervise the Smith River floating operation and help make it a wonderful experience.

For reviewing my book from the Native American perspective, I am indebted to historian, college instructor, storyteller, poet, and writer Dr. Joe McGeshick, a member of the Sokaogon Chippewa tribe, who was raised on the Assiniboine and Sioux reservations in northern Montana. I also wish to thank Dr. Shane Doyle, a member of the Crow tribe and an instructor of Native American studies for Montana State University.

Down at water level, I thank my brother, Kevin McCafferty, for organizing our expeditions down the Smith River, and Joe Gutkoski. Joe has floated the Smith more than fifty times, and his insight into the river's history and pictograph sites proved invaluable. I also thank authors/river explorers Alan Kesselheim and Marypat Zitzer for allowing me to steal the identity of their three-legged dog Beans, who is Cochise in the novel.

For inspiration during the writing of the book, I often turned to a limited-edition print of a Monte Dolack painting called *Smith River in June*. Monte painted this landscape masterpiece for Montana State Parks' seventy-fifth anniversary, and he has come closer than anyone in portraying the splendor of this canyon in an artistic medium.

Of course there would be no *A Death in Eden* if not for Dominick Abel, my literary agent, and Kathryn Court, the publisher of Penguin

Books, and her team, including Victoria Savanh, Bruce Giffords, Ben Petrone, and Sara Chuirazzi. They are the best.

For their early morning moral support, I thank my friends at Wild Joe's—Kaila Gill, Erica Brubaker, Sarah Grigg, Sydney Knox, and Sammy Haight.

Last but far from least, I thank my wife, Gail, my first and best editor, and my children, Jessie and Thomas, for journeying with me down the Smith and through life.